A Second Chance

a novel
by Vasily Mahanenko

*Books are the lives
we don't have
time to live,

Vasily Mahanenko*

Invasion
Book 1
Magic Dome Books

A Second Chance
Invasion Book #1
Copyright © Vasily Mahanenko 2019
Cover Art © V. Manyukhin 2019
English translation copyright © Colin Parker 2019
Published by Magic Dome Books, 2019
All Rights Reserved
ISBN: 978-80-7619-071-9

All Books by V. Mahanenko:

The Way of the Shaman LitRPG Series
Survival Quest
The Kartoss Gambit
The Secret of the Dark Forest
The Phantom Castle
The Karmadont Chess Set
The Hour of Pain (a bonus short story)
Shaman's Revenge
Clans War

The Alchemist LiTRPG series by Vasily Mahanenko:
City of the Dead
Forest of Desire
Tears of Alron

Dark Paladin LitRPG Series
The Beginning
The Quest
Restart

Galactogon LitRPG Series
Start the Game!
In Search of the Uldans
A Check for a Billion

Invasion LitRPG Series
A Second Chance
An Equation with One Unknown

World of the Changed LitRPG Series
No Mistakes
Pearl of the South
Noa in the Flesh

The Bard from Barliona LitRPG series
(with Eugenia Dmitrieva)
The Renegades
A Song of Shadow

You're in Game!
(LitRPG Stories from Bestselling Authors)

You're in Game-2!
(More LitRPG stories set in your favorite worlds)

Table of Contents:

Chapter 1

WHENEVER YOU experience hardship on a cosmic scale, you turn to a higher power. You might formulate it differently each time, but the sense is always the same: "Why me? Can't somebody else get sick, or die, or lose something important, just for a change?"

Stupid, pointless questions, yet it's a rare person who doesn't ask them in time of woe. To keep your feet you have to be either dead cynical or deeply religious. Or a project manager, in which case forecasting and accepting risk is part of the job. I belong to this third category, so when I received news of my redundancy, I didn't stress over the question of my uniqueness, because it was bound to happen sooner or later. My miscalculation lay elsewhere – time frames. Occupied as I was with a two-year government project, I figured I was employed until at least its completion, during which time I would develop several of my own business ideas, so that afterwards I could look to the future with confidence from the panoramic window of my own high-end office. It didn't happen.

In a world where Imitators – robotic systems with limited artificial intelligence – were taking over more and more jobs, there would soon be no place for the common man. Nobody now remembers how enthusiastically people greeted the first prototypes of the Imitators, originally designed for use in the hazardous manufacturing industries. And then quietly, with none of the original press and Internet fanfare, the robots established a firm foothold in education, medicine, industry, everywhere. Imitators didn't get tired, didn't demand wages, and completed their tasks precisely and punctually. Ideal workers. It was only after the mass layoffs that people wised up to what was happening. The powers that be declared the replacement experiment a success, and started kicking crowds of people out of their jobs and onto welfare. Pickets and protests were organized, but it was too late. The powerful and the moneyed of the world understood that the pros of replacement seriously outweighed the cons. In fact there really were only two cons: the general social unrest, and the resultant, ever-growing criminal situation. The government, garnering the support of interested parties, came up with a remarkably original solution – the virtual world of Barliona.

Relieved of work and a purpose in life, people needed, aside from food and housing, a new ideology. The total-immersion game was presented as the only escape from the drab calamity of existence. The government was aggressive in its promotion of the new virtual messiah to the masses. Everywhere glistened with conscription advertising images, ratings of game achievements were compiled, and new virtual celebrities smiled from media screens. Barliona was awesome, seductive, and carefree. But the real clincher was that in agreeing to a new life in Barliona, people were giving themselves over to total government welfare.

Municipal residential facilities were built in outlying districts – two-by-three-meter concrete box rooms, with no windows, kitchens, bedrooms, or toilets, but this was compensated by continuous-immersion pods, fully equipped for all your needs. Newly unemployed citizens, who could no longer provide for themselves, would sign a contract with the municipality and receive ownership of such accommodation, along with a lifetime paid account. They were obliged to spend no less than twenty hours a day in the game, including sleep, and were generously allowed to pass the remainder of their time in the real world.

The idea went down like a bomb. The first to rush into Barliona were droves of adolescents, only too happy to cast off their everyday cares. Accompanied by their whoops of joy, agreements concerning self-imposed exile were signed by unemployed newcomers, freeing up space on the Earth for those who had the money for a real life. Those who escaped to Barliona on the social program became known popularly as "vagrants," and nobody was offended.

The old residential suburbs were demolished, making way for new garden suburbs, sports and entertainment complexes, and vibrant mansion communities. The world changed its image, bowing to the will of the rich, with the tacit disapproval of everyone else. That was how natural selection usually worked.

"So what are you going to do?"

I sighed to stifle my irritation. In the last week, pretty much everyone had been bugging me with that question. My parents, ex-colleagues, friends – faux and true. But if my parents really were concerned, everyone else did not always hide their glee. And why should they? Those who had managed to hang onto their positions sensed their superiority, and those who had already been enlisted to the armies of unemployed were relieved they weren't alone. But absolutely everybody was dying to hear how I planned to remain solvent. Suddenly I developed a cunning plan.

"So what are you going to do?" Matty poured us another drink each and waited patiently. He wasn't one to gloat over the misfortunes of others. He was a childhood friend, one of the family.

"First up, I'm going to celebrate my divorce and the fact that I have no children." Not a great joke, but that evening was no time to be serious. I was just elated to see Matty for the first time in five years.

"Well obviously. Although I'm not convinced," he sniggered, frowning.

"Uh-huh. You were always pussy whipped. Relax, your wife's not here," I laughed, remembering Matty's other half. If there was ever anyone who shouldn't be complaining about family life, it was Matty. They were one of those rare couples who were blissfully happy raising children together. At least they were five years ago.

The first couple of shots washed away the stress of recent days. It really was great to see him and forget our problems for a while, and the booze unwittingly drew us into nostalgia.

We'd met on the first day of the first year. Neither of us shared the general excitement about starting school, and the example of my elder sister had shown us clearly that our happy-go-lucky yard games would be replaced by lessons and homework. Matty hated kindergarten and school. We stood together, panting under the burden of either existence or our school bags, and brushing aside everyone else's bouquets of flowers. Common troubles bind people together, and boring lessons and constant knuckle rappings from a spiteful teacher made us almost brothers. We were together throughout school. We fought, teased the girls, and received beatings from our fathers when our mothers tired of threatening us with the belt. At the time it seemed it would always be like that, sticking together through thick and thin because we were a gang.

But after school we went our separate ways. Matty hadn't found studying particularly easy at school, so higher education wasn't even a question. He was, however, a wizard with his hands, and with my help he enrolled on a college course in car mechanics, and found work in a nearby workshop, where he soon earned the respect of all the men. Then all of a sudden he met Liz, married her, and had kids, immersing himself in family life, but looking supremely happy with it. It's strange: as a car mechanic you'd think he would have been more worried about losing his job, but he assured me he had a reliable client base. As one of his regular clients used to say about the switch over to Imitator mechanics: "It's like pleasuring your woman with a vibrator when you have your own eager hands, a fully working member, and a head on your shoulders."

I had a different fate in store. A bachelor's degree, a second bachelor's degree, and a prestigious internship followed by a fulltime job in an incredibly high-end corporation. I started as assistant manager, and was then chief project manager in charge of implementing ERP-class information systems for thirteen years. It sounds terrifying, but all I actually did was ensure my juniors fulfilled their functions proficiently and on time. I soon got out of the habit of working with my own hands.

At first I hooked up with Matty once a week, discussing problems and sharing news, but those meetings became less and less frequent: once a month, then once a year, and for the past five years we didn't even call each other. Turns out I suck as a friend. Occasionally I would remember him and swear I'd finish work early the next day and call to ask how he was doing, or even pop round to see him, but I never got round to it. It's hard when you're working yourself into the ground fourteen hours a day. That's why my ex left me. She was sick of going to sleep and waking up alone.

I was laid off a week ago, and out of the blue Matty shows his face. Even though he hadn't phoned, he apparently kept abreast of my successes by looking at posts and photos in social networks. He was just wary of letting friendship get in the way of a "big boss," which amused me, but at the same time shamed me. Time had left us rungs apart on the social ladder, but my dear friend remained nothing but a true human being.

"You haven't answered me," persisted Matty.

"Matty, why do you keep banging on like that? We're having a good time, don't go and spoil it." I hadn't noticed my temper rising. I took a couple of deep breaths and added, "I'll find something. The Imitators can't replace everybody. They haven't taken over everything."

"Another round?" As if to disprove me, an Imitator-waiter appeared. Its subservient physiognomy irritated, but we couldn't refuse the offer, otherwise we would have to leave the establishment. The owners kept a strict eye on guests so they wouldn't be distracted from spending money. "I remind you that you can receive a discount by stating your Barliona login. The size of the discount depends on your character's level."

"Oh wake up, Bro, these monsters are everywhere," hissed Matty angrily, unembarrassed in front of the robot. "You know who doesn't have them? The army. Because it's more interesting to fight with live soldiers – you can be a real hero, even a spy. Intrigue all round, why the hell not? An RPG,

7

in reality, with a Cargo 200 bonus. And they're way creative. All of them."

"What are you getting so wound up about? I thought everything was hunky dory with you?" His over excitement was getting to me. Surely it was me who had problems? And here he was getting all emotional.

"Hunky dory? What would you know? Five years ago everything was fine. Then it all went wrong." All of a sudden Matty wilted and looked glum. He drained his glass of vodka.

"The repair shop closed three years ago. Almost all the customers went over to the Imitators. They're fast, reliable, and free. That's a car manufacturer's lifetime guarantee for you. What could we offer to counter that? Exactly, nothing. Although we took the piss as best we could. We put a huge display stand of family photos by the entrance. Children, wives, parents, dogs. Get it? Pictures from a family album all about happiness. So that when the client picked up his pride and joy, he understood he was feeding someone and would have to come back."

Shocked by the news, I swallowed the lump in my throat. "Why didn't you call me?"

"What for? To say, 'Hi, mate! How's it going up there on Mount Olympus? Still building Hell's Kitchen for us?' You were building shelters, weren't you?"

"I was," I said. Up until then it had just been installing and setting servers for the social shelters. A government contract. Yet another project with no reference to specific people or goals.

We were silent, each thinking our own thoughts.

"Liz left. No money coming in, children to feed. Josh Spenning had a thing for her ever since school. Maybe you remember him? He's doing well for himself now, moved to a rich part of town, suggested she moved in too, he'd keep her. The kids are with her, and now they've got loads of toys, clubs, sport... I see them once a week. That's how hunky dory it is." Matty spoke reluctantly and softly, as though afraid of what he was saying.

I felt even more wretched now, thinking I could have found out for myself, if only I'd been interested in his life. I could have been there to support him. Matty's family was everything to him.

"I'm such an asshole. I never called you once to ask how you were. You didn't call either, and no news is good news."

"Forget it. I'm not pissed off with Liz. What do I have to offer them, apart from a shelter? By the way, they're not bad little mansions. Well played!" he chuckled.

"Don't start. I'm sick of it myself." I'd asked for it, envisaging a pod in a concrete anthill as a home for my best buddy. "If I can't find a job, I'll move close to you, we can be neighbours."

"Bro, you know me, I didn't drag you here out of self-pity," said Matty, shaking off his melancholy. "I've got a proposal for you. How are you with Barliona?"

"Not good. I started a couple of times and gave

up. I can't be sitting in a pod with my job. It's not my thing anyway. Are you trying to entice me into your game? An 'Introduce a friend and receive a bonus' promotion stunt?"

"Something like that." He wasn't offended. "Listen, I've been in the game three years, and I haven't done half bad, for a vagrant. I've got money, connections. But I'm not blind. I see the clan officers taking most of the loot and leaving us with next to nothing. There are hordes of vagrants in Barliona now, so the clans don't cling on to us so desperately. If they're dissatisfied with something, they're told to get lost. A paid account, on the other hand, is something else. This is what I've thought up. It's not easy to earn money in Barliona, but it is possible. First, you need your own clan. While you've got money, you can subscribe, create a character, organize your own business. Remember school: I do the handiwork, you do the brainwork. How long did you spend just learning to manage things, Bro? Plus, with a paid account, you'll have kudos and bonuses all over the place."

Reference information

Account types
Social one-size-fits-all – A pay-as-you-go account for people living in social housing and prisons, with a compulsory contribution to the government of 30% of all

income. In the game, players with this type of account have their name underlined in red (cannot be hidden).

Commercial account, beginner – An account with a monthly fee of 11 credits, without bonuses. Most popular with schoolchildren and students.

Commercial account, basic – An account with a monthly fee of 525 credits. Bonuses: Experience +1, Reputation +2.

Commercial account, premium – An account with a monthly fee of 2100 credits. Bonuses: Experience +3, Reputation +5. Favourable terms and offers from the game bank. Opportunity to become a member of the top private game clubs.

"You're suggesting I waste my time and money in Barliona, just to end up in a shelter even sooner? Instead of looking for a job? And swapping my commercial account for a vagrant one? Yeah, right!" The sceptic in me was fuming. "If only it was all that simple, Matty. Then half of us would be Mahans. Dream on!"

"Who knows? Maybe it is a dream. But you

have to believe in something. And I believe you'd make a damn good clan chief. We can find earners, buy a castle. I'll do the creative stuff. We'll earn a ton of cash, and everything will turn out all right—" He was interrupted by an electronic signal from the device on his wrist.

The Imitator came over: "Matthew Lavery, your reality time limit expires in thirty minutes. A taxi is waiting for you by the entrance. Payment will be debited from your account."

Matty rolled up his sleeve and shook his metal bracelet. Everyone on a social contract had one, to monitor their whereabouts, time-management skills, health, and other important stats.

"Damn convenient piece of kit." He winked. "If you change your mind, give me a buzz. And good luck in the job search."

He rose from the table, thought for a moment, and necked another shot.

"The pod will flush me out anyway, and the way home will be more chilled," he explained before waving goodbye. "Lead on, oh soulless one!"

The Imitator saw Matty out and returned. "Another drink, or would you like to move to the VIP lounge?" The machine could see my account balance and was doing its utmost to reduce it. The VIP lounge entailed live serving personnel and doubled prices. Otherwise it was no different from the general bar.

"No, I'm good, thanks. Debit payment from my account."

"Your companion has already paid the bill,"

said the Imitator, before escorting me to the door. "Would you like to use the Sober Driver service?"

I declined, informing the robot I had autopilot, and climbed into my expensive car. Apart from a huge headache and no free time, my job as project manager had also provided me with a decent income. The car drove past blocks being readied for demolition. The alcohol and the conversation with Matty evoked thoughts of social inequality. High-rises were being knocked down, and new mansions built in their place. Mansions like mine – large, comfortable, and expensive. I'd never given thought to where the people would go. An entire district, hundreds of twenty-story buildings, a thousand flats in each, and each flat housing a family. Surely they can't all be in Barliona? Now was probably not the best time to think about it.

The following morning was fine and sunny, unlike my physical and mental state. I hadn't been that drunk for ages. My head pounded mercilessly, and my body begged to be horizontal again. It was only the nauseating, electronic, "Incoming Correspondence" signal that prevented me from dying in peace. The sound came from the Smart Home management module, and indicated receipt of a letter from the management company. Taking a couple of shaky steps, I accepted I wouldn't be able to cope without the robodoctor, and trudged through to the kitchen to deal with my hangover.

Dear Mr. West, the management company Everything for a Present Future would like to remind you that your prepaid, one-year lease on a mansion in Sector 2, address: House 43, Street 2, terminates four months from today. Your current account balance is sufficient to extend the lease for two years, including advanced payment of utility charges.

Considering the absence of weekly deposits into your account, the management company would be happy to offer you a comfortable flat in Sector 5 at a price to suit you. You can browse all the options by following the link below. The price of a one-year lease includes: a two-room flat with standard conveniences, direct connection to Barliona, and secure parking. The management company has studied your levels of social and intellectual development, and has selected the most suitable neighbours for you.

To extend your lease or apply for a housing swap, look in the My Profile section of the main menu.

We are pleased to be of service to our clients, and to make their future a comfortable present.

Fuck off with your joyful concern! I've only been unemployed for a week.

Sector five was a high-rise ghetto on the outskirts of the city, a concentration of human desperation, crime, and all manner of disease. Even the police didn't bother showing their faces around there. Why would they? Let the dregs destroy themselves. Fewer people equals fewer problems. There was only one way out of there – into a long-stay pod, and I wasn't ready to give up my place in the sun, in the literal sense of that expression.

Submitting to a momentary fit of rage, I flipped the finger at the entirely blameless management module, and extended the lease on my comfortable and expensive domicile for another year.

I spent the whole day checking my email, sending my resume to some of the bigger companies, and phoning work contacts. Nothing. Out of twenty companies, only seven responded, all of them with rejections. Project managers had been replaced with the new generation of Imitators. Looking at the employment sites was fairly damn joyless too. Every job offer had loads of replies, whether it was for a VIP-establishment waiter or a specialist in microelectronics. White-collar workers were no use to anybody. Reading forums, phoning acquaintances, and lunch with a particular big cheese proved no cause for celebration either.

By the end of the day I was seriously ready to contemplate Matty's proposal. People on the forums agreed about one thing: Barliona was now pretty much the only place where you could earn anything at all. So for want of anything better to do, I decided to do some homework on the subject, filtering out the adverts. A rigorous analysis of the information available took me two hours, and my conclusions indicated that Matty's suggestion was not an option. The game was created for people to spend money, not earn it. What the vagrants called earnings was peanuts compared to my usual take-home, and even then they hoarded it, scrimping on everything and paranoid about anyone taking anything. The comfort and security of your personal assets came at a price. Absolutely everything cost money, from use of the Bank to a Scroll of Flight to expanding your inventory. All this convinced me Barliona was designed to relieve players of their money, time, and reason, and in no way to provide them comfort in their declining years.

An "Incoming Correspondence" notification flashed up. On autopilot I opened my mailbox. With all the stress and fatigue, my brain had switched off.

Greetings, Mr. West. We have perused your resume, and would like to invite you to an interview at our company for the position of project manager. The interview will take place...

"Yeees!" I shouted, without even reading the details. My body was gasping for any opportunity to make up its deficit in feel-good hormones. For the first time ever I regretted not having someone close to share this small piece of non-binding good news with.

The company inviting me to interview was not a giant in some market or other. In fact I could only find a couple of mentions in the Internet. No scandals, quantum leaps, or participation in tenders, and oddly, everything I could glean about my potential employer came from their own website. A supplier of network equipment, with its own consulting and commissioning departments. Just what I was looking for. In years of managing projects, I had studied all this stuff in such detail I could work as a manager, architect, or design engineer. If they'd let me prove myself, that was.

My reply was quick and concise: *Your offer is interesting, I am familiar with the company, I will definitely be there.* Almost immediately I received confirmation that my letter had been read, and a few seconds later a contact request appeared in the messenger application of my mail client:

hrs@rightdecision.com requests to be added to your list of contacts.

WTF? There's a real live employee sitting there? The system clock read 1:00 a.m. I clicked on "Accept Message."

> *HR department: Good evening, Mr. West. Please forgive me for disturbing you at such a late hour. I saw your letter and decided to reply.*
> *Brody West: Good evening. No problem, I'm not sleeping anyway.*
> *HR department: We arranged your interview for tomorrow at midday, but unfortunately the head of the department is flying out at 10:00 a.m. You can wait until her return, or come to the interview at 8:00 a.m. tomorrow.*
> *Brody West: Tomorrow at 8:00. Thank you for warning me.*
> *HR department: ;) Pleased to be of assistance. We will expect you tomorrow at 7:50. I will order a pass for you.*

What the f...? A smiley from a real live HR

employee. And a live interview. Could it be a joke? Job interviews went virtual eons ago. My last live interview was about ten years ago. Nothing but a waste of precious time. Maybe this was just a test? To see how much I valued my time, and theirs.

> *Brody West: You mean I have to come to the office? Why not use conference call? Especially since the head of department is flying out.*
>
> *HR department: There's nothing to be afraid of ☺ Live interaction at work is a company policy. Our staff consists only of people.*
>
> *Brody West: Why?*
>
> *HR department: That's not for me to say)) Come and see us and you'll find out everything. Good night.*
>
> *Brody West: Good night.*

I was intrigued, to say the least. Good night? I googled Right Decision Ltd. with renewed vigour, but learned nothing new. Old links concerning charity affairs, and their website. That was it. There was no information whatsoever in the Internet about companies which had opted out of Imitator services. Some random company with a load of inconsistencies. How could you provide network equipment for Imitators, without even using Imitators?

hrs@rightdecision.com was still online. The silence of the empty house was stifling, and I wanted to continue our chat, the more so because my curiosity was getting the better of me.

Brody West: Can I ask you a question?

HR department: As long as it's just the one, and it's not about work)

Brody West: Why did you write to me here? You could have called tomorrow or advised me in a letter.

HR department: I saw the "Message Read" notification and figured you really needed a job)

Brody West: So you took pity on me?

HR department: That was your second question) See you tomorrow.

So much for the chat. A cup of camomile tea was more comforting than the abortive chin wag, and I went to bed.

The interview with the head of the project management office was a walk in the park. I was tested on my knowledge of my professional sphere, asked to elaborate on details of successfully completed projects, and, as is usual, to comment on problematical situations, before being informed that on the whole I fitted their requirements. The working conditions suited me, as did the salary. The office manager waved away my questions about the project, saying I would find out everything if I got past the big boss, and after wishing me success, he headed off to an exhibition of new Imitator prototypes on a different continent. If only I lived like that.

A girl entered the conference hall and said,

Book One: A Second Chance

"Good morning. Could you please fill in these forms, and I'll take you through to Mr. Williams's reception room."

I silently took the papers from the outstretched hand of the clearly recent school leaver. She sat down opposite me, trying to look important, but her hastily gathered hair and ink-stained hands ruined her businesswoman image.

Paper forms? A ballpoint pen? Yet another anachronism to add to the list of the company's quirks. I hadn't held real documents in my hands for years. I'd even forgotten what a pleasant sensation quality paper could produce.

"My name is Helen. I'm your personal HR manager. If you have any questions, please ask."

"Hello, Helen. Was it you I spoke to today?"

"Today?" The girl frowned and wiped her forehead with dirty fingers, smearing ink on it. "No, yesterday... Ah, yes. I mean today."

So this was who I had to thank for the successfully rescheduled interview. This young homely creature, on her first day at work. It explained a lot, especially the smileys. At that age feelings of compassion haven't yet atrophied, and the desire to show one's worth runs high. Not to worry, we've all been there; it passes with time. It was a good job our chat hadn't got off the ground; otherwise I would have been feeling very embarrassed just then.

"Helen, thank you for organizing the interview. You're a very responsible employee." I flashed the girl a friendly smile to thank her for her consideration. "Your diligence is literally written across your forehead."

I demonstratively wiped my own forehead, unsure how to drop the hint while not offending her sensibilities. At first she just frowned and mirrored my gesture. Then the penny dropped and she squealed.

"I've smudged my forehead again, haven't I? I just can't get used to this thing actually writing. Styluses aren't messy like that."

I smiled politely again and busied myself with filling in the standard HR forms, while Helen cleaned herself up with a tissue.

Twenty minutes later the sweet, though very young, HR girl led me to reception and handed me over to a real office shark. It was etched into everything from her stylish coiffure to the tips of her high heels. The high-class secretary was arranging documents, and with such dignity and focus that doomsday itself paled before the importance of the task. All I merited was a curt glance from her severe and impeccably mascaraed eyes, motioning me toward a visitors' chair. Not a single word. But who needs words anyway? Words would only have spoiled the whole magic of that silent, yet evocative film.

It was entertaining to see a real live secretary in action. Due to the efforts of directors' wives, secretaries had been among the first to be replaced by Imitators, relieving honest women of that particular headache. Were I conscious of my own uniqueness, I might well behave that way too.

Book One: A Second Chance

The internal telephone on the table rang. "Yes, Nathan... of course," said the secretary in an incongruously pleasant voice. She replaced the receiver and, looking at me coldly, nodded toward the office door. "You may go in."

A semidarkness reigned in the room, diluted by the light of a projector. On a small screen I saw the first slide of my resume. Nathan Williams was sitting at his desk and unhurriedly poring over the contents. He cut an interesting figure: expensive suit and tie, manicure, watchful stare, and no sign of plastic surgery to conceal his age. I had read on the company website that the owner of Right Decision Ltd. was over ninety, and for that age he looked amazing. In the comments it mentioned that he did not use a medical pod on principle, having on the staff a human doctor, who was just as ancient as him. Looking at his wrinkled face, that was easy to believe. His liver spots didn't add to Williams's charm, but in no way did they affect his working capacity. His mind remained ever alert and inquiring.

"Take a seat," said Nathan with some effort. His hoarse, forty-cigarettes-a-day voice was more suited to a ship's captain than a businessman. The slides changed on the screen – a photo, achievements from my previous places of work, personal information. I didn't recognize the last slide, which contained information from the security service. There couldn't be anything to be ashamed of. A career in a prestigious company obliged you to take good care of your personal and business reputation. Reaching the end of the presentation, the owner asked:

"Brody, what is your relationship with God?"

Only now did I notice the Bible on his desk and a large crucifix on the wall. Both objects looked very expensive, and several bookmarks made of torn pieces of paper protruded from the book.

I don't know what my face reflected, but long-forgotten obscenities swam up in my head. Fuck! You have to warn people in advance about corporate policies like that. I wasn't an atheist, but I preferred not to have anything to do with God. At all. You could call me an agnostic – I believed there was something somewhere, but it didn't encroach on our lives and did not demand worship. With regard to faith, that was enough for me. But what do you say when your only source of income is at stake? I searched desperately for a correct response.

"I am christened. That was my parents' decision. But I don't go to church."

"You misunderstood me. I wasn't asking about your relationship to the institution of faith. I was asking about your relationship with God."

"That's a very personal question, Mr. Williams. I need a job, and I don't know how to answer your question in order to get it."

The old man laughed. "Brody, there are no correct answers here. I'm just interested to know what sort of person wants to work in my company."

"I think I would best describe myself as an agnostic."

"Thank you for your honesty. People are

losing their faith. It's tragic, but not without reason. Barliona can also be used to control the people, can't it? Hehehe."

I didn't know what to say, and shrugged my shoulders. I wanted this to end soon, and with some degree of certainty. It was crappy practice to philosophize on the subject of citizen-control techniques during a job interview.

"Tell me, Brody, what is good about faith? Why do people believe in God?"

"Because it's easier to overcome hardship. Some people don't have enough strength of their own, and faith supports them, humbles them. It's like an element of psychotherapy."

"Good. I like your answer. You've probably noticed certain peculiarities of the company. I shall explain. It's connected with my faith, and that, as you correctly stated, is very personal. Consider everything which doesn't fit into a normal framework for you, to be the folly of a pious old man. When all is said and done, what does it matter if I give you the opportunity to pay for a villa in sector two, and at the same time don't demand that you share my feelings? Right?"

He laughed again. With a couple of unconventional questions, he had checked my resolve in a stressful situation, and defined the limits of what was admissible. Whatever underpinned his methods of business organization, he acknowledged the right of his employees to choose their own faith, but demanded the same of them. It does no harm in this business to remember who pays who, and for what.

"And now to business. Tell me about yourself."

I breathed a sigh of relief when I heard this more familiar interview phrase. In view of the fact that my life story had recently flickered across the screen, the request was obviously loaded. A classic test of attention to detail. Without touching on information already provided, I had to flesh out my resume. Which was all well and good, but the facts needed sifting through scrutinously, otherwise the security service would not have done its job properly. Knowledge of such details allowed relations with the security team not to be spoiled from the word go. I had a set piece ready for just this situation.

"Brody West. Thirty-five years of age. Divorced. Employment history as project manager – over thirteen years. Three major and twenty-five smaller projects successfully completed. I prefer to use Gantt charts, and PMI methodology, considering other methodologies superfluous or inadequate. As tools for Gantt charts I use—"

"Enough," Nathan cut me off, twiddling his fingers nervily. A company owner is the last person who wants to hear the jabberings of a potential mid-level manager, which was exactly what I was banking on. "Have you been told about the project?"

"No. But I'm ready to take on anything lawful. My experience enables me to manage any size of project concerning the construction of network infrastructure. That's why I'm here."

Book One: A Second Chance

Williams was quiet for a while, concentrating on the restarted presentation. After rubbing his red eyes, he pressed a button on the desk with a shaking hand and said, "You've got the job. But there are conditions. Go and have everything explained."

The secretary came in and stood by the door, holding it open. I said goodbye to Williams and left. The lady followed me out, sat down at her desk and, in a businesslike manner, held out a file of documents, saying, "Brody, here is the decision of the personnel department concerning your candidacy. The director has already approved it."

The file contained my slides printed out on copy paper. When I got to the Conclusions page I was flabbergasted. "Avoids solid social relationships outside the workplace? Seriously?" The conclusions of the local psychologists stated categorically that I had problems communicating with other people outside work. When was I supposed to socialize and establish these "solid" relationships, if I was at work from eight in the morning till ten in the evening? I stared at the secretary, demanding an explanation of what this had to do with the company. She took the file back and flicked through it.

"The conclusions are based on an analysis of the last four years of your life," she began. "You have no family, friends, or interests. Even in Barliona you're represented by a level-ten character. Your entire life is work. You are in a risk group."

"What risk group?" I asked, gobsmacked, still not quite grasping what they were trying to tell me, and unable to get my head round the surreal situation. The secretary slapped the file shut.

"The company is not interested in hiring employees with a risk of developing depression or neurosis from loneliness. If you notice, we pay particular attention to interaction, especially real-world interaction. Even our electronic document flow is kept to a minimum. Brody, has anyone ever *made* you work thirteen hours a day?"

"No, but work must be completed on time." Apparently the lady and I lived in different realities. In mine, any boss was happy if a person lived at work and for work.

"Mmm. So, you're a good project manager, but managing your working time is beyond you, right? Or were you just afraid to leave the office before the management?" She raised a mocking eyebrow. A secretary able to play with facts! "I must tell the girls to register you for the time management course. Don't worry, it's a common problem now. The director considers it necessary to remind employees about the importance of free time, socializing, and other pleasures."

"So to work for you I have to get married? Or will sexual relations with a long-standing partner suffice?" Angry that strangers were teaching me how to live, I couldn't resist a touch of sarcasm.

"If sex is supplied to you on a contractual basis, it doesn't count," replied the secretary, utterly unabashed. "Brody, do you need a job?" I nodded gloomily, and she smiled at me almost humanly. "Then let's dispense with these attempts to rub me up the wrong way. We are currently recruiting a team. The project begins in ten months' time. Your professional qualities are impressive. Your personal ones are cause for alarm. The latter is a priority for our company, but the former permits us to give you a chance. Attend our training course. Of course it's not exactly what you need, but you have to start somewhere."

"And how will you know when I no longer cause alarm for your psychologists and HR people?"

"That's no problem for them. While you're on the course, they'll watch you and suggest an individual approach to solving the problem."

"For example?" I already didn't know what to expect from these people.

"Anything at all. You can make it up for yourself. Meet up with friends, take interest in their lives, have lunch with your parents more often. If you find a steady partner, it can only be a good thing. Or join a clan in Barliona. You can socialize there. The main thing is that it should be just for fun, and not for the pursuit of some work-related goal. Understand?"

"I understand," I replied unenthusiastically. It irked me that people had weighed me up and were now giving me their recipes for normalcy.

"It's important for us to evaluate your ability to communicate with people outside work. During this time, Nathan is willing to employ you officially as an intern, with a salary of twenty-five percent of a project manager's full pay. If you accept, sign the last page. There's a pen on the stand."

Vasily Mahanenko. Invasion

Biometrics had long since replaced personal documents in our state, and a handwritten signature had lost all meaning. Your fingerprints and the retinas of your eyes were always with you, and when you held them to the scanner, you weren't worried about forgeries.

Tired of the weirdness and excessive questions, I just wrote my surname. I didn't have a specific flourish for these situations, because these situations didn't arise. I would deal with everything as it happened, since there was no other way out. I needed any work I could get, because I wanted my own house, a real piece of meat, and the real sun.

"Welcome to the company, Brody. Training begins in one hour. Helen will show you the way." The secretary folded my signed papers meticulously and filed them away.

"Okay, um..." I hesitated, realizing I didn't know her name. "How should I address you?"

"Victoria."

"Victoria, I still haven't been told anything about the project," I said, reminding her of the purpose of my visit.

"All information upon completion of your training. Helen, show Brody to the training hall."

The course turned out to be standard communication training, the likes of which I'd seen a gazillion times before. Never mind seen, I used to run them myself. For a good half hour, myself and seven other unfortunates were subjected to tired tropes explaining the importance of communication and live contact with coworkers. Badly, and by the wrong person. Little Helen, standing by the board, studiously drew adaptation graphs, recited wise quotes, and even read a short piece on the history of the Imitators, without understanding the first thing about it herself. It was clear she had mastered the methodology well enough, but she'd never actually been to an event like this. The result was a master class in how not to conduct a training session.

With my experience and the necessary knowledge, out of sympathy for the girl I gently seized the initiative and organized a Brownian Motion business scenario. One of the best ways to acquaint people with each other is to take the heat off by showing the need for nonverbal communication. It was curious to watch people who were used to exclusively digital interaction, blushing and becoming flustered in their attempts to think up new ways to greet another person – at first tactilely and silently, then tactilely and verbally, and by the end just verbally. After touching another person twice, they now found it difficult to readjust and greet them with only words.

Following this I introduced a standard scenario called, "Find five positive features of your neighbour," which forced them to enter into dialogue, communicate, and draw conclusions about somebody based on that communication. Helen forgot completely about her role and became actively involved in the game, and by the end of the session, the atmosphere was certainly warm, if not friendly. Eventually came the moment I'd been dreaming of since the very start – they let us go home. On the way out of the hall I was intercepted by a stern-looking woman, who turned out to be the head of HR and Helen's direct boss.

"Brody, I'd like a word with you."

I went back into the hall to see Helen, now wearing headphones, tidying up and shaking her tousled head in time with the music. Seeing her superior in the doorway, she quickly removed the device and tried to adopt a serious look. It was comical, just like in school, I swear.

"Brody, these sessions are not suitable for you," announced the lady. "You've clearly had experience of something similar before. When was that?"

"Way back at the dawn of my rebellious youth. And since then I've often conducted them myself."

"You can tell. You helped me a lot," Helen chipped in.

"Helped?" the boss teased her. "He did your job for you. Should I give him your wages? It's shameful."

The dressing-down had been friendly enough, but the girl's eyes sparkled with tears. The lady and I pretended we hadn't seen anything. To encourage snivelling in the workplace was the height of unprofessionalism. We were agreed on that.

"The training is pointless for you." The lady steered our conversation back on course. "You were clearly in your element. You need taking out of your comfort zone, and we have a number of solutions.

Please take a look at these."

An image flickered on the screen. At last, a glimpse of automation, a hint that this might yet be an IT company!

"A company trip to an exhibition of modern art... A fishing competition... A blind date... A character upgrade in Barliona... Stop, rewind! I agree to the training." And I'd thought we were done with idiocy for the day.

"Brody, concentrate on the matter at hand, which is to take you out of your comfort zone." She was relentless.

"I have another suggestion. You and I are business people, right?" I wasn't about to give up so easily, so I said, "You still have to do the adaptation course for the others. I can help Helen, teach her. For that we can keep... an upgrade in Barliona, and we can forget about my personal life."

She wasn't exactly fired up at the suggestion, and she fixed me with a heavy stare. But I didn't yield. Assistance came in a very unexpected form. Helen.

"Oh, Grandma, say yes. Brody can help me with my training, and I'll help him with his upgrade. And I'll introduce him to my friends."

The boss's stern manner disappeared in an instant, and she said to her granddaughter, "Helen, there is no 'Grandma' here! How many times do I have to tell you? Here I am Maria," said Maria before turning back to me. "Very well, Barliona it is. It's good enough for your purposes. I see your case isn't too far advanced. With your acumen, Brody, you need to build your career using social connections."

"And I will," I chuckled, looking poignantly first at Maria and then Helen. "So what's happening with Barliona?"

"We have a checklist for that kind of adaptation too."

The projector displayed a list of ten items.

	SOCIALIZATION VALUES FOR A BARLIONA SCENE	Numerical value
1	Develop your character to required level (candidate chooses parameters)	50
2	Become a full clan member or create your own clan (clan size in both cases min. 20 people)	—
3	Pass a dungeon at any level as part of another group	20
4	Receive Friend status from other players free of charge	5
5	Fulfil socially important tasks which provide no game advancement	50
6	Give assistance free of charge to random players when they complete tasks	20
7	Ask for insignificant help from Social category players	10
8	Extended verbal communication with another player	>=2,400 min per 6 mths.

9	Participate as a contestant in 2 festivals in Barliona	2
10	Receive 80 Agreeability points from a Barliona NPC	2

"On top of that, you will lead the course and teach Helen for six months, and then I will approve your socialization." The HR manager had pronounced my sentence.

"I'll be playing at home," I warned.

"You can play in the nether world for all I care… God forgive me," she replied. I was beginning to take a shine to the lady. "But you will spend two hours every day in the office. I shall be checking up on you personally. Now off you go, I'll be expecting you tomorrow."

I went home via the nearest Barliona office. I urgently needed a new pod with the standard frills, and the only game-connection devices at home were a dusty old helmet and gloves, the kind long since discarded by everyone.

Barliona had almost as many outlets as KFC or McDonald's. Each office had its own unique fantasy design based around a real object in the game: a medieval castle, an earth-goblin burrow, or a witches' hut. The person who dreamt all this up was a genius – it was both advertising and immersion in the game. And you couldn't miss it.

The office I came across was stylized as a country tavern. Everything was so real I could hear the creaking of worn steps under my feet, and the sweet aroma of food played with my empty stomach.

The interior furnishings and decor also seemed authentically medieval. As you would expect, keeping house behind the oaken bar was an Imitator-innkeeper, and several "customers" – devil-may-care pirates or highwaymen – were drinking beer, playing dice, and poking fun at the serving girl. The most active and noisy were the Imitators; the rest of the crowd consisted of holograms. There wasn't a single person among the office staff.

"Good day to you, lord. What is your desire? I see this is your first time with us." An electronic menu appeared on the counter.

A new client is a favorite client!

In order to become our client, select a type of pod:

* *General continuous-immersion pod (GCI). Supplied free of charge. All standard features: medical unit; sanitation unit; bed sore prevention and massager; pleasure/pain impulse sensors; feeding tube.*
* *Professional continuous-immersion pod (PCI). Supplied for an additional fee. All standard features, plus extras: full tactile sensation unit; olfactory centre; fitness module, allowing increase of real physical characteristics (agility, strength, endurance)*

whilst playing.

• Professional transitory-immersion pod (PTI). Supplied for an additional fee. All the extras of the PCI pod, but without some standard features: medical unit; sanitation unit; bed sore prevention; feeding tube. Continuous game-connection limit – max. 3 hours. Interval between connections – min. 1 hour.

Familiarize yourself with the terms of the contract and the user agreement.

A multipage text appeared, of the kind which, due to the nature of my profession, I was used to reading in full and with care. Cutting corners wasn't an option anyway, because the system monitored my eye movements and turned the page accordingly. It was impossible to just scroll to the end of the documents and touch a finger to the scanner to confirm my agreement with the contents. I didn't learn anything new – just the customary buck-passing from the administration to the player. I'd prepared identical documents myself and knew all the nuances. There could be no fault-finding – if I died or went bust, it would be my own fault.

The system confirmed that my eyes had followed the text from start to finish, and opened a new window:

Touch any finger to the scanner screen.
Congratulations! You are a new, and therefore favourite, client!
Select a type of pod and take the test to define the limit of your tactile sensation
GCI | PCI | PTI

TEST

Choosing a pod wasn't all that straightforward. The GCI was free, meaning I would save some money, but it was damn unpleasant when you could feel the feeding catheters, the urine-collection bag, and whatever else inside your body. My body mass, now in three figures, had long been hinting at exercise. The household robodoctor was forever complaining about my blood pressure and sugar and cholesterol levels and suggesting a diet and exercise plan, but I would refuse, citing a mad rush at work, a bad mood, the release of the new Star Wars film, or just that it wasn't Monday. Ultimately the choice was between the long-stay and short-stay professional models, and the advantages of the long-stay were obvious: I would fulfil the socialization tasks quicker, the inbuilt medunit would make sure I was losing weight and, significantly, in six months' time I would be able to give the pod to Matty. I'd be doing him a good turn. And I still felt guilty. Some things are worth loosening the purse strings for.

Book One: A Second Chance

No sooner had I signed the contract than a crew of service engineers left for my house to install the pod, without even waiting for it to be fully tested. The pods gave the user a whole range of tactile sensations to make the playing process as realistic as possible, but each one had its own sensitivity threshold, and so that the user didn't accidentally go schizo from overdosing on pleasure or pain, they ran checks before fixing the settings. My figures settled at roughly 30% pain and 80% pleasure. With high parameter readings, the conscious became addled or switched off altogether. In this respect I was statistically average – it would be easier to fuck me to death than beat me to death.

"Would you like to open an internal game bank account? If you do this the same day you sign the contract, we will offer you a discount." As befitted any good worker, the Imitator was trying to flog me optional extras.

I had read up on the Bank and the internal game accounts the previous evening, so I knew it was the same bells and whistles as the immersion pod. When a character regenerated, half the money they had at the moment of death remained at the place of death as loot. Beginners, of course, had nothing to lose, but as your level rose, so did your income, and thoughts of losing it would begin to torture everyone who was progressing. The Bank offered an automatic transfer of money to your game account, bypassing any pockets. No cash meant you couldn't lose it. Only vagrants refused, because for them, losing half their money was no scarier than the commission for opening and maintaining a virtual account.

"What terms are you offering?"

"Fifty-three credits to open the account; a yearly service subscription of fifty-eight credits; the commission for account transactions is two percent of the sum of the transaction."

"I hope that's without the discount?" I understood vagrants very well.

"The discount applies only to opening an account. Without it the fee is seventy credits. You can also merge a real account with a game account."

"No, I'll keep the game account separate."

"We have a promotion at the moment. If you top up your account with between one thousand and ten thousand credits, you will receive an additional twenty percent from Barliona. There is one small condition – you cannot withdraw the money for three months."

What a surprise! The last free gift I received was from Santa Claus. And that was bought by my dad. My account balance was no secret to the Imitators, and they were trying their hardest to con me into converting real money into game money, in strict accordance with their raison d'être. The less money a client had in reality, the less desire they had to return to that reality.

"Transfer fifteen thousand credits to my game account." Even so, the offer was very tempting.

"Would you like access to a mailbox?"

"That will be all, thank you." I brought the conversation to a close. Being blessed with a brain,

I would decide everything else after reading some forums and guides, and after a chat with my personal expert, Matty.

When I got home I was cheered by the news that the installation and setting of the pod would drag on into the late evening. I called Matty.

"Hi, buddy! Can you talk?"

"Hi, Bro. I always have time for you. Just wait a second and I'll log out."

If anyone was going to diss modern technology, it certainly wasn't me. You could call somebody even if they were in their pod. The main thing was to know their number.

"Has something happened?"

"No, I just wanted some advice. I'm having a pod installed. Can you tell me how to go about starting? I killed off my old guy."

"So you decided to go for it?" he said, thrilled. I didn't want to go into details over the phone, so I responded with silence, but Matty wasn't expecting anything else. "Cool! You've made my day."

"Uh-huh. Listen, you said you'd worked it all out. Let's meet and you can tell me who to play and where to begin?"

"Great!" He was genuinely excited. "But only in two hours, okay? I've got to finish a quest against the clock. Some guys are waiting for me. Then we'll discuss everything. Shit, Bro, we've got big work to do! We're gonna kick Barliona's ass for sure!"

Matty hung up, and I dialled the next number. I had a training session to prepare for.

"Peter, hi, it's Brody West. All good, thanks.

Oh, you know already? I've nearly found one, that's why I'm calling. How are you? Great. Listen, remember we ran that communication course years ago? Have you still got the teacher training and preparation plan? It should be on the server in the archive somewhere. Yeah, with the course. I fancy giving it a go. Yes, I know it's all out of date. Can you send it in an e-mail? Thanks. I owe you."

Before meeting Matty, I had just enough time to fry myself an enormous marbled steak. While I had money, no one was going to stop me enjoying a slap-up meal.

We arranged to meet in the park zone just outside the city. Anywhere else would be difficult for him to get to. The social shelters were being built a ninety-minute journey from the edge of the city, and the reasons were compelling enough. Firstly, to minimize time spent by social citizens among the Free. The less a vagrant saw of normal, comfortable life, the fewer improper thoughts they would have; and if such thoughts did arise, then their realization would not be far off – an hour tops. Secondly, so that endless concrete anthills wouldn't ruin the green splendor the city had become.

The park zones were being developed directly outside the city specifically so the vagrants would have somewhere to stretch their legs. Beyond them was an exclusion zone which only public transport was permitted to enter. The state very charitably paid to deliver the wearers of metal bracelets from their shelters to the park zone and back. To get to the city you had to take a taxi, and pay for it yourself.

I sat on a bench with a parcel of warm food on my knee and a bag of our favorite beer beside me. It was already evening, though at that time of year, twilight draws in much later, so I saw Matty's gangly, jogging figure from a long way off.

"Hey! It's cool you came." He was panting, but it didn't stop him rejoicing at seeing me, and at a little physical exertion. We embraced, and he plopped himself down beside me.

"Ah, living it up two days running! Decent food." Matty took his wrapper and got stuck into his kebab. His stomach would organize a revolution out of sheer joy.

"What do they feed you? If I'd thought, I would have grabbed something more substantial," I said, opening two cans of beer. I'd already forgotten how easy it was to talk to Matty about simple earthly matters. At work everyone used office speak, even if they were talking about some new dish on the set lunch menu.

"Powdered gruel, like what they give babies. Very little pleasure involved, it's just to clear the pipes out so they don't get gunked up. So go on then, tell me. We haven't got much time." Matty somehow managed chat between mouthfuls.

I took a swig of beer, then told him everything, just like at confession.

"Yes, you're in trouble now," he said. "Do you really want to work there? If you ask me, the people in Barliona will be more normal than there."

"Matty, they're offering me something

Barliona doesn't have and never will – reality. Sorry, but I want to live here."

"Yeah, I get it. You don't have to explain. In six months you'll completely disappear."

"No, I like the idea of the clan. Let's try it. Six months for set up and development, then we'll need a powerful advertising campaign. Then I'll hand over management to you, and only login for a couple of hours a day."

"Like that, huh? What the hell do we need advertising for?"

"No offense, but even a genius director won't lead an all-vagrant clan to the top. We need advanced players with gear and money. It would be good to find a Maecenas or two. The Phoenixes and the Legends made names for themselves first, then people came flocking to them. Now they always have plenty to choose from. A well thought out advert is half the battle. So, Matty, we create a clan, we establish connections, we organize the collection and processing of materials, we do quests, we sign contracts with NPCs. And that's it – we're the victors in life. All we have to do is start and finish."

"You've already drawn up a plan?" asked Matty in awe.

"Yeah, just now," I admitted honestly. "They're installing me a pod too, but I haven't got a clue. That's why I called. Come on, we've only got half an hour left."

"You're right. It's just a bit sudden." Matty snapped out of his daydreaming about a happy future, and looked balefully at his bracelet. "If only

I could take this bloody leash off. Anyway, listen. A new continent has just appeared..."

Reference information

Continents in Barliona

Astrum – a continent for players in North America

Kaltua – a continent for players in Africa

Calragon – a continent for players in Europe

Celestial – a continent for players in Asia

Ratrandia – a continent for players in South America and Australia

Stivala – a continent introduced in the latest version of Barliona, with no geographical reference for players

---

For the remaining thirty minutes, Matty gave me the gist without going into too much detail. He really did have an idea. While doing some Blacksmith and Engineer business, he'd wangled a rare quest connected with materials on Stivala. After the first settlement of the new lands, players began to mine resources and sell them at auction. Prices for demon ore were exorbitant, but it was still snapped up in seconds. Matty pushed the boat out too and bought a little ore and some other ingredients, whereupon, for perhaps the first time in the game, fortune smiled on him. After you created an object, the system offered a unique handicraft task, only it demanded resources and funds. He couldn't boast either of these, but if he had a reliable clan, it might all work out. That was when he found out I'd lost my job, and he was struck by a ray of hope.

I needed to create my character on another continent, get busy with some Mining and Lumberjacking, bust a gut while making others work too (demanding ten percent to the clan), build a castle on the new continent to house the main stores, and wait for Matty to show up. His last piece of advice concerned expenses imperative for a comfortable game: an account in the game bank, a mailbox, and a communication amulet with a game number. But I knew all that anyway. That was pretty much it: our master plan to nail some unreal megabucks.

I wanted to discuss the rest of the details over the phone, but Matty rejected the idea categorically. Pods and phones were wired, and great ideas stolen without scruple. We parted on that good note, and without me saying out loud what I thought of the plan. At first glance it looked utopian. At second glance too. But what did I know about game economics? Nothing. Before you've done any digging around for yourself, it's silly to speak of the reality or unreality of any plan. Who was I to criticize without an alternative to offer?

Returning home, I poured the first of that night's succession of coffees down my throat, and fell to digging. For three hours I scoured everything available, all the way down to advertising descriptions, guides and official reference materials, until my head was in pieces. Most of what I read was almost worthless, and any essential information on the new continent was only to be found in fee-paying resources. Game specifics, extras, bonuses, advancement tips, videos – everything cost money, and sometimes quite a lot. Apparently this was due to an announcement by the Barliona Administration that people would no longer be able to influence the mechanics of the game. Some recent, large-scale bribery cases had forced the Corporation to take extreme measures – complete replacement of the development and support team by Imitators. Programmers, scriptwriters, designers, cartographers, project developers, and testers were all laid off. Now nobody could spill any beans. The market reacted instantly, and prices rocketed. Not so much on legacy content, but you could easily make reasonable money from selling new content.

I decided not to use the sellers' services, preferring to rely on my own experience. On the official site, the most valuable information about starting the game concerned a bonus for commercial accounts. If a player created a new character but left the choice of race, class, and initial location to the discretion of the game, they received a bonus. Since I had no thoughts on the matter, and I only wanted Matty to see the right continent, I was delighted at the opportunity for random generation and the extra bonus for my lack of initiative. As long as the bonus was of use, of course.

Vasily Mahanenko. Invasion

When I finished the theoretical preparation for immersion in Barliona, the clock showed I only had three hours plus journey time before work. It was too late to think of sleep, so I decided to check out the pod.

Years ago I dreamt about a huge grand piano in the middle of the living room. That dream, adjusted for time, had almost come true. In the middle – though not of the living room; and huge – though not a grand piano. In its dimensions, the professional pod for continuous immersion in the virtual reality of the Barliona game world was consistent with an unrealized dream. Maybe someday I'd enrol on a course and climb in there to play Vivaldi or Chopin.

After pressing some buttons and carefully studying my new toy, I froze with indecision. To climb in or not to climb in?

Hell, bring it on! This ultra-modern coffin was thought out to the last detail. I didn't actually have to climb in to it, like in the vampire films, because the pod adopted an almost vertical position for loading and unloading the passenger.

Inside, to my surprise, there were no horrible probes, tubes for biowaste, or other suchlike fittings. Or rather there were, but they only appeared and were aligned while the pod was returning to its horizontal position, so the player didn't experience fear or discomfort. I didn't even notice the roof closing. A platform came out, I stood backwards onto it, and it went back in, depositing me into a chamber in the lower part of the pod, at which moment a hoop was lowered onto my head, taking over control of my brain. Absolutely no feeling of claustrophobia or being buried alive. Cool!

I stopped sensing my body. All around was boundless and pristine space. And a message before my eyes.

Welcome to Barliona

Description: *We are delighted to welcome our new player. The initial settings of the pod are fixed. The sensory perception filters are set in accordance with your individual characteristics.*

Important: *You are entering the pod after a long absence from the game. Be advised that the Barliona game mechanics have been significantly revised. You will find a description of the changes on the official game site. A redenomination has been conducted, equating the value of gold in the game with the value of credits in reality.*

The system confirmed I'd read the message to the end, and the message changed.

Select a faction
Kartoss | Malabar | Free Lands | Random

All the available selections were lit up in red. All I had to do was fix my eyes on an item, and it would instantly change colour to green, changing back as soon as I looked at another item. All clear with navigation.

There were actually many more factions in Barliona, but for our geographical location only these were available. Matty played for Malabar, so I didn't worry too much about my own selection there. The user agreement said the pod was able to read the upper layer of my thoughts. I fixed my eyes on "Malabar" and mentally pronounced, "Malabar."

Select a faction
Are you sure?
The "Selection Assistance" option
provides the player with reference
information concerning each faction.

"Yes. I don't need any assistance. My selection is Malabar."

Selection accepted: Malabar

Select the race you would like to play
for
<List of races available in Barliona and
their descriptions > | Random

"Random generation." This phrase was the key to loading the scene I'd read about on the website.

Random generation of character selected
Necessary action: *Define parameters for random generation (min. 4).*
Parameters:

- *Faction*
- *Race*
- *Class*
- *Name*
- *Appearance*
- *Geographical reference*
- *Initial location*

I shifted my gaze from one parameter to the next, making my selections, until only geographical reference was still red. Players from different factions could easily communicate and collaborate with each other, the only question being language barriers. Still, let's go for it!

Geographical reference selection
Necessary action: *Select geographical reference for your character. After confirming random generation, you can only change your race or class after 30 calendar days.*

Parameters:

- *Choose continent*
- *Go back*
- *Cancel random generation of character*

Vasily Mahanenko. Invasion

"I need the continent of demons – Stivala. I confirm random generation of all other parameters."

Instead of a message or a progress bar, in front of me appeared a gray-bearded and long-robed elder holding a staff. Resting his hands on the staff, he bowed his head in a dignified manner and said, "Greetings to you, Free one! You have taken a decisive step." The old man pursed his lips deferentially and stroked his beard. "Such valour is worthy of reward. Barliona needs brave heroes, and it is encouraging that you are one such. Welcome to Barliona, hero Kvalen!"

He knocked on the ground with his staff, then crumbled into a cloud of pixels, leaving the parameters of my character in his wake.

Initial settings generated
- **Faction**: Free Lands
- **Race**: Tiefling
- **Class**: Demon hunter
- **Name**: Kvalen (name from "reserved" list)
- **Appearance**: Customized appearance of player
- **Geographical reference**: Lok'dar, continent of Stivala
- **Initial location**: Demon-Hunter Training Camp

What's a tiefling? Never heard of... demon hunter... I can run around as a hunter... Kvalen is, well, Kvalen, who cares? All the rest we'll deal with later... "Start game!"

The white space darkened, and a ball of mist appeared ahead. It grew, curled, and stretched, forming a silhouette. The figure gained substance and was complemented with features, and when the mist dissipated I saw a horned, tailed, and hooved creature looking back at me. WTF? My first thought was, "That can't be my guy! It's a goat! All that's missing is the beard!" In response to my indignation, a somewhat sparse beard suddenly sprouted. Shit! And where's my bonus?

The creature eyed me aggrievedly. Its pitch black eyes had no whites. I looked it sceptically up and down, and gave the mental order to "give us a twirl." This is what they call "customized appearance of player"? The gray canvas coat didn't hide my spare tire, and the novitiate's pants refused to stay up on it. Way to go, tolerance! Although it's true I was even fatter in real life.

So, tieflings are humans with tails, hooves, and goat's horns. If I bumped into my ex in Barliona, she would definitely say, "I always knew it." She would also add that it was a hint at my subconscious and a manifestation of my real alter ego. Ugh, I was definitely going to change it in a month. I could just imagine Matty's face.

With that thought, I decided to learn how to change my parameters. The beard had materialized, after all. I began mentally saying what I wanted to change, and assessed the results. The original image really was a work in progress waiting to be tweaked. I altered the length and ramification of the horns, the appearance of the tail, the colour of the skin and eyes, and various other things, until I got bored.

Since the game was 18+, I ordered the tiefling to undress, and appraisingly sized up its figure. "I want a six-pack!" The game responded humorously by drawing six beer bottles over the bulging belly. Ha ha! "Okay then, I want a sinewy, muscular body with fifteen percent body fat. Oh, excellent!"

My gaze shifted down. Well, it was my customized body, and nobody had actually complained. I decided to leave it as it was. Making peace with my character's image, I found the Save button with my eyes and read it mentally. Another message appeared:

Birth of a Tiefling scene launched
Description: *The race-specific Birth of a Tiefling scene launches every hour. Next launch in 32 minutes. You will be put to sleep while you wait. We wish you a pleasant game!*

The tiefling assumed a sprinter's crouch before charging in a flash toward me, horns down. I felt odd and tried to step out of its way, but couldn't – I didn't have a body. At the last moment, when I realized collision was inevitable, I screwed up my eyes and... felt nothing. No impact, no pain. But I couldn't open my eyes.

The feeling of space suddenly changed. There

was no time to even pin down or keep track of the moment. I was just suddenly aware of myself drowsing in a comforting liquid and experiencing fantastical blissfulness. I floated with closed eyes, occasionally bumping into something soft and warm, rejoicing in my own being, and that of the warm, soft thing, and in our bumping. I loved this thing, and I loved our gentle physical contact, and it responded in kind, for in the ocean of bliss there was room for all. There was no need to waste your breath on spite and aggression. Everything around was invoked to give us happiness.

"Arise, my children! Your hour has come. It is time to emerge into the light," a delicate and seductive voice sang out. Only a mother could speak so tenderly.

Mother. I wanted to approach her, and was afraid to upset her with my inertia. I must hurry! I reached out toward the voice, straining to open my eyes.

It wasn't easy, but I tried. Mother would be angry if I was blind or came last. She didn't like failures, and ate them straight after their birth. There was no place for weaklings among demons.

I broke out in a cold sweat from head to toe. What freaking demon? When I understood the absurdity of my own thoughts, I opened my eyes. Then I screamed. From shock. A normal reaction for a person who finds themselves swimming in a lake of molten lava. The world around was so natural, its colours so deep and voluminous that my vocal cords seized up with fear and my cries were cut short. I managed to save my conscious by concentrating on the game interface buttons, which did not disappear even when I blinked. My brain accepted this as a weighty argument in favour of virtuality, and was calmed. *It's just Barliona, I'm in virtuality, surrounded by a pod, nothing more. Everything's fine.*

I breathed out heavily and looked around. There really was a lake of lava surrounded by cliffs. The horizon line was hidden some distance away, behind the tall, rocky barrier. Leaden clouds hung low in the sky, showering rain down on me through the thunder and lightning, though the water drops evanesced before they could reach the ground. The lava did not burn; quite the opposite, it was warm and comforting.

Aside from me, another dozen heads were swimming in the lake. Oddly, I couldn't see a single other player among the newborn tieflings. They were all NPCs. In a state of ecstasy from their unity with the lava – primogenitrix matter – they also floated with eyes closed.

My hand reached out by itself to touch my new accoutrements. Curious sensations. Neither the tail nor the horns felt alien, just like I'd had them all my life.

Completing my examination, I swam a little front crawl, all the while contemplating my fellow clansmen. Until I realized my mistake – I was not alone here from the real world. Alongside me was a player from the social shelters, for some reason bearing the simple name Eredani.

Reference information

Character names

Within Barliona every character's name is unique. To provide uniqueness, and to satisfy players' desire to be named as they choose, composite names are used, consisting of two or more words. There is also a register of "reserved" simple names. This is a fee-paying service. Reserved names can be used free of charge by Premium Account holders, or when a player selects random generation for his character (min. 3 parameters). Simple names are also assigned to prisoners, using min. 10 letters.

When the player noticed me, I nodded to him in greeting, but instead of replying, he pointed to something behind my back. I turned round and immediately began paddling backwards and swearing loudly. It was going to take a while to get used to Barliona. On the shore of our jacuzzi stood the higher demoness Ireness, and behind her, chained to the wall, hung an array of tormented and barely alive beings: orcs, humans, elves. The demoness made a pass with her hand, and one of the victims doubled up in pain. The creature, a onetime paladin, choked on his own shrieks, before his body went limp and gray, and another tiefling surfaced, luxuriating, beside us. A life for a life was the name of this sanguineous scene.

Vasily Mahanenko. Invasion

Turning again to the vagrant, I saw him swimming with broad strokes toward the opposite shore. A sensible decision. I had no desire to hang around under Mother's gaze myself, so I swam after him, carefully detouring around blissed-out tieflings. We reached the rocky shore at almost the same time, but I chose to climb out a little way from Eredani.

I pulled myself half out of the lava and was immediately pierced through by a savage cold. Once upon a time my wife had convinced me to buy a cryochamber, saying something about rejuvenation and rebooted immune systems. Still young and in love, I allowed myself to be talked round without going into the details, but by the time I was wearing wafer-thin clothes and strange footwear with metal heels, I felt most out of sorts. I entered the first chamber without a fuss, simply because I didn't know what to expect, and was greeted by a temperature of -60. I had to be manhandled into the second chamber (-120) by my colleagues, motivated by the fact that it was already paid for, and assured I wouldn't notice the difference. Only then did I realize what the iron heels were for: those fuckers outside could hear if I'd died or still hadn't quite yet attained the grade of White Walker. The only thing that got me through the ordeal without strangling anyone, was remembering I was a real man and could not disgrace myself in front of my dear lady.

Similar sensations awaited me when I hauled myself out onto the shore. But seeing Eredani, who had pulled himself out first, produced a muffled

"Woah, shit!" and dived straight back in, and understanding there was no one around to flaunt anything to, I followed his example. Immediate relief and drowsiness, and no wish to exit the lava again. If anyone felt so inclined, they could dig me out.

"In the name of the Light!" A ruckus to wake the dead came crashing through the thunder and the snarlings of the demoness. "Die, spawn of the Abyss!"

Lightning bolts skidded across the lava and produced a light, but nevertheless unpleasant, prickling on the skin. New dramatis personae entered the stage: a sparkling gold warrior, a girl dressed in snow white, and a heavyset, bearded man with a shield twice his own size. My little knowledge of game classes and races was enough to identify a paladin, a priestess, and a warrior. Or alternatively, a human, a she-elf, and a dwarf.

"You're too late, light boy!" hissed Mother, adding ultrasonically, "They are all mine!"

My body quaked at the shrieks of the primogenitrix, and the upper part of my viewer was occluded by a slew of vibrantly coloured pictograms. Mother's debuffs did us no harm; the demoness guarded her children most attentively.

Reference information

Buff
A positive status effect on a player, created by increasing one or several of their characteristics. A buff may affect

a player indirectly, increasing, for example, their Agreeability to NPCs. The duration of a buff may be specified, or may last until cancelled by the player.

Debuff
A negative status effect on a player, differing from direct damage. As a rule, for any stat which may be increased by a buff, there is a debuff which decreases it.

"You have no power in this world!" answered the paladin no less loudly. He raised his hammer up to the heavens, where it shone brighter than the sun. "In the name of Eluna!"

"Bastard," said Eredani, wincing with pain. The paladin had fixed the whole vicinity with light magic, unconcerned for our wellbeing. The slightest movement was enough to burn your whole body mercilessly, and it occurred to me that thirty percent pain was too much for me. Trying not to move, I observed the unfolding spectacle. The scriptwriters had gone a touch overboard on pathos for my liking.

"Your paladins were the first to be sliced up," laughed the demoness, blind to the light emanating from the hammer. "But do not weep, they did not die in vain, for they allowed my children to enter Barliona. It is their home now and you cannot banish them from it. See how strong my children are. It was the power of the paladin's death cries that made them this way."

"Beast! Go back to where you came from! I banish you!" cried the priestess, and the white Eluna merged with the yellow light of the paladin's hammer. The demoness could not hold off this two-pronged attack and she began to wither, as her recent victims had. I remembered from the guides that fire could not harm a higher fire demon, and only sacred light could have any effect on them. Ireness was in a really bad way, and in her death throes she threw out crimson threads to her prisoners, mummifying them on the spot. The instantly released power she kept for herself, though there was little of it, and she was not about to die quietly:

"You shall never achieve anything! This world will be ours!" The demoness scattered like ash, and all was still. Gone was her monotonous gnarling, gone were the prisoners' wails, gone was the thunder. And in that ringing silence, the footfall of the paladin rang out like the blows of his hammer.

"They are all dead, Bartalin," said the girl sadly, after inspecting the prisoners shackled to the rock face. "She took their souls with her. I cannot revive any of them."

"Lorgus, unloose them." Even when he wasn't shouting, the paladin's voice was powerful. "The brothers deserve a proper burial."

Servants appeared and, under instruction from the dwarf, began to release the mummies from their chains and lay them on stretchers. The paladin and the priestess approached the lake.

"Spawn of the Abyss!" said the paladin with ill-disguised hatred, and spat. His spittle evaporated before it hit the lava.

"Do not be so harsh, Bartalin. They are the sons and daughters of our brothers." The priestess was more tolerant toward other races. "Children are not responsible for the sins of their parents. Give the volcanic tieflings a chance."

"You ask too much for the demons! There is only one place for them in Barliona – the eternal chains of the demonologists!"

"They are not demons, Bartalin." The she-elf was insistent. "Our blood runs in them too – the blood of elves, of humans, of dwarves, of orcs. Do not let the memory of that blood die. There are ever fewer warriors. Ireness will return. Be prepared. Instruct the tieflings and send them to fight her. Better a half-demon should die than a human or an elf. We will choose those who can stand against the will of Ireness, we will purify them, we will train them, and we will send them into battle."

So that was the way it was! Mercy came in no pure form. The priestess saved us not out of kindness, but for the sake of her fellow tribesmen who were hunted and killed by Ireness. Expendables – that's what tieflings were to the she-elf. Hypothetically, Ireness could only have killed us. We were unfit to be used as food or for bearing new children.

"As you please, Abigail," the paladin relented. "Do with them as you will."

Book One: A Second Chance

The priestess nodded. An inexplicable force drew me up out of the soothing hot liquid and left me hanging in the air. The cold immediately fettered my body and my mind, but before I blacked out, I heard the order: "Lorgus, we need more stretchers! We are taking the tieflings with us."

My consciousness returned in a couple of seconds; at least, that's what the system clock showed. I was lying inside a warm dome, which is why I no longer felt cold. The lake among the cliffs had transformed into a stony dungeon with steel bars at the window and a small iron door. Apart from myself, and two wizards holding up the dome, there were also two elves: the familiar snow-white Abigail, and a certain Uldaron, dressed in leather with chainmail reinforcements.

"I'm not sure," said Uldaron, looking me over like a horse at the fair. "Too many disadvantages, too much hassle. The fiery nature and demonic essence will need suppressing, otherwise he'll die. But that will make him weaker. What do I want with a warrior like that? The first weakling he runs into will knock him down with a stick."

"His enemies are demons. He has good defense against them. All the rest is irrelevant. He's a Free citizen, he can come back from the Gray Lands. If they knock him down with a stick, he will get up, dust himself down, and continue. Such warriors are exactly what we need now."

"Then let him be a warrior!" muttered Uldaron, dissatisfied. "Why make a demon hunter out of him?"

"Because these are the only two left," said the priestess. "You should have come to the assembly on time. Then you could have chosen your own Free citizens. They all came. Uldaron, you know you can't not take them. Either you take them, or your training camp will be closed down and all the recruits redistributed. The choice is yours."

"Oh, I'm riddled with doubt now," he quipped. "Let me think. So, either they shut down the training camp, or I take these two waifs. I really don't know, it's such a difficult choice."

"Quit clowning around. Consider the tieflings a challenge."

"Purify them and dispatch them. I'll figure it out as we go along." This was already the second NPC to concede an argument to Abigail. Did she have high Charisma or something? On the surface you wouldn't say so.

"Brother Lektor, he's all yours," called Abigail, and another priest entered the cell. This time a human. I got goose bumps just from the look of him. Brother Lektor had a malicious look about him. Not spiteful, but just that – malicious. And heavy.

"Dome!" he ordered, swinging his censer harder and filling the cell with smoke. The wizards lowered their hands, and the heat sphere around me disappeared. "Now get out!"

The NPCs vanished into thin air, and for the third time recently the cold descended on me. I hunched over on the floor, searching convulsively for the Escape button. However, either the cold affected my brain that way, or I wasn't allowed out according to the script, because there were no buttons on the status bar. The game did not want to release me until the end of the scene.

"Don't hold your breath, you're not going to die." Gentleness was not brother Lektor's strong suit. He waved the censer above me until I was totally enveloped in black smoke. The cold left me, giving way to weakness. The priest proceeded to whine a prayer in a mind-numbing recitative in an unfamiliar language, and then sprinkled my head with a gray power. Resigning myself to my current situation, I shut my eyes and waited for the end. The cold was gone, and sooner or later the script would finish.

"I name you Kvalen!" After the purification process, Abigail preferred to endow me with my name herself. "Henceforth you are a tiefling – half-demon/half-human. Arise, Free citizen of Barliona!"

I tried to get to my feet, but it was futile – my body was wooden. Every movement was a struggle requiring maximum effort. My sensations and perception of the world were too natural. During the scene I forgot a couple of times that everything around was virtuality. Which is why I remained lying on the ground, waiting for whatever would happen next. I wasn't in the habit of putting myself out much in the real world, and I couldn't make myself overcome pain just like that and stand up in a virtual one. It wasn't about pressing buttons in a comfortable armchair.

"And this is a demon hunter?" asked Uldaron in disgust. "He can't even get up off his knees. Take him to the training camp. I hope he'll have the brains to escape from there by himself."

Birth of a Tiefling scene completed
Description: *Race-specific Birth of a Tiefling scene completed. We wish you a pleasant game!*

Some control buttons appeared on the progress bar, and I pressed Exit. Fuck Barliona with its continuous immersion! I should have agreed to that fishing date.

Chapter 2

JUMPING AROUND the room, shivering, while trying to get dressed, I couldn't seem to get my foot into my trouser leg. Shit, why was it so cold? It felt like the next ice age had decided to kick off in my house. Having eventually dealt with my clothes, and tapping out a Morse-code message with my teeth, I skipped sprightly to the kitchen in search of something warming. Oddly, the thermometer was showing the usual 23°.

Bundled up in a blanket and armed with a cup of cognac-laced coffee, I hit the Internet to find the answer to the perennial question: WTF? The cognac entered my system in small doses and was exclusively for medicinal purposes. Namely to warm up and calm down. It worked.

The seasoned gamers on the forum assured me the cold I was experiencing was absolutely normal after the first few immersions. It was like a phantom pain, the body continuing to feel what it had recently experienced in the pod. With time the brain became used to virtuality, and would react appropriately to changing conditions.

Next in line for research were the tieflings. Who were they, and what did you eat them with? Ha ha. If I was honest, I didn't understand the nature of the bonus I'd undertaken all this for. The more I read about Kvalen's race on the official website, the more questions I had for the developers.

Reference information

Tiefling

A closed race. A half-demon, born of a fire demon and a creature of another race. Appearance depends on the demon parent, but all representatives have horns, a tail, hooved lower limbs, and monotone black eyes. In order to adapt to life in Barliona, tieflings have lost their demonic power, fire resistance, and enhanced survivability. Their demon ancestry has resulted in Barliona residents' negative attitude toward half-demons.

Race abilities of fire tieflings

- *Increased basic value for Agility (+3 each 10 levels) and Intellect (+3 each 10 levels)*
- *Increased fire resistance (+50%)*
- *Increased demon magic (+30%)*
- *Increased resistance to demon magic (+50%)*
- *Total-darkness vision*

Race weaknesses of fire tieflings

- *Decreased basic value for Strength (-3 each 10 levels) and Stamina (-3 each 10 levels)*
- *Increased damage from Barliona magic (+30%)*
- *Inability to study Barliona magic*
- *Weak reaction of healing incantations to Barliona magic (-50% to healing)*
- *Growth rate for Agreeability to NPCs decreased by 50%*

A search for the term "closed race" bemused me. If the guides were to be believed, players could not choose their own race, class, or anything else marked "closed." However, apart from myself there was another player swimming in the lava, and he was on a social contract. Interesting.

Over and over I reread the information and weighed up my prospects. I categorically disagreed with the developers that having a goat as your character was a great bonus, but there was nothing I could do about it. According to the rules of random generation, I would have to run around cloven-hooved for a month, maybe longer. Things weren't looking good. Not only would NPCs be hostile to me because of my demon genealogy, but players would also turn up the heat.

I didn't know how to go on. If I deleted my account and created a new one, I could only recoup my money in three months' time. And the refund system was very unclear. I wasn't about to risk my savings, so I wrote an official enquiry to client support concerning a refund and having being made a tiefling. Everything by the book.

"Hi. Are you asleep?" After finishing my letter I called Matty, only glancing at the clock when it was already too late.

"Hi," he replied croakily, before yawning into the microphone. "Yes."

Sleep in Barliona was never sound, but social players had no choice. They had no time or place to relax.

"Shit, I wasn't thinking."

"Bro, call whenever you like. There'll be time for sleep."

When I understood how stupid my reason was for waking him up at half six in the morning, I hesitated. "I wanted to ask you... I've created myself a character."

"Ah," he said and was silent, either groggy from being half asleep, or surprised at the fervour with which I'd dived into Barliona. "Great. What's your name? Height? Weight? Are we going to wet the baby's head?"

"Horns, more like. They called me Kvalen. Have you heard of tieflings?"

"The half-demons? I read something in the news. I don't remember. What, have you made yourself a tiefling? They're hardcore!"

"It wasn't me." I had to confess what a genius I was to have found such a great random generation scene. "I'm sitting here wondering whether to delight in my goat-legged bonus, or delete it in a month."

"Ah, that's why you're calling?" Matty sighed with relief. "I was worried something had happened. Ditch it and create a new one. The simple name is cool, but it's not worth the hassle – nobody likes demons. It'll be a massive pain in the ass. Even demonologists are getting strange looks. It's not much of a bonus."

"I can't delete it straight away, only in a month. What am I going to do? A whole freaking month on my butt, then start all over again?"

"Well... let's meet today and discuss a strategy. I'll think of something to keep you busy for a month."

"Why bother meeting? I'll call you when I get back from work." It occurred to me that every time we spoke Matty suggested getting together.

"No, let's have a beer," he insisted, although he quickly added, "Or are you busy? In which case we can meet tomorrow."

"I'm not busy. It's just a ninety-minute journey for you. And what the hell for? Just don't say that evil foes are tapping our phones and stealing ideas." I heard a deep snuffling sound, one that I'd known since childhood. Matty was brooding. "Well? Say something."

"What is there to say?" he mumbled. "Just a bit longer and I'll be back, Bro. In there I'm a druid with a unique task. Out here I'm a vagrant whose wife and kids have left him. Nearly everyone's gone from our block. They live in Barliona. And all the rest come out looking angry and bottled up. You can't talk to them, or have a drink with them. I reckon I'll lose it soon and get stuck in there. I've already got no reason to leave the pod every day. I see the kids once a week, and that's for an hour. I don't have time for anything else."

I felt for him, but didn't know what to say. I'd always felt awkward when it came to showing sympathy and support. "Okay. I'll just sort work out, buy some beer, and be on my way to yours. I'll call."

"I'm not going to say no. I'll be waiting," he said. I was just about to hang up when he said, "Wait! I've just thought about your tiefling. Nobody knows anything about them. Or about demon hunters. It's a new race, a new class, a new continent. Just smell the cash! Don't be too hasty about leaving the training camp. Go for a walk, have a look around, make a video, draw a map. You can do a lot of trading in a month, make some contacts in the top guilds. What's wrong with that? Then you don't need to delete your guy."

"Agreed. I'll do some thinking." Whichever way you looked at it, Matty was right. I hadn't seen any rates for information about the new continent. With the proper handling, my goat had a good chance of becoming a golden antelope.

"Matty, can you do me a favour? Sometimes I don't get obvious things, just because I don't think about them. Next time tell me straight, without that spy paranoia. You heard it yourself – I'm socially challenged. I've even got a psychologist's note."

"Go to… work, socially challenged. Pack it in with the self-reflection. I'm going to sleep."

The situation with Matty worried me more and more. Was I a friend or what? He definitely needed dragging out of the shelter. Yet again I prowled the expanses of the Internet, trying to work out how to restore him to normal society. After flicking through a couple of legal reference bases, I realized I knew lots about turning citizens into vagrants, but nothing about the reverse process. My entire experience was not enough to render the legal documents unambiguously. They'd done it deliberately. It was advantageous to the government to have everybody sitting in Barliona instead of exacerbating the situation in the world with their irrelevance. With the thought that I needed a consultation with a good lawyer, I closed my laptop and went to work.

All contemporary learning had long since been transferred to virtuality. People slid into their pods to mingle with teachers, other students, and simulation programs, getting excellent results in no time and with minimal expense. But Right Decision Ltd. didn't cut corners, and out of a sense of duty I decided to comply.

Helen was waiting for me in the empty hall, ready to absorb the wisdom of my experience. Just like a million years ago, instead of a tablet she had a graph-ruled exercise book and a ballpoint pen. Where did she even manage to find them? Couldn't you find an ink pot, my little eager beaver? Instead of the expected lecture, I dumped a stack of printed sheets in front of her.

"Right. We are not going to waste each other's time. Memorize this lot by Monday. Inside out, down to the last comma. If you learn it earlier, call me and we can start putting theory into practice. If not, I'll punish you on Monday."

"How?" Aghast, Helen looked from the papers to me and back.

"I don't know yet." I frowned and said, "Helen, don't think about the punishment. Concentrate on fruitful work."

"I'm not asking about the punishment," she said, raising her voice. "How am I supposed to learn all this? Don't you have an electronic version? I could throw it in the emulator and listen to it in the pod."

"Not likely, my girl! It wouldn't be corporate to use the blessings of civilization like that. What's your character in Barliona?"

"A paladin."

"There you go. You like facing hardship head on. Open the first page and read it to yourself. If you don't get it, read it again. Quote it from memory. If you make a mistake, read it again. Repeat the cycle until you've learnt it all by frigging heart. During this time I will allow you to use swear words in conversation with me, to make the learning process easier."

"I... I'll tell grandma! This is absolute nonsense!" shrieked the girl.

"Then I'll punish her too. I choose the teaching method. Of course if *grandma* doesn't agree, everything's open to discussion," I said calmly.

"Hch-hm," resounded the diplomatic cough of the HR boss from a speaker. "Maria sees no need to interfere and revise the terms of your socialization. Old methods of instruction are just as valid as new ones."

I broke out in a wide smile. "As you wish."

"We're not allowed to spend personal time on work. Had you forgotten?" continued the girl stubbornly.

"You will learn everything by end of business today," stressed Maria.

"But there are two hundred and thirty-six pages of font size ten! I'd sooner die than learn all this using your old-fashioned methods."

"Helen! Don't be so childish! Have you been given a task?" barked Maria in such a tone it went right through even me.

"Yes," said the girl in a whisper. Grandma was perfectly capable of becoming a strict department head when she saw fit. The faded Helen collected her papers and headed for the door.

"Helen, why are you such a muddlehead? No one's taken the scanner away," her beloved grandmother grumbled after her. Helen paused for a second, and with a shriek of, "Thanks, grandma," flew off to fulfil her task.

"Maria, I could use a lawyer," I said before the lady signed off. "I want a consultation on a personal matter. Would that be possible?"

"It would. They'll help you in reception. Come and see me afterwards. And Brody, don't scare the girl. Otherwise it'll be me doing the swearing, and we don't want that now, do we?" came the reply, before the intercom shut off.

I could have argued with Maria about how to educate the youth, but she was right, I genuinely didn't want that. After quickly squaring everything with Helen as planned, I went to reception, where Victoria was leafing lazily through pages on a tablet. I approached and strained my neck to have a peek at how the director's assistant entertained herself when left to her own devices. No doubt reading valuable advice from silly women's magazines. Noticing my interest, she turned off the screen, not allowing me to confirm my suspicions.

"Good morning, Brody. How can I help?" Her right brow was raised high, demonstrating a disparity between her polite tone and her real feelings concerning my early appearance. A display of true professionalism.

"Good morning, Victoria. Could I talk to the company lawyer concerning a personal matter?"

"What matter?"

"A personal one."

"Brody, what kind of lawyer are you interested in?" she asked, rolling her eyes pointedly and making me feel stupid.

"A civil one."

"You can talk to me."

"You're a civil lawyer?" I didn't believe her.

Book One: A Second Chance

"Does that make you feel uncomfortable?" Victoria could work her eyebrows superbly.

"No, not at all." I shrugged. I wouldn't have been surprised if she earned some extra cash cleaning the office after work. You never know. "I need some advice concerning a citizen-welfare contract."

"Brody, could you dispense with the verbiage and be a bit more specific?" She still looked relaxed, but I discerned a barely noticeable change in her posture.

"I have a childhood friend. I recently found out he's on a social contract. How can we get it annulled?"

"You want to become socialized in favour of your friend?" Her voice became icy. "That's a bad idea, Brody."

"No, I just want to help him. And please don't lecture me." I drew forward. She wrinkled her nose.

"Have you been drinking?" she asked.

Jeez! How keen is your sense of smell to sniff out a drop of cognac?

"Just coffee." I urgently had to regain face and feign unease. "I had a pod installed late last night, and decided to try total immersion. I didn't get any sleep, and this morning I mistook a bottle of cognac for a bottle of syrup. It happens."

Victoria narrowed her eyes sceptically. "You do understand how stupid that sounds?"

"I understand," I said, smiling widely. "But it's the truth. You've seen my resume. No problems with alcohol. So what about this consultation?"

"You'll get your consultation. But first tell me, why do you want to restore someone who's already given up and gone to Barliona?" The secretary looked like someone who was confident in her right to demand answers. I tensed.

"He's my only friend."

"Okay, so you get your friend out. What then?" She narrowed her eyes further, unpleasantly now, and leaned in toward me. "If you don't succeed, you are aware that your friend will burn up? Will you be able to forgive yourself?"

I felt uncomfortable with the turn our conversation had taken. Victoria was conducting the interrogation harshly. However, my gut feeling was not to get pissy, but to calmly convince her of the seriousness of my intentions.

"Burning up" was a real threat for people who were forever returning to the shelter. Not for everyone, of course – for about ten percent – but it was enough for folks to start talking about the problem. Something broke inside people, robbing them of their self-awareness. All that remained was a body, and the ability to eat, sleep, breathe, and defecate. In all other senses they were as good as dead. Interestingly, the luminaries of science could find no evidence of damage to the brain on either a physical or a spiritual level. There was also the question of what was worse: disappearing into Barliona forever, or burning up.

"I'll have nothing to forgive myself for. I'll sign him up for retraining. You can't do that in the shelter, because the social pods are only connected to Barliona servers. He'll get certified, and then we'll find him a job. The Imitators aren't everywhere."

"Repeat that to yourself more often." The lady averted her gaze, and now answered me as a generic lawyer. "Citizens on a social contract may have their contract annulled only if they can provide evidence of financial security. It might be a work contract, in reality or virtuality, it doesn't matter, but the main thing is it's not short-term. Or if the citizen is a dependent, according to family legislation. But that's irrelevant to you. Or are you related?"

"No. Do they demand a regular income?"

"It must be equal to or more than minimum wage. There are no stipulations concerning the kind of work. General director or street sweeper. But it must be official. You can also register your relationship, in which case we'll consider it as a factor in your socialization." There wasn't a trace of a smile in the woman's eyes. I wondered if she was always like that, or it was just a reaction to my question.

"No, thank you. We'll get by old school. For the training period I'll take him on as a driver or personal assistant. I've seen my neighbors do it. It shouldn't raise any questions."

"No, it shouldn't. Brody, I must repeat that if you can't find your friend a job, after he returns to the shelter he may burn up completely. And you'll have no more friends." There was a hint of something other than human sympathy in Victoria's voice. "Have a good think before signing a contract and registering him with the municipality. And it would be better if your friend decided for himself if he really needs this or not."

It was a harsh point, but fair, though nobody in the world could have convinced me we wouldn't make it work. After thanking Victoria and taking my leave, I went to see Maria. No lessons were planned for that day, and I wanted to sort Matty out as soon as possible.

"Brody, Nathan likes the way you've got into the swing of things. He thinks that for the period of your training you can run a course for all candidates."

"Why all? We could just work with the ones that are taken on."

"The company can afford to work with everyone. Even if we reject a candidate, a course like that will still be useful to them. Don't forget, people have lost their jobs. Live interaction will encourage them and help them determine their future."

"I understand. What will I have to do?"

"Design a five-day course. Candidates will be sent to you every week in groups of five to seven. When you finish on Friday you will write me a short report. As a former director you will immediately see who works well in a team and who is a lone wolf. You evaluate only their professional qualities and whether they can adapt or not. Helen will help you with everything, and study at the same time. Then later she'll take over."

"Okay. I'll have everything ready by Monday."

"I would expect nothing less." Maria nodded her satisfaction and sighed. "Brody, stop this nonsense. What was wrong with the pod? It's a quick and effective way to study. You can only reject the blessings of civilization to achieve certain goals, not out of spite."

"That's the way it was, Maria." I pretended I didn't know what she was talking about. "Firstly, Helen must be able to solve problem situations. Secondly, since it didn't occur to her to use the scanner, she would have learned to calmly get into a routine. I understand your loyalty to her, but the youth need conditioning."

"The youth indeed. I understand your position. Have a good weekend."

Organizing a work contract was no problem. The Imitators in the municipality blocked part of my finances to provide six months' salary, accepted my pledge that I would provide the employee with permanent accommodation, and gave the go-ahead to annul the social contract. Now I just had to convince my friend.

"Ahh, that's good," said Matty, taking a large swig of beer. I stretched myself out beside him and was quiet, allowing him to offload. "Just to sit and look, and not worry some bandit's about to lynch you from behind. Not to have to hide or be on the look out. To appreciate what you're eating. Can you hear my stomach rumbling? Music to the ears! The last year's been terrible. Sometimes I climb out of the pod and punch the wall till my fist bleeds. It's nothing to worry about, I'm fine. In the pod you quickly forget what it is to feel, but punch the wall and you immediately understand that it's for real out here. Blood, pain, friendship, love. And that you climbed out into reality for a good reason. Get it?"

"I get it, Matty. Actually, I have a proposal for you." It seemed like the right time. "Come and live with me."

"Yeah right. I'll just throw off these leg irons and run and get my stuff," Matty sniggered and shook his bracelet. "This is no place for vagrants."

"I'm not joking," I said, getting out my tablet and showing him the documents. "By decision of the municipality, I can hire a personal assistant, and provide them accommodation and a stipend of a thousand credits a month. Official employment with all the trimmings. They've already approved the annulment of your social contract. If you agree, that is."

"Bro...," his voice faltered.

"Matty, don't get all emotional. I need a friend, not an assistant. Alive and healthy. And your kids need you too. I'm not doing this for the laugh, so don't think I am. You're going to be working like a dog. In six months you've got to finish the course and get certified. Staying in the shelter is not an option. You know your pods are only connected to the game. Engineers will always be in demand, and with certification you'll find work in no time."

"I haven't got anything to pay for training with," he said, turning gloomy. "Banks don't give loans if you have a shelter back story."

"I'm not a bank, and I'll give you one. You can pay it back when you find a job." I tapped on the screen and showed him a list of vacancies for engineers. "Look how much work there is. Get trained up, get certified, and off you go. Barliona isn't going anywhere. There'll be plenty of time for playing. Well, what do you reckon?"

"I'm thinking," he mumbled.

I gave him a minute, then said, "Finished?"

"Finished what?"

"Thinking."

"No."

"Thinking about burning up?"

"What freaking burning up? Leaving Barliona and burning up are the same freaking thing! I don't want to be a burden on you."

"Don't be stupid. Put your finger on the scanner and let's do this. You're not going to be a burden."

"What, that's it?" he asked incredulously. I nodded.

"You're kidding," he muttered and touched the screen. A metallic clicking sound, and the bracelet unlocked and fell into his lap. The liberation was symbolic – the manacles were off but didn't disappear, a reminder of the time factor and the dwindling finances. We had half a year to get our feet on the ground.

We went straight to the municipality, where we handed in the tag of slavery and officially confirmed Matty's status. Then we went to the sales office for a new pod. He refused point blank to accept a professional model, and I didn't force the issue, as I understood how he felt. I didn't forget myself either, reducing my pain threshold to ten percent and buying a mailbox and a communication amulet. Together they cost me nearly two hundred and twenty credits. No small sum for standard gaming communication gadgets. We took the installation guys home with us. After the age it had taken to install the professional model, the standard pod only took half an hour.

"Jesus! What on earth do you need a mansion like this for?" Matty entered the house and was immediately impressed.

"Andrea wanted to live in sector two, so I rented this as soon as my salary would allow. Then she left, and I couldn't be bothered to move. I got used to it."

"Shit, you're an oligarch! I bet you've got a miniature golf course in the back garden."

"Uh-huh, and a wine cellar." It was amusing to see Matty in such wonder. I was so used to it I'd stopped noticing.

"Where's this wine cellar? Are you going to give me the grand tour?" he asked.

I tried to insist on a full excursion, but he didn't want to hear it. As a result, we sat on the steps in the cellar, uncorking bottle after bottle. That day Matty didn't even find out about the pool room and swimming pool. Never mind, all in good time. He had his restoration to celebrate, and nobody has nerves of steel. He wound down to the max, me officially keeping him company, and as soon as he passed out I lugged him up to his room and onto his bed, to have a good sleep and then remember what a hangover was. Without the robodoctor. It would be good for his health to sober up by himself. Who was complaining about not having any feelings?

After wandering around the house for a while, trying to get used to not living alone anymore, in lieu of dinner I slipped into the pod. Everything else could wait. Now I wanted to sort out those tieflings and demon hunters, since all the information on them in the Internet I'd have to pay for. A few minutes of initiation, and my hooves were shining in the dull rays of the Barliona sun. Welcome back. Kvalen, in his familiar canvas pants and shirt, with no protection, was resurrected in the middle of a small temple made of sand, surrounded by smooth boulders. Up ahead, about two hundred meters, were some wooden buildings like old barracks, whence came a ringing sound, shouts, and a nasty smell. No, not a smell. Something imperceptible, without distinct qualities, yet invoking an unpleasant sensation of chill. Trees grew all around, and try as I might to make anything out through them, I could see nothing. Only tables of properties popping up and obscuring the already limited view – common maple, crumbly oak, heather shrub, magnolia vine. I gave several mental orders, after which everything began to appear only on request. There was now a good view of the mountain range concealing the horizon line. I could even see the snowy peaks without binoculars. The location was picturesque and fairly sizeable.

"Are you going to be admiring the view for long?" An unpleasant voice distracted me from studying the landscape, and alongside me materialized an NPC marked, "without level". The human called Tarlin turned out to be a demon hunter like me. His face was disfigured with scars, as though it had suffered a bear clawing, his right ear was completely gone, and he had a prosthetic left hand. But none of that stopped him from training new recruits, for Tarlin was the drill sergeant of the training camp.

"I don't know," I replied. My previous Barliona experience had taught me that picking a fight with an NPC for no reason was more trouble than it was worth.

"I'll give you a pointer." He was courtesy itself. "You see the barrack? You have precisely thirty seconds to reach it. If you don't make it, you're toast. A fast-track plunge into the Abyss. What are you waiting for? At the double, march!"

I couldn't remember the last time I'd run anywhere, so I decided straight away to challenge the sergeant. Slowly, maintaining composure and dignity, I left the temple and headed for the designated barrack. Generals didn't run, they relocated decorously. If you set off at a gallop so much as once, someone was guaranteed to put a saddle on you or harness you to a cart. Like I had nothing better to do than run!

"So that's the way it is, huh?" Tarlin said knowingly, before the ground suddenly disappeared from under my hooves. My back and buttocks hurt like hell, and the space in front of me began to spin at an incredible speed. I didn't immediately realise that the instructor had grabbed me by the tail and begun to whirl me round like a hammer. And in the same way, like a hammer, he launched me toward the barrack. I had the wind knocked out of me first by the flight, and then by the sensation of free fall. It wasn't classified as dangerous, so it wasn't blocked by the system. My crotch tickled unpleasantly – I'd always hated fairground rides and everything to do with them; even skiing and skating made me feel sick.

No matter how I tried to level myself out in flight, maneuvering my arms like an eagle its wings, it was all in vain. I hit the ground horns first, and the impact knocked my combative mood for six, despite my ten percent pain threshold.

Damage sustained

Health decreased by 99: 1500 (fall to ground) - 0 (physical protection)

Remaining Health: 1 out of 100

I managed just one convulsive breath out before Tarlin was by my side, repeating the throw and reducing the distance between me and the barrack. Then again. And again. I didn't sustain any more damage – HP had frozen at one and didn't wish to decrease all the way to zero, which would strip me of the possibility to avoid competing in athletics competitions as a missile. In the nursery – for a training camp could not be anything but – it was impossible to destroy a player.

"The exit's over there. Go and wave your

attitude around in the wide world!" With one more throwing motion, Tarlin hurled me all the way to a shimmering sphere, a one-and-a-half-meter ball of lightning, and the second I landed, electrical charges flickered over the surface of the portal. Next to it, stiff like an idol, stood a small demon. Its pathetic mug and total absence of wit indicated that its skin was all that was left of it. The Light ones had burned out its essence, leaving him one function – to manage the portal.

Reference information

Portals in Barliona

Static: *Connects two points in space. Operated by subjugated demons. Not available for acquisition by players for personal use. Located in large cities or key points in Barliona.*

Breach: *Has a static point of departure and a dynamic point of arrival. The static point is operated by a subjugated demon, whose level must be at least five times higher than the level of the lock. The portal takes energy directly from the lock. A portal demon cannot be bought; it can only be subjugated, have its essence burned out, and be tethered to a portal.*

Custom: *Created by three Wizards. Enables transfer to any point on the continent. Cost of maintenance: 30% Energy per minute; Energy potions may be* *used during maintenance.*

Teleport scrolls

Created by wizards, both NPCs and players. Enable transfer from any point on the continent to a specific point indicated in the scroll. Cost of using scroll always set according to zone 5.

Scale of distance and cost

Barliona charges a fee for using all types of portal. Players may set a surcharge to make a profit, usually 10–20% of cost of transfer.

- *Zone 1. 0–50 km. Cost: 11 gold*
- *Zone 2. 51–100 km. Cost: 32 gold*
- *Zone 3. 101–200 km. Cost: 84 gold*
- *Zone 4. 201–300 km. Cost: 137 gold*
- *Zone 5. 301+ km. Cost: 210 gold*

After creating a character, any player could leave the nursery without training if they considered they had the strength to bring all comers to heel. All abilities could easily be gained automatically, without instuctors. This was done for those impatient ones who thought the wide world more attractive than the nursery. I was not one of them; I had plenty to do in the training camp.

Tarlin took my silent inaction as a sign of resignation and, readjusting his grip on my tail, dragged me back to my point of rebirth, clearly longing to see me run. A couple of times the interested faces of demon hunters flashed by, among whom I could make out a human, an orc, two elves, and not a single tiefling. The players grinned as they watched me go. Evidently it wasn't every day they got to observe the taming of a shrewish half-demon.

When we got back to the point, the instructor flipped me over onto my feet. Drums and flutes began to play in my head from the abrupt change of position, and I felt sick again. It seemed my vestibular apparatus was not yet adjusted to the new reality. Tarlin produced a flask, forced my mouth open, and poured the contents into me. I had to swallow, or else I risked choking. The nausea passed immediately, and my HP shot up to maximum.

"The barracks! Thirty seconds! At the double, march!" Tarlin rapped out, making no secret of his hostility.

This time I didn't argue. It isn't a sin for generals to run during hostilities. I shot off so fast my hooves sparked, but when I got to the designated point, I froze and considered how I felt. In the real world, any acceleration without warming up meant wheezing and giddiness; here I didn't so much as pant. I liked the feeling of having an agile, lissom, strong body. Tarlin stood next to me and didn't intervene. He waited patiently until I familiarized myself with my recently created character. I opened the characteristics window and became absorbed in reading.

Characteristics window for player Kvalen							
Main parameters				Additional parameters			
Experience	0	of	1,000	**Item**	**Unit**	**Quantity**	
Player level	1			Account balance	GP	18,000	
Race	Tiefling			Physical attack	units	4	
Class	Demon Hunter			Magic attack	units	4	
Main speciality	-			Protection from physical attack	units	0	
Learning speed	0			Protection from magic attack	units	0	
Life	100			Chance of critical strike	%	0.15	
Energy	100			Chance of avoidance	%	8%	
Main characteristics				Fire resistance	%	50%	
Characteristic	**Scale**		**Limit**	**Base**	**Total**		
Stamina	0	of	1,000	1	1		
Strength	0	of	1,000	1	1		
Intellect	0	of	1,000	1	1		
Agility	3	of	1,000	1	1		
Additional characteristics							
Characteristic	**Scale**		**Limit**	**Base**	**Total**		
Not specified							
Not specified							
Not specified							
Not specified							
Specialities				Specialization			
Speciality	**Scale**		**Limit**	**Base**	**Total**	**Specialization**	**Unit**	**Quantity**
Not specified							
Not specified							

What first caught my eye was the absence of Liveliness. The very same headache which had made everyone more attentive to the game. You'd constantly had to remember how long you could run, jump, use your abilities, and carry out physical activities. Even I, a lowly level-ten player, had my fill of sorrow with Liveliness. One day I was whacking a hare in a clearing, but didn't notice my Liveliness level in time, and dropped to the ground like I'd been poleaxed. I couldn't stand, couldn't sit, couldn't move my arm. There was no one about to pour water into my mouth, so I lay there, enjoying the clouds and waiting for automatic recovery. The fluffy beastie, however, didn't wait, and began to gnaw at me like a carrot, forgetting it was a herbivore. Level one hare-mob gnaws level-five player! If Barliona had a Darwin Award for the stupidest death, I would definitely have won it. And more than once. Now there was no Liveliness, and you could work out actively and not worry about getting tired. It's probably the only time when advocates and opponents of changes in Barliona were united – without Liveliness the game became more dynamic and easier to master.

I did a few squats, eyeing the table carefully. Nothing changed, but the 3 on my Agility scale showed that skills grew during the process of carrying out an action. The four turtles supporting the mechanism of Barliona were included in the Main Characteristics block, and were called Stamina, Strength, Intellect and Agility. All parameters depended on them, from Energy and Health, to Attack and Chance of Avoidance. Each characteristic had its own scale of growth. Squats didn't increase anything, but running at full speed had an impact on Agility. The people on the forums were right – now the scale filled up only as a result of real physical exertion. You couldn't boost Agility by sitting in a chair, dangling your feet and picking your nose. You had to run, swim or jump, balls to the wall. Then mass would grow too, just like in reality. When you gained a new level, your main characteristics automatically increased by a point and you earned two bonus points, which you could spend on either additional characteristics or a specialization. You couldn't boost the four turtles like that. If you hadn't assigned your bonus points within five minutes of levelling up, the game did it for you. If there was nowhere to assign them, they burned up. Not very nice, but very convenient for beginners. Especially those who didn't like spending time to "think," considering it a relic of the past.

There was nothing else of interest in the characteristics window. Attack and Protection had some formulae, but I wanted to deal with them with a calculator, and in reality. There was no reminder of the bonus for registration, which was disappointing. Everything else was pristine.

"Twenty-eight seconds!" Tarlin waited for me to get bored of looking at my virtual doll, then continued to roast me. "Two hundred meters in twenty-eight seconds! Were you running on all fours?"

"I can't go any faster, I need to train," I said honestly. In the real world, honesty and self-criticism were an excellent way to disarm your opponent. Why shouldn't it work in Barliona?

Vasily Mahanenko. Invasion

"So what are you doing here when the training camp's empty?" The instructor abruptly changed the course of the conversation. Now I was guilty of not training. Which was better than being seen as a weakling.

"Can you begin by enlightening the unenlightened?" I stuck to my guns. "Which course is meant for newbies? I don't want to turn up at the advanced one and have everyone die laughing at my failure. Who would be responsible for their deaths?"

"You're going to retch like a pregnant tortoise on the first one anyway." The impervious instructor waved a hand in the direction of the assault course. "It's that way. The instructor's name is master Gurt. Muster is every six hours. Latecomers and no-shows take a dive into the Abyss. You'll be living in this barrack. Go and register, then get training, newbie. I don't want to see you until you've completed the course with full marks.

Task received: Step 1. Start of training
Description: *Class-specific task. Complete newbie assault course. Minimum completion score: 7 out of 10. Completion time unlimited.*

Reward:

- *Experience: +5*
- *Reputation with Light of Barliona faction: +1*
- *Access to next training step*
- *Bonus for course completion*

Book One: A Second Chance

with full marks: +1 to all main characteristics

First up I went to check out the barrack. It was almost empty, only one of the twenty bunks occupied. The game obligingly offered me the choice of the free ones, and since I wasn't planning to spend the night in Barliona, I put my hand on the bed closest to the exit.

I froze. Only now did it strike me how easy it was to walk on hooves; no less so than on feet. And I might have been born with a tail. Focusing on my glutes, I wiggled my buttocks. A good looking lad! Pfft, a good tail, and it would come in handy in the game, as a third lower limb or an extra argument in a fistfight. The main thing was to tense the right buttock at the right time. Imagining my backside clenching there and then in the pod, I couldn't resist a sarcastic smile. So that was it, the tieflings' bonus – a toned butt for free! I would have to push the idea to the masses on a women's forum. It was quick and cheap, and if you waved it around like a huge fan, in a month you could be posting "before and after" photos.

"What are you smiling about, goat?" A gruff voice returned me to the game. Here we go!

Two level-three players barred the way to the training camp. Braksed the elf and Kurtune the human, sharing the second name Vartalinsky. They must have been brothers, at least in mind. Outwardly the pair looked very different from the players hovering behind them. If the rest wore

94

simple shirts and pants, and many even had no shoes, Braksed and Kurtune were not badly kitted out: full leather armor, rings, chains, helmets, and heavy belts with several bags. Even by my inexperienced reckoning they were dressed more than sufficiently for level three of a closed location. What were guys like them doing in the nursery?

"Smell the light!"

Something bright lit up in the hands of the elf, and the light produced an unpleasant chill in my body, making me twitch. The same feeling as when I was reborn in the temple. Back then I'd thought it was a smell, but I was wrong – it was the effect light magic had on me. The closer it came, the worse the pain and shivering. Reflexively I shoved a fist out in front, wanting to punch the scumbag, but it went straight through him unhindered. They couldn't lay into me on the training camp, but ruining a tiefling's physical and mental health with light magic would be a piece of cake.

"I don't get it," frowned Braksed, turning a blind eye to my attempt at retribution. "Why isn't he doubled up?"

"You're all fingers and thumbs," said Kurtune. "Give it here."

He grabbed the shining sphere and set it to maximum brightness. These guys were a team because they worked well together. My body felt the chill once more. I'd reduced my sensitivity threshold to ten percent just in time.

"What's going on here?" Supervising Instructor Drumm appeared just as the pointlessness of the Vartalinskys' actions was becoming apparent. The menacing werewolf, covered from head to toe in thick fur, looked funny in his demon hunter's leather clothes, but his natural charm, bestowed on him by Barliona's artists, precluded any joking on the subject. His contemptuously raised upper lip bared sharp fangs, and the look he gave everyone around was particularly noteworthy. It was the look you gave to the dead wood beneath your feet.

"Let's exorcise demons!" laughed Braksed and Kurtune, ignoring the charisma of the NPC. I breathed a sigh of relief – there were even school kids here! These two were no older than twenty, and had no brains and no brakes, but enough attitude to pave a road out in the sticks. Mommy and daddy had given them money, but not bothered with manners. The gilded youth in all its loathsome glory. Adolescents who had lost their minds to overindulgence and tedium. Multiply that by the opportunities of Barliona, and you get players with no mind disobeying the rules.

"The light of Eluna has little effect on tieflings. If you want to banish a half-demon, ask your parents to buy you a brain." NPCs could also pick out the golden guys. "Have you completed my task?"

"No." Kurtune stroppily screwed up his face. "We've still got two hours."

"I'll be waiting for your results. Put the Drop of Light back where it belongs. You'll be penalized for using it." Drumm cast another disdainful glance over us and went off to attend to his business. The scene was boring without him, so I went to find the newbie assault course.

"Flea-ridden mutt," spat Braksed. "Three thousand gold!"

"Forget it, our folks will cough up." Kurtune waved it away and called to me: "We haven't finished with you, goat-boy!"

He got no reaction, so he caught me up and blocked my path. I walked through him like he wasn't there. Blatant disregard was one of the most terrifying punishments for them. At home they were used to everyone licking their asses, and they expected the same here. Braksed shouted after me that he'd find me in reality and chastize me, but all my attention was now on the training camp.

Next to the portal was a small muster station. On one side of it stood barracks – four for players and one for instructors. On the other side were two assault courses enclosed by a low fence. A newbie course and a basic course. Beyond them were another two – the mid- and high-level courses, along with an obscure wooden tower similar to a high diving board. "Minimalism and practicality" was evidently the guiding motto of the cartographer who created this place. A huge hullabaloo and the shouts of the instructors – the training process was in full swing.

"We haven't finished with you yet!" I caught one last threat from behind me before I stepped onto the course and all external sounds disappeared – the magic fence had superb sound insulation inward, only letting noise out. Nothing should distract a student from his training. The newbies' course consisted of ten obstacles one after another. You had to walk, crawl, run or jump, avoiding swinging axes, spiked clubs, firewalls, spears, and other devices that would hamper your painless transfer from point A to point B. There were no safety mats or stage props, only red-hot iron and fire. There was a player on the course as I arrived. He skipped nimbly under the swinging chopper, flew between the incandescent slabs, scarcely touching them, scrambled adroitly over the barbed-wire net, and frustratingly didn't react in time to a spike appearing from out of the ground.

"Seven out of ten, an excellent result," boomed master Gurt, a green orc. "Marcon the Spoiled, I give you access to the basic level. Access to this course remains open to you until you complete all ten obstacles. Next!"

Marcon's fall didn't send him to be regenerated – with one HP he lay on the ground and waited for a healer. The next player stepped onto the course. He passed the first three tests with relative ease, but a powerful blow to the chest on the fourth knocked him out.

"Three out of ten. Waste of space!" Gurt was not happy with progress. "Number four to the start!"

The number "11" appeared in the upper part of my viewer – I had evidently received an electronic ticket to join the queue of fortunate souls. The bad news was that I had to attempt the course without any previous training.

"Number four to the start!" repeated Gurt

louder. Number four was in no hurry to take his place, making everyone wait. Players milled about, exchanging quizzical glances and wondering whose turn it was. "Eredani!" Gurt shouted out a familiar name. "Where the hell are you? On the course, at the double!"

Out of the corner of my eye I saw something move over by the fence. Eredani sat and looked gloomily at the course, ignoring the instructor and everyone else.

"You want to go back to the Abyss?" asked Gurt, and the tiefling twitched. Begrudgingly Eredani stood up and moved slowly to the start, dragging his flaccid tail. After clambering up onto the platform, my horned fellow tribesman shivered, closed his eyes, and took off at a pace. The first obstacle was the slabs crashing into each other. Even I, who had never stepped on a course before, could have got through, but not Eredani. The slabs collided, crushing the tiefling to the sound of his doleful "oofs" and "aahs", and a second later we watched empathetically as a compacted briquette fell to the ground.

"Again?! Nought out of ten. Waste of space. Next!"

The duty priestess restored the tiefling's health, and Eredani quietly headed back to his place by the fence. I went a little closer to the course, to train mentally along with the players attempting it. It would soon be my turn, and none of my predecessors had got further than the fifth obstacle, which was making Gurt all the more angry and disconsolate. When my turn came, the orc just waved a paw, unhopeful of my success. I didn't let him down. The first obstacle really was too elementary to embarrass myself on, but next came the spikes popping up from below, and no matter how long I studied them for, I could see no pattern in their appearance. As a result I crashed out straight after the first obstacle.

"One out of ten. Waste of space!" Gurt had a good look round the group and said, "Get training! You're demon hunters, not legless, blind pieces of meat. You've got to be quick and agile like the hare, not slow like the tortoise. The next test is in five hours. Get to work!"

The training camp shimmered and faded, and in its place appeared ten simulators, the same as on the course, only you weren't required to have completed the previous levels. Players rushed to their problem sections to work on their movements. Several demon hunters were able to train simultaneously on the same piece of equipment, passing effortlessly through each other's projections. Each had its own virtuality, which was both good and bad. Good because you could observe and repeat the movements of an experienced player. Bad because you could become confused with all the projections, and not notice a trap under your feet. Before joining the others, I wanted to clear up an important question with the instructor.

"What's the point of training?" I asked Gurt as he approached. "We're newbies. Shouldn't you be teaching us abilities?"

"If it's abilities you need, the portal's just there," he said irritatedly and pointed at the twinkling sphere. "You can have abilities and skills and everything you desire. While you're here, you do as I tell you. And right now I'm telling you the Abyss awaits you. I was going to send Eredani again, but since you're so inquisitive, you can go instead. I can't stand loudmouths. I'll be waiting by the tower in twenty minutes. If you're not there, you're out of the camp. Now get training!"

Two timers appeared in my viewer: one – a countdown to my Leap into the Abyss; the second – my estimated time to the tower. Very convenient. Even if you wanted to, you couldn't forget and you wouldn't be late. I tried to make eye contact with the other players to ask about the jump, but they were aware of Gurt's temper, and looked away to concentrate more painstakingly on their exercises.

The lone tiefling Eredani remained sitting by the fence, not even attempting to climb onto the simulators. Just the chap I needed. Gurt said he'd been in the Abyss. Eredani watched distrustfully as I approached and sat down next to him.

"I've been sent to the Abyss. Can you help?"

If you want to get in with someone, make them feel superior. A request for help is a good start, because you can kill several birds with one question: show him his importance and your helplessness, and most importantly, discover more about him. That way you'll know immediately if he's a degenerate.

"How? Go instead of you?" Eredani's voice

was neither friendly nor malicious. It was the voice of someone who wanted to be left alone.

"No, I'll be fine. But there's nothing in the guides about the Abyss, let alone about jumping into it. I'm led to believe you've been there. What can I expect?"

"A thousand gold," he said. But of course! A player from a social shelter couldn't not think about money. A thousand gold was an average monthly wage in our world. Not bad for a simple question.

"I see. Forget it then. Good luck in the game." I stood up, determined to pass at least one obstacle before the Abyss, despite still not understanding what for.

"Wait," said Eredani. "How did you end up a tiefling?"

"You mentioned something about a thousand gold," I shot back. "I'll tell you with pleasure."

"An exchange? Information for information?"

"Sure." I sat back down. I saw nothing wrong with disclosing the secret of my birth, since any player could read about it on the site, but I'd just heard about the Abyss for the first time. "You first."

"Agreement."

That one word made me take Eredani seriously. And when I read the text he gave me, he gained my respect. He didn't offer me a standard agreement on ten pages of unintelligible text, but rather a one-page document in which our exchange was clearly described. You have to work with contracts for many years to be able to whip up a sample like that out of thin air.

"It's a quality text, thank you." I signed the document.

"Thank you for what?"

"For the pleasure of reading a literately drawn-up contract. There are too many windbags around. Lots of clever phrases, but no common sense."

"Are you a lawyer?"

"No. Their documents need editing too."

"What's a bright fellow like you doing in Barliona during working hours? Have they abolished office slavery?"

"Waving my tail about and butting folk with my horns. Let's make it a closed agreement." I wasn't about to divulge my personal information to the first person I came across.

"Okay. How did you become a tiefling?" Eredani shot the first question. I calmly told him about the bonus and my random character generation. Everything was open source, so he could check for himself. A green tick appeared next to my name on the list of current agreements. Barliona was acknowledging that I'd fulfilled my part of the contract.

Eredani was silent for a time, staring blankly ahead. I was just beginning to worry about him, when he suggested another exchange.

"I don't want to say it out loud," he explained and sent me the text of another agreement. "A free piece of advice for the future – keep quiet about how you became a tiefling. It's a closed race, not accessible to players. They're running tests at the moment. Most likely you were taken on to test the effect of the bonus on class and race balance."

He was quiet again, allowing me to read the new agreement. In order to give information to another player, you needed writing implements and paper, which cost money. So as not to spend money on paper, the cunning bugger had put everything he knew about the Abyss in the text of the agreement. Regardless of his level one, Eredani was far from a newbie in Barliona.

Scrolling down to the right place, I immersed myself in reading. What was a leap into the Abyss? A long rope was tied to the player's legs, and he was pushed off a platform into a separate location called the Abyss. Most demon hunters hauled weapons out of there. Then they purified them using Eluna magic, and gained enhanced attacking properties against the beasts of the Abyss. Some managed to retrieve armor, others – accessories. Players had even begun trading extracted objects. But there was a minus – every leap was accompanied by maximum possible pain. Jumpers had to remember that the Abyss was not intended for live players. Even if you turned sensations completely off, the leap enabled an Abyss debuff, which increased sensations by ten percent and was disabled only when you left the training camp. Anybody could survive one jump; some could survive two; only the few could survive more. However, as Eredani had written, this was all irrelevant to tieflings, for in the Abyss you were looking for weapons. Your task was to lasso yourself a demon, suppress it, and use your abilities to constantly recharge your remote demonic essence. In this lay the enormous difference between our class of tieflings and the other races. Everyone else used light magic, while we used demon magic. Parallel paths of development, which is why they were running the test, because they needed to evaluate the balance of the class. Eredani hadn't written anything about capturing demons, because he logged out for his leaps. Basically he hadn't told me anything directly useful to me. General information about everything and nothing. You call that experience? Barliona, however, was satisfied, and with a second green tick, the agreement was closed.

"I overheard your question to the instructor. We could do another exchange of information," Suggested Eredani.

"For what?" I asked. Eredani was turning out to be quite the wheeler dealer.

"What did you leave behind in Barliona?" For some reason he was curious about my presence in the game.

"That's personal information, and I'm not exchanging it for the nonsense you gave me. I can read about training on the forum myself. I haven't asked why a social player with so much experience is only on level one and his sensations aren't turned up to the specified thirty percent."

"And you are right not to ask," he sneered. "You won't be told where to get off."

"Fine. I'll go and try a couple of obstacles before the jump. Thanks for the agreement, it'll come in handy as a template. By the way, I'm Brody."

I extended my hand. Being called by your real name in Barliona wasn't the done thing, although it wasn't forbidden either. As a profoundly real person, it was far more usual for me to call someone Dave than AFingerUpYourNose. The tiefling's eyebrows shot up when he understood my gesture; he wasn't expecting it. There followed a second's bewilderment, before he shook my hand:

"Victor. But I prefer Eredani."

"Noted. Good luck in the game."

I only had time for the spike obstacle. On the first attempt I understood that the spot where the spike appeared from rippled ever so slightly just before it shot up. Just a second, but in theory it was enough to skip away. In training the spikes didn't cause any damage, only pain, and you were flung to the ground, just like in the real thing. After three attempts I understood it wasn't my day. I didn't move my leg or my arm or my tail out of the way in time, and each time the spikes knocked me down.

The timer began to flash red – I had to get to the tower fast. The navigation arrow showed me which way to go, and I sprinted as fast as I could. Again I had no shortness of breath or decrease in speed or any other parameter. I felt like Superman, moving mountains without turning a hair. I even jumped a few times while I was running, to check how high you could go, and I left the ground by a whole two metres. Working as a counterweight, my tail allowed me to hold my balance going round corners. Oh, to have skills like that in the real world!

"Up there." The duty priestess at the entrance to the tower pointed the way up some stairs, and I bounded up them two or three at a time. Were my adrenaline levels running high or something? It seemed the only explanation for experiencing such exhilaration from controlling my body. I liked being a quick and nimble tiefling.

Gurt was waiting for me on the upper platform with a rope in his hands. There was no one else around.

"You're not just a demon hunter. You're a tiefling," he began, tying the rope round my ankles. "There are different demands on you. In the Abyss, close your eyes and feel your essence. They may have burned out the demon in you, but you can't fool Mother Nature. She'll show you what to do next. Find a demon in the Abyss, subjugate it, and drag it out here. We'll make a demon hunter of you, not an empty husk. When you want to get out, tug twice and I'll pull you up. Go!"

You have started the Taming the Demon scene

Description: *You can use demonic abilities only after subjugating a demon. Complete the test and gain access to abilities.*

Reward:

• *The following abilities will become accessible to you: Demon*

Book One: A Second Chance

Subjugation, Demon Retribution, Demon Strike, Automatic Attack, Tail Strike.

- *You will be able to gain new abilities as you level up.*

The orc gave the rope a tug to check its strength, and pushed me off the platform. "Fu-u-u-ck!" was all I could shout. He should have warned me. An announcement flashed before my eyes, but I couldn't read it. I tried to help myself as best I could by waving my arms and tail around. It suddenly became cold, and a sharp pain pierced my whole body from the tips of my toes to the top of my head. Even my horns hurt, although I had somehow forgotten they even existed.

By the time I felt a massive jolt bring an end to my fall, the platform was high above me. The Abyss was aptly named – visibility was zero in the murk. I gradually became used to the nagging pain, and tried to get my bearings. First I brought my hand right up to my eyes – nothing. Something was most definitely absolute: either the darkness surrounding me, or the transparence of my body. At least the interface icons were in place, so I wasn't strictly one-on-one with nothing. Taking a deep breath, I took Eredani's advice and began to flail my arms about, trying to latch onto something. My hand touched cold metal. Whatever it was, it was sharp, cold, and had a handle, and that was enough for me, so I took it. I waved my free arm around some more. Nothing else. Now it was time to use Gurt's advice. I hadn't a clue what "feel your essence" meant, but I obediently closed my eyes and tried to tune into sensations. I was still in pain, but it was tolerable. The tip of my tail began to itch, so I clenched my buttocks, leant my head back, and scratched it with a horn. Two of the body parts I'd gained in the game had already come in handy.

Progress of the Taming the Demon scene
Progress description: *You were able to perceive your own demonic essence, and you can now invoke a demon.*

Special conditions: *You are granted a bonus for the random generation of your character. The rank of your subjugated demon will be 3 higher than standard.*

At last! The first mention of the generation bonus. I was already beginning to suspect Barliona had successfully forgotten about it.

"Mother weeps for her sons," came a drawled and sinister murmur. "She is grieving. Help her! Come back! Become one of us!"

My eyes filled with tears. Mother! I have betrayed you. I defected to the enemy, became one of... What was all this? Why the hell was I getting these obsessive thoughts?

Regress of the Taming the Demon scene

Book One: A Second Chance

Regress description: *You lost perception of your demonic essence.*

Like that, is it? After chasing the tiefling out of my head, I had become Brody West again. The rope twitched. The supervisor had felt a change and wanted to know if I was ready to come back up. I wasn't. I was all fired up.

My tail brushed against my horns again, advancing the progress of the scene. The ominous murmur was right on cue. My head swam, like after a shot of vodka on an empty stomach, but this time I was mentally prepared. Again I pitied the outcast Ireness, deprived of her children, and I felt utterly discouraged by the knowledge of my own treachery, but a small, stubborn part of my conscious sneered insidiously at these emotions thrust upon me. My identity didn't go anywhere, but it slackened the reins and allowed the situation to develop by itself. My head hurt from being in two consciouses simultaneously, but the pain was even an advantage just then. It was much sharper than the pain inflicted by the Abyss, and it helped me focus.

"Ireness wants you back! Come with me!" The dismal murmur rang out right next to my ear. The enforced conscious rejoiced, recognizing the voice of Ireness's daughter, the archdemoness Aniram.

Reference information

Hierarchy of demons in Barliona
Supreme Demon: *A creature without*

level. There exist only three Supreme Demons, who are the heads of their houses. They answer directly to the Emissary of Chaos. The Supreme Demons fight each other continually for territory. In Barliona they can only dwell within a one-mile radius of the Ziggurat of Defiance. They are the strategic commanders of the invasion.

***Higher Demon:** A creature without level. The generals of the army invading Barliona. They answer exclusively to their own Supreme Demon. Depending on the strength of the Supreme Demon, at any one time between three and ten of his Higher Demons can dwell in Barliona. They are the operative commanders of the invasion. Their residence time in Barliona depends on the will and strength of their Supreme Demon.*

***Archdemon:** An officer of the army of demons invading Barliona. They are copious in number and strong, and subject to the invocation and suppression of their will. They command demons and lower demons, and are always surrounded by their corteges. They can dwell in Barliona for 6 hours, after which they are banished to the Abyss for 18 hours. Their residence time may be increased by means of sacrifice.*

***True demon:** A deranked archdemon.*

Subject to the invocation and suppression of its will. A lone wolf. They can dwell in Barliona for 12 hours, after which they are banished to the Abyss for 12 hours. Their residence time may be increased by means of sacrifice.

Demon: *A soldier of the army of demons invading Barliona. They are strong and have a human intellect, due to which they are not blocked by Barliona. They are subject to the invocation and suppression of their will. Lone wolves, although they can unite into groups. Demons of different houses feud with each other, and are occasionally prepared to cut deals with citizens of Barliona in order to banish a demon of a rival house to the Abyss.*

Lower demon: *The cannon fodder of the army of demons invading Barliona. Copious in number and devoid of intellect, they are not blocked by Barliona, because it sees them as aggressive animals. They conform to a herd instinct, and are subject to the invocation and suppression of their will. They run in packs, and if for some reason they become left behind, they enter hibernation.*

The overwhelming joy of seeing my elder sister all but totally engulfed me, but I managed to retain consciousness by using mathematics. Previously, whenever a member of a project team did something stupid or openly sabotaged a job, I would mentally calculate the square of a three-digit number. You can't shout at your subordinates; you can only discuss their degeneracy with their direct bosses in the hope of getting a more suitable replacement. I tried as hard as I could. Mathematics allowed me to handle my emotions then, and it helped me to focus now – Aniram was whispering something to me about Ireness and her inner turmoil, and I was squaring 329. Waiting until I could feel the aura right up close to my ear, I took a wide swing with my free arm, trying to catch the archdemoness. My hand fell on something cold and hairy, and was soon gripping a hefty clump of hair.

"What are you doing?" she asked, before I tapped the rope twice with my pick. Gurt reacted instantly, and I shot upwards, dragging the archdemoness behind me. She tried to free herself without hurting me, but as soon as a glimmer of light appeared, she sank her talons into my shoulder and started to howl, "No-o-o!" We exited the Abyss together.

"Don't let her slip away!" shouted the orc. Swearing, I took my newly procured instrument between my teeth and, securing my grip on Aniram's hair, held her like a loved one, enwreathing her with all my limbs and my tail. She squirmed frenziedly, biting and scratching, and beating me with her tail. Her HP dropped instantaneously to one and froze. The archdemoness's luck had run out – she couldn't kill me in the training camp.

"Stone! Hoop! Seal the outer boundary!"

Concise orders were given. The death throes of my captive gradually abated, and my body was wracked with a chill. I opened my eyes. Alongside Gurt stood Uldaron, the head of the camp, and Abigail, the priestess who had purified me. The latter's hands glowed, creating a light dome. Aniram wilted completely into a rag doll.

"You can let her go now," commanded Uldaron. I unclenched my fists, and the prisoner collapsed to the ground. The light of Eluna was concentrated on the archdemoness, releasing me from my distress. The orc helped me to disentangle myself and stand up.

"Not a bad catch." Gurt grabbed the pick from me, nearly knocking out my teeth in the process. "Well balanced. Sturdy. Could take a lot of heads off."

I looked dubiously at the ordinary-looking pick. If you removed the dark fog curling around the handle, it was no different from any other. Gurt turned it this way and that, clicking his tongue, before reluctantly giving it back to me.

Demon Pick of Power

Description: *A rare object, used for mining ore.*

- *Damage: 10 (Physical)*
- *Mining +1*
- *Strength +1*
- *Stamina +1*
- *Possibility to exploit Demon Seams without forfeit*

"Go and see master Dheire," Gurt advised me. "He'll teach you to use the pick correctly."

"Don't distract him, Gurt," said Uldaron with a reminder of the reason for our mini-muster. Aniram was drained off all willpower, and sat staring into space. "Go, Kvalen. You must be bound."

I obeyed, though entering the dome of Light was particularly unpleasant.

"I had to burn out your internal demonic essence, otherwise Barliona wouldn't become home for you," said Abigail. "But we have found a way to return tieflings to combat. The spurious power of a demon. You can use your abilities again, though I should warn you straight away that your demon must remain a demon, and conscious. You can't clap on everlasting chains like the demonologists. You are obliged constantly to crush any attempt to resist. Remember, every thirty minutes that you use your demonic abilities, the demon will try to hurt you. If it succeeds in taking the upper hand over you, it will return to the Abyss, and you will have to endure the subjugation procedure again. Now get ready! You must put your demon to sleep and strengthen the bond. I shall restore her will."

Two new buttons appeared on my Abilities panel. One was flashing fast and furious, inviting me to fulfil Abigail's demand and complete the subjugation scene. I followed the directions and Aniram disappeared. At last I was a real player with abilities.

Training a Demon scene completed

Abilities gained:

Demon Strike: *You project purified demonic energy at your opponent, inflicting 100% damage to their Attack parameter. Range: 50 meters. Cannot be used in motion. Requires an active demon. Cost: 20 Energy.*

Demon Retribution: *A passive ability. You subjugate a demon and gain the ability to use demon magic. The demon resists subjugation, creating a diversion once every 30 minutes. The demon chooses the optimal strategy to ship you to the Gray Lands. If you die, the demon is freed and returns to the Abyss.*

Demon Invocation: *You invoke/dismiss your subjugated demon.*

"A good catch," said Uldaron praisingly. "It's not every tiefling who can fish out an archdemon first time round. If you can get along with it, you'll become a worthy warrior. Abigail, purify the pick."

The priestess directed the light of Eluna onto the procured object. I was concerned the properties of the pick might change during purification, but apart from the fog, everything remained in place.

"Let's go." The orc motioned me toward the newbies' assault course. "I want to see how you use the abilities you've gained."

Task received: Demon Strike training

Description: *A regular task. Use the Demon Strike ability successfully five times in succession.*

Reward:

- *Experience: +5*
- *Reputation with Light of Barliona faction: +1*

I went with my gut feeling – no changes. The fact that there was an archdemon somewhere close by, albeit asleep, was a matter of indifference to me. Throwing the pick over my shoulder, I trudged off after Gurt.

"Kvalen, wait a second!" A player hailed me by the entrance to the course. Shukir the Vaunted, a level-three human. He wasn't as well equipped as Braksed and Kurtune, yet he was also clearly no simple player. His leather coat sparkled with chainmail reinforcements, and his patchwork pants looked built to last, but the most striking thing distinguishing him from all the others was that he was wearing shoes. I stopped and waited for him as he hurried toward me.

"An interesting show you put on up in the tower," said Shukir genially. "I've been here a week, and that's the first time a player's emerged from the Abyss hugging a demon. Can you show me the video? I want to have a look at the beast's mug. We have to know who we're up against, otherwise it's scary as hell. I'll even pay you. I haven't got much gold, but I can find twenty."

"You just want the face?" I asked. Shukir made a good first impression, especially after Braksed, Kurtune and Eredani. He told me about his problem, asked for help, even offered to pay... Wait a minute! That was a classic manipulation ruse. And as if to confirm my suspicion, he added:

"Actually, the whole jump would be better. I still have two more jumps, and what if I bump into one of them? Did the pick come from the Abyss too? What are its properties? Here, take the twenty."

Crafty fucker! Offers an exchange, gives me twenty gold, then mentions the pick, shifting my attention to it. If I was less cynical, I'd have taken the money and gladly helped the afflicted soul. Then I'd have kicked myself. Barliona is no reality – a verbal contract and the voluntary wish of each participant in the deal is enough. I would have to part with my video. But Shukir was overlooking one thing – two could play at that game.

"No, twenty's not enough." I dug my heels in, playing the simpleton, and declined the exchange. A demon was nothing compared to what the camp chief whispered to me after the jump. My Reputation had flown way up.

"Give me a break!" Shukir didn't believe me. He couldn't not say anything; he didn't like demons.

"I swear on Barliona! Up there Uldaron told me how to become a worthy warrior. Only an idiot would leak information like that for twenty. And anyway, I should probably offer it to the Phoenixes first."

I was enshrouded in a snow-white glow – Barliona had accepted my oath. You weren't allowed to misuse such affirmations of your words, on pain of punishment, but this was a fitting moment.

"Consider you've already offered it to the Phoenixes." Shukir persevered, taking the bait. "I'm here on their behalf."

"You're lying." I eyed him warily. "Why would they want to reset a player? Thanks, of course, but I'll contact them directly later. Maybe. Or maybe I won't. Rumor has it the Dark Legion is also buying up information."

"A hundred gold for the video of your dive." Shukir upped the stakes dramatically. "And another fifty for the pick."

I was about to milk him a bit more, when Eredani suddenly crawled out of his corner and unceremoniously butted into our conversation.

"Kvalen, don't agree. A video from the tower is worth substantially more than that. You're being taken for a ride."

"Butt out, Eredani, I'm done with you." Shukir's amiability faded.

Eredani paid him no attention and continued to talk me round, but I was sceptical of his desire to help.

"There aren't many demon hunters. Even fewer tieflings. Tiefling demon hunters are in single figures. You should already have worked out for yourself the specifics of our mechanism. If Uldaron told you something, keep it to yourself!"

Keeping calm on the outside was difficult.

What the hell was Eredani doing minding other people's business? I had to wrap it up, but leave my net cast wide for the future. "Eredani's right, Shukir. Sorry, but I'm not ready to sell information from Uldaron just yet. I should study the market first, otherwise I'll be underselling myself."

"A thousand gold right now for the full video from the tower!" Shukir had lost his patience.

The negotiation was back on. I pretended to be looking for support from Eredani, and unexpectedly noticed the shadow of a smirk flit across my congener's face. It was fleeting, barely noticeable, but so articulate that the answer came to me instantly. "Get outta here! Ten for the whole thing, not a penny less."

"Are you out of your mind?! Where did you get a price like that from? I'll give you fifteen hundred for the lot. That's for your eyes!" Shukir was seething. It was time to make a concession, otherwise the whole deal would break down.

"Three thousand, but only for the clip of what Uldaron told me. That's my final offer. I'm not going to haggle myself into a loss." I wasn't best pleased with myself, and waved a hand to drive home the point.

"Deal!" Shukir threw me a clipboard viewer. Shit! Three thousand gold for a few seconds of video! Had everyone gone nuts? I'd have to put in thirteen hours a day for two weeks to earn that sort of money. What was happening in people's heads that they were prepared to pay so much for a chunk of computer code? The most important thing now was to keep a lid on my jubilation.

I didn't even have to cut Uldaron out – the system did it automatically. I just needed to check the excerpt didn't include anything unpaid for, and press the Exchange button. Slightly short of three thousand entered my account – the Bank was fastidious in regard to its two percent – and the system made a suggestion:

New specialization available: Trade

Description: *Your ability to drive a hard bargain is impressive. You are a true trader. Every specialization point increases your discount with NPC-traders from 0.1% right up to 50%.*

Accept! As a potential clan chief, this specialization was compulsory.

"You?!" roared Shukir after looking at the video. The system obligingly censored the player's vocal outrage which followed. "Where's the information about levelling up?"

"That's all the boss told me," I replied nonchalantly. Of course the advice to "Gain the upper hand over the archdemon" wasn't worth three thousand gold, but I wanted to teach Shukir a lesson. If you're going to manipulate people, you must be prepared to be manipulated yourself.

"Give me my money back, you bastard!" demanded Shukir. It was verging on the orgasmic to observe his ire-distorted face.

Book One: A Second Chance

"The terms of our verbal agreement have been fulfilled, and you've received all the information. If you have any objections, refer them to a lawyer." I could be quite headstrong when the need took me. "If you don't require any more information, I won't presume to detain you further and distract you from the game. Have a nice day!"

I turned around and unhurriedly entered the newbie course. Shukir tried to stop me, yelling threats of divine retribution, but it fell on deaf ears since I had no intention of returning the money. The troublemaker didn't have access to the course, so he couldn't hound me there. Eventually things quietened down – the Phoenixes representative had been making a lot of noise. Although no, I was still being shadowed. Eredani stood beside me and, his eyes on everyone training, announced, "I want my cut. I reckon I'm due half."

I'd been expecting it ever since he'd come over and tried to help. I turned silently and expectantly toward him.

"Everyone around here knows Shukir," he said. "And his business. I knew he'd latch on to you after your tussle with the demon on the tower. Everyone knows you're a newbie in Barliona, down to the last deer. When I saw you were going to milk him, I decided to help out a bit. You wouldn't have been able to finagle him out of three thousand on your own. He's not stupid, but he is a tightwad. The least you could do is return the favor."

"So that's your game," I said. The first time we spoke, I'd taken Eredani for a reasonable guy.

Evidently I'd been too impressed by his agreement. Matty was right – Barliona had changed. If before people had played for the enjoyment, now it was for the money. Everyone wanted to make a profit, and preferably at the expense of others.

"Sorry, Victor. I didn't ask for your help. Plus you nearly ruined the entire negotiation. Newbie doesn't mean idiot. If you think I owe you, there's a Dispute Settlement button in Settings. The lawyers will sort it out. Good luck in the game!"

"So you're not going to give me my share and earn my goodwill?" Eredani had lost all sense of proportion. It wasn't a nice feeling to be wrong about people.

"What do I need with someone so generous?" I asked sarcastically.

"I suppose you don't," he agreed and backed down. "Good luck in the game."

Dismissing the tiefling, I went to find the supervisor. Gurt was standing by some sparring dummies and looking impatiently in my direction. The instant I reached him, he boomed, "You took your time! Invoke the demon!"

The Invoke Demon button began to flash, like a prompt for retards. One click and Aniram appeared. An animated buzz from the direction of the simulators indicated the archdemoness had been spotted, but she paid no attention to the folks around her. Her hate-filled gaze was fixed on me alone. Her hands and feet were manacled by a white cloud, so, unable to get her claws into me, she was trying to burn through me with her eyes. Poor NPC!

If only she knew how often I had to put up with looks like that in the real world. Especially when I had to remove someone from a project because of their incompetence.

"Traitor! You will be cursed and banished from the Abyss!" Getting no reaction to her stare, Aniram had to add some big words. The orc peevishly screwed up his face – the demoness's voice enabled debuffs. They had no effect on tieflings, but everyone else in the vicinity got an unpleasant earful.

"Tell her to shut up," said Gurt, retreating from us and drinking a white liquid from a flask. I specifically observed the orc to see the result – the debuffs disappeared as if by magic. I assessed my abilities and pursed my lips, dissatisfied, as not one of them allowed me to control the conscious of the subjugated demon. I decided to follow the old-fashioned route, and said:

"Don't open your mouth unless ordered to do so!"

"I'll tear out your heart and ram it down your throat! And without any orders from you." Aniram didn't bat an eyelid. "You'll be begging me for death. Mother will reward me."

No new debuffs appeared. So that was how Demon Retribution worked! Aniram hadn't attacked *me*, but everyone else, to damage me in training. In confirmation of this, a countdown timer appeared in the upper part of my viewer: Minimum time to next diversion. I chuckled – it would seem my "pet" had a mind. What was the point of creating a diversion if I was ready for it? She would save up her strength for thirty minutes and strike when I was least expecting it. It didn't exactly make for a comfortable game.

"Select a dummy and perform a Demon Strike," ordered Gurt, reeling from the debuff.

The next button began to flash on the panel, and several of the dummies closest to me lit up in white. I knew the game was played by people with varying levels of education, but such detailed prompts were excessive. Highlighting the nearest target, I pressed the button. Aniram bent over backwards, and a dark cloud burst from her breast. It flew toward me and into my hands, arousing a feeling of oneness. Memories of the warm lava and Ireness's soft voice zipped through my head. My body reacted, quaking in ecstasy, something it had sorely missed. My fingers tensed spasmodically, and a snow-white flourish struck the dummy. Task progress: one out of five. The buttons flashed again, making me go into Settings. Of course! The Newbie parameter was selected in Game Regime. By default, Barliona tried as much as possible to guard people against thinking, doing everything for them. I selected "lower than average", and the flashing ceased. That was more like it! Completing the remaining strikes was no problem. Aniram put up no resistance, and didn't try to stitch me up; she just bent over and gave me part of her demon essence.

Demon Strike training task completed

Reward:

- *Experience: +6, until next level: 994*
- *Reputation with Light of Barliona faction: +3*

I was seriously distressed at the damage I'd caused. Demon Strike was a magic ability, and given that my Intellect was lower than low, and I had no magic weapons, twelve Damage points was not easy on the eye. Were I to lock horns with even a level-one player with a hundred HP, I would have to use the ability ten or so times. In that time any half savvy player would tear me to shreds and have time to spare. Conclusion – don't engage in open PvP without being properly kitted out. The bonus from the basic commercial account increased Experience by one point and Reputation by two. I was itching to buy myself a Boosting Gem, but no sooner had I opened the in-game store and seen the prices, than the desire evaporated all by itself. Spending that sort of money just then was stupid.

Reference information

Training speed and Boosting Gems

Training speed – *The parameter determining how quickly a player gains Experience. A coefficient increasing Experience. Default setting 0%. Increases due to obtainment of a special Boosting*

Gem. A player may have only one Gem at any one time.

Boosting Gem – *An object increasing the speed of training. Can be obtained only from the game administration. May not be resold to another player. Types of Gem and prices:*

- *Gem +10%, minimum +1 experience. Price: 1,050 gold*
- *Gem +20%, minimum +2 experience. Price: 2,100 gold*
- *Gem +30%, minimum +4 experience. Price: 3,150 gold*
- *Gem +40%, minimum +6 experience. Price: 4,200 gold*
- *Gem +50%, minimum +8 experience. Price: 5,250 gold*

"If you train hard and always use your abilities, you'll grow into a worthy demon hunter." Gurt officially signed off on my task, and returned to the other recruits. The orc's words struck me as strange, and I opened my character window. Indeed, five Demon Strikes had increased my Intellect by five points, one for each strike. 995 more strikes and I would increase my Intellect by one point. How freaking simple! I had to hammer away at a dummy for half a year in order to bump up a characteristic to a more or less respectable value.

I dismissed Aniram, but the countdown to the next diversion didn't stop. More bad news. I couldn't do anything to my pet, I couldn't freeze the timer, and I couldn't use my abilities without a demon. Too many "I couldn'ts". Deciding to see what this would lead to, I went over to the simulators to polish up my moves. I got so caught up in the feeling of control over my own body that I lost track of time. I hated running, jumping, and squatting in reality – my unwieldy body and shortness of breath constantly resisted my desire to exercise. There was nothing like that here. I literally flew through the simulators, and the logic of it all became clear – a demon hunter had to be quick and agile in order to escape danger. We weren't supposed to get mixed up in open conflict with enemies. Our core rotation was: leap away from opponent, keep opponent at a distance, constantly batter opponent with Demon Strikes. No Leeroy Jenkins here!

The next two hours I spent working hard on completing obstacles. Fortunately for me, Marcon the Spoiled didn't content himself with seven out of ten, and stayed on to practice the last three. I shadowed him on the simulators, trying to remember each movement, but then he suddenly disappeared to reality. His character faded away right in the middle of an obstacle, as a result of which I and the rest of the brethren following him all fell to the ground. Some sooner, some later, but everyone collapsed. I was the first. My Agility scale rose to 748, and I at last felt depleted. No physical fatigue, only mental. At the end of the day, repeating the same thing over and over is hard work. I needed to switch off, so I decided to take a stroll around the training camp, but as soon as I exited the assault course, my body was seized by that familiar chill.

"You again! Smell the light!" Braksed was once again ensconced in his battle station next to our course. I ignored his cloying odium, far more concerned as I was with the state of Eredani, who was lying on the ground, hunched over in a most unnatural position, wheezing, and tearing at his chest with his fingers. Braksed laughed, pleased with the result, and that was the last straw. I was no great philanthropist, but I couldn't stand open travesties of justice. I couldn't damage the player directly, but Braksed himself had given me a fantastic idea. Aniram, my dear, enter!

"What the hell?!" The elf stood transfixed. The archdemoness's spectacular entrance did not go unnoticed. Her wings spread wide, Aniram hovered above me, intent on flattening me like a bug as soon as the light of Eluna touched her. It still hadn't occurred to the aggressor to switch off the Drop of Light.

"I will drink your soul! I will make you pray for death!" Her target had suddenly changed. I wasn't going anywhere, so her priority was now to rid herself of the light she so hated. A deafening crack, an earthquaking tremble, and all around was rent with the wild shrieks of a pack of lower demons. Aniram had called up six canine beasts, and pointing her wings at Braksed she roared, "Kill!"

The dogs rushed to obey the order, and the noise from the camp was joined by two abominable sounds: the wail of the security system, and the cries of Braksed being torn apart. A player's pet, just like a player himself, could do nothing to an opponent, but this restriction did not extend to invoked animals. A shadow flickered and the pack was dust. Drill sergeant Tarlin was the first to reach ground zero, but it was too late – Braksed lay prostrate, one HP to his name, emitting toe-curling screams. The lowlifes had had a splendid romp, and Braksed now understood the need to visit a sales office to decrease his pain threshold. He'd been so panicked he hadn't even thought of exiting virtuality to escape the demons' jaws.

The satisfied Aniram folded her wings, devoured me with a bloodthirsty look and, spraying everything around with her hatred, spat, "You're next, traitor!"

Tarlin frowned, and I hurried to get the archdemoness out of harm's way. If he killed her, I would have to dive into the Abyss again, something I wasn't burning with desire to do. "Pick up Eredani and follow me," he ordered. "You attacked a Free citizen. Punishment awaits you!"

Upgrades gained

- *Experience: +6, until next level: 988*
- *Reputation with Light of Barliona faction: increased by 3*

Yeah right! What were the bonuses for?!

Chapter 3

CAMP COMMANDER Uldaron listened to Tarlin stony-faced. According to the instructor it just so happened that, out of the blue and in broad daylight, a tiefling had decided to seize power in the camp, by invoking an archdemon outside the training area. Brave Tarlin had nipped the half-demon's insidious plan in the bud, and now wanted a reward for his saintly trouble. I was about to call the sergeant a mercenary scuzzball, when Uldaron set everything straight by explaining the reward Tarlin was speaking of:

"Absolutely no frontline! I need you here," the commander cut in. "If you want a reward, open your purse and I'll fill it with cash."

Tarlin screwed up the features of his already grisly mug. He was most dissatisfied with that particular choice of reward.

"So what actually happened?" Uldaron was playing the intelligent commander, wanting to clarify the situation and allowing his underling to have his say.

"The youngsters swiped the Drop of Light from the assault course and started training with it in an undesignated area," said Tarlin. "I didn't intervene. Thought I'd punish them afterwards. Then Kvalen showed up, invoked the demon, and

133

ruined the training session."

"Training session?!" I strongly resented this interpretation of events. Had I not been an indirect participant, I might even have believed Tarlin, if it wasn't for Eredani's resuscitated, though still limp, body testifying otherwise. I brought up the text of the user agreement, found the relevant paragraph, and said, "That wasn't a training session, it was a violation of the user agreement. You allowed a player to be tortured and dealt a level of pain incommensurate with common sense. Section five, clause forty-two, sub-clause three."

There was a pause in the conversation. Eredani wanted to say something, but only had enough strength to squeeze out a brief mew. Uldaron and Tarlin froze, their eyes filled with the snow-white of the loading indicator, and unexpectedly for me, the surrounding space spoke:

"Dear player! Your appeal to the dispute settlement service has been accepted and considered, and a decision has been taken. Please be informed that according to section one, point thirteen of the user agreement, no infringement of the playing process has been recorded in regard to player Eredani. Thank you for your appeal to the dispute settlement service. We wish you a pleasant game!"

The text of the user agreement scrolled down and stopped on the following point:

The standard user agreement does not extend to players convicted by a court decision of crimes specified by criminal legislation. For this category of player there exists a separate user agreement approved and confirmed by the Penal and Penitentiary Commission.

I saw Eredani in a new light: he wasn't a vagrant, he was a jailbird with one-hundred-percent sensory settings; a player who was allowed to kill, rob, and persecute with impunity anywhere in Barliona; a criminal who had been able to flee a coalmine or an ore mine or a logging camp by paying to have his red armband removed. That's why he couldn't bag a demon – nobody could withstand the hundred-percent pain of the Abyss if they were conscious. The system ensured I had fully grasped the true nature of my new acquaintance, before unblocking the NPCs, who continued to act out their algorithms as if nothing had happened. NPCs turned a deaf ear to anything which concerned the real world.

"Yes, training session!" The drill sergeant's voice was metallic. "Braksed acted just as any demon hunter should. He tried to banish a demon."

"Tieflings are not demons." Uldaron came to our defense, although he was ultimately only on the side of truth. "Kvalen and Eredani are Free citizens, helping us rid Barliona of the beasts of the Abyss."

"This is no place for them. They can't control their own demons." Tarlin refused to budge. "I don't want to come running every thirty minutes to wipe everyone's backsides."

"Agreed, something must be done with the

demon. So you teach the tieflings what to do."

"Me? No, chief, you're not going to offload this pair on me. I'll quit, hide, desert, but I'm not having anything to do with tieflings. I have a short way with demons – a knife to the throat and back into the Abyss."

"That's unnecessary, Tarlin. An instructor is obliged to fulfil his duties."

"An instructor is obliged to teach combat with demons," retorted Tarlin. "External, not internal. If you want to instruct them, send them to Hermit. If anyone can explain to them how to deal with their essence, it's him. Outcasts should work with outcasts. End of." He looked defiantly at Uldaron.

The boss sighed dolefully and shook his head. "If you think I'm going to fire you for your insolence, you've got another think coming. Who's going to teach the recruits? Shut up and get to work, or I'll pack you off to the priestesses to embroider some lace. But you're right about Hermit, he can help the tieflings. I'll send them to see him just as soon as they've completed the course."

"These losers? The whole course?" snorted Tarlin. "Fat chance. The most they're capable of is seven out of ten. Maximum."

"Done!" Uldaron slapped his palm on the table. "Kvalen and Eredani complete the newbies' course and go to see Hermit. They finish training when they get back. We'll see what the outcast can do with them."

Task received: collaborative tuition

Vasily Mahanenko. Invasion

Description: *A class-specific rare task. Make your way to Hermit and study with him.*

Reward:

- *Experience: +5*
- *Reputation with Light of Barliona faction: +1*
- *You will learn to negotiate with a subjugated demon.*

Restrictions: *You must complete this task together with player Eredani.*

Penalty for failure/refusal to complete task: *expulsion from training camp.*

And there you have it – the particularities of the upgraded Barliona: the generation of tasks during the process of player development. The Imitators responsible for our location had tweaked the basic conditions, adding points unacceptable to me, which I declared immediately:

"Why do I have to complete the task with him?" I nodded in Eredani's direction. "I don't want to burden myself."

"Because you're in the same boat now," said the boss.

"What's that supposed to mean?" I asked.

"It's all very simple." Uldaron's eyes once more filled with the white haze, as control of the NPC was taken over by a more advanced Imitator. "The

Barliona Corporation has received from your employer a request for cooperation. The terms have been accepted, and the criteria imported into the game. You can read about them in a special section. We are trying to socialize marginal players, which is why we've introduced a counterclaim. Confirmation has been received from your employer concerning the acceptability of the changes."

What? Why didn't I know about this? Oh shit, I set the higher level not for retards! Who was a retard now? I rummaged around in the menu and opened the table of socialization criteria. There was just one point of difference from the document I'd signed: <u>Help players complete tasks a total of twenty times; one of these players must be marginal</u>. The "One of these..." was the very same "counterclaim," which I hadn't signed in the real world.

"You could give us a map." Eredani rose to his feet and approached the camp commandant. "Where do we find Hermit?"

"Fair enough." Uldaron produced two pieces of paper from a drawer and laid them on the table. "We can't be dispatching you into the unknown."

Eredani took his copy of the map and nodded toward mine. "Take it. Let's go to the barrack and discuss tactics. We're going to be working together for some time."

I approached the table and took the map. I didn't know what I'd got so excited about. What difference did it make if Eredani was a criminal or not? We would complete the task, and he could go to hell. I would have words with my employers on the Monday. It was bad practice to alter signed documents unilaterally. That would need the kibosh putting on it.

Map upgraded

Description of changes: *You have received a fragment of a map of the demon-hunter training camp and adjacent territory.*

Familiarization percentage of current location: *10%.*

"We'll be passing through the lands of N'Got." Eredani had studied the map in a matter of moments. "Who's that?"

"An archdemon," explained Uldaron. "The training camp is situated on one of the islands of Stivala. Five archdemons have based their prides there. N'Got is the weakest of them. Part of your training will involve driving beasties out of his lands."

"You mentioned five but only named one. Where are the others?" Eredani continued to hustle the NPCs, but they'd already told us more than they wanted to. Tarlin, who hadn't yet contributed to the conversation, said irately:

"Right now you should be thinking about how to complete the course and get to Hermit, not where to find all the archdemons. You have twenty-four hours to complete the task and set out on your search."

Task update: Step 1. Start of training

Book One: A Second Chance

Description of update: *A simple task. Complete the newbies' assault course together with player Eredani. Minimum completion score: 7 out of 10. Maximum completion time: 24 hours from time of task update (23 hours 59 minutes remaining).*

Reward:

- *Experience: +5*
- *Reputation with Light of Barliona faction: +1*
- *Access to next training step*
- *Bonus for course completion with full marks: +1 to all main characteristics*
- *Bonus for course completion in group: +1 to all main characteristics*

We made it to the barrack without any problems – no "Smell the lights" or "Give me my money backs." Aniram's performance and, most importantly, Braksed's resultant wails had poured cold water on all potential hot heads. Everyone avoided us, unsure what to expect or how to defend themselves. Which suited me just fine.

"You can't enter the barrack without permission," said Eredani, settling down onto his bed. "Nobody will disturb us here." Not a muscle twitched on my face. He hadn't given me permission to enter the barrack, so were I not already registered there, I would surely have smacked my nose on an invisible partition. The tiefling knew a second occupant had appeared, and this was his way of checking whether it was me. No questions or superfluous words, just a timely unexecuted action. I didn't know whether to be happy about it or not. I liked Eredani's methods, but I didn't like him applying them to me.

"Let's start with the essentials. My name is Victor," said Eredani, but immediately he did so, his face was obscured by a thick white fog. A second later it dissipated, leaving a testy scowl. He was disgruntled with something.

"We have three attempts left. Let me outline the situation so there are no questions. The court has forbidden me to give out any personal information which could be used to identify me in reality. This is monitored by a separate Imitator, and all I have to do is open my mouth, point, hint, or drop a clue, and it blocks the attempt and issues a warning. Four warnings and I get sent to the mines. Pay no attention to my appearance. It's changed and is nothing like the real me. Any questions?"

"No," I replied. I wanted to think everything through first. Sent? Not returned, but sent? I recalled the widely and aggressively advertised story of the Mahan. The shaman began his journey in the ore mines, and by the time he was freed he was at level twenty. Eredani didn't just arrive in the wide world at level one – he passed through the tiefling birth scene alongside me. And he did it like a Free player, which is why I thought he was a vagrant.

"Good. We're clear on that then," he said. "Now I want to emphasize that I'm not happy about being a burden. On the contrary, I'm a very useful source of information about the game. And I have a lot, even if it is about the old Barliona. But the central points will hardly have changed. The key thing is still the same: kill or be killed, buy or be bought."

"All of a sudden you're the very epitome of candor," I noted. "What happened?"

"I need help. I can't cope with the training camp on my own. At first I thought you were from the Corporation, sent to check up on me, which is why I scrutinized you, studied you. After you stood up for me, I realized you were a newbie and didn't know a thing about me. The voice of Barliona cannot prevaricate. Who are you? What do you need from the game? What conditions do you have to fulfil?"

"Too many personal questions. And free ones at that."

"Agreement? I'll show you my worth. You'll definitely benefit from collaborating with me."

"Agreement," I nodded. "I'll answer one question, and we'll see what you can offer me."

"Why did you come to Barliona?" The tiefling had contrived to ask a question, the answer to which involved a lot of information. Following his example I began to edit the text of the contract, adding information bit by bit and waiting for a green tick.

Fussy Barliona was only satisfied when I wrote about my employer and my plans to create a clan. And I had to mention both points, as only one wouldn't have counted as fulfilling my duties. Did they have lie detectors or something?

"That... changes... everything... drastically," said Eredani. "Very drastically. Take this, it'll come in handy."

I read the new information sceptically. It was the structure of a clan, with contract templates, a description of the main functions of each role, and requirements for creating your own clan. There was an addendum to the final point: if you made an initial equity capital investment in the clan of thirty or forty thousand gold, the NPC-registrar would take it as a serious intention and allow you to choose the location of your clan castle. Somehow or other I could have found or cobbled together each of the points by myself, but the addendum came most opportunely. There was no information about it in open source.

"That's a fraction of what I know about clans and establishing, organizing, and managing them." Eredani continued to big himself up. "Because of my status, I can't create a clan on my own, or be a treasurer or deputy, but I can be an adviser. However, if one of your tasks is to create your own team, I'd like to be part of it. I can be of use to you."

"Isn't it a bit soon to be making decisions like that? You know nothing about me and my financial situation, yet you're already prepared to advise."

"You were discarded as superfluous, but you still managed to find work in these difficult times. You even agreed to an internship. That speaks of tenacity and character. That's number one. You bought a professional pod. As a new employee you couldn't take out a loan, so you used your own means. You're a good project manager, so you know how to manage a budget. I'm willing to bet you spent no more than ten percent of your resources on the pod." Eredani cocked his head in expectation of my answer. I did the math and nodded. "You see? That's number two. Number three, you decided to create a clan. That means you don't just have the resources, financial and human, but you also have a plan. You can't be a good project manager if you're an opportunist. Believe me, I know what I'm talking about. Add to that my knowledge and experience, and you have yourself an interesting enterprise. Is that sufficient to make a decision?"

"Absolutely. Why aren't you in the ore mines?"

"I made a plea bargain, so they let me out into the wide world. With specific restrictions and constant control, but the wide world all the same."

"Okay, so you have experience. But what do you want?"

"Peace and quiet," said Eredani seriously. "There are many like Braksed, and I need protection. I want to finish the training course, wringing as much out of the locals as I can. When we set up the clan, I want my share and a say in making clan decisions. Nothing too excessive, but I don't want to take a back seat either."

He'd called the NPCs "locals." I'd heard that term before, but nobody used it anymore. It's what players had called NPCs at the dawn of Barliona, fifteen or sixteen years ago.

"And in return you just share information, yes?"

"Not only information." Eredani chose his words carefully, not wanting to receive another warning. "I know a lot about how to establish relations with the locals, and how to get to the Emperor. In order to indemnify everyone, you and I sign a cooperation agreement. I'll prepare the text."

"I need to think about it," I said. It wasn't good to make hasty decisions. "I suggest taking a break from plans and concentrating on our current problems. We've got twenty-four hours to complete the newbies' course. We'll set up a group, work together, go to see Hermit, and then draw up the contract. That way we'll see if we make a good team."

"I wouldn't expect anything less," agreed Eredani. "Send me a group and organize a chat. Some things it's better to type and not say out loud. And another thing. A non-disclosure agreement. Whatever we learn from each other stays between us. We can't give or sell information to third parties. It's not a fact that we'll stay together after completing the camp. We need a safety net."

The group interface didn't add any new information about Eredani. A level-one player with the standard hundred Health and Energy points.

"And the last thing. Before we go to the

course, we need to open our main specialities. Nothing unique or too specific, but they must increase quickly and without too much effort on our part. I would advise Trade or Cartography. Minimum effort, maximum benefit."

"I get Cartography, but Trade as a main a speciality? Why?"

"Trade is actually very important for us, but it's no good to me. Traders are prejudiced against prisoners. As a basic speciality, Trade provides a discount of up to fifty percent, and if it's your main speciality, traders might offer you under-the-counter goods, stuff you can't usually get hold of. I can't remember the exact probability coefficient, we'll have to wait and see afterwards. The thing you won't find in official sources is that the main speciality of the chief extends to the entire clan, which is an advantage."

"Does Trade increase only with NPCs?" I asked.

"No, with players too. It's increased by any activity which involves exchanging something for money. Auction, direct buying and selling, information, even transferring a large sum to another player."

"What about management specializations? As the head of the clan, wouldn't it be better for me to have those?"

"It is true lots of clan chiefs take them, only for some reason no one thinks about how to increase them. Don't forget about the restriction – basic specialities can only be twelve points higher than your main speciality. Let's say you take Manager. Specializing in managing groups of over one hundred people. Where are you going to find so many people now? And even if you find them, how are you going to level them up? Manage them all personally? I thought you weren't planning to live in Barliona. Brody, you understand perfectly well you can't read too much into a name. Everything must be to the maximum. Leveling up is an advantage to the player and to his clan."

"Okay, you've convinced me, I'll take Trade. What are you going to take?"

"Cartography. For three reasons. Firstly, maps are like gold dust. Secondly, we can make scrolls. And thirdly, for every ten Cartography levels, Intellect increases by a point. So you take Cartography. And Skinning too, that's extra Agility. Indispensable to tieflings."

"Maybe it's worth taking something else for Stamina then? They're going to reduce it every ten levels."

"Mining, but it's pretty dreary work. Smacking ore with a pick sucks. I hope I won't have to bother."

"We'll see. I have a pick." I showed Eredani my weapon. He toyed with it a while before announcing:

"Change of plan. I'm taking Mining. And yes, you'll have to give me the pick."

"I'll sell it to you if I don't need it," I corrected him. He'd started bossing me around.

With a detailed shopping list, we set off to see Dheire, the camp's specialities instructor. Eredani had no money, so we drew up another contract to the effect that I would pay all his expenses, and as soon as he'd earned enough money, the game would settle our accounts for us.

"Greetings to the young tieflings!" Dheire the gnome welcomed us. He was sitting in the middle of his workshop doing what you would expect of a specialities trainer in the nursery – meditating to relieve the boredom. Newbie-level demon hunters would think about anything but developing their specialities.

In his shoebox of a room my attention was drawn toward an abundance of food packets: duck, pork, chicken, ravioli, and noodles, as well as dozens of tubs of various strange combinations of dishes. I was lost for a few moments, trying to work out what had caught my eye, but I snapped out of it upon receiving a not insubstantial prod from Eredani. According to our provisional arrangement, my partner prompted me in the chat, but it was I who had to speak to the NPC. A peculiarity of game chats was that you had to write literally *in* them – using a virtual keyboard. No "power of thought" or "freedom of the mind," just simple mechanics.

"And greetings to you, master Dheire." I obediently read out the first message from Eredani.

"What crooked horns you have. You won't find a wife with those horns. And what an ugly tail!" Dheire shook his head in sympathy, and I got it – He was a Chinaman!

"Have you... already... eaten?" I asked a completely different question to the one in the chat. Eredani coughed subtly behind my back, for which I whacked his leg with my tail as if to say, "I can cope on my own."

"Oh yes, thank you, I dined very heartily," said Dheire, nodding his bobblehead.

"And what did the master eat?" I was now sure.

Eredani: *I don't get it. What's with the ad-libbing?*

I tried to type an explanation, but gave up. Typing wasn't one of my strong points.

Eredani: *Did I miss something while I was making myself at home? Is this some new way of conducting negotiations? Are you going to ask him about how often he passes stool?*

I was impressed with my partner's typing speed, but wisely I didn't reply; I just continued to grin at the master.

"I had ravioli, noodles, and a little beer." A smile broke out on Dheire's face, and his Agreeability to me increased a little. "What brings you two cloven hooves to me at this late hour? Too sick to train? Haven't eaten?"

Eredani had got worked up for nothing. The directness and wealth of food would give any player a hint at the master's citizenship of the Celestial Empire. Some mistook the frankness of the Chinese for discourtesy, but not me. When he mentioned my horns and wife, I'd immediately felt a warmth in my soul, as if I'd met an old friend. How nervous I'd been until I figured out how to make the egg-noodle lovers work.

"The time to study is upon us," I explained. "In order to dine well, we must first study well."

"Study is the most important thing in the life of any creature," said Dheire. "Directly after food. What would you like to eat, um, I mean what would you like to study?"

"I have plenty of money and I would like to study Cookery." This one utterance triggered two different responses: delight in Dheire, and surprise in Eredani. Another hint at my frivolity appeared in the chat, which wasn't something we had discussed in the barrack.

"How pleased I am that you came to see me!" Dheire had heard the phrase "plenty of money" and bloomed. "Are you going to make that most important of specialities your main one?"

"To begin with we shall see what we can learn. Fried rat is easier to buy than to cook oneself."

"How dare you say that?!" he said, outraged. "Correctly prepared rat meat is impossible to buy, and can only be cooked by oneself. It is a shame that we have a problem with rats in these parts."

"How many pieces of meat do we need, and which particular kind of rat?" I asked, reading Eredani's first relevant question.

"Twenty should do." Dheire brightened up again. "Any meat, so long as it's rat."

Task received: Rat meat supplier

Vasily Mahanenko. Invasion

Description: *A rare task. Dheire – mentor of the demon-hunter training camp –asks you to bring him 20 pieces of any meat described as "rat".*

Reward:

- *Experience: +5*
- *Reputation with Light of Barliona faction: +1*

"So, teach us Cookery, and we'll go looking for rats." I vocalized Eredani's hint a second time, and *We leave now!!!* left me in no doubt he'd sniffed out something interesting.

"Why not?" Dheire rubbed his hands in anticipation of a good deal. "Ten gold from each tiefling, and the speciality is yours. Chef's kits – that's another ten each, and of course twenty recipes at five gold each. Two hundred and twenty gold, and you're both on the way to becoming top Barliona chefs. I must warn you, no haggling! This isn't a market, and prices are fixed from upstairs."

"Thank you, we'll think about it." Eredani literally dragged me out of the workshop. "It was nice to meet you."

"Hey..." Dheire wilted when he realized no purchase was going to be made just then and he wouldn't get any money. "You come here, you disturb me, and you don't buy anything? How can I do business with folks like that?"

Book One: A Second Chance

My recently raised Agreeability to the gnome dropped back down to the standard twenty.

"Brody, let's agree on something: if I make a suggestion, you do it straight away and without winging it." Eredani laid into me the second we stepped out of the administration building. "Even if you think I'm wrong, do as I say. I have more experience, so don't ruin the game. Don't make life difficult for me until I screw up at least once, okay?"

"Okay," I consented. "What happened?"

"This is a tricky task. It depends on financial input." Eredani quickly calmed down. "The key phrase was 'any meat'. The higher the quality of the meat we give Dheire, the better the result. The best meat comes from level-two-hundred rats on the third level of the drains in Anhurs, the capital of Malabar. One piece costs twenty gold or more. Plus the auction's cut, that's ten percent of the deal price. If you're willing to spend nearly five hundred gold, let's go for it."

"Five hundred for a task?" I had trouble containing my sarcasm. "Okay, let's discuss the viability of that. What do we stand to gain from this task?"

"Recipes, a discount, Agreeability, a rare commodity." Eredani listed the benefits. "Anything that'll help us here and now."

"My thoughts precisely. Whatever we get will be useful for newbies. Who can we sell this stuff to, in order to recover our investment? That's half an average month's wages. If we're going to spend money, we need to know we'll definitely get it back.

Preferably twice over."

"Okay, let's work it out," Eredani chuckled. "The cost of any rare item coming from demon hunters has a coefficient of ten, possibly even more. Shukir is evidence of that, since the Phoenixes are prepared to pay thousands for any information that will help them become even stronger. Whatever Dheire offers us, we can sell it here, to Braksed or Kurtune. They've got money. If we can't earn anything here, we'll get to the wide world and sell to the Phoenixes or the Legends of Barliona. We'll definitely make our gold back, and we'll be in possession of something rare."

Eredani's arguments were hard to dispute, but my entire being objected to the thought of paying out five hundred gold without a clear idea of how to get it back. I hated working as a wingman.

"Here's the number of a human who works at the auction. If you decide to risk the cash, call him. Say you found him in the Internet. He puts good money into advertizing. If you decide against it, call him anyway. Ask him to buy you a few gold's worth of simple rat meat and e-mail it to you. We need to close the task."

Eredani left the decision making to me and stepped aside. If he thought the responsibility would weigh heavy on me like a granite slab and I would hurry to call a strange number, he was wrong. I had already made a decision. "The task has no time restriction. Let's stick to the plan, and train first. We can always come back to the rats later."

"Also an option," he agreed. "Then we take only the necessary specialities, without all this Cookery lark. Why the hell did you ask Dheire about what he'd eaten? That's not what we came to see him for."

"What do you mean? I was boosting our Agreeability. I'm pretty sure that NPC's a Chinaman. It was written all over his workshop."

"What makes you think that? There was no Chinese paraphernalia, no chopsticks, no fans. And what's food got to do with anything?"

"Food is a big thing for them. A consequence of hunger. If you're in favor with a Chinaman, instead of greeting you he'll ask you if you've eaten. Then he'll quiz you about what you've eaten. He's showing interest and concern. His workshop was full of boxes of food, didn't you notice?"

"I noticed. I just didn't think anything of it," said Eredani.

"Pork is an allusion to sweet and sour pork. Duck – Peking duck. And so on. If a Chinaman doesn't eat at the right time, he'll do your head in with his whining. I once had the pleasure of working with some representatives of that magical country. I nearly missed my deadlines trying to get used to their idiosyncrasies."

"So you're an expert on the Chinese?" He regarded me with interest.

"No. To understand them you have to be born one of them. I just worked with them for a while. Why?"

"Nothing. Forget it." He waved it away. "Let's

go back and see your Chinaman."

Dheire was overjoyed at our return. However, no sooner had he learned that we planned to study only our specialities, with no recipes, than he lost interest and after that spoke begrudgingly through his teeth. He was getting no money out of us, so why waste time on a couple of tieflings? After opening Cartography and setting it as our main speciality, the gnome was about to meditate again, but Eredani demanded he sell us Cartographer and Chef's kits. If the first of these was clear, the second required explaining. Many specialities in Barliona opened automatically if the player completed tasks specific to the speciality. Cookery and Mining were two of these. To open Cookery you simply needed to cook something; for Mining – to strike some ore with a pick. I was grateful to him for this, because it was good to save forty gold. Maybe this Eredani wasn't so bad after all.

You have chosen your main specialization: Trade

Description: *Your ability to drive a hard bargain is impressive. You are a true trader. Each speciality point increases your discount with NPC-traders from 0.1% right up to 50%. A feature of your main speciality is that traders may offer you goods that are not readily available, depending on your speciality and Agreeability levels.*

Book One: A Second Chance

The level of your other specialities may not exceed that of your main speciality by more than 12 points.

"Set Cartographer straight away," said Eredani. "The maps should update automatically. We need to keep our input to a minimum, so get used to scanning for detail. Open Settings – Specializations – Cartography, tick Read Personal Data. Done it? Excellent. Now we'll update the map of the training camp. Calculate the distance to our barrack – how many meters is it? Calculate the size of the square, and the relative position of the barrack. The position and orientation of the teleport, and how far from it to the training areas and the barracks. The paths separating the courses. You see the hill by the trees? Calculate the distance to it, its height, and position relative to other objects. The key thing in cartography is noticing details, and doing it here and now, not wasting valuable time watching videos or rendering maps from memory. I understand it's difficult at first, but the more you do it, the quicker you get results. You'll begin to note details not only in Barliona, but in reality too. It's a very useful skill."

I agreed with him on that. Details were everything to us. I had come across this tracking technique before, but never used it for its true purpose, which is why I rejoiced at every point gained on my Cartographer scale. The map became more and more detailed as I gauged distances, heights and depths. But the most effective method for levelling up was names. By marking the central square "square," and the shimmering sphere "portal," I immediately boosted my Cartographer scale up to a hundred.

"Well done," said Eredani. "Detailization without labelling is no good to anybody. Players and locals alike understand nouns, not coordinates. So always ask where you are, it'll help you develop. And another thing – self education. When you get out into reality, find time to look at the rules for map-making, and the particulars of cartography and orienting yourself in your surroundings. Without being tied to Barliona. Just the rules. It'll help enormously. For some reason everyone gets fixated on the game and forgets about reality."

It took us an hour to get to the newbies' assault course after thoroughly exploring the training camp. It wasn't a large area and did not allow either myself or Eredani to increase our specialities by even one point, but we did lay some groundwork – 572 points out of 1,000. All we had to do was to step out of the camp and our Cartographer characteristics would jump up to level two.

"Marcon, come here a minute. A spot of business for you," I called to the local leader. The nimble elf was winding down his training session on simulator ten, about to complete the newbie assault course and receive his bonus reward.

"Greetings, Tieflings!" he said, approaching us with a radiant and friendly smile. The others grumbled because we'd hijacked the player everyone was copying. Marcon was all puffed up with himself.

"Did you see that? I've nearly done all ten. Plita goes, 'I'm gonna do you now!' And I go, 'Ain't gonna happen, not on my watch.' So I duck down, crawl, and slip through. Awesome! Whoever was behind didn't have a clue what to do, and the ones on the platform go, 'Thwack!' Hilarious! Anyway, what did you want?"

"We want to do the newbie assault course."

"What are you standing here for then? See what everyone else is doing? Come on out here, y'see, and hop onto the course. Get your head down, run through here, crawl through there, and it's, 'Yeah! We did it!' "

"We just bet each other we could pass a couple of obstacles first time round."

"Nah, it won't happen, not first time," Marcon said and started dancing, parading some fancy footwork. "I've been dancing the cha-cha-cha here for three days. Step here, step there, turn, crouch, and bow. Every simulator has its own dance. You have to feel it."

"That's why we came to you," said Eredani. "We can dance, we just don't know the right moves. Show us the whole thing on the ground, and we'll repeat it on the simulator. What difference does it make where we practice dancing, on the ground or in amongst the pendulums?"

"Hmm..." Marcon scratched his head thoughtfully.

"Five hundred gold." I decided to give him a hand making the right decision.

"Each," he said all too quickly. At last

somebody in the game knew the value of money.

"Each," confirmed Eredani. "What are these moves then?"

What followed was something akin to an epileptic fit, and I immediately wanted to unsee it. Marcon started pirouetting, and Eredani copied his movements to a T, as though he'd done nothing else all his life.

"Hmm..." said Marcon for the second time, before sharply throwing his arms out to the sides and bending them alternately at the elbows. Raising his knees high, he began to strut around Eredani like a peacock, simultaneously nodding his head in time with the music that only he could hear. Eredani joined in, dancing even more wildly than Marcon. The tempo upped, and the dancers whirled their arms like windmills, tap dancing, egging each other on and looking every bit like cocks fighting over a hen. Everyone stopped training to observe the wild saltations of the elf and the tiefling. Even Gurt deigned to marvel at the spectacle.

"A ritual Zimbali dance?" The orc was surprised. "I haven't seen that for ages."

Eredani and Marcon couldn't even think of stopping. The absence of a Liveliness scale allowed level-one players to show everything they were capable of. Marcon succumbed first. Bending for the nth time at the waist to an angle of 45° and spinning about himself, he stumbled and fell. The contest, or whatever it was, ended in a one-sided victory for my new partner, although the elf wasn't remotely upset and ran to embrace Eredani, forgetting they were in different virtualities. Flying boldly straight through the tiefling, he undashingly ploughed the ground with his nose. Where had all his dancer's grace gone?

"Yes!" The tumble didn't dampen his spirits. He picked himself up and continued to gambol around Eredani, bowing to him. "Marvelous! You are a master of the school of Rivaldo!"

Eredani held himself modestly. After adjusting his pants, he waited for a pause in Marcon's caperings, before asking, "What about these dances then?"

"No problem, brother." Marcon just would not stop. "I'll teach you, I'll show you, and I'll spell out every single movement. We'll begin right now. Dear Mother of mine! A master of Rivaldo's school, a demon hunter! Level one! And you thought you'd outdance the horned ones with those skills? Oops, you're horned yourself!"

"Marcon, time!" My partner reined the motormouth in.

"Of course, of course. I can't believe it – the master is here! So, ten obstacles – ten dances. The first is the waltz. You don't mind my being so straightforward, do you, master?"

"Don't call me that," winced Eredani. "It was a long time ago and a different character."

"And I could only get as far as master," said Marcon as though he hadn't heard. "I just can't get my head around acrobatic dancing. That's why I became a demon hunter. Here I'm going to level up and get my master's."

"Waltz!" Eredani cut him off. "What's wrong with him?"

"Ah, it's all very simple. The first simulator goes, 'I'm a waltz fan.' And you go, 'Okay, I'm just going to tie my laces.' As soon as you see the first slabs, you go, 'A-a-nd one-two-three, one-two-three, one-two-three.' The main thing is to constantly move forward, a-a-nd one-two-three, one-two-three."

Marcon held his arms out in front of him, supporting his invisible partner, and began to waltz. He did it beautifully. Eredani, not remotely embarrassed in front of the assembling rubberneckers, joined in with the movements being practised. As for myself, it was too difficult – despite my having passed the first simulator no problem without any dance moves.

"Kvalen, don't just stand there!" said Marcon, not stopping for a second. "Join us! One-two-three, one-two-three. The first simulator is not the only waltz. Seven and ten also like a bit of a Tchaikovsky twirl."

I shot a look at the whispering players, mentally spat, and joined Marcon. I didn't care how it looked to others; the main thing was the result. The waltz for me was no terrifying ordeal, because it had been my ex's dream wedding dance. Considering my efforts sufficient, Marcon moved on to the second test – the floor spikes.

"Quickstep. Up onto your hooves, imagine your partner and, as soon as the front spikes pop up, it's: 'Y-e-a-h!' And you're off! Six steps, turn, two steps back, turn, and gradually step out to the end.

See how easy it is."

Once more Marcon took his imaginary partner in his hands and leaped, so long and quickly you'd think someone had stepped on his heels.

"It ain't gonna happen," said Eredani despondently. "Your tail gets in the way, your balance is off."

"That figures – my butt weighs me down! I need a partner!"

Eredani and Marcon looked in unison at me. "We're in the same group, we can work together. I'll lead," Eredani suggested. Then I understood what he meant.

"No!" I protested. "Never mind that I'm not a dancer. I need a female partner!"

"You can trip the light fantastic with men too. I won't mind," Eredani chuckled and held his hands out in invitation.

"The first obstacle will be easier with a waltz," agreed Marcon.

I shook my head.

"Kvalen, don't be so childish." Eredani changed tactics and began to play on my sympathy. "There are two options – together or alone. Personally, it would be easier to dance with you than pick spikes out of my ass every time. That's why I failed the first test. When your sensitivity is at one hundred percent, a spear in the butt is torture. Be a man. A master of the school of Rivaldo has a fantastic sense of rhythm. It'll be fine."

"What is this school anyway?" I muttered. Everyone, myself included, knew I would have to consent, but I just couldn't make myself fall into Eredani's arms.

"Rivaldo is personal ballet master to the emperor of Malabar. His dance school is the best in Barliona."

"And you studied there?"

"That's classified information," whispered Eredani so the elf wouldn't hear. "I'm not allowed to talk about it."

"It's just that... I'm going to film it," Marcon informed us. He wasn't asking; he was stating a fact. "Two dancing cloven-hooves. Hilarious! You should entwine your tails. It'll be easier. And more erotic. I'll upload the video and we'll be inundated with likes."

And you couldn't complain, since according to the Barliona agreement a player could film anything he fancied. After taking a deep breath, I took a step forward and felt Eredani's hands on me. He pulled me so close that just a fraction more and I would have lashed out and punched him in the face. Nonetheless, he led superbly, and I really could sense the professional in his movements.

"You've forgotten your tails! Entwine! That's it! Now one-two-three, one-two-three. Kvalen, not so tense! Feel the rhythm!"

"Just relax and let me do everything. It won't hurt," said Eredani, fanning the flames. I couldn't curb my temper any longer and exploded. I wasn't ready for such close contact. With this Barliona I would soon forget what a comfort zone was.

"What are you up to over here?" Gurt loomed

over us. "This is a training course, not a ladies' finishing school! Either train or get out of here! In two hours there's a test. Just you try and fail it! I'll pack the lot of you off to the Abyss."

"Let's go to the barrack," suggested Eredani. "We need to work on these dance moves."

For the next two hours I wished only that what happened in the barrack would stay in the barrack. Eredani span me all over the place, now pulling me to him, now throwing me to the side, now swooping me up in his arms and flying forward. Under Marcon's tireless commentary, we jumped and ran, honing our movements, and when the time was right, we went back to be tested.

"Eredani!" boomed Gurt. "Where the hell are you? On the course at the double! Kvalen, where are you off to? It's not your turn yet."

"There's nothing in the rules that prohibits us doing the course together," said Eredani. "We're tieflings. We were ordered to stick together, and together we shall stick!"

"You're just going to get in each other's way!" scowled Gurt, but stood aside anyway. "Well, if you insist, do it together. And don't even think about failing the first obstacle, or you'll be off to the Abyss together too!"

Eredani glowered at the course and said quietly, "Just remember – waltz, quickstep, mazurka. Rythmically, and fluidly. Positions! And go! One-two-three, one-two-three!"

A few seconds later the newbies' course was ripped through by a shout from Gurt. "One out of ten! Wastes of space, both of you! Next!"

"Kvalen, don't close up like that." Eredani squirmed after the spike, then began lecturing: "The longer you close up, the longer it'll take us. The first obstacle was ideal. The second you started well, but fumbled the turn. When I pick you up and turn you around, just relax. The whole game depends on that, so remember it."

What I needed to remember remained a mystery, for Marcon completed the newbies' course. "Ten out of ten! Genius! Marcon the Spoiled, I proclaim you a true demon hunter! You have nothing left to do on the newbies' assault course. Give my regards to Haldei, the supervisor of the basic course. I am sure that anyone like you can complete it with full marks."

"Ye-e-e-s!" Marcon jumped for joy and hurried over to us. "Master, I did it! I have become dance. I have become rhythm. I've done this course. Let's go, quickly! I made a mistake on the tenth test. It's not a waltz, it's a foxtrot. In four hours I'll make even Kvalen a novitiate of the school of Rivaldo. Let me into your group. You need to polish up your steps."

Nobody asked me about anything, but Eredani accepted the new member into the group, and training began all over again. While all the newbies were jumping and running on the simulators, we were doing pirouettes in the barrack. As soon as I made a false move, Marcon would appear and correct an arm or a leg or a turn of the head, until he got a perfect result.

Then everything stopped.

Book One: A Second Chance

"Muster! Two minutes until muster! Everybody to the square!"

The ringing announcement hung in the air. Running out of the barrack, I saw a column of light above my allotted place. The game didn't believe I would cope with the commotion, and had come to my aid. Eredani stood beside me, and Marcon went to join a group of more advanced students. When all the brethren had taken their places, the difference between the players was obvious. There were fifteen newbies, and we stood behind everybody, at the back of the square, clothed simply, half of us with weapons. Next were the basic- and mid-level players, who were more presentable, about forty of them, I guessed. There were only a couple of high-level players – Braksed and Kurtune. The last group I wasn't even aware existed – the graduates – those who had completed all the courses, but for some reason stayed in the training camp. The biggest and best-equipped group, there were at least two hundred of them. Their clothes could compete with Braksed's, but were excessively funereal and blood-stained for my taste. I even spotted Shukir the Vaunted, the Phoenixes representative. Players whispered among themselves, congratulating each other, their smiles never leaving their faces – typical of people who have just finished a difficult project and are waiting for their just rewards. Interestingly, I didn't see any other tieflings among the new recruits.

"Brothers! Today we present the world with fifty demon hunters!" Uldaron began his speech triumphantly. "Our heroes have dispatched T'Mir and R'tan to the Abyss! For the first time in my memory, those two archdemons have left the island, and they will need a week to return. N'Got and L'Kri are also in the Abyss, and peaceful times are upon the island. Let us pay tribute to our heroes!"

"What a coordinated raiding team," whispered Eredani. Overpowering an archdemon without a tank, without healers. Good lads. The clans will be interested in them."

"There were five archdemons on the island," I reminded him. "He only mentioned four. If the fifth is no cause for Ulderon's concern, then..."

"Then it's not worth speaking about out loud," said Eredani. Which was true – why state the obvious aloud? There was a dungeon on the island.

"As a reward, each combat participant will receive the demon-hunter-training-ground graduate's honorary ribbon! Wear it with pride, and annihilate beasts of the Abyss wherever they may be!"

The players shouted rapturously and lit up with a snow-white glow – on top of their ribbons, they had all gained a level. Celebratory music rang out as the newly decorated heroes filed one by one into the portal. For them the training stage was over. They were followed by another hundred-odd players who hadn't graduated – not everybody was willing to wait a week for the rebirth of the archdemons. The training camp thinned considerably.

"Next muster in six hours! Dismissed!"

"Kvalen, time is pressing." We returned to the

barrack, and Eredani turned up the heat. "If we don't complete the newbies' course now, we never will. I have a new timer – in three hours I'm going to be switched off for maintenance. Twenty-four hours. We'll fail the task and be kicked out of the camp. Do you understand what I'm saying?"

"I'll try."

"That's the whole point, you don't need to try. It's impossible to make a dancer of you in two hours. Your task is to lean correctly and at the right time. I'll do all the rest."

"Kvalen, imagine yourself in the jungle," Marcon butted in. "All around are lianas, snakes, and spiders. You say, 'I must save Marie Antoinette!' You take a big breath and 'Bam!' You defeat everybody and save your loved one. Don't think about the dance or the test. They don't exist. There is you and the jungle!"

"I've never heard so much rot in my life."

"No, our flexible friend is right." Eredani supported Marcon. "You really are overthinking the dance. I have a solution, but I need your consent."

"Consent for what?" I didn't like his tone.

"For discomfort. Untick Settings – Customization – Automatic Update, and increase the Aridity scale there, in Customization. Let's say by fifty percent, that should do it."

I carried out Victor's demands and winced as a warm, dry wind blew on my skin. Despite being quite unpleasant, it was tolerable. Instinctively I wiped nonexistent sweat from my face, and the system suggested returning the settings.

"You get used to air like that quickly, so we must hurry." Eredani sensed all the charms of the island of demons. "Concentrate on sensations. Feel the blast of heat. Forget about dancing. Let's go!"

Two hours later I knew exactly what Eredani wanted from me. I could not relax and rely totally on my partner, because he couldn't carry us both. At the same time I couldn't tense up too much, at the risk of knocking him out of rhythm. In the end I managed to find the right state of detachment and allow him to lead me. The hot wind really did help, averting my thoughts and relieving excess muscle tension.

"You're a long way from becoming a dancer, but with the necessary application, even a tiefling like you can float like a butterfly," said Eredani, evaluating my efforts. Two hours of non-stop one-two-three should have crippled me, but Barliona exceeded all my expectations, and I wasn't even tired.

"What about my money?" said Marcon. I raised an inquiring eyebrow, and it wasn't very convincing – tieflings' facial muscles were wooden. I had to explain:

"You'll get your money after we complete the course. No advances."

"But..." Marcon tugged his ear in disappointment. "But we agreed."

"We agreed you would teach us how to complete the course. Where are the results of that agreement? R-i-i-ight – *complete*. Which hasn't happened yet. How do I know you showed us the right combination? That's our safety net."

"Kvalen, don't be like that. Pay him." Eredani was on the player's side. "He's earned the money honestly. We're on our own now. It has nothing more to do with him."

Marcon looked as though he'd lost faith in humanity, but I didn't care. If it was a total-immersion game, then I was a tiefling. Faith in people had nothing whatsoever to do with me. And anyway, what was all this desire to throw money about left and right? First results, then payment. That's the only way.

"As soon as we complete the course, Marcon will receive his thousand gold. That was the arrangement. Let's go, time is pressing, the test has started."

The downhearted Marcon lead us to the newbies' course and wished us luck. He couldn't enter it anymore. We made it just in time for the end of the test; there were two players left in front of us. Gurt sighed heavily, looking us up and down, and asked, "You're going to do it together again?"

"It's not against the rules."

"Get on with it." The orc waved a hand. "If you can't do two obstacles, you both take a dive into the Abyss. I'm not horsing around here. Begin!"

"Kvalen, I'm not going to make a farewell speech," said Eredani heavily. "Either we pass, and go looking for a dungeon, or we leave the camp and go our separate ways. Into position, we begin with the waltz. And one-two-three, one-two-three..."

The state of detachment I'd been practicing

for two hours came immediately. I concentrated firmly on the hot wind, only the edge of my conscious noticing the tests-passed indicator. One – the crashing blocks were behind us. Two – the spikes appearing from the floor couldn't touch us. Three – the poleaxe pendulums were powerless against our reels. Four – the horizontal, fiery flashes could only lick at our reverentially bowed heads. Five – the whirling propellers raised their white flag as soon as they heard rumor of our sirtaki. Six – The crossbow bolts made but a few small holes in our clothes, unable to cope with our mind-boggling gyrations. Seven – the barbed wire and densely packed stakes prostrated themselves before our fine waltz, and our tails allowed us to scramble through without interrupting the dance. Eight – the horizontal and vertical blades glanced uneventfully off each other and ushered us through with a dull clang. Nine – the fire from the ceiling and the spikes from the floor and walls were too lethargic for our movements and could only disturb the air. And ten – a variable foxtrot; Marcon wasn't wrong. Slabs fell from the ceiling, the floor collapsed beneath our feet, and fire and jagged metal attacked us from all sides, but we danced on, progressing mindfully toward our cherished goal – the red flag.

Characteristic improved
- *Agility: +1*

Achievement gained: unrivalled newbie
Description: *You passed at least four*

obstacles on the newbie assault course at the first attempt. Your agility and ability to foresee danger are impressive. Before you leave the training camp you will receive a Newbie buff: a twofold increase in experience, reputation, and growth rate.

Bonuses:

- *+1 to all main characteristics for passing 6 tests in a row at the first attempt*
- *+2 to all main characteristics for passing 8 tests in a row at the first attempt*

Additional characteristic accessible: Luck

Description: *Your ability to foresee danger is impressive. You have grabbed the bird of luck by the tail and do not intend to let it go. Every characteristic point increases your probability of developing special techniques (critical strike, chance of improved haul, blunder, etc.) from 0.1% up to 50%*

Step 1 task "Start of Training" completed

- *Experience: +12*
- *Reputation with Light of Barliona faction: +6*
- *Access to next training step*

- *Bonus for completing course with full marks: +1 to all main characteristics*
- *Bonus for completing course together with Eredani: +1 to all main characteristics*

"Oh, mother." Eredani produced a throttled whisper. I turned around to see him doubled up on his knees and moaning loudly, his face buried in the platform. It was like the system's white light going into meltdown.

"Help!" I shouted, but he grabbed my leg with a trembling hand and wheezed:

"Don't, I'm fine. It'll pass in a minute. Aaah!"

The tiefling's voice gave no hint of pain or suffering; quite the opposite, it was the groan of someone in a state of ecstasy, or orgasm. I watched stupefied as he came down from his sensory phantasmagoria. Several players rushed to us, concerned by Eredani's condition, but nobody knew how to react, since his HP was normal, the course was completed, and he was lying on the platform and grunting fit to dub a porno.

"That's enough lying about!" Gurt's bass returned everything to normal. The glow around Eredani went out, and he was able to get to his feet, albeit unstably, due to his recent pleasure injection. "Ten out of ten, and eight of them at the first attempt! Geniuses! Eredani and Kvalen, I proclaim you true demon hunters! You have nothing left to do on the newbies' assault course. Give my regards to

Haldei, the supervisor of the basic course. I am sure that anyone like you can complete it with full marks."

Task received: Step 2. Basic training (class-specific task)

Description: *Complete the basic assault course. Minimum completion score: 7 out of 10.*

Reward:

- *Experience: +5*
- *Reputation with Light of Barliona faction: +1*
- *Access to next training step*
- *Bonus for completing course with full marks: +1 to all main characteristics*

"Did you get an additional characteristic?" Eredani had found the strength to operate his limbs and was clinging to me for dear life.

"Yes, it's hanging right in front of my eyes."

"Accept it!" he commanded. "It's one of the most important in the game. Let's go to the barrack. We need to hire Marcon."

The dancer was waiting for us by the course, and before anyone could say anything, I threw him an exchange and handed over twelve hundred gold. Even his elfin ears expressed their surprised joy.

"That's a bonus for your patience and the result. Things like that are always rewarded."

"Marcon, come with us." Eredani put a gentle arm round him. "We have to talk."

"Master, I'm always happy to talk." Marcon's familiar smile crept back to his face. He hadn't been duped, he'd been paid, and he'd got a bonus. What wasn't to be happy about? I tried to imagine why Eredani needed a dancer. We would return from Hermit, and Marcon would bring us all the obstacles on the remaining courses on a platter, and I would have to pay. From the easy newbies' course we took away +5 apiece to all characteristics. Say, five levels. Plus the doubled experience, reputation, and characteristics scale values. Which all gave reason to suppose they might award the same, or even more, for completing the basic course. It was worth splashing out.

I wasn't wrong. Eredani had won Marcon over so expertly the latter was willing to pay for the right to help us complete the training camp. Yes siree, the master of their mystical dance sect had asked us for help! The artful tiefling had even drawn up an agreement with the elf – he couldn't teach anybody else and had to keep mum. This time I didn't begrudge him the advance, and gave him five hundred gold up front. It was a lucky day for Marcon.

"What happened to you?" I asked Eredani after Marcon headed off to the basic course. "Was that some sort of hidden bonus for total immersion?"

"Why hidden? It's an absolutely official, even obligatory, bonus for prisoner pods." He shivered at the memory. "D'you want one? Join our ranks. Every time specialities or characteristics level up, you're overcome by such total immersion that a romp with a real woman in reality is nothing in comparison."

"There was nothing like that in the film about the Mahan," I said, remembering everything I knew about the Shaman.

"There was a lot missing from that. Films about the Shaman are just an advertizing fairy tale. Damn marketologists don't think about the youth at all."

"So, you're going to spasm like that every time? That's not normal. It was like watching a flasher."

"How sensitive you are! We weren't given the choice. You think I like rolling around in front of everyone?" Eredani didn't appreciate the subject. "I must warn you, for the first ten or twenty level ups, I can't guarantee to keep my head. Is that a problem for you?"

"I'll get used to it. The main thing is it doesn't happen when we need you."

"I can't guarantee that either. I have thirty minutes left. We move out to Hermit in twenty-four hours, when I return. What plans do you have?"

"None. Get out into reality, sort out some business. By the way, I forgot to say, when you and Marcon were dancing for the first time, trying to work out who was best, Gurt was very interested. He said it was a 'ritual Zimbali dance' and he hadn't seen it in a long time. Does that mean anything to you?"

"Hmm," Eredani thought. "You wouldn't think it to look at him. It's strange an orc should know so much about dances. The ritual Zimbali dance is a creation of Rivaldo and his school. It's made up and has no historical or cultural background. Where could an orc have seen it?"

"You're the game expert, you think about it." Delegation was my favourite pastime. When they couldn't be bothered to do something for themselves, a savvy boss would find an expert in the field and put them in charge. If they coped with the task, the boss was "da man" for finding the expert employee. If they didn't cope, it was, "What did you expect? We work with whoever they give us!" The expert got sacked; the boss got rewarded. I loved being a project manager.

After saying goodbye to Eredani, I settled down onto my bed and pressed the Exit button. The time had come to check up on my hungover housemate. In the eleven hours I'd spent in Barliona, Matty should have slept it off, if his habits hadn't changed with the years. The rainbow flickered, and the warm hoop was removed from my head, returning me to a familiar reality. The roof had already slipped aside and, when the platform tried to eject me from the pod, I fell flat on my face slapstick-style. My outstretched hands didn't save my head from contact with the oak parquet, because either my strength or my muscles had failed me. The lights in my eyes went out with a dull thud, and an unpleasant noise rang in my ears.

Book One: A Second Chance

When the pattern on the floorboards became distinct, I tried to stand. It didn't happen. I wasn't in pain, but I felt an all-over weariness and a quite human listlessness. Cool, conditioned air flowed over my body, so I hadn't lost sensitivity. I clenched my fingers and toes a few times to make sure, but I had no strength for anything more. I couldn't even close my mouth. My furry cheeks were moist with spittle, and my brain couldn't decide what to do: ignore it all and sleep, or debate the root cause of my condition. Faulty pod? I'd sue. Have a nap, wipe away the spit, and sue. Or was this the next stage of bodily adaptation? I didn't remember reading about it. What else might happen? Forget it. It seemed I'd made my decision – sleep.

I don't know how long I was out for, but I was woken by a hoarse and anguished cry.

"Bro-o-o-dy! Bro-o-o-dy!" The groaning receded or drew nearer depending on the location of Matty, who was wandering the house, lost. I felt better, so I sat up and pulled on my pants. I was rejoicing that I wouldn't die alone and naked on the floor of my own house, when I felt the need to lie down again. What was happening?

"Just a minute, Matty. I'm going to have a quick lie down, then I'll be with you," I muttered, gathering my energies. But he got to me first.

"Brody, here you are," croaked the relieved man with the green face. Bent almost double and clutching the wall, he began incoherently to explain the hubbub. "I woke up... so terrible... everything strange... don't remember what happened yesterday... This is it, I thought, I'm finished..."

The lover of vintage wine apparently felt nauseous, and like a meandering bullet headed for the toilet. I made myself more comfortable on the floor and put on a T-shirt. I would just lie down a touch longer, wait for Matty, and we'd go to the kitchen for the robodoctor. Or he would bring it to me. Whatever, everything would be alright, although it was a pity I hadn't thought the day before that Matty wouldn't be so much hungover in the morning, as poisoned, having spent three years in a pod.

Through my drowsiness I heard a shuffling, and a warm body lay down on the floor next to me.

"Bro?"

"What do you want, juicehead?"

"Why're you lying here alone? Doing yoga or something?"

I cussed obscenely. Looking at Matty's lean figure, I realized accompanying him to the kitchen was not an option. If Matty was a welterweight, there was surely enough of me to make a couple of full-bodied heavyweights. Bolivar could definitely not carry double. "Crawl to the kitchen and fetch the robodoc."

"Okay... Just don't shout at me... I'm just going to lie down for a bit, and then I'll go," he wheezed, curling up into embryo pose. "What happened to you?"

"It happened. Off you run."

"Just a sec, Bro," he said, struggling up from all fours and staggering to the kitchen. And falling head over heels down the stairs, or so it sounded.

Further events unfolded fast and dramatically. Matty brought me the robodoctor, and together we fixed on the sensor pads.

"Blood pressure critical. Pulse week. Temperature low. Emergency ambulance callout. Sector two, block 557. Patient Brody West. Doors unlocked." The robodoctor transmitted the preliminary information and also sent my address and code by Internet.

The ambulance arrived precisely three minutes later. The Imitator took a blood sample, confirmed the robodoctor's initial readings, and asked what symptoms I was experiencing and how it had all started. Then it froze, scanning the blood and receiving data from Barliona's medical servers. "Acute physical exhaustion, overdose of painkilling medications and a preparation that lowers blood lactate. Confirming your consent to conducting medical procedures."

Being way out of touch with disease, pharmaceuticals, and medicine in general, I had no idea what lactate was, who had lowered it or why, who had given me painkillers, or how I'd managed to have an overdose. After my confirmation, I was carefully carried into the bedroom, given several injections, and hooked up to a drip. "Diagnosis confirmed. All procedures conducted. Improvement in condition of patient planned for three minutes' time."

"And the reasons for this condition?" I asked.

"What possible consequences, and how do I avoid a repetition?"

"The settings of your fitness module correspond by default to those of a statistically average person who leads an active life. Your level of physical fitness is very low and corresponds to a sedentary way of life aggravated by poor diet and nonadherence to a daily regime. You spent eleven hours in Barliona, engaged in intense physical exercise, and ignored the exhaustion warning."

"I didn't get any warning!" I protested.

"Information from Barliona's servers state the opposite. Notification was sent. You closed the window yourself. For confirmation of this information, contact Barliona technical support. You have an increased level of lactic acid in your muscles from prolonged and intense exercise. The in-built medunit gave you painkilling injections and medicinally reduced your lactate level before your exit to reality, as specified by established parameters. There are no consequences for your body, except for temporary weakness. The pod's medunit firmware has been updated, the fitness module is set to rehabilitation levels, and the necessary medicinal preparations for muscle recovery have been ordered and will now be administered automatically. We recommend you abstain from immersion in virtuality for twenty-four hours. The cost of services rendered has been debited from your account. Thank you for using our service."

A thousand credits left my account,

enhancing my already somber mood. I searched through the memory for all the messages I'd received, and there was nothing about exhaustion. I was justifiably angry at my situation and the fact that I'd even been blamed myself. I would log into Barliona, look at the record files, and get myself some compensation.

Considering it had fulfilled its salvatory function, the Imitator had removed the drip and was preparing to leave, when Matty drifted into the detection zone of its olfactory sensor. Following another natural cleansing session, he'd stepped into my bedroom with the robodoctor in his hands.

"Attention. The air contains above-normal concentrations of the products of ethanol decomposition. The figures correspond to heavy intoxication. Should procedures be conducted for the accelerated removal of acetaldehyde?"

"What?" asked Matty, shying away.

"No, no. Thank you. We'll cope by ourselves," I said, louder than necessary, when I realized how much Matty's decontamination might set me back. My portable robodoctor could cure a hangover absolutely free of charge.

"You are requested to confirm you have no need for medical attention," the Imitator said to Matty.

"I confirm. You're free to go," he replied proudly and dismissively. The smart machine obediently left the house.

"Switch the robodoc's regime from diagnostic to treatment. Select 'cure hangover' and 'conduct full body cleansing,' I said, after evaluating his condition.

Even for edifying purposes a person shouldn't suffer for too long, otherwise it's not so much edification as torture. I'm all for humane education. In a matter of moments the robodoctor returned Matty to a reasonable condition. His green pallor disappeared, and his cheeks blushed with a modest ruddiness, emphasizing the dark bags under his eyes, but even progressive medicine was impotent against those.

"Phew! I thought I was going to die. I'm never gonna drink like that again. Ever." The rescued man stretched out blithely in his chair and closed his swollen eyelids.

"Yes, Matty. Sorry, but not a drop from now on. Not you, not me. First training, work, and family. Everything else can wait. Agreed?"

"What, we can't even have a couple of beers?" he asked.

I shook my head. "For the next six months it's prohibition. Then we can get drunk either to drown our sorrows or to celebrate."

"Agreed." He nodded and shuddered. "Describe exactly what happened to you."

"A mutiny on board. Or rather in my body," I giggled in reply, not knowing how to explain intelligibly. A turbid story had emerged along with the warning, which according to the records had been given, but in actual fact hadn't. "I hired a call girl because I was thinking of losing some weight. And I lost some weight."

"I get it," Matty guffawed and slapped his knee. That's your comfortable life screwing you up. I didn't recognize you in the café."

"I don't recognize myself," I said, remembering the fat, always sweaty man who looked at me every morning in the mirror. "Are you seeing the kids tomorrow?"

"Nah. They're off out of town today to Liz's parents. I haven't told her anything yet," he said, his voice quavering. "I figured I wouldn't say anything yet. I want to find a job first, settle in... find my own home..."

"Absolutely right," I said, supporting him and not wishing to belabor the subject or poke my nose into someone else's business. The physical exertion was taking its toll, and I wanted to sleep again. "Let's not do anything today and catch up on some sleep. I'm a bit sick of Barliona."

"What about training?" asked Matty, yawning heftily.

"We can leave everything till Monday. You need to recover too, after yesterday and your pod time."

I didn't remember Matty leaving. Sleep overcame me quickly, and my conscious switched off even before that.

We slept all day Saturday and, feeling relaxed and chipper, I spent nearly all of Sunday drawing up a program of five-day courses. First work, then Barliona. Matty sat in the Internet all day, seeing which were the most in-demand and highly paid jobs, picking courses, and occasionally coming to me for advice. Then he fixed the settings in his pod and connected it to the educational servers, before once more analyzing the job market. I had to stop him making hasty decisions – he was itching to begin a new life there and then.

The day's designated workload was nearly done, when I received an e-mail from Barliona's tech support.

Dear user!

We are pleased you have joined the multitudinous and multifaceted community of Barliona.

Re: your inquiry №BR–1443–1. In accordance with the user agreement, we inform you that deletion of a character created by random generation is possible only after one calendar month, about which you were warned during the process of launching the selected scene. Deletion of a game bank account including withdrawal of all funds is possible after three calendar months, in accordance with the rules of the New User First Deposit promotion, which you agreed to when you opened your account.

Deletion of an account including loss of all funds is possible at any time convenient to you.

The Barliona team expresses its regret that the suggested closed tiefling race did not satisfy your expectations. We consider it necessary to inform you that at the present time, testing and checking of the race are being conducted on real game servers. The race will become accessible to a wide circle of users in three months' time. We hope you will show *tolerance toward your character and change your mind about deleting it. All proposed bonuses will remain valid after testing is finished. By way of supporting your loyalty to the tiefling race, we offer you favourable conditions for depositing funds into your game account: you will receive an additional 50% of the deposited amount. To execute a transaction follow the **link**.*

Thank you for helping us improve Barliona. It is only thanks to you that our virtuality is worthy of reality.

With best regards, the Barliona team.

I didn't know what to say. I understood what an idiot I was, but that loyalty bonus was just taking the piss. They would hardly have gone bankrupt by offering something a bit more substantial. All that remained was to hope I was right after all, and that there hadn't been any exhaustion warning. Then I'd take them to the cleaners for the risk to my health.

After the letter I decided I would definitely stay a tiefling for a month and think about it later. Of course I could leave the nursery right then, transfer the money to Matty, delete the account, and deposit the money in a new one, but I still had business in the nursery. The second possibility – transfer the money to Eredani – I didn't like at all. I didn't trust such an experienced jailbird.

After dealing with some personal affairs, I hurried to look at the records, but standing in front of the pod and having already removed my T-shirt, I stopped myself short. Virtuality could wait. Neither myself nor Matty had been outside for two days. With the thought that priorities needed setting out correctly, I dragged him out of his pod, and we went to the only local open-air cinema without glasses and similar high-tech gizmos. I hadn't been there in ages. Matty grumbled that we could watch a film in comfort at home, but it wasn't entertainment on my mind. Of all that gibberish the psychologists had written about me, they were right on one thing – I had forgotten all about live interaction with people I owed nothing to, and they me.

When we got home we argued ourselves hoarse about choosing the right specialities for him. He could only think about his work experience, and I – about the need to retrain. It was into the wee small hours when we finalized a list of courses, and too late to dive into Barliona.

I spent half the following day polishing up my internship obligation.

"And on that note ends our first meeting. I hope you at least take away the main point, which is how to recognize and resist attempts of subtle influence and manipulation from others. Tomorrow we begin the theme of conflict, and we'll be developing our skills in solving problem situations. As homework, try to remember an instance of conflict in your experience. Not necessarily work, it might be domestic. Describe how you felt and how your opponent looked, what the outcome of the disagreement was, if any, and your suggestions for reconciliation. See you tomorrow."

"What's all this for?" There was always one

brainiac. "Who needs these live conflicts? It's been years since everybody started resolving problems using electronic document flow regulations. Are we going to be employed or not?"

I completely understood the feelings of those present, having myself recently been in their shoes, but everyone must do their job, and mine was to conduct communication courses.

"Young man, have you studied carefully the specifics of the organization you wish to work for?" I regarded my audience intently. That day there were seven of them, and they were easy to classify: the potential leader, his disciples (clear and latent) and his various opposition, and the low-profile loner. It didn't matter which social category you created your group from – these classes were always represented.

"Why study it? I'm spending my time on these courses without any guarantee of a job." With the tacit approval of the rest, my pluckiest listener was expressing the general unease. Uncertainty and fear for the future had transformed into vexation and were looking for an outlet.

"I can't guarantee you'll find a job," I said, looking the inquirer right in the eye without raising my voice. "But I'm doing everything I can to increase your chances. The company does not use Imitator labor and prefers live interaction to electronic document flow."

There were no further questions, and the group headed for the exit, for some reason Helen among them.

Vasily Mahanenko. Invasion

"Helen, where are you off to? You and I haven't even started," I called out to my individual project.

Changing course sharply, the girl flew back to me and started to babble excitedly, "Brody, that was so cool! I would never have thought we were surrounded by manipulators. You explain everything so well. I want to go home and watch the seminar again. It's a great topic. Can I show it to my friends? You show everything so clearly. You can feel your professionalism straight away. I want to do that too. Can I watch the video again now?"

"Helen, did you do your homework?" I had watched the children's show with a sad heart. The actors were gutsy, but not convincing. Helen hesitated, losing her passion in a trice.

"No... Yes!... No."

"Yes or no? Make your mind up," I prompted her. The earlier we jumped to it, the earlier we could leave.

She thought for a moment, then adopted a decisive look, and with defiance in her eyes said, "I didn't do it."

I understood it wasn't going to be an easy fortress to take. Oh, Helen, Helen! Fine. That was just the right time to give her a lesson in acting technique. Lower the shoulders, chin down for deeper grief, swallow, and greater dismay in the eyes.

"No? Well, if you didn't do it, you didn't do it. Off you pop. Tell your grandmother I'll be along for the documents in a minute." I turned away to gather my things, while Helen froze in indecision.

"What about telling me off? What documents?"

"Why tell you off? You're a big girl, you heard everything yourself. I get the job if I teach you, but you don't like my methods and you don't want to study. That means I don't get the job... Anyway, go... I still have to call your parents and disappoint them. Good luck in your job," I said vaguely, without turning toward her, and wiped my forehead and eyes. Check and mate, little girl.

"Brody, are you manipulating me?" she asked, unsure. Damn, she was clever. I had forgotten I'd just been sounding off for four hours. "I've learned everything."

"Have you? Really? What was all that about then?" I turned round to her, maintaining my plaintive expression.

"How could I not have done it if grandma was listening to you? It's just that the guys said you were... old... um... you had an inflated ego... and you were just mocking us. And I thought and thought and decided to leave. Maybe you'd forget..."

"Fine. Let's say I believe you. Chapter one, paragraph three. Define your own character type according to values-based orientations."

"Easy!" She smiled and adjusted her wayward hair. "Somewhere between realist and traditionalist."

"It seems you have learned it. Question two. Chapter three – today's topic. Paragraph two. Define the most effective means of manipulation for your character type."

"Appeal to sense of duty. You have to make me believe somebody's fate depends on me, and... I knew it! Brody, that's... that's not fair!"

The clever girl turned crimson with indignation, and I didn't conceal my victory smile.

"Now I can see you've learned the theory, but I don't agree it's not fair. You heard for yourself I'd get the job if, among other things, I taught you. I simply hyperbolized your significance a tad. Now we're going to put our methods of manipulation into practice. I'm going to feed the other students to the lion – that's you. Attack! Manipulation, Helen, is something people use all the time to achieve their goals. But not always maliciously. You're judging me now for my dishonesty, while you're no angel yourself. Who's just been singing my praises and lying? The student utterly deserves the teacher."

Helen blushed and said, "Forgive me. I won't do it again."

"I forgive you, but I will do it again. And more than once. There's a new task for tomorrow's lesson. Here, learn this."

"Just the one?" Surprised, the girl took the piece of paper. "What's this?"

"Your role. Tomorrow we're going to study conflict, and you have to yell this at me. Think you can do it?"

"Can I do it?" Helen repeated the question enthusiastically, scanning the text, her expression becoming excited, even predatory. "Of course I can, Brody. What if I get carried away and start improvising? Would that be a problem?"

"As long as you keep it decent and remember that if you start shouting, your grandmother will come running. Other than that you have complete artistic freedom. And stick to the main plot line," I sniggered.

"I understand. See you tomorrow." With that, the girl with the off-white mop ran off to rehearse her premiere role. And with a sense of a duty fulfilled, I went to find out why the terms of my socialization had been unilaterally altered. Maria wasn't around, so I was forced to go and see the boss.

"Hello. Is Mr. Williams in?"

"He's gone to a meeting," Victoria informed me. "Is it about the changes to the agreement?"

"You're uncannily discerning and well-informed." I looked with interest at the secretary-cum-lawyer-cum-God knows who else. No matter what you asked, Victoria had all the answers. Some kind of joker in a skirt. Maybe it was actually her in charge, rather than Williams?

"Maria didn't have time to speak with you herself, so she asked me. The company is aware that the original agreement was violated, but there was no alternative to the amendment made by the Barliona management. Otherwise we would have been deprived of the possibility to monitor the socialization progress of all our candidates. Surely you don't think you're the only one socializing this way?"

I shrugged my shoulders as if to say I hadn't

thought about it. I couldn't care less about everyone else.

"As compensation you are permitted to remove any one of the ten points, except for the one that has been amended. Do you agree to that?"

I was tempted to haggle for eight instead of nine, but I resisted. The Corporation had only altered one point, and offered me the chance to remove one, and of my own choosing. It was totally fair, and it wasn't worth getting fresh, or else they wouldn't hire me.

"I agree. Can it be documented?"

"Naturally." Victoria nodded calmly. "An additional agreement has already been drawn up."

I arrived home in an excellent mood. Matty and I had lunch together, then dove into our pods – him to study, me to hit Barliona. Eredani was waiting for me.

Chapter 4

"I SEE YOU WERE in no hurry," Eredani greeted me. Barliona returned me to the same place it had let me go – the barrack. My partner was lying on his bed and studying the ceiling, still oblivious to all. The reason for this was the Vartalinskys, who were hanging around outside the barrack windows, finding fault with every player who walked by.

"On weekdays I'm busy until lunchtime," I said, explaining my absence but deliberately not going into detail, so as to define the limits of our collaboration. "Any news?"

Eredani sat up and scratched his ear pensively.

"Marcon's worked out five of the fifteen obstacles on the basic course. He needs another three days for the rest. The Phoenixes and the Dark Legion have already got wind of us completing the newbies' course, and I've been approached with an offer to buy the dance. I promised to think about it. Don't scowl like that. Sooner or later everyone'll learn the details. If we can pass the basic course with bonuses, I reckon we should sell the information while it's fresh and worth something. I've made an agreement with Marcon that he's only going to work with the clans via us. In return he'll get thirty percent of sales, plus I'll help him with school of Rivaldo Master's-degree training sessions. That's all my news. Any objections?"

"None at all." I was in complete agreement. "Did you figure out Gurt's interest in dancing?"

"Not yet. I had more important things to do. Look, this is a crude map of our island." Eredani unfolded an image on the bed. Part of the training camp was more or less detailed, but most of the rest was an empty oval, the only features being some hills and a mysterious red 'X' in the north-west.

"The Vartalinskys weren't around at the weekend, so I had a stroll around the camp, chatted to the locals. I can't say it was profitable – nobody here's going to open their mouth without an incentive, but I did glean something useful. Nobody goes near the hills to the west – great fat mobs and it's a long way from the camp. I think we need to look for our dungeon there. I saw lots of level-six graduates and even a couple of sevens. You can't level up like that near the camp. What I'm trying to say is we won't get to the dungeon just the two of us. The mobs will eat us. We need a team, but I don't know how to put one together yet."

"Marcon?"

"We need about ten players," said Eredani shaking his head.

"You sure know how to stump a guy," I said. "We'll get back from Hermit and check out some people. Then we'll have a think."

We were about to leave the barrack, when through the window we saw the Vartalinskys had waylaid a player and were gesticulating wildly to make a point. "Have they been here long? The beasts of the Abyss not enough for those vampires?"

"Two hours. As soon I got back they made a beeline for me. I barely made it into the barrack. They wanted to follow me in, but couldn't, and now they're lying in wait out there, wanting to get even or have some more fun. Young thugs. Living proof that idleness and money corrupt the youth."

"Don't whine, you sound like an old man," I said, wincing at his complaint. "How are we going to get out?"

"I am an old man. We need to think. How much time have you got today?"

"Plenty, but I don't want to go nuts, I have work tomorrow. Maybe we could buy some of the armor and weapons people have dragged out of the Abyss? We don't want to be stuck in this hole like rats."

"No." Eredani's response surprised me. I thought the tiefling would be glad to boost his strength and survivability at my expense. "I had a look at what they're offering. Nothing but rubbish. Nothing even remotely like your pickaxe. If you want to kit yourself out, you've got that telephone number. Only I don't know how much beginner-level, full leather armor costs nowadays. Prices in Barliona have changed drastically since the update. One piece of advice – don't spend any money. Did you see the graduates' clothes? You can't buy that, you can only hammer it out. Don't forget, in the next couple of months, maybe even weeks, we'll level up a few dozen times, and everything you buy will have to be thrown away or sold for peanuts."

His words were uncomfortably true, which dinted my self-assurance. Everything was right there in plain sight, so why hadn't I made these logical conclusions myself? Was I getting old or something? Or perhaps my brain wasn't working after my spell of exhaustion? Exhaustion? Oh no! I'd completely forgotten to check the records. I went straight to Settings, warning Eredani I would be busy for a few minutes. A search of the key word "exhaustion" produced only one message:

Attention! Your body's limit for transmitting impulses from the game to reality has been exceeded. You are strongly recommended to exit the game and reduce your transmission threshold to Rehabilitation level.

I looked at the other records from around that time, and sighed as I recalled there had indeed been a message. As I was plunging down the abyss, shaken by the jump and the pain, I'd accidentally swiped the warning window to the side, and afterwards conveniently forgotten about it. Yet another game reminder that my horns were no accident. What a doofus!

Eredani patiently waited out my investigation before asking, "Is there something I should know? To avoid surprises."

"No, it's personal." Again I thought divulging details would be superfluous. "Shall we go then?

Hermit will be tired of waiting. We'll take the Vartalinskys with our bare hands!"

As I stepped out of the barrack, my body was seized with an unpleasant sensation. Those jerks had found a way to damage me after all. I bent over, heaving, sensing the proximity of a very powerful Light object, and heard satisfied chuckles from away to the side.

"Well hi there, cloven hooves! Not feeling too well? Should we call the instructor?" The Vartalinskys were enjoying from a distance the spectacle of a fallen tiefling.

My eyes were welled up with tears, but my peripheral vision could make out a small ring swaying off to my right. If it wasn't for the wind, the artefact would have been difficult to spot. Well done lads! They had learned from their mistake, and were now afraid to hold the Light in their hands. My nausea was crashing down in waves – the closer the ring was to me, the worse it became. I heard a dull "Oof, ahhh!" behind me as Eredani left the barrack and also felt the Light. He sank to the ground, and all I could think of was to shove him back into the building with my foot. My hoof struck his jaw, and he groaned again as he disappeared back inside. Not great, but my intentions were good.

The Vartalinskys produced peals of idiotic laughter at the sketch. I wanted to wring their necks, then wait for my next rebirth and wring their necks again. I was convulsing now not from the Light, but with rage. Before that moment, if someone had told me I was capable of such strong emotions, I would never have believed them. Motivated by my anger toward those fools, I reached for the ring and pulled it off its rope, all but losing consciousness. The Vartalinskys were silenced. Looking in their direction, though seeing nothing for the red mist, I threw the booty into my inventory. Eat dust, bastards! You picked a fight with the wrong guy. I felt better immediately, and not just psychologically, but also physically. There was no aftertaste from the evil ring in my virtual pocket.

"Hey!" Braksed flew to my side and said, "Return the ring, goat-man!"

My body was still shuddering from close contact with a Light object, but I ignored it and glared at him, my horns lowered and ready. Sensibly he took several steps back, and, figuring he'd had more than enough of my attention, I called to Eredani, "Let's go, we're expected." My partner was back on his feet and waiting for the end of the show. It was a good thing I hadn't kicked him too hard.

"Are you deaf or something?" Braksed couldn't decide what to do next. He was afraid to approach me, but he couldn't lose the ring. "Return the ring! It's worth more than you'll ever earn in your life."

We moved silently toward the exit from the camp, the Vartalinskys following us but scared to come closer or get in our way. "We've put you on a counter, you freaks!" shouted Kurtune. "You owe us twenty coins and the ring. If we don't get the gold today, tomorrow it'll be twenty-one!"

"Twenty-two!" Braksed corrected him.

"The counter increases by two coins every day," agreed Kurtune. "You have no idea who you're messing with."

Eredani: *Aikido? Karate?*

Kvalen: *Difficult childhood with an elder sister. We survived as best we could.*

I was still slow at typing, but when the occasion arose I tried to hone the skill. Eredani read it and laughed throatily, wiping his face.

Eredani: *At least the action movie 'Brothers and sisters' is more interesting than the drama 'Fathers and children'.*

Kvalen: *Are you talking about yourself?*

Eredani: *I'm talking about the adolescents back there. Give me a description of the ring. What are they so worked up about?*

Large platinum ring of Eluna

Description: *An epic object. Encrusted with a Drop of Eluna, the ring emits Light, stripping dark entities and demons of their power and desire to do evil. Level requirements: 250. Creator: the Mahan*

- *Intellect: +20*
- *Stamina: +20*
- *Faith: +10*
- *All dark entities and demons within twenty meters of the ring receive a Weakening debuff, reducing all characteristics by 40%*

- *All dark entities and demons within twenty meters of the ring receive a Giddiness debuff, reducing all characteristics by 40%*
- *Once every minute, the player receives a Blessing of Eluna buff, increasing damage inflicted on all creatures by 20%. Buff action period: 10 seconds*

In my opinion, the characteristics were astonishingly low for a ring of that level worth ten thousand gold.

"So that's how they did it," muttered Eredani. What he meant by that, I decided to find out later.

To the accompaniment of the half-witted youths' primitive threats, we left the square, skirted around the instructors' barrack, and arrived at the gate. The perimeter of the training camp, with the exception of the part which bordered with the Abyss, was marked by a three-meter palisade. The exit was closed by a gate and guarded by unfamiliar demon hunters and several priestesses, all NPCs.

"Exit prohibited until completion of courses!" said a guard menacingly, blocking the Vartalinskys' path.

"How come they can leave?" complained the youngsters. "They haven't even completed the basic course."

"They can leave," the guard confirmed, and opened the gate for us.

"Return the ring!" shouted Braksed one last

time as we exited the camp.

The world around us, together with its soundscape, changed as if we had left the grounds of a verdant Egyptian hotel for the inhospitable clutches of the barren desert. Only instead of the odd date palm, there were gray spiniform cactuses with no needles, a vibrant purple sky, and red rocks and sand beneath our feet. The background mountains alone remained the same as when I'd seen them from the temple on my first day of immersion.

A flickering dome fully protected the training camp and its plentiful greenery from the impact of the local climate. Leading away from the gate, a well-trodden path forked after approximately thirty meters, one prong heading straight for the mountains, the other turning to the right, rounding a small hill, and disappearing into the gray cactuses. The hill was topped by the picturesque ruins of a once great fortress, amid the stones of which could be seen the figures of graduate players. The howling of the dry wind was cut with explosions, the players' cheers, and the death rattles of demons. The fiefdom of N'Got was going shamelessly to rack and ruin, until such time as its leader could harness enough power to return to Barliona.

"Fu..." Eredani flopped to his knees and lit up. His Cartographer level had jumped up to two. I wasn't so observant and still had 172 points to go. Watching him languish was not pleasant, so I turned away, but he soon revived and stood up next to me to see what was happening among the ruins.

"Shall we go to the fortress?" I asked.

"On the way back. I have no abilities – that's minus one. You have an uncontrollable demon – that's minus a half. Half a warrior instead of two is not a condition I'm willing to sign up for.

"We could enlist somebody to the group," I said, seeing a player called Diabettis approaching us. He leaped dextrously and landed on a small mob, squashing it flat. His next jump, bolstered by a quick spell, destroyed a jug-eared demon venturing out from some rocks. The hunter acted in a supremely self-dependent manner, displaying no false majesty, nor incurring foolish penalties.

"On the way back!" insisted Eredani, setting off along the track and veering to the right. "Diabettis will be counting on us both, but he'll only get half a player. There's no need to throw him under the bus."

"Have it your way," I said, dousing the thrill of the battle that was kindling inside me. Demons weren't terrifying monsters; if anything they were comical, big-eared, level-three beasties across the board. You took one by the tail and smashed it on a rock. A couple of hits and the client was ready.

"Can you explain what's wrong with the ring?"

"Nothing. I noticed it's changed since the update. Doesn't it seem strange to you that a level-250 epic ring has only thirty plus characteristics? I didn't get it at first, but then I realized –levelling up. Clothing has taken a back seat, and now the most important things are levels and plus characteristics. Where would vagrants have got the money for a ring like that? The Corporation has adjusted all objects. The emphasis isn't on characteristics now, it's on additional bonuses. Look at the ring – three boosts on top of the pluses. That's very cool and very interesting. Everything's based on percentages and adjusted to the player. Numerical values are a formality. Take your pickaxe for example – a rare object with two bonuses, while an epic object has three bonuses. That means a legendary might have from four to six boosts, and I'm not even going to mention scales. But that's just me speculating. When you get out into reality, see what they say about it on the forums."

"Why don't you look yourself?"

"Because prisoner pods are not connected to the general information field."

Reference information

Classification of objects in Barliona

Common: *The most widespread kind of object in the game, with no additional characteristics or bonuses. Created by players or bought from NPCs. May be sold to other players, including after personal use. No level restrictions.*

Unusual: *An object with one random plus characteristic and one bonus. Created by players or bought from NPCs. May be sold to other players, including after personal use. No level restrictions.*

Rare: *An object with two random plus*

characteristics and two bonuses. Created by players or bought from NPCs. May be sold to other players, including after personal use. Level restrictions apply.

Epic: An object with three random plus characteristics and three bonuses. Created by players or bought from NPCs. May be sold to other players before personal use. After use, not transferable to other players. Level restrictions apply.

Legendary: An object with five random plus characteristics and five bonuses. Created by players or bought from NPCs. May be sold to other players, including after personal use. Level restrictions apply. Object may be stolen from inventory, with 10% probability it will remain on the ground when player dies.

Scale: An object with seven random plus characteristics and seven bonuses. Acquired only from NPCs. Not transferable to other players. No level restrictions. Object may not be stolen from inventory, and does not fall out when player dies.

Divine: An object with ten random plus characteristics and ten bonuses. Received only for distinguished service to Barliona, awarded personally by the Emperor. Not transferable to other players. No level restrictions. Object many not be stolen from inventory, and does not fall out when player dies.

Book One: A Second Chance

We rounded the hill, but couldn't see a single living being. No demons, no rodents, no snakes, no nothing. The players had left us bare rocks and sand. Being used to my solitude in reality, I lagged behind Eredani in Barliona. He didn't mind; he simply scooted over to the side of the path and drew level with me. We walked some distance apart, but could still see each other.

"Kvalen, come here!" he called and knelt down. His tone was casual and his frame was green, so I didn't hurry. His horned head was bent low over a red prickle.

"Demon clover," he explained, and scooped some sand aside with his hands. "To pick it correctly you need Herbalist skills of at least four hundred. Then the cut-line becomes visible. Try and pick it."

Eredani stepped aside, and I crouched down to look. I knew the picking technique – when you studied a plant in detail, a twinkling stripe should appear, along which you could cut or tear while preserving it intact. If you slipped, you got a handful of straw that was no good to anybody. There was no stripe, but I estimated where it ought to have been, gripped the stalk closer to the base, and snapped.

New speciality received: Herbalist
Description: *A gathering speciality. You are becoming a true master at seeking out herbs. From now on you are capable of sensing and finding herbs in the very shyest recesses of Barliona.*

Object received: demon clover pollen
Description: *A common object necessary for specialities. Use: gather 100 pollen and receive one demon clover.*

Improvement gained

- *Experience: +12, until next level: 964*

"Wonderful news," said Eredani joyfully. "I knew reason would win eventually. I just didn't think it would take so long. Has your Herbalist level increased?"

"Only the scale by two points," I said, becoming absorbed in the variations. "Although experience has made good progress."

"Now I understand the logic of the upgrade," he said. "Objects have indeed lost their leading role, and players' ascent is now only defined by their level and received characteristics. Even if someone on level one pours millions into the game and buys themselves a bunch of scale objects, they won't suddenly become hella strong just like that. Only by going up through the levels."

"Which have become freaking difficult to achieve." I echoed Eredani. "I got a bonus for the pod, and a twofold experience boost for the newbies' assault course, but for the flower I only got one percent of the level."

"Who said it was going to be easy? The fat cats must be able to feel their privileged position, otherwise they'll stop spending money. Mark this spot on the map – plants regenerate every twenty-four hours. In Settings find Herbalist and tick Automatic Detection. The higher your skill, the further away you can detect herbs."

There was nothing wrong in what Eredani said, but his continual fatherly tone was irritating. "Do this, don't do that." I quietly obeyed his commands, but it was increasingly difficult to keep my cool. My nature demanded that I display self-sufficiency and prove I had long since grown up and wised up.

"You do what you like, but I'm going to try some hunting." Eredani could wait for the way home if he wished, but I wanted to level up right then. He shrugged his shoulders and moved further away, not wanting to be on the receiving end of my archdemoness's "bonuses." If I was honest, I didn't believe she would do me any damage. Surely the developers could never realize that moment so wrongly? Who would chose to be a tiefling when they come with such baggage?

Aniram appeared in all her glory – threatening, wings wide, shackled in light fetters and, which was especially concerning, silent. No "I'll grind you to a powder," or "I'll drink your blood," or "I'll defecate under your door." She merely glared down at me from her two meters, and made no attempt to summon a beastie from the Abyss.

I waited. Her contempt remained exclusively passive. Taking that as a good sign, assuming I was correct, and being a real man, I set off on the hunt.

N'Got's minions were level-three, jug-eared snakes, which looked like nagas who had been sick since childhood. Slightly over a meter long, they had a scrawny torso, undeveloped limbs ending in long, black nails, enormous ears, and two horns which they used to cling onto stones. The demonettes evoked anything but fear. I wanted to sit down and scratch the cute little things sympathetically behind the ear.

When the players had shuffled off around to the other side of the hill and couldn't see me, I extracted the anti-snake from between the stones and activated Demon Strike.

Damage inflicted

You have inflicted 15 damage: (20 Magic Attack) - 5 (protection of vassal of N'Got). Total Health remaining: 285 out of 300

The demon screeched and lunged to take retribution for its desecrated honor – it was the only explanation for such aggressive behaviour; fifteen HP lost wouldn't anger it that much. With a fearful squall the overfed maggot targeted my leg, but an opportunely stamped hoof stopped the graceful attack in its tracks and, just to make sure, I sealed it with a second Demon Strike. The snakelet got off lightly with fifteen damage, and attempted to bite my hoof. Fuck you! The attack didn't decrease my Health, but it did tickle, so I stepped on the demon's head and pinned it to the ground. Now I could open the records. I had inflicted sixty-one points of magic damage, but due to the level-difference between me and the demon, that became threefold less. A formula was even provided: damage = A/B, where A is player attack strength, and B is opponent level divided by character level. Accordingly, the higher the opponent's level, the less damage they sustained, and vice versa. Such entertaining mathematics.

While I was sifting through the records, Aniram moved closer to the hill and struck the area around it with such supersonic power it made me jump. "Come hither, brothers! Annihilate the traitors who have cast aside their essence! Come!" When she was done screeching, she bared her sharp teeth in delight, clicked her tongue, and folded her wings. "Soho!"

The stones began to rustle as N'Got's flunkies rose to the archdemoness's call. Deprived of their master, they could not resist her will. Twenty bat-eared heads poked out from the surrounding stones and, smacking their chops, surged toward me. The first to attack was the flattened snake, which writhed, jumped, and sank its teeth painfully into my leg.

Damage sustained

Health level decreased by 30: 30 (bite from vassal of N'Got) - 0 (physical protection). Remaining Health: 570 out of 600

That hurts! A hoof to your snout, you ungrateful creature, not a tickle behind the ear!

Vasily Mahanenko. Invasion

For the first time in total immersion I had been attacked by a mob, and I could say with absolute confidence that I could do without such experiences. I kicked the viper back toward the ruins. The flight was short but ultimately pointless, because after hitting the rocks, the demon merely shook its head and bolted back in my direction.

"Go, Kvalen, go!" Eredani shouted almost in verse and, leading the way, took to his heels. After weighing up my chances against a horde of miniature, flap-eared monsters, I set off after him.

"Had a bit of a hunt now?" he asked ironically after letting me catch up to him, though his legs didn't stop working to whisk him further from N'Got's domain.

"Save your breath, you'll need it," I replied in irritation, although I understood his irony was justified.

"The radius of demon agro isn't usually more than a kilometer," said Eredani, continuing to mock me. You'll have enough breath. Just look at the bonus! Attention, right!"

I looked toward where he was indicating, and saw Aniram. Her manacled hands did not preclude her maintaining balance, and her leather corset strikingly underlined those features which indicated unambiguously that I was host to a demoness as opposed to than a demon. Those features moved in time with her run and arrested all my attention, leading me to trip over a stone and very nearly fall. Just how did Eredani manage to notice everything? To be on the safe side I sent the double Ds packing, together with Aniram. Or to be more accurate, Aniram with her double Ds.

The demons dropped behind after a kilometre, but we ran on another five hundred meters just to be sure, before stopping. Up ahead the track became a neglected path, then disappeared completely. Evidently few players ventured that far from the camp, since at first glance there seemed to be no demons or booty. After ten minutes we came to a full-flowing river about twenty meters wide. The black water looked strange and was bubbling vigorously.

"That's not water." Eredani squatted down on the bank to inspect the unknown substance, but was wary of putting his hand in. "It looks like air-saturated sand."

"I don't care what it is. I'm more concerned about how we're going to get to the other side."

Nowhere could I see anything resembling a normal means of crossing a river, even on the other bank. Only a thin pole resting on small struts stretched from one bank to the other, half a meter above the surface, challenging us to test our tightrope skills.

Hoping for a Cartography boost, I scoured the opposite bank. Beyond the ever-present, gray, spiky trees I was surprised to see an exuberance of green and yellow vegetation, and just as I noted the height of the mountains, the system at last recognized my attempt to compare the relative sizes of objects.

Improvement gained

- *+1 to Cartography speciality*

"Piece of cake," Eredani chuckled and ran nimbly across the pole to the other side. The bridge, which was scarcely big enough for a human foot, didn't even bend under the tiefling's weight. This was the first time in Barliona I had encountered deviation from the usual laws of physics.

Kvalen: *I'm amazed! But I never was a big fan of the circus.*

Eredani: *How strange. You're one hell of a clown.*

"You motherfucker!" I said good-naturedly, as I stepped onto the bridge with growing interest in the nature of the simmering, black liquid. What would happen if I fell in? I wasn't much of a wirewalker, so after a second's hesitation I lay down on my belly and began to pull myself along, slowly, carefully, and much to the annoyance of my partner.

Eredani: *I'll be free before you get across. Summon your demoness. You run pretty fast when she's around.*

"Motherfucker," I reiterated. "Why are you getting my goat so much today?"

The question was rhetorical, so he couldn't hear it. After three metres I relaxed – it wasn't as terrifying as it seemed at first. However, at a certain point I relaxed my legs a little too much and lost my grip. In a flash I tipped upside down and my horns skipped along the surface of the river. Hanging on under the bridge was difficult, as my hooves kept slipping, and I was about to right myself when I realized my tail was half dangling in the river. It really was like quicksand. It did no damage and caused no unpleasant sensations, although that was it for the positives of the experience, because something bit painfully into my tail and tried to pull me in. I roared in agony, and jerked the appendage out.

Damage sustained

Health level reduced by 20: 20 (river demon bite) - 0 (physical protection). Remaining Health: 580 out of 600

Health level reduced by 20: 20 (river demon bite) - 0 (physical protection). Remaining Health: 560 out of 600

Twisting my head, I saw a fish the size of a well-fed cat attached to my tail. The terrible beast was clinging to its prey not only with its teeth, but also with its inexplicable hands. Crying, "Get the fuck off me, you fucker!" I wagged my tail from side to side, trying to throw the demon fish off, but it wasn't happening. It continued gnawing at my tail, at the same time grizzling and exuding acrid fumes.

"Let go of the bridge!" Eredani somehow appeared alongside me, taking my hand and wrenching me back up onto the pole, whence I shot back to the bank. The fish didn't give up, whizzing after me like a smoking comet and continuing to inflict damage. That was the last straw. Jumping onto the bank, I grabbed my pick and began to spin on the spot, like a dog chasing its tail, and after a couple of misses, I landed a hefty thwack on the demon fish.

Damage inflicted

You have inflicted 42 damage: [19 (physical attack) - 5 (protection from river demon)]*3 (boost coefficient for being in the air). Total Health remaining: 158 out of 200

A quick read of the description was enough to stop me spinning, and I struck the level-two beastie frenziedly. Five hits and it shimmered and dispersed into the air, leaving behind a small red flask.

Improvement gained

- *Experience: +14, until next level: 950*

New speciality received: fishing

Description: *A gathering speciality. You are becoming a true master fisherman. From now on you are able to sense and catch shoals of fish in all Barliona's water sources.*

I accepted the new speciality and showed Eredani my catch – a flask containing demon blood. "Not a bad catch," he said, pleased. "Hide it. You can sell it after the camp."

"Carry me to the other side," I said. "I won't make it on my own."

"No can do. I'm still not used to this body. We'd risk falling in together. Have you noticed the bridge is bigger?"

I looked at the pole, and it was indeed wider; not much, only two centimeters, but still.

"Kvalen, do you like fishing?" Eredani asked mysteriously, before demanding elliptically that I shove my tail back into the river.

"Have you lost it?" I said angrily. "I'm not fucking fishing. If it's so important to you, you shove whatever you want wherever you want."

"I can't, it'll hurt. And I'm a pretty useless fisherman. If you don't want to put your tail in the river, walk over the bridge. It's not my problem. I'll be fine anyway."

"I'm going to crawl on my belly." I wasn't going to give up.

"Get a move on then. Experience doesn't just gain itself. Have you not noticed just how fortuitous your fall was? Stick your tail in the river!" Eredani was trying another tack.

Instead of my tail, I tried dipping my pickaxe in, but the demons audaciously ignored it, so I was forced to turn my back to the river and squat down. If I was a water demon, I would demand satisfaction for just one glimpse of a backside hanging over my home. I was in no hurry to put my tail back in, because although my HP had recovered, memories of being bitten were still fresh. It wasn't critical, but it still hurt.

"Do you like fairy tales?" Eredani asked out of the blue.

"No. And I hate it when serious people tell them," I muttered, slowly lowering my tail.

"What a bore you are. And so proper." He continued to sermonize. "Now say the magic words: Fish be caught, large and small."

I laughed. "I know that tale. The wolf's a fucking idiot."

"Pull! Pull!" he shouted.

My tail flew out of the river, dragging another level-two demon out into the air. Two steps, pick in hand, tail forward, five strikes – and a new flask of blood appeared in my inventory, while my Fishing scale increased by two points.

"The wolf's not an idiot. It just wasn't the right fish," Eredani said philosophically. "But ours is. Look, the bridge is another two centimeters wider. Kvalen, you need different bait. You're only catching small fry. You're a serious guy, but you're wasting your talents on trifles."

He was winding me up. I did some math: to be sure I'd get across, I would need to catch no less than ten demons. Then the pole would be wide enough that my vestibular apparatus could coolly withstand the walk.

With every demon caught, I had to wait longer and longer for the next one to bite. If I snagged the first five beasts almost immediately, starting with the sixth I had to wait with my tail dangling in that strange substance. It was still difficult to call it water. The tenth demon took over a minute, during which time I felt several impulses to give up and just go for it, but Eredani insisted on ten. As usual he didn't explain, but his reasons became clear as soon as the last beastie was impaled on the pickaxe.

Improvements gained
- *Experience: +14, until next level: 824*
- *Booty received: 1 demon blood*

Achievement gained
Level-one threat to demons. *You have destroyed ten demons, without dying once. Your skills are staggering. Damage to all demons is increased by 5%. To reach the next level you must destroy 100 demons, without dying once (progress: 10 out of 100)*

"I'm not going to hang around here until I go blue in the face!" I warned, after reading the text.

"You won't have to. We've caught all the small fry," said Eredani. "But admit it, it would be cool to get ten percent to damage."

"Ninety demons! It's me, not us, who's going to be catching them for six months!"

"Still, I wasn't joking about the bait," he said enigmatically. "Let's go to the middle of the bridge. You go in up to your waist, and I'll hold you. There's a theory we need to test."

"Tell me first," I said obstinately. "I don't want to stick my butt back into the unknown."

"It's not your butt, it's your tail," he corrected

me. "If I'm wrong, you'll just sit there, that's all. If not, then... Put your legs in and wave your tail from side to side."

"What the hell for? Are you using me as live bait?"

"We agreed you would do everything without question until my first mistake. Now stick your ass in the river!" My co-player had adopted an authoritative tone, worthy of someone used to giving orders, so I evaluated the situation. No matter how much it galled me, we really had agreed on my unquestioning subordination until his first slip. It would be unprofessional to disobey him twice in one day. And anyway, it was only a game, so I was there to enjoy it.

I moved forward a little and climbed down into the river, holding onto the bridge. Nothing happened. Apparently we had caught all the river demons. However, Eredani reminded me to wag my tail, so after shooting him a hostile look, I obeyed his order.

The yank on my tail was unexpected and unthinkably hard, and before I knew it I was in up to my neck, only the strength of Eredani's hands preventing me going completely under.

Damage sustained

Health level reduced by 30: 30 (river demon bite) - 0 (physical protection). Remaining Health: 570 out of 600

Health level reduced by 30: 30 (river demon bite) - 0 (physical protection). Remaining Health: 540 out

Book One: A Second Chance

Health level reduced by 30: 30 (river demon bite) - 0 (physical protection). Remaining Health: 510 out of 600

My new assailant was quicker and more powerful than its predecessors. It dragged me down to the bottom, chewing my longsuffering tail. I groaned, ready to dig my own teeth into whatever was at hand so as not to plunge further, but Eredani hauled me out of the river just in time. Lightning quick, I shot to the opposite bank – fuck fishing! On attaining my long-awaited target, instead of immediately finishing the demon off with my pick, this time I knocked it to the ground with a hoof – enduring more pain was more than I could cope with.

"Don't let it slip back in!" Shouted Eredani, running after me. "But don't kill it!"

The level-three river demon, the size of a dog, billowed smoke into the air and paddled with its hands, trying to get back to its familiar environment. Its skin was peeling, and it howled, crawling desperately toward the river – its only chance of salvation.

I aimed a blow and brought the pick down on the beast's tail. The game mechanics did not fail me – the weapon sank deep into the ground, impaling the fish. It howled even louder and twitched violently, so I leaned on it and clasped its maw shut with my hands so it couldn't snap anymore. It did continue to whine and fume, however, since exposure to air acted on river demons like fire.

"Pain! Feed! I want to feed! I don't want pain! I want to feed!" The skewered beastie unexpectedly spoke up in the language of the demons, but strangely I understood it. The specifics of my origins were making themselves known.

"Ask it where the treasure is," demanded Eredani.

"Pain! I don't know anything! I want to feed! Pain! Home! Feed!"

"Answer!" Eredani commanded threateningly. "Where's the treasure?"

"Feed! Give me food! I don't know anything! It hurts!"

The demon's skin was drying out quickly and sloughing off from contact with the air, causing it pain. Eredani scooped out a little of the water-sand and pour it over the captive, upon which its skin ceased to peel, and it sighed with relief. But only for a second, for the sand soon slid off, and the pain returned.

"Where's the treasure?" We continued our interrogation, repeatedly providing sand relief.

"In the water!" the demon wailed sorrowfully. "I don't know anything! Give me food! I want to go home! Pain!"

Additional characteristic accessible: executioner

Description: *Your ability to extract a confession from prisoners is impressive. Every characteristic* *point increases the probability of drawing out a prisoner and eliciting information by 0.1% right up to 50%. Prisoner mortality decreases by 0.1% right up to 50%. The shadow clans of Barliona will be interested in you.*

I was momentarily taken aback, trying to grasp what the system meant. As if all I needed to be happy as a pig in shit was the interests of the dark side of Barliona. Thieves, criminals, outcasts, and other scum. Eredani was more than enough!

Pressing the Decline button, I told my partner to sprinkle the demon once more.

"If you tell us where the treasure is, I'll let you back in. I won't kill you."

"Bullshit! Food! Give me food! Bullshit! I don't know anything!"

The questioning wasn't going well. The demon was crying more from pain and hunger, than saying anything constructive. I determined to be as firm as I knew how.

"It's not bullshit! You and I are of one blood. We are children of demons." My God, what was I saying? I – a human with two university degrees and a serious profession – was fraternizing with a demon fish in some ridiculous virtual game. The world had gone mad, and I together with it. "I ran into some bad luck and was purified, but inside I'm the same demon as you! Help me, brother! Let me relieve you of your suffering, and return you to the river. Tell me where the treasure is. I need your help. Don't you want to go home? Now where's the fucking treasure?!"

"It's there!" howled the demon, succumbing to our demands. "In the water! Under guard! Food! Feed me! Pain!"

Additional characteristic accessible: Charisma

Description: *Your ability to persuade and win others over is impressive. You have a strong personality and the ability to be a leader and reach out to creatures. Every characteristic point increases the probability of receiving a hidden task from NPCs by 0.1% right up to 50%. Every characteristic point increases Experience gained by you and players under your leadership by 0.1% right up to 50%.*

Even without Eredani's advice, I accepted the new characteristic. I'd read lots about it, and knew its particular requirements and the rules for receiving it – without the appropriate charisma in reality, it was impossible to receive it in the game. You didn't just learn overnight how to persuade people and be able to lead them. Even in life it wasn't something you could learn specially.

"Why are you torturing an animal, you

heartless fiends?" A thundering roar immobilized me and enabled a cluster of debuffs, while Eredani hit the ground like a croaking mummy. I heard heavy, but quick steps, following which a red and somewhat muscly paw with black claws hoved into my field of vision. The paw took hold of the demon, but I protested:

"That's our quarry!" It was none too convincing, but I was heard.

"Oh it's yours, nobody's denying that. But you either kill it, or let it go! It's not good when the strong torment the weak. Can't you see the animal's in a bad way out in the air? Stay here and await my order!"

This last phrase was directed at the demon. A quiet glug, and I felt the prisoner's relief in my guts, before the demon flapped a couple of times and disappeared down to the riverbed to lick its wounds. The beclawed paw lifted me up and turned me to face its owner. The higher demon Argalot was a boss without level, and in addition the local Hermit. I sized up the Adonis. The wholesome and rather attractive muzzle might have adorned the covers of novels about weak women and strong men. The red skin with its dark veins looked diseased, but what did I know about higher demons? For all I knew it was the highest expression of brutality. The athletic, two-meter figure and fine wings provided the finishing touch to this exemplar of masculine perfection. I wouldn't have refused such a flying machine.

"Who put you up to catching demons with

your tail?" Argalot placed me on the ground and disabled the debuffs. At last I could breathe normally. "What if there were crocodiles around here?"

"Result!" Eredani got up by himself. "We caught the boss."

"What boss? That's small change," said Argalot dismissively. "The boss of the river demons dwells in the depths of Lake of Tranquillity. What would he be doing in the shallows of the River of Darkness?"

My partner fell on his knees in a white glow. His Cartography had been boosted by a level, arousing more pleasant sensations. He was boosting up quickly compared to my Cartographer, which had only just reached a quarter of the scale.

"Let's go. It's time to do business," said Hermit, waving an arm somewhere toward the interior of the island.

"Are you not going to ask who sent us and why?" I said, throwing my partner a bewildered look.

"Uldaron sent you here. I don't know why he sent you, Kvalen, but Eredani needs to catch a demon. Have you been in the Abyss?" he asked my partner.

"Yes," replied the other curtly.

"I see. The Abyss was too much for you. It happens," said Argalot, shrugging. "So what brings you here, Kvalen? Along for the ride, or couldn't cope with the Abyss either?"

"No, I coped. I just can't cope with my demoness."

"Demoness?" the lord of the island sniggered. "What sort of man can't cope with a woman? Summon her and let's have a look at this sweetheart of yours." I did so, and a second later Hermit said, "Holy Abyss! This little jalapeno gets top marks on the Scoville scale!"

Aniram squealed and adjusted her hair coquettishly. If demons could blush, she would have reddened like a poppy. She folded her wings and batted her eyes, clearly wanting to look hotter. Even her horns sharpened. Were she might type, she would have been a veritable beauty.

Kvalen: *Come on then, Barliona specialist, explain what the Scoville scale is.*

Eredani: *Ignoramus. It has nothing to do with Barliona. It's a scale of the pungency of hot peppers.*

Kvalen: *Meaning Aniram is a hottie? I was wondering what jalapeno had to do with anything.*

"Lovely." Argalot walked around Aniram, voicing his approval. "Her capricious and feisty character is chiselled into her face. I love girls like that. It's not going to be easy for you, Kvalen. Now I understand why you're here."

"He will be trampled and debased," Aniram pitched in with her unctuous voice. "I'm going to beat him to a pulp and drink his soul!"

Argalot embraced her, unfazed by our presence.

Eredani: *Something like that. Except that Argalot is brazenly lying to her. A jalapeno is nothing to a real pepper connoisseur.*

Kvalen: *Out of male solidarity, let's not judge*

him for one little schmooze, hey?

"Aniram, allow me to show you my estate. Should you behave yourself, I shall ask Kvalen to remove these white ropes," said the demon, indicating the demoness's bound hands.

"I shall be as good as pie, my Apostate," she said, breaking into a smile. Her tone sent shivers down my spine.

"What about our catch?" I said, remembering the fish. "The river demon owes us treasure."

"He's not going anywhere!" Argalot waved an irritated hand. "Who needs that addled egg. Although... Eredani, come here!" Eredani approached Hermit apprehensively. "Take the river demon in your hands and close your eyes. I'm going to bind you."

"I don't want a lower," Eredani protested. "Kvalen's got an archdemon, and you want to slip me this piece of crap? You could at least give me a regular."

"If you want a demon or an archdemon, take a leap into the Abyss!" said Argalot irately. "Take what you're given! When you level up to a hundred, you can change it. Free citizens have access to five ranks of demon: lower, regular, true, arch, and higher. Each hundred levels you get the opportunity to change the rank of your subjugated demon. Kvalen pulled his archdemon out first time, but it's three ranks higher than authorized, and he can't cope without my help. Aniram is enough to get him to level four hundred, but then he'll have to replace her anyhow. By the way, my dear, take note of that.

The quicker your master levels up, the quicker you will return to the Abyss."

"He's not my master, Apostate," said the demoness, correcting him. "I will return to the Abyss much sooner. Just as soon as I've crushed his head."

"I suppose that's another option," Argalot agreed. "Eredani, take the demon and close your eyes. You're stuck with the fish until level one hundred."

My partner kneeled stroppily down and fished out the demon. Unable to stand up to the higher, despite him being called Hermit, our former captive had stayed close to the riverbank, occasionally breaking the surface to remind us of its presence. Argalot threw a sphere over the fish, like a drop of water, and it was comfortable with that and didn't howl again. Eredani closed his eyes, and Aniram shrank back away from Argalot, as lines of light projected from him, just like those from the priestesses. This was a huge shock to everyone, since the nature of the beasts of the Abyss did not presuppose the use of Barliona magic, but Argalot didn't care. He shrouded the hands of the river demon in snow-white manacles and made a few tweaks, before a gong sounded to announce that the binding was complete.

"Hide it," Argalot ordered. "When we get to my dwelling, you can show how you coped with the Demon Strike. And you, Kvalen, dismiss your moppet for the time being."

Eredani's expression remained unmoved, but

a certain fidgetiness gave me to understand he was impressed with the demon's ability to work with the white ropes.

"Why do they call you Hermit?" I asked. We were moving out toward the heart of the forest, but it was boring to walk in silence.

"Many years ago I left the Abyss and made it to Barliona," Explained Argalot. "The spirit of Barliona accepted me, permitted me to stay, taught me the local magic, and gave me students, whom I raised to be the first demon hunters. The demons could not forgive my treachery. The supremes and highers call me "Traitor". Such small fry as your Aniram do not look for trouble – sword law is soundly embedded in demons' blood. That's why I am her Apostate – one who has turned his back on his home. To the rest of these negligible beings I am the local god."

"Why do you hang out here? You could help in the battle against the demons, or work as a supervisor in the camp."

"I did work there, while everyone was happy with Uldaron. But his camp provides too few hunters, and they're all weak. Many wanted to pursue their own interests, and not everybody got involved in the war against the demons. Certain individuals desired to expand their own sphere of influence and fill their purses, deposing my student from his position as leader. To begin with they shouted that Uldaron was a traitor, in cahoots with a demon. Even his subordinates were not pleased to have me working in the camp, so I was forced out.

When the storm dies down, I shall return. I just need to bide my time. Welcome to my humble abode. I seldom have guests, so I live as I choose."

Hermit's cave was a typical confirmed bachelor's pad, meaning it looked more like a garbage dump than a living space. Gnawed bones, sticks, and other detritus were strewn all over the place. Beneath the ceiling was a perch where, judging by the claw marks, Argalot liked to hang out.

Our host motioned with a paw toward a dark corner of the cave and said, "Eredani, show us what you can do. I want to be sure everything went smoothly with the binding."

My partner did as he was told and summoned his fish, which hung in the air in the balloon-like sphere Argalot had created. Eredani rattled off five seamless strikes, earning the demon's praise.

"Now I see it is a demon hunter who stands before me. So Uldaron decided to inflict your further training upon me? Didn't want to bother himself? Never mind, I shall have words with him about that. I will train you. Now you have demons, you must learn to parley with them. You can either guess how to do that for yourselves, or I can tell you. What would you prefer?"

"Is there a difference?" I asked, immediately getting a kick from Eredani. Clearly there was.

"Certainly. It is far more useful to guess for yourself. How much more useful, I shan't tell you," said Hermit, grinning.

"We're all for a bit of guesswork," said

Eredani. "Will there be any clues?"

"Clues?" Argalot's face twisted with ire. "Are you serious?"

"They don't have to be direct clues," I said. "We could play chess, and if we win, we get a clue. And if we lose, we don't. I dare say it gets a bit lonely here, on an island, nobody to play with?"

In the glimmer of the torches appeared a chessboard. I could reasonably suppose that Argalot at least respected the game, but I'd been on first name terms with chess since early childhood.

"An interesting idea. Only we'll be playing demon chess, agreed?"

I turned to Eredani, but was met with a clueless look. Demon chess was apparently something new for the Barliona guru.

"I shall explain the rules." Argalot waved a hand and transformed the cave. Or rather the cave disappeared. And we were transformed into giants looming over an enormous chessboard.

"This is a battlefield. Half belongs to the demons, and the other half to the citizens of Barliona. You'll be playing for them, and I for the demons. My goal is to seize your territory and kill everybody. Yours is to get any figure to my end and hold it there for a couple of turns in order to gain weapons from the invasion. Meanwhile do not forget to protect your lands."

"And that's the whole difference?" I asked, not really understanding the logic of the name of the game.

"No. In demon chess it's not so much the

territorial position of a figure that counts, as its strength. Let's say you decide to take a bishop with a pawn." To make his point, Argalot took two elaborate miniature figures from a bag – a blue warrior and an enormous red monster. "According to your rules, the pawn takes the bishop. According to mine, if the pawn makes a move on its own, the bishop doesn't worry overly. It ignores it or steamrolls it – whatever's easier."

"That's not all, surely?" Eredani asked, becoming interested in the parameters of the pieces. Attack, defense, HP. Everything just like in Barliona, but in chess form.

"Of course not," said Argalot, grinning mischievously. "We'll add a little spice to your forces. This is the chess Argalot, and just like in real life, he'll be playing for you."

An exact copy of Argalot appeared on the board, and the demon stroked the figure lovingly. Purified demon, unpurified demon – no difference. All demons were renowned for their propensity toward narcissism.

"It's a strong, almost immortal figure. But it's sluggish. It can move one square every turn. And this is you. You'll be playing as your own class."

Two horned and tailed figures appeared on the board, of which I instantly recognized one as Eredani, and the other, with some difficulty, as myself. My partner couldn't resist twirling his figure to have a good look from all sides.

"What does the class give us?"

"Accessible spells and abilities. The first game

is a test, the second for ratings." Argalot tipped the figures of his own army out onto the field. Demons of all colors fell onto the board, jumped to their feet, and ran to take up their positions, just as though they were alive. A huge army of lowers and regulars was joined by a dozen archdemons, four highers, and one supreme. I looked at the properties of the supreme and understood we were goners if the creep got as far as our army – total annihilation of everything alive within a radius of ten squares. Opposing anything of such power would be nigh on impossible.

"And this is your army. Behold!"

He upturned the second bag and spilled the figures of archer-elves, warrior-dwarves, human priests, horses, and several catapults onto the field. Our half of the board became a fortress, with towers, a wall two squares thick, an entrance with hefty gates, and a moat one whole square thick. The figures shinned deftly up the walls and prepared for battle. We also had officers: Eredani, Argalot, supervisor Tarlin, and I played the roles of higher demons; Uldaron was the supreme, the commander-in-chief of our army, and just as sluggish and powerful as his opposite number.

"And finally your spells." Argalot continued to surprise. He overturned a large deck of cards onto the table. "Every turn you take one card, which you can use instead of an action. One turn – two actions. I'll give you an advantage – we'll imagine I have two opponents, each playing for themselves. Ready?"

"Ready," said Eredani and I in chorus. The

rules were unusual and therefore interesting, so we just had to try it out.

"The demons invaded, so they begin."

As was to be expected, we lost the first game. We fended off attack after attack, and also encountered another unpleasant peculiarity of demon chess – after being destroyed, the beasts were reborn from the Abyss every three turns. Our forces weren't. We fought like gods, defending every inch of the wall. The slow supreme, able to move one square every five turns, managed to crawl to the middle of the castle and use his Assimilation ability to turn everyone into desiccated mummies. Uldaron was busy fighting three highers at once, so he couldn't come to our assistance, and was killed a couple of moves later.

"The game's fixed against us," concluded Eredani. "You can't win when your opponent's strength is boundless."

"Defense tactics are defeatist tactics," agreed Argalot. "It's impossible to defeat demons by defense alone."

"Are you saying the invasion will inevitably lead to the downfall of Barliona?"

"If everything remains as it is, then yes. In order to survive, we must change our consciousness radically. Are you ready to play on, or shall we begin your training?"

"Play. But first I want to change our classes. I'm a priest and Kvalen is a paladin," announced Eredani, and the figures transformed so that Eredani's figure was robed in white, and mine wore golden armor and carried a shield and an exquisite, twinkling sword.

"That's a tad impromptu, but I don't remember it being against the rules. Shall we begin?"

Kvalen, your task is to take the paladin's card every other turn. Find me a Bubble. Move Argalot toward the right flank, then to their rear. We're going on the attack.

Once again the demons charged our castle. The smaller ones were cut down in droves, because instead of pawns Eredani had placed archers at the front, which destroyed the enemy as they approached. The more powerful figures took a little longer, but the catapults helped. First time around we'd used them too late. I acted strictly according to my partner's instructions – I had about ten cards of different suits, and one Bubble. My Argalot had already reached the right flank and was ready to move to the rear. The enemy threw its main forces into the fray. The arch and higher demons went on the attack, sacrificing their own pawns left, right, and center.

"Thundercloud!" Argalot buttressed the officers' actions with a card, and the chess field was enshrouded in a dark veil. The paint began to peel off the archers and pawns, and their HP dropped.

"Mass dispel!" Eredani made a counter-stroke, purifying his warriors. Evidently it was more convenient to play against demons as a priest. "Hammer of Justice!" The archdemon closest to the wall covered his head in terror, for hanging over him was a gigantic (by chess standards) hammer of pure Light.

"Move forward. Shield of Ursula!" One of the highers moved a square closer, and above the head of the archdemon appeared a dark sphere, protecting it from damage by our hammer.

"Dispel. Move catapult!"

"Move. Shield of Ursula."

"Dispel. Move catapult!"

"Demon roar. Dark immunity."

"Summon angel. Benediction of the wise!"

"Move. Move."

"Catapult. Catapult." The archdemon twitched for the last time and faded. A crashing stone sent him back to the start.

"Dark mold!" Argalot's resolve deserted him for the first time. He was shattered not to have been able to keep the archdemon alive, and forgot to perform his second action.

"Dispel!" Eredani returned the favor, forgoing his second action.

"Strike of Gildar!"

"Sphere of assimilation!"

"Face of fire!"

"Wisdom of the fallen!"

The combatants had utterly forgotten about making moves, operating using only cards, of which they had both built up plenty. Wanting to see their enemies respond quicker to the spells, they weren't using their second actions. But I was – on the sly, casually, and not interfering in the battle between my partner and the demon. As soon as Argalot had made his move, I would move my figure one square, take a card, and give it to Eredani. He would unleash a retaliatory spell, slapping the card down on the board distractingly. They had both forgotten about me and were now staring unwaveringly at each other.

"Armageddon!" the demon guffawed joyously, as an mushroom cloud sprang up over the fortress.

"Bubble. Bubble," Eredani responded unflappably, and the figures of the chess Argalot and Uldaron began to flicker in a golden sphere. I moved the figure of the demon one more square and wanted to take a card, but it wasn't to be – Argalot laid his clawed paw down on the deck.

"Not so fast," he said. "You must be alive to use the cards."

Our turn was over, and the spells came into effect. The towers, walls, archers, warriors, and even Eredani and I simply disappeared from the chessboard. Armageddon spared nothing and no one. Uldaron stood alone, his head held high in expectation of the demons. The explosion had caused them no damage. Born of fire, they experienced only pleasure in the inferno.

"Game!" Argalot clapped his hands in delight.

"Not so fast." Eredani threw the phrase back. His self-possession was enviable. "Your turn."

"Move supreme. Move... Wait! There were two bubbles! What?"

At last Argalot beheld the consequences of my actions – our officer figure had reached the end of the board. Only one square remained. It was occupied by a fat demon, but it was no match for me, either in terms of damage, or of HP. One move and the officer would begin to receive weapons against the invasion.

"The order has been given," said Eredani. "Make your move. You may not use a spell."

Argalot exhaled heavily and treated us to a hostile glare. One of the higher demon figures moved a square closer to Uldaron, and our supreme could easily have crushed the lone, unprotected adversary, but that was not our plan. In two turns he would be reborn and undoubtedly appear alongside a figure we needed.

"Miss a turn, miss a turn," Eredani said. I made my move, flattening my opponent and taking his position. Just a little patience from our figure and the game was ours.

"Curse you!" shouted Argalot in a fit of rage. The space around us roiled, collapsing the chess set and bringing back the cave. He accepted his loss and said, "You have one clue. Listen..."

"Stop!" I said, raising an admonishing hand. "I know the correct answer."

"Well go on then, wise ass," said Hermit, locking his fingers. "How do you parley with a demon?"

"Give him what he wants?"

"Are you asking or answering?" Argalot said, not taking the bait.

"That's no problem with my demon," Eredani piped up. "It's more animal than sentient being. Simple demands, simple desires. Just food and no pain. You relieved its pain, so all I have to do is feed it and hope it doesn't demand a lady fish."

Hermit laughed. "True, true. But don't worry, it won't need a girlfriend. It'll manage by itself somehow." I didn't have time to think about how a demon fish could satisfy its basic instinct on its own, before he explained: "You're demon is a hermaphrodite. Just feed it. But what with?"

"Are there any rats in this area?" I asked, remembering Dheire.

"Rats?" Argalot was genuinely surprised.

"Yes. Are there rats on this island?"

"There were on the Island of Darkness. What do you want with rats? Are you going to scare Aniram?"

"Master Dheire charged us with bringing him twenty pieces of rat meat. He's a going to teach us a recipe, and then we'll have something to feed—"

I didn't get to finish my sentence. Argalot laughed so hard the walls shook. "Give demon-rat meat to Dheire? Ha-ha-ha! That cook, that would-be Celestial acolyte? Ha-ha-ha! You know why he went into cookery? Because demons are afraid of fire. Uldaron won't let him go, makes him train recruits, and he holes himself up in his little room and doesn't show his face. What if some demon shows up? And you want to take him demon rats?"

"He said it can be any meat, as long as it's labelled 'rat'," said Eredani, backing me up. "Where is this Island of Darkness, and how do you get there?"

"Well, I have warned you, but the decision is

yours," replied the demon. "If you go out of the northern gate of the training camp and head due west, in three or four kilometers you'll come to the Lake of Tranquility. It's this big puddle of concentrated Abyss, and the River of Darkness flows out of it. It's a big lake. In the middle you'll find what you're looking for, but it's difficult to get there, which is why recruits have never taken rats from there."

"It's here, yes?" Eredani unfolded the map in front of Argalot. "Here's the lake, here's the island—"

"No," said the demon in exasperation. "That's completely wrong. The shoreline is shown wrong, there's no outflowing river, and the island's in completely the wrong place."

"Can you help us correct it?" I asked. "A master is called a master because he doesn't make mistakes. If master Dheire says any rat will suffice, he must accept demon-rat meat. And in future he should choose his words more carefully."

"This map will get you to the island," snorted Argalot.

"Then tell us the easiest place to get to the island from. We need to know both shorelines, the features of the landscape, places where we can find ore and demon clover."

"Why?" he asked, surprised again.

"Because we're only level one, and there'll be swarms of demons in places like that. We need to avoid needless confrontations."

"There's nothing like that on my island," he

said. "No demons anywhere near the clover and ore."

"That needs checking," I insisted. "Show us where they are."

"Like I have nothing to do but schlepp around the island with you," said Argalot dismissively. "Why don't you tell me instead what you're going to do with that beauty of yours. Feed her too?"

"First I'll have a word with her." I summoned my pet. "Aniram, what will stop all your carping?"

"Your brains and soul," she replied cheerfully.

"I've heard that before. What about knowledge? I can tell you about Barliona."

"Why do I want to know about a world that will soon be invaded? We shall recast everything and erase your history. There will be no reminders left that Barliona was once inhabited by non-demons. I will annihilate you and gain access to all the interesting places of *our* Barliona!"

Kvalen: *Come on, adviser, any ideas?*

Eredani: *She doesn't need knowledge. Or gold. She's a demon. The easiest thing is sacrifice. Offer her ten souls a month.*

Kvalen: *I'm not doing that. She wants access to interesting places. What does that mean?*

Eredani: *Could mean anything. A beautiful canyon, a dungeon, something new and unexplored.*

"You will receive access to a dungeon." Eredani had given me an idea. On the island was a new, as-yet-unexplored dungeon. "You can visit it as often as you like."

"Pfft! Who do you take me for? What's there that I haven't seen before?"

"The fifth archdemon of this island," I said. "Argalot, what's his name?" The demon needed a prod. "You promised us a clue. Now would be the time to give it. What's the name of the archdemon in the dungeon?"

"Hmm," said Argalot pithily. "You've got me there. His name's G'Rot. He's the chief of the Path to Enlightenment dungeon."

"G'rot lives in this hole?!" We'd managed to get a rise out of the ice-maiden. "That trickster! Who does he feed on? Where does he find his victims? Why doesn't Barliona wrest him away?"

"You can put those questions to him personally," I said, clinging to Aniram's interest. "I plan to reach his dungeon in a month. If you're as good as gold, I'll let you speak with him before I send him back to the Abyss."

"A month?! Are you delirious?" She was outraged. "A week! I'm prepared to give you a week of peace if you take me to G'rot!"

"Not happening. I have to be in the training camp for three weeks. They won't let me out any earlier. And I need another one and a half weeks to get to the dungeon. A month in total. If you want to speak with an archdemon who has never left this island, agree to my terms."

"Two weeks. That's my last word on the subject," said Aniram. "If you don't take me in two weeks, I shall refuse to converse with you for a month. I shall root out the most devious means to destroy you, and sooner or later I will prevail. I will exterminate you and return to the Abyss! Two weeks, not a day longer. Now I know where he is, I can speak with G'Rot after I'm freed."

"I don't accept your terms." I had to decline. "Just as soon as I complete the training camp, I'll summon you again, and we'll discuss the terms of a truce. Argalot, let's finish our training. I understand the principle of parleying with a demon, but right now I have nothing to offer her."

"But I do." Argalot was unexpectedly accommodating. "What about access to the Barrows of the Fallen?"

"You're bluffing!" said Aniram. "A level-one Free citizen cannot have access to them."

"He doesn't have it. But I do. Name your price, archdemon. How many *weeks* are you prepared not to pester your host, in order to get to the Barrows? Bearing in mind that I'm not negotiating. If Kvalen considers your first and, for the record, only offer insufficient, the Barrows will remain inaccessible and will drop off the radar when your invasion takes shape."

The demoness snarled, but didn't dare argue with the stronger demon. "Five weeks!" Aniram hissed. "I'm willing to give you five weeks of peace and quiet for access to the Barrows of the Fallen. That's enough for the traitor to complete the training camp."

"Not you," Argalot corrected her, then pointed at me and said, "Him. It is your host who will have access. Do you agree?"

"Yes!" she said suspiciously quickly. I wasn't about to sign up for something I didn't understand, so I decided to check:

"What are the Barrows of the Fallen? Is it dangerous to go inside?"

"It's a demon burial place," explained Argalot. "Many years ago some demon spies intruded into Barliona. They were captured, and so that the information they'd gleaned did not fall into the hands of the supreme demons, they were confined in a place now known as the Barrows of the Fallen. There they rest, beneath the bodies of their vanquishers. With time, some of the barrows have deteriorated, and some of the demons been unfleshed, while some of them were able to return to the Abyss. Our little beauty is dying to know the names of those residing on this island, for which she is willing to leave you alone for five weeks. Is it dangerous? No, it is not. If you don't suffer from claustrophobia. It's cramped in the Barrows. The guard will not permit you to do anything stupid. The location will be marked on your maps."

"I agree." All said and done, I had no choice.

Collaborative Tuition task completed

Reward:

- *Experience: +13, until next level: 811*
- *Reputation with Light of Barliona faction: +6*
- *You have learned how to negotiate with a subjugated demon*

Vasily Mahanenko. Invasion

"You have five weeks to deliver Aniram to the Barrows. If you don't make it, she will refuse to speak with you for two months," said Argalot. "I shall be expecting you at my place immediately after the trip. You must continue with your training. Uldaron has clearly neglected you. You're useless."

Task received: continue collaborative tuition
Description: *A rare, class-specific task.*
You have completed your training with Hermit and were able to interest him. Visit the Barrows of the Fallen and afterwards return to Hermit for further instructions.
Reward:
- *Experience: +5*
- *Reputation with Light of Barliona faction: +1*
- *Agreeability to Hermit: +20*

Map updated
Description of changes: *Entrance to Barrows of the Fallen marked. Guard forewarned of arrival of two Free citizens and their demons.*

It had become clear that the seemingly attractive bonus from subjugating an archdemon was actually a headache. Just like any woman, Aniram had a penchant for information. To satisfy her curiosity she was even willing to make a deal with her own subjugator. But where was I going to find so many interesting places in the lower levels? After the Barrows I might be able to negotiate two weeks in the dungeon, but that was all. I had nothing else.

Argalot froze, and Eredani nodded toward the exit. It wouldn't do to overstay our welcome.

"To get to the Barrows, we'll have to go through L'Kri's lands," the tiefling noted. Hermit was showing in every way that the audience was at an end, but my sneaky partner was up to something again.

"He's in the Abyss now. His demons are being destroyed by recruits. We'll manage," I said, after reading the reply in the chat.

"Agreed. The main thing is not to lose seams and clover. I'm sure after a couple of rebirths we'll be able to find all the places they occur, and learn to avoid demons."

"There's nothing near them!" said Argalot flaring into active mode once more. "Why would demons hang around something which can't be devoured?"

"As I was trying to explain," I said patiently, "there are always Free citizens idling around objects like that. Strictly speaking, they can be devoured."

"That's absurd. There are only lowers and regulars on the island. They're not that clever."

"Aniram, if you were the head of a pride, would you give the order to keep watch over places where prey was guaranteed?" Eredani came to the rescue, and my pet answered very quickly:

"Hunting? Oh yes, I love hunting! If I had my

way, I would personally capture them all and crush their heads!"

"Even Aniram, who lives in cloud-cuckoo-land, understands that ambushes are unavoidable," Eredani concluded. As far as I was concerned, the demoness hadn't given an answer at all, apart from the inevitable "crush them all," but Eredani had twisted her words to suit himself.

"No, you are definitely trying to pull one over on me! I repeat, there are no small demons hanging around the seams and clover!" Argalot raised his voice to ram home the truth.

"So if we get eaten there, we can easily make an official complaint, yes?" The wily Eredani cast his line, and the fish immediately bit:

"Yes! Here are the coordinates of all the demon seams and clover on my island. If you're ambushed by a demon near even one of these, I'll... I'll think of something to recompense you with."

Map updated
Description of changes: *Your map shows all the locations of demon ore and clover on Hermit's Island.*

I weighed up the changes: the seams were marked with plus signs; clover with circles. There turned out to be surprisingly few natural resources on the island. No more than ten of each. Although each ore location contained two chunks, which was convenient. The nearest point wasn't far, compelling us to go and open Mining. However, Eredani was on a roll.

"How do we know you've removed all the demons? There aren't any on the island. We go and check everything's fine, we go to the Barrows, we get ambushed."

"I'm sick and tired of you!" Argalot was yelling now. "There are no demons near the seams! Take it! If you stumble across so much as a single ambush, I'll give you all an object."

Task received: search for trouble

Description: *A unique task. Check locations of demon seams and demon clover in the eastern part of the demon-hunter training camp location. If you find an ambush near them, you are entitled to a reward from Hermit.*

Reward:

- *Experience: +5*
- *Reputation with Light of Barliona faction: +1*
- *One epic object from Hermit's collection, consistent with your level and specialization*

Map updated

Description of changes: *You have received a fragment of a map of the eastern part of the demon-hunter training camp location with locations of demon ore and clover* *marked.*

Familiarization   percentage   of current location: *60%.*

Improvements gained

- *Charisma: +1*

"Now beat it!" Hermit snapped, then shoved us out of the cave and blocked the entrance from the inside with a rock. The audience was officially over.

"If you don't mind, I'll decline Charisma," said Eredani with thinly veiled elation. "That was beautifully played. Shall we take a stroll around the island? By all accounts it's safe." I certainly had no objections. The closest thing to us was a patch of demon clover, so we set off in search. "Pull it!" he said, pointing at the plant.

"You do it," I said. "You need to open Herbalist too."

"Kvalen, there are two things I can't stand – fishing, and collecting garbage, like mushrooms and herbs. People of my age like to wander, to enjoy the silence and solitude. Some simply like to walk through the woods with a knife. I don't get that, either in reality or in Barliona. With a pickaxe I get it – stamina needs boosting. But everything else... count me out."

He was adamant, so it was me who had to harvest the five plants we found. Although he had no aversion to the ore. Gripping the axe confidently, he began to pummel a seam, aiming at the gaps between large rocks. One minute. Two. Three.

Eredani struck and struck again, but he looked more and more perplexed. In five minutes he managed to dent the durability of the seam by just ten percent. It was time to remember Liveliness again – had they kept it in Barliona, it would be no picnic for us.

"An hour on one seam?" After another five minutes Eredani stopped for good. "What's going on?"

"No speciality?" I suggested.

"Durability is dropping. That means I'm doing everything correctly."

"Maybe the difference is in your levels. To extract demon ore normally, you need four hundred Mining, which you don't have, so pay the price. Strike – you'll still get the result. There's no point wasting time."

Eredani continued to work and grumble. In total he put in fifty-two minutes on the seam, on autopilot for the last two percent, bored of the monotony. I was fine, lying there and enjoying being lazy, occasionally looking up in the hope of spotting a fleeting demon. Hermit's island was indeed barren. The higher demon had rid it of all the little ones, driving some out, gorging on others – the bones in the cave must have come from somewhere. As a result, when Eredani glowed his white glow, he didn't even fall to his knees. In fact he reacted with remarkable calm, bordering on glee. After all, when you'd had enough – physically or psychologically, it didn't matter – the effect of the rapture was not so strong anymore.

"You're doing the next one." He handed me the pick and lay down beside me. "If it's the same shit at the mines, I don't want to go there. Take this, your inventory's bigger." He gave me a small, dark stone. I turned Matty's coveted object over in my hands – a dark metal, opalescing whimsically in the sun's rays. It was quite heavy, but nothing that could have been worth fifty-two gold, which was precisely how much Matty had paid for one chunk of demon ore at auction.

Eredani gave me a short lesson on where and how to strike, and I spent the next hour rehashing his feat, trying to obliterate the seam. Before I got the hang of it, I hit my own hooves a number of times, then realized it was no use hammering mindlessly away as I'd previously thought. You had to know precisely where you were hitting, why you were hitting, and who all those miscreants were.

New speciality gained: mining
Description: *A gathering speciality. You are becoming a true master at seeking out and mining ore. From now on you are capable of sensing and finding ore it in the very shyest recesses of Barliona.*

The seam flickered and disappeared, leaving behind it another chunk of ore. My Mining scale increased by a whole two points: one for the seam, one as a bonus. Considering there were a thousand units in the scale, I would need five hundred standard hours to increase Mining to level two. Eight hours a day for sixty-three days. Had Barliona really been simplified?

"We need another one," said Eredani. "After gaining a speciality, loot-gathering speed should increase."

Common sense told me he was right, but my heart insisted the opposite was true. Never before had I done such monotonous physical work for so long. My idleness protested against all attempts to banish it and, shameful though it was, most of me was on its side. We got to the next seam, and Eredani, spitting on his hands all businesslike, gestured for me to begin picking away. The traitorous thought occurred that I was in a position to buy ore instead of mining for it. I had always valued my personal time. Nobody knew the cost to me of rallying myself to start work. Even me. One strike. Two. Three. I got stuck in and forgot about everything else. Just me and the seam. Ten minutes flew by in an instant, then the seam winked and bestowed my improvements on me.

Improvements gained
- *Experience: +14, until next level: 711*
- *Object received: 1 demon ore*

"Just what we needed to prove," said Eredani. "Ten minutes on a seam is more like it. Let's go on. There are another five seams."

We left Hermit's island three hours later,

256

exhausted but happy.

"How much time do you have?" asked Eredani when we arrived at N'Got's ruins.

"It's late, but I can find two or three hours. Any suggestions?"

"Diabettis, can you come here for a minute?" Eredani shouted to the player jumping about on the rocks. What a dedicated demon hunter! We'd been to Hermit's and back, and he was still terrorizing the ruins. Having leveled up to eight, Diabettis continued to pound the big-eared level-three demons. He was gaining no experience, but his goal was clear enough – boosting his achievements. The more you beat demons, the better you became at it.

"Just a second!" The player finished off the next jug-eared head to emerge from the rocks, and in a couple of bounds was with us. "What did you want?"

"Let's work together. You'll cope admirably, no question. Although the group kill count will increase quicker. That's what you're doing here, yes?" Eredani had read the player and was now applying pressure to his weak spot. Neither of us, however, were expecting the response we got from Diabettis:

"One hour of collaborative leveling up costs two hundred gold from each player. We work for a minimum of two hours without breaks. In that time you'll get level three. The mobs here are level three, occasionally four. All regular, I haven't seen any rare ones. You can wallop actively yourselves, or you can stand to the side and kick your heels, there's no difference. If you agree, pay me eight hundred and accept me into your group. There are three of us. The other two are working inside the ruins."

"What about loot?"

"We have no interest in demon blood. If something significant shows up, we roll the bones. If you need blood, bung in another fifty gold on top and take the lot. Are you in?"

I looked questioningly at my partner, and he nodded. He was interested.

Eredani: *Brody, I can't make you. It's like with the rats, the decision is up to the budget keeper. That's you. I want to say one thing – gaining level three in two hours is well worth it. Way more than four hundred gold from each of us."*

"Send the group, businessman." I made the decision quickly. Leveling up in Barliona was difficult, and it wouldn't hurt to skip straight up to three.

"I see nothing offensive in that word." Diabettis received his money and added us to the group. The frames of another two level-eight players became accessible – Maestro and Yasya Tishkin. It was the first time I'd seen a female demon hunter, and it crossed my mind they'd split us specially into different virtualities in the training camp. But Yasya Tishkin was evidence that girls could also be interested in demon hunting.

"Everybody swings it to the best of their ability. We can play, so why not make some money out of it?"

"Are you planning to establish a commercial

clan?" The idea was close to Eredani's heart.

"It's already established. Ultium, Free Lands. We work with Kartoss and Malabar. Leveling up, dungeons, rare mobs. Anything you desire, for your money."

What happened next I would call, "slaughter of the innocents." Diabettis, Maestro, and Yasya acted as a well-orchestrated unit, each on their own plot and not interfering with each other. The speed with which the level-eight players massacred the level-three demons was astounding. Kills worked out at two per minute. I gained level two after thirty-four mobs, or fifteen minutes of active farming – the pod bonus experience point and the boost coefficient together showed themselves large as life. There were no complications with distributing characteristics – Luck and Trade gained their own point apiece. Level three came after fifty-nine demons, level four after seventy, and level five, the last one for that day, after eighty-three. I didn't have occasion to summon Aniram, as I spent the whole two ours collecting demon blood. I didn't make it to where Yasya was gambolling deep in the ruins, so I had to be content with what Diabettis and Maestro's demons had left behind. 173 demon blood and not a single gold coin were the results of our leveling up. Although if blood was worth even five gold, those two hours would pay for themselves.

Achievement gained
Demonbane 3rd rank: *You have destroyed 250 demons, without*

dying once. The strength of your skills is impressive. Damage to all demons is increased by 15%. To gain the next level you must destroy 500 demons, without dying once (progress: 256 out of 500)

"Are you going to extend?" Two hours had come around too quickly. Without the pod bonus, Eredani wasn't advancing very actively, but he had managed to gain level four and, unlike me, he'd helped Diabettis a lot. In two hours his hungry demon had attempted to attack his host four times, but had only succeeded in calling up more beasties. However, with a level-eight player nearby, we had no problems. Quite the opposite in fact – Diabettis didn't have to run around the ruins in search of new victims, because they came looking for us.

"That's enough for today," said Eredani, not forgetting my time restriction. "And it's getting pointless leveling up here. Do you go to the other locations?"

"We do, but it's hard to find buyers there. We only go there if we have a direct order. To T'Mir and R'Tan's locations. If you want to get level eight, you're most welcome. The mobs there are fatter, there are more rare ones, and our services are more expensive. Five hundred per person per hour, and we work for a minimum of four hours."

I looked at the updated map and saw that the lands of the two archdemons mentioned were just beyond the Lake of Tranquility. At least ten kilometers away.

"Leave us a number," Eredani said. "Will you be in the training camp for long?"

"Sure, this is my direct number. We plan to work here for another month. Then there'll be another gang, so the location won't be without our services. If you decide to level up, warn us in advance. You were lucky today – we finished all our orders before evening and reached all our targets. We usually get hired immediately. You could join us – tomorrow we're going to T'Mir's location, two clients, so we could take you two along. Experience doesn't get cut until there are ten players in the group."

"Thanks, but we'll be staying in the camp for a couple of weeks." We had to decline the generous offer. It was remarkable how effectively people adapted to life in Barliona. It would take the group two hours to reach the location, where three hours of farming demons would earn the gang three thousand gold. Two hours back, and each would receive one thousand gold for seven hours' worth of personal development. Because Diabettis would also gain Experience from level-five demons. The guys had got themselves a nice little gig.

The camp was empty except for a training session on the high-level course. Eredani snarled. Or coughed, I couldn't tell. The training players were the Vartalinskys.

"I know who Diabettis will be leveling up tomorrow." Juxtaposing facts wasn't a problem for me. The Vartalinskys were working steadfastly on gaining access to the wide world. Not lacking money, they wanted to level up good and proper before trying to get their ring back.

"They might become a problem." Eredani said what I was thinking. "Outside the training camp they can attack players."

"We'll be here for three weeks, if not longer. I don't think those kids will have enough patience to wait so long."

"I very much hope not. Since we have no particular plans, you don't have to come tomorrow. Marcon can only train us in three days."

We went to the barrack, and I pressed the Exit button with relish. It was time to relax from Barliona.

Chapter 5

T UESDAY BEGAN buoyantly. When the star-to-be burst into the hall, the audience were already seated. Slamming the door for effect, Helen accused me of making her stay at work late and said she couldn't continue like that. I responded that if an employee couldn't handle their duties within the specified timeframe, it was their problem. Apparently, if I hadn't laden the employee with tasks beyond her official duties, she would have been able to go home to her boyfriend earlier. After I strongly recommended that Helen spare me the details of her personal life, we switched to discussing personalities. The girl acted with feeling and abandon, and I genuinely believed she hated and wanted to strangle me. The group observed the scene impressed and silent, and I observed their reactions.

When a pale Maria appeared in the doorway, it was time to wrap up the demonstration. Moderation in all things.

"Your blouse is torn." I told Helen the first thing that came into my head, overtly loudly, before adding in a whisper, "Get behind me, I'll cover you."

She blinked several times uncomprehendingly, but on seeing her grandmother she came to her senses and ducked behind my back. It was so natural I could barely repress a smile. She had immersed herself in her role so deeply that she actually believed in the revolt against her despotic boss.

"As you are already aware, my dear listeners, the subject of today's session is conflict. Thank you to my assistant." I clapped, and the group joined in. "Thank you, Helen. You may take your seat. Who can name the method I used to snuff out the emotional outburst?" While the audience was answering, the blushing Helen scampered back to her desk, and her grandmother left the room looking relieved.

The subject of conflict was painful for many. Even the group clam didn't hold back from the discussion, which I considered a small personal victory. The most heated arguments erupted around the question of whether it was worth avoiding conflict. Some thought it an excellent means of solution, while others saw it as no solution at all, but rather as cowardice. I arbitrated, gave them some homework and, with a sense of commitment fulfilled, drew the lesson to a close. How easy it is to intellectualize when the matter doesn't concern you personally.

I arrived home in a fine mood to find Matty in the living room. The steely car mechanic was trying to fathom the art of origami using kids' Internet clips.

"You think that'll help?" I asked, alluding to the legend of the thousand paper cranes and the granted wish.

"You never know," Matty grinned and launched his paper bird. "I told the kids that in school you and I used to make paper ships, and they asked me to teach them. I found some paper on your desk and decided to remember our youth."

"Childhood, Matty, childhood. Let's have something to eat." I was so hungry I could have guzzled half the robocook menu.

In the kitchen we were bummed out to find the robocook broken – It never rains, it only pours – and I was about to submit a request to have it fixed, when Matty hustled me away from the machine, saying, "Let me have a look."

It's not that I didn't trust my friend, but I didn't want to invalidate the service guarantee and have to mend it at my own expense. However, watching the former engineer confidently remove the touchpad, I kept my mouth shut.

"Duck soup. Make some coffee. This is five minutes' work." Matty retrieved a device from his room and connected it to our magic porridge pot. I glanced over his shoulder into the electronic bowels of the machine and was flabbergasted. How the hell could anyone understand anything in there? But he was right. After tinkering for a minute, he replaced the panel, and the robocook signaled its readiness to work.

"Will you just look at that!" I was blown away. Able only to work with my brain, I was always amazed by people who could conjure with their hands under the leadership of their brains.

Book One: A Second Chance

"Nothing to it," he said, dismissing my wonder, blind to his own skill. After observing him at work, I was more convinced than ever that things would work out for Matty.

Two days without Barliona had flown by so quickly I didn't want to go near the pod. Unfortunately, I had to.

"Bang on time!" Eredani diverted his attention for a second from the gesticulating Marcon. They were working on a series of movements in the center of the barrack. "Don't plan anything for today. Training's likely to drag on until morning. Set your pod timer for tranquilizer injection. And positions!"

My hand reached treacherously for the Exit button, but I checked myself. Plus five to all characteristics had cost me yet another shameful evening. Although I must admit I wasn't the only one suffering. Marcon and Eredani were trying as they might, but transforming a hippo into a graceful fallow deer in such a short time was only within the power of a deity.

"Bravo! You've stopped treading on our toes!" said Marcon praisingly. "In two hours we've worked through ten tests. Have you not thought about Rivaldo's school? Kick the door in and shout, 'I have references! I can outdance you all! Prepare the festival podium!' "

"For jokes like that I might just give you a little scratch with my horns." I was finding the training hard, but the festival joke reminded me of my job description, which included participation in two festivals. "Do dancers have festivals?"

"But of course!" replied Marcon emotionally. "Two or three a month. When I get my master's degree I'm going to open my own dance school. Festivals are cool. You can earn some cash. I'll arrive and say, 'I'm a master of the school of Rivaldo! Everyone bow before me!' And that's it – the top prize is mine. I'll give you second place. You've convinced me. Positions!"

Marcon's inexhaustible positivity and chattiness were making me lose my composure. He prattled on about seemingly random stuff: dancing; the specifics of cleaning swimming pools in fall without Imitators; the new space shuttle which had ferried the next group of settlers to Mars; ground squirrels, which were becoming extinct. A true fucking man of art!

After another four hours of intensive training, my torturers decreed I was ready. The fifteenth and last dance I found particularly difficult. Marcon wasn't able to orchestrate anything practical for a pair, so I had to leave the group and align my own projection with Eredani's in order to repeat his movements to the centimetre, and that took up most of the time.

"Welcome to our fans," laughed Eredani, indicating a small crowd of players collected at the entrance to the basic assault course. Apart from the Phoenix Shukir, there were several level-one newbies and a couple of level-five players.

"Have you already agreed to sell?" I was gutted my partner had said nothing about his initiative. He could have warned me.

"Yes. I am bringing our plans to fruition. The Phoenixes, the Heirs of the Titans, the Dark Legion, Ingenium, Exorsus, even the Legends of Barliona showed an interest. In your absence I spoke with them all. Today is open day – we must showcase our wares for the people. If we make it through, there'll be bidding. If not, we won't be able to rely on business relations."

Shukir stepped to the front and threw us a proposal to join the group.

"I want to consider your parameters before the start of the test. Don't think you can pull a fast one on me again."

We just shrugged and accepted the proposal.

The rest of the players joined in. "Include me. And me." Without reservation Eredani updated the group personnel. I looked at Shukir's frame and was filled with unwitting respect. Three thousand HP on level six was no mean feat.

"So you decided to show your faces, you slackers!" shouted master Haldei, the basic course instructor. "Why've you been hiding in the barrack? Quick march to the start! Pass less than three and I'll send you to the Abyss!" The orc muttered something else and stepped aside. "Ready?" Eredani took his position. "On the count of three!"

I performed the pair routine with full marks, but the individual routine created problems. As we were all in one group, we had to do the fifteenth test one after another. Why the hell hadn't any of us thought about that? I naturally went second, trying to keep my distance without lagging behind, and maintain the tempo while not losing concentration. A mammoth task. My temples pulsed, but I kept going. When Eredani finished, success was almost palpable, which made losing my balance a meter from the finish and taking a sledgehammer to the face especially galling. I flew high into the air, and after somersaulting at the apex of a beautiful parabola, I felt a sharp pain in my coccyx, and my flight path changed. While all thought scattered like ash, and I struggled to understand what was happening, the ride ended. My partner had managed to catch me and drag me to the finish line.

"That's cheating!" roared Haldei. "Kvalen didn't pass the whole course!"

Time ticked by, but the system was in no hurry to acknowledge my result, just like the previous time.

"He's at the finish line!" Eredani retorted. Circles whirled before my eyes, and I kept prudently quiet. "He passed the test! In full!"

"Charlatan!" The supervisor was angry. "He got smashed in the face by a hammer! His last obstacle doesn't count."

"Let the chief arbitrate!" said Eredani stubbornly. "I demand a fair trial!"

"You have no right to demand anything!" Haldei screamed, completely incensed.

"But *I* have." I'd caught my breath enough to join in. "I completed the course! I'm standing on the finish line and I demand my reward! In full, for all fifteen obstacles!"

My announcement was far more serious than

the words of the right-deprived prisoner, so the chief appeared on the square, as if he'd been standing by the entrance waiting to be called. Uldaron looked first at us, then at Haldei, and finally at the frozen recruits with video pictograms above their heads, before asking calmly, "Why is the course empty?"

Haldei screwed up his eyes and was silent, miffed at his superior's presence. We didn't hurry to justify ourselves either, and in the meantime Uldaron continued, "I asked why the testing has stopped. Two demon hunters are standing at the finish line arguing. That's most irregular. If you've finished the course, well done! Now move on to the next one and don't obstruct everyone else. Enough of this farce. Just so you aren't inspired to repeat this in the future, I'm placing a ban on doing the course as a group. Only one at a time. Does everybody understand?"

"Kvalen didn't compl..." Haldei began, then thought better of it. Uldaron turned and strode from the basic training zone. The orc spat in our direction and snarled, "Fifteen out of fifteen! You have nothing left to do on the basic course, so fuck off to the mid-level course! I will pass on the chief's words to master Drumm over there. You complete the course one by one! Now get out of here!"

Achievement gained: basic conqueror
Description: *You passed all fifteen obstacles on the basic course at the first attempt. Before leaving the training camp you will receive a*

Basic Demon Hunter buff: a fourfold increase in experience, reputation, and characteristics growth rate (supersedes Unrivalled Newbie buff).

Bonuses:

- *+8 to all main characteristics for passing 15 obstacles in succession at the first attempt*

Step 2 task "Start of Training" completed

- *Experience: +28*
- *Reputation with Light of Barliona faction: +12*
- *Access to next training step*
- *Bonus for completing course with full marks: +1 to all main characteristics*

Task received: Step 3. Mid-level training

Description: *A class-specific task. Complete the mid-level assault course. Minimum completion score: 15 out of 20.*

Reward:

- *Experience: +5*
- *Reputation with Light of Barliona faction: +1*
- *Access to next training step*

- *Bonus for completing course with full marks: +1 to all main characteristics*

Restrictions:

- *You must pass the mid-level course alone.*

"It would have been better if they hadn't recognized your result," the crabby Eredani said and exited the course. "The developers have taken quick advantage of the opportunity, and now we can't waltz in pairs."

"What are we going to do?" I said, jumping to the ground. A priestess next to me made two passes with her hand and restored my HP. The sledgehammer had smashed it down to 1.

"Train and run! It's every man for himself. Sorry, but I can't back you up like here. You're going to be dancing every day. Marcon will work out a test, show it to me, and prepare the next one while I'm working with you. There's no other way. Let's go. It's time to open the bidding."

We left the training course, and the expert jury continued to grow.

"Plus nine to all characteristics for the whole course," Eredani said in summary. "It would be the same if we'd completed the whole newbies' course. That's thirty-six pluses for four courses. I'm willing to teach you the movements, in detail, analytically explaining each obstacle. We'll video everything. I'll dictate requirements and necessary skills to the candidates. Thirty-six pluses for the current characteristics growth rate isn't a bad bonus for level one. But the decision is yours."

"How much?" asked Shukir the businessman.

"There are two prices. One – twenty-five thousand gold, per clan, for the course. How many you train is up to you. One, two... You can get all Barliona over here, it's not a problem for us. Or two – five thousand gold per clan for the course now, plus twenty percent of all profits from players who level up using our method, until they achieve level thirty-six. In the second case, if anyone pays to level up, we take one third."

"Sounds like a rip-off." Shukir frowned.

"Go and breed perch in the lake then," said Eredani curtly. "You can see the result, it was filmed. You must understand the advantage if you're not a total idiot. We're passing the courses one by one now. Personally, I wouldn't want to hold you back. Discuss the details with the curators and make a decision by the end of the week. In a month, maybe less, it's going to be problematic to buy a pass."

Leaving the clan representatives to their thoughts, we were on the way to the barrack to continue training, when somebody called to us.

"Hey, guys, wait up!" Level-one player Luckyrain the Almighty caught us up and ran alongside us, but backwards, telling us to stop.

"What do you want?" I asked. He was clingy and didn't induce a desire to stop and chat.

"Let me into your group. You won't regret it, brothers. I really need to level up."

"Twenty-five thousand and you're in," snorted Eredani. The player blocked our path and made us stop.

"I have serious money problems. But I also have valuable information."

We passed him on opposite sides and continued on our way, but he wouldn't give up. "River demon treasure!" He tried another tack to grab our interest. I was ready to stop, but Eredani shook his head barely noticeably.

"Surprise, surprise. Any player knows a pride of demons has its own treasure. River demons, N'Got, L'Kri, all of them. It's a classic."

"I see you're on the ball," said Luckyrain. "But not every player knows where to look for it. I do."

"Folderol," said Eredani, not slowing his pace. "We're not interested."

"The Island of Darkness on the Lake of Tranquility." He blocked our way once more. "The boss of the level-seven river demons is a huge, overfed crab. He hangs out in the lagoon on the island. So, brothers, do we have an agreement?"

Eredani: *What do you say? A lowlife like any other, but he knows a lot.*

Kvalen: *I say it sounds like a crappy trailer for a crappy thriller. Are you suggesting we extort the information, then do him in?*

Eredani: *Clown.*

Kvalen: *Rather a clown than a distrustful moron. If he leads us to the treasure, what's the difference if he's a lowlife or a lousy intellectual?*

"How do you know about the island and the

lake?" Eredani stopped and scrutinized the player.

"I bought it. Or a friend slipped it to me. What's the difference? I'm sharing it with you fraternally." Understanding he had us hooked, Luckyrain rubbed his hands with glee. "So, I have the exact coordinates. You get me there, and I'll take you to the boss himself. We bump him off together, and split everything three ways."

"Not happening. We teach you, you give us the coordinates, we go alone."

"Don't take me for a sucker," he said, the smile falling from his face. "Together, or I find someone more accommodating. See how many clans there are around? Anyone would give me a couple of purses' worth for treasure like that."

"For treasure in the nursery? There won't be anything in it but low-level tripe," Eredani sniggered.

"I'm doing demon hunter for the third time because of that tripe!" Luckyrain shouted, his eyes bulging. "I came to you because you're alone and I need company. If you don't want to go together, choke on it!"

Eredani: *I've got a bad feeling below my tail. He showed up in the nick of time.*

Kvalen: *Get yourself checked out for digital tapeworm. What if total immersion's become completely realistic? Eredani, what on earth have we yielded to him for? We have nothing to offer apart from your tapeworm.*

Eredani sighed, showing exactly what he thought of me, and continued: "Last question: how are you planning to get to the Island of Darkness?"

"I have everything worked out, brothers." Luckyrain took from his inventory a small wooden boat which, judging by its size, must have taken up all the free space in there. "As luck would have it, it's a three-man boat. That's why I came to you. So, am I in?"

"Training starts tomorrow at nine in the morning. Don't be late," said Eredani, finding no reasonable grounds for refusal. The boat had been his final argument. Luckyrain broke out in such a beaming smile I also began to think it was a set up. Nevertheless, an agreement had been reached, and we returned to the barrack. I paid Marcon for the basic course, and Eredani explained the new rules, expecting to hear a protest, but the dancer was oddly pleased:

"One at a time? That completely changes things. Every time I was like, 'What am I going to do? How do we do this as a pair?' That's why it took me so long without a partner. For individuals I'll draw up the middle level in two days. Twenty tests – pfft! That's nothing if your desire is to become a master."

"We must start training tomorrow," said Eredani. "You pass two simulators and you teach me. I'll deal with my partner myself."

"Gotcha. I'm already on it," Marcon said and made for the exit.

I said goodbye to Eredani and was about to exit to reality, when I saw him lie down on his bed, and it occured to me I had a life waiting for me outside this digital stage set, while he really was trapped in there, and for the long haul.

"Victor," I said, deliberately calling him by his real name, "maybe I should buy you some books?"

He looked at me keenly. "I wouldn't say no. I'm sick of lying here contemplating the burden of my sins. My brain is atrophying."

"Just a minute and I'll ask my friend. He can send something now, and tomorrow I'll fetch you whatever you fancy." I took out the communication amulet and toyed with it. No buttons to dial – only search, list-scrolling, and creating a copy of itself to give to another player. I copied mine, opened my mailbox, and sent a letter to my friend Keiron Marley. Not wanting to wait around until he read it, I logged out and called Matty in his pod.

"I've sent you an amulet. I don't suppose you have anything to read in Barliona?"

"I do, but only what I'm reading myself. Is it urgent?"

"Yeah. Give me what you've got."

"No problem, but I must have it back. I haven't finished it."

"Whatever you say, O lover of detective novels. I'm waiting."

In the attachment were three books. Without looking at them, I transferred them to Eredani, who inspected them and, instead of expressing gratitude, threw them on the floor.

"Good joke, Brody. Much appreciated." He stared at me like a crazy man.

In my confusion I shifted my gaze from the

tiefling to the books and read the titles. *How to become an effective member of society. Time management for beginners. The way to success through self-improvement.*

Thanks a lot, Matty! However, understanding the irony of the situation, I didn't let it get to me. "Screw you! I didn't know what he was going to send. I figured a detective novel or some pulp fiction. He never used to read anything else."

"These aren't yours?" Eredani asked skeptically.

"Do I look like the sort of person who would read that?"

"Do I?" He justly threw my question back.

"If you don't like them, let me return them to their owner. That's all there is until tomorrow."

"Leave them. I'll read them as satire." He looked at the tomes on the floor with the contempt they deserved. I made a mental note to give Matty a talking-to for reading that shit, asked Eredani what sort of books he would like, and logged out.

The next two weeks were routine and dull: work, dance till I dropped in Barliona, sleep, repeat. Everything at work was running smoothly and, in my view, successfully. Matty was finishing his first course and preparing for exams. He looked more confident and had developed a sense of purpose, which could only be cheering news.

A hard-work vibe reigned in Barliona too. Three clans were interested in us completing the course: the Phoenixes, the Dark Legion, and the Heirs of the Titans. Exorsus and Ingenium declined

– spending that sort of money on newbies was excessive. They made several attempts to convince Eredani to lower the stakes, but he stood firm. The rest of the clans chose the first scheme. All financial transactions were done through me, as Eredani was too poor to sacrifice thirty percent to the government.

Luckyrain appeared once, the following day, when we were in the process of coming to an agreement. He asked us to send him the video, and said he would be training later and alone. This pleased Eredani, and they drew up a contract: we would provide the video of the completion of all the courses; he would not resell the material, and as soon as we finished the courses he would take us to the river boss and give us all his information concerning the treasure.

Marcon broke down the mid-level course in a record one-and-a-half days, then spent the same on training Eredani. We got stuck on the course exclusively because of me. For one-and-a-half weeks, five hours a day, I danced to my partner's tune and tried to internalize it. When he flew off the handle, he would tell me precisely where to go, before stomping off to train his new students. Things were a lot easier with them. The clans accepted Eredani's demands on the players, and provided quality performers. In four days, all nine of them had finished the middle course and were on a level footing with me. Even with a head start I managed to come last.

Eredani was so upset he didn't want to speak

with me, and the only reason he didn't stop was that he couldn't admit to failure when he saw I was putting my all into it. I was even strutting my dance moves out in reality.

Eventually our collective efforts were rewarded.

> **Achievement gained: mid-level conqueror**
>
> **Description:** *You passed all twenty obstacles on the mid-level course at the first attempt. Before leaving the training camp you will receive a Mid-Level Demon Hunter buff: a sixfold increase in experience, reputation, and characteristics growth rate (supersedes Basic Conquerer buff).*
>
> **Bonuses:**
> - *+10 to all main characteristics for completing 20 obstacles in succession at the first attempt*

The local victory bolstered me no end, and I felt like a hero. Had someone told me a month ago that I could dance complex trails faultlessly, I would have laughed in their face. I knew my own talents well enough, and dancing did not number among them.

"Greetings, brothers!" Luckyrain was waiting for us by the exit from the course. "Change of plan. My guys can't wait any longer. If we don't move out for the treasure today, they'll find somebody else, and we'll have to wait three weeks for a new boss to be born."

"How do we get out of the camp if we haven't finished the higher course?" I asked. "That's not what we agreed."

"Agreed, didn't agree... I have to go today, no two ways about it. Brothers, are you coming or not?"

"Did you hear Kvalen?" Eredani raised his voice.

"I heard him, brother, I just don't get it. What's the problem with leaving?" A piece of paper appeared in our temporary partner's hands. A regular, everyday piece of paper, except for what was written on it. The scroll, signed by Uldaron, sanctioned one single exit from the camp to three players, irrespective of their progress.

"We're not taking a step until we know where you got that." Eredani outlined our position clearly, and I was in total agreement.

"I bought it. One hundred gold per player. What, you didn't know?" His surprise was too natural not to be genuine.

Kvalen: *Did you know?*

Eredan: *No, but I concede it's perfectly possible.*

We weren't planning to leave the camp, which was why we hadn't thought about it.

"Just so you don't think I'm trying to dupe you, you can pay me later, when we find the treasure." Luckyrain continued with his persuasion campaign. "I can't wait. What about it, brothers?"

"Okay," I said, looking at the clock. The next day was Saturday – no work – I could afford to be a bit late.

"Alright! Wait, I'll go and get something for the journey," Luckyrain said and ran off toward the barracks.

"I don't like him," Eredani said, watching him go.

"Why not? He seems fine so far."

"That's the point. I can't put my finger on it, but something's not right. What's he doing hanging around us? Said he needed to level up, but didn't want to train with us; pops up like a jack-in-the-box then disappears; has watertight answers prepared for every question. If this wasn't the nursery, I'd think he was trying to scam us. His boat is a three-seater."

"The Vartalinskys? They haven't left the camp."

"Don't be daft. This is too complex for them. Those kids wouldn't wait so long planning revenge. What for? They kill us outside the camp, we get reborn and reappear here. We have to go and have a look. Aside from time and possibly our lives, we have nothing to lose."

"Let's go, brothers!" The cheerful Luckyrain was back.

There were no problems leaving the camp. The paper really was signed by Uldaron, not by Luckyrain himself in a fit of artistry. It was three kilometers to our target, so I decided to put the time to good use. According to Hermit's map, between the camp and the Lake of Tranquility were three patches of demon clover, and I made frequent excursions to the side in search of flowers. The first time Luckyrain said nothing; the second time he muttered something poutingly; the third time he exploded. According to him we were wasting time and being distracted from the main task. There were so many players in the location that someone might easily get to the treasure first. The mob restart was in three weeks, and he couldn't possibly wait the same time again.

The lake was a vast black bubbling cauldron, just like the River of Darkness, and stretched to the horizon. The island was invisible from the shore, despite being only two kilometres away if the map was to be believed.

"Let's get loaded up, sirs." Luckyrain took out the boat, jumped into it, and took the oars. "Lake demons don't attack objects, so don't be afraid. As far as they're concerned, there's no boat and no us."

We reached the centre of the lake quickly and uneventfully. Luckyrain was a skilled oarsman and might have been doing it all his life. The island rose out of the water and was looming out of the mist, and with every minute our escort became more and more excited, while Eredani became gloomier and gloomier.

Kvalen: *What's wrong?*

Eredani: *It's an ambush.*

"Turn round!" he ordered. "Let's go back! I'll pay more."

Luckyrain wasn't listening and began rowing

all the more actively as we approached the island. Eredani waved a hand and summoned his river demon.

"Go back, I said!" yelled the tiefling, hanging menacingly over the seated player.

I looked all around, but couldn't understand why he thought we were about to be ambushed. As if his behaviour wasn't odd enough, Luckyrain's reaction was even odder – all he could do was snicker.

"Don't get mad, *brother*! I can't go back. I've already spent the money for you. The only way is forward. And put your anchovy away. Get hostile with me, and I'll throw you back to the mainland to swing in your pick in the ore mines. Do I speak the truth?" The player laughed impudently, straining at the oars.

"You speak lies, you mercenary son of a bitch!" Eredani said and activated Demon Strike. The level-one player had no chance of survival, and he flew away to be reborn together with his paddle. Eredani's username became highlighted in red to show he'd been marked as a killer, just as he himself tensed up in expectation of consequences he alone could perceive. He closed his eyes, but nothing happened, and when the bow of the boat touched the shore, he shuddered and opened them.

"They weren't lying, I have no restrictions," he said, confusing me. Then he looked nervily at the island before continuing: "Kvalen, grab your pick and row! We have to get out of here."

I trusted myself to his experience and pushed

off from the shore, but we'd only gone two meters before the hungry demon fish created a small diversion. Little baby demons appeared in the boat, unable to do any significant damage to us players, but perfectly able to chew holes in the bottom of the vessel. With every passing second it looked more like a sieve and sank lower into the watery sand, until we were forced to bail out onto the shore, where we could only watch in impotent anger as the wooden structure became wood shavings. Demon termites. The things they think of, huh?

"How did you know about the ambush?" I shouted at my partner. "Is this all because of Eredani's secret past?"

"Don't you notice the strange silence?" Eredani backed right up to the water's edge, not taking his eyes off the trees flanking the beach. "We were led out here to the slaughter."

"We or you?" I asked the burning question and joined him in retreat.

"They can't have sniffed me out," he said unsurely, shaking his head.

And in confirmation of his words, a voice droned along the beach, "Hi, ti-i-eflings! Here you are at last!"

He sighed and said, "The fucking Vartalinskys. Right now I'm almost pleased to see them."

Braksed and Kurtune stepped out from the treeline. They had bought themselves level eight and become a serious threat. Yet they still weren't half as dangerous as the mechanism that was crawling behind them. The level-150 Red Executioner looked like a dentist's chair with a set of pincers and a load of mechanical arms and clamps, and did not bode well for any being detained by it.

A scroll appeared momentarily in Braksed's hands, melting away just as quickly after casting a spell.

Debuff received

Weakening: *All your characteristics are decreased by 50%. Duration: 30 seconds*

"What the f...? Where from?" Eredani's voice was shaking.

"Did you celebrate too soon?" I laughed, appraising the reincarnation of the instruments of the Inquisition.

"That torture golem is used by representatives of the dark side of Barliona. If I fall into its clutches, kill me."

"I see you're familiar with our toy," laughed Braksed. Did you shit yourself? Now do you understand who you're messing with, goat-boys? You're going to be on your knees begging me to take the ring back."

"And the money. Don't forget about the money," chipped in Kurtune. "Those fuckers ripped the clans off for three hundred thousand."

The Vartalinskys rushed us at the same time as the debuff. They ran quickly and nimbly; you could tell they'd completed the camp. But we weren't going to be whipping boys: jump to the right, roll, foot sweep, tail blow. The PVP regime flashed red and warned that for the next eight hours, experience would pass me by. I didn't give a damn. The result there and then was important.

"Fuck, my eyes!" Kurtune hissed and grabbed his face. Luck plus ability had blinded our opponent for six seconds.

"Don't let them get away! Don't just stand there, stop them!" Braksed hadn't expected such fleet-footedness from us. Another scroll appeared in his hands, and before I could stop him, he managed to activate it.

Debuff received

Deceleration: *Your speed is decreased by 50%. Duration: 30 seconds*

It was unbelievably hard to move; every step had to be fought for. I felt like I was on the ocean bed, with the entire mass of water pressing down on my head to underline my insignificance. By this time Kurtune had recovered his eyesight, but could think of nothing better than to dump me on the ground, bundle on top of me, and pummel me, each strike decreasing my HP by 167.

"Don't kill him!" cautioned Braksed. "Just hold him. I'll get the other one."

Kurtune stopped whacking me and twisted my arms. He had strength in spades and handled me with relative ease. Even though fighting off Kurtune and two debuffs was unrealistic, I did not give in, unleashing my primary weapon. Aniram, my child, come to me!

"Oh, what a darling little thing! I want one!" Aniram appeared not far away, but didn't even notice our horseplay. All the demoness's attention was on the Red Executioner.

I didn't care about her indifference; the ability could be used anyway. A couple of seconds, and a text appeared in front of my eyes.

Damage inflicted

You have inflicted 178 damage: (188 demon damage) - 10 (magic protection). Health remaining: 1,422 out of 1,600

"Bastard! Brak, he's released his beast," Kurtune shouted, and I had the wind knocked out of me by a heavy punch. After two seconds I caught my breath and repeated the demon strike. And again. And again.

"Fuck you!" Strikes hailed down from above, as Kurtune hit hard, but without direction, which only helped me – I craftily freed my hand and flipped over. The demon strike stopped him for a moment, the debuffs became inactive, and it was time to take the initiative. Mid-level course, test number seven! Low break dance. The drill sergeant's square-bashing had not been for naught – I even remembered the names of the elements. A backspin tossed Kurtune to the side, where I windmilled him, spinning on my back again and knocking his teeth out with my hooves. I continuously tail-whipped his face, disorienting him and making him recoil, and every two seconds Aniram knocked him senseless with a demon strike. Of course I couldn't simply trample him under hoof, because his protection against physical attack was so good his HP didn't drop by a single point. All my drive was concentrated on making the little vampire's brain reel so he couldn't sense his superiority. Windmilling helped me twice: once, as he was reaching for a health-restoring potion, my hooves knocked it away from his mouth just as it became accessible for interaction; and again with the cycle: demon strike – two seconds' spell-casting while windmilling, making him stagger backwards – another strike.

"Shove your paid-for levels up your ass, you brainless child," I said, dispatching the player to be reborn.

Achievement gained: killer
Killer, rank 1: *You destroyed another player. Your bloodthirstiness knows no bounds. Damage to all players is increased by 5%. To gain the next rank you must destroy 100 players (progress: 1 out of 100)*

Swiping aside the message, I rushed to help Eredani, but I needn't have bothered. What could possibly happen when a well-equipped, level-eight newbie and a naked and experienced level-five player with high characteristics get into a fistfight? Only one answer to that. Eredani had wrestled Braksed to the ground and was hoofing some sense into his head. The Vartalinsky tried to shield himself with his hands, but the strikes were hard and loud. And utterly innocuous. In order not to let his opponent gather his wits, Eredani was also systematically using demon strikes. Braksed had no protection against magic, and with a final blow to the head, his figure dispersed into the air. The player left the game, leaving the tiefling battering a puppet.

"Sadistic juvenile!" shouted the emotional Eredani, continuing to pummel the spot where Braksed had been lying. "Stupid little rich boy! Wanted to see someone else's pain, huh? Wanted to torture someone, huh?"

It was the first time I'd seen my partner so seriously riled. He couldn't calm down, and ran along the beach, lashing at his sides with his tail. I tried to distract him by saying, "In the boat you said you hadn't been deceived. What were you talking about?"

Eredani stopped and looked at me as though trying to remember. "If a prisoner makes the first move on a player, they're sent back to prison. I had a special agreement concerning that, but I couldn't check it." He took several more steps before he stopped and went limp, his emotions all gone. "Something must be done about those animals. The Red Executioner is a line that normal people don't cross in their right minds," he muttered, deep in thought.

I nodded my agreement. "I take my hat off to your intuition. Fancy sniffing out an ambush just from the silence," I said, expressing my admiration.

"What intuition, Brody? Have you been boosting cartographer?" he asked ironically, pointing at a towering rock near the beach. Only then did I notice the body of a rat-like demon lying on it in an unnatural pose. The Vartalinskys had slain all the small beasts, so they wouldn't interfere with them meting out their righteous justice to us. The rich kids thought it superfluous to collect loot from the beasts, and left them to wait twenty-four hours for self-destruction. I surveyed the beach and saw more than a few little bodies.

"What are we going to do with the executioner?" Eredani diverted my attention from boosting cartographer.

"What can we do with it?" I shrugged. "Two minutes ago I didn't have an inkling such things existed in Barliona."

"For me it's a good sign. I say we destroy it. We could sell it, of course, but I don't think we need that kind of money."

"Whatever you say." We approached the torture device. Prematurely sent to be reborn, the Vartalinskys hadn't been able to put it in their inventory, so it was now available to any player. Loot! Only this loot didn't come with much joy attached.

I had already drawn my pick and taken a swing, when Aniram spoke up. "Stop!" I froze and looked quizzically at her. Her wings jerked in displeasure. "Why are you destroying such a useful item?" She was obviously hatching a plot.

"What do you suggest we do with it?"

"If you don't need it, give it to me." She forced a stiff smile, trying in that feminine way to get what she wanted. "I'll be an angel for a week."

"No deal. This thing must be destroyed." My convictions wouldn't let me exchange the loot for the demoness's submission.

Aniram froze in indecision, and I took another blow.

"Wait! Why are you being so hasty? I have another suggestion. Let me destroy it." She was working hard to communicate with me without cursing. She tried to remove the contempt from her voice, but it wasn't convincing. "M... m-m-m... master."

Well I never! Her beautiful face twitched in revulsion, but she didn't back down.

"Why?" I asked, grinding my teeth. "Come on, Aniram? Why do you want to destroy the golem yourself?"

"Why? Because I want to!" Angry at having to justify herself, she stamped her foot and flapped her wings.

"Well that's settled then." I shrugged and gripped the pick more comfortably. "You're not getting anything for free."

I took a demonstrative backswing, aiming at the executioner, and it was enough to break the demoness. "I want to consume the essence of that golem. I don't have one like it in my collection. I promise you a week of obedience." Jerking her head up, Aniram stared into my eyes and added firmly but questioningly, "Master?"

"Master." I nodded my agreement and took a step back.

The demoness hung over the torture chair until it exuded a white mist, which she inhaled. She shuddered, rolled her eyes back, and sneezed, causing the device to scatter in a fine dust. The consumption of its essence was over.

Eredani: *I see your lady friend is not lacking ambition. She has her sights on becoming a higher demon.*

Kvalen: *I can see that.*

Reading the reference information had eventually helped me, and I was now able to find my way around Barliona without my partner's help. For an archdemon to become a higher, it had to gather its own army and defeat one of the reigning highers. Consumption of an essence was fundamental in the creation of an army, because the archdemon gained the possibility to spawn demons specialized in specific roles – warriors, magi, torture devices. The higher the level of the essence consumed, the stronger the warriors.

"What about your devotion to Ireness?" I asked Aniram, before sending her to rest.

"Only the very strongest are worthy of devotion," she said, glaring. I had seen and heard enough to understand that the sneaky demoness was planning to unseat our mother, but I wasn't too worried by her monkey business.

The Island of Darkness was not big – smaller than our training camp – and we soon found the lair of the river boss. The two-meter crab lay on its back with its pincers spread freakishly out to the sides. The Vartalinskys hadn't left us a single emaciated demon rat, annihilating them all, so our cunning plan to shock master Dheire dissipated like smoke.

"They cleaned out everything," said Eredani after searching the cave. "No treasure, no boss, no moral satisfaction. Let's go. We have a new obstacle – three kilometers of breaststroke and lake demons. And all without boosting experience."

I can't say the return journey was easy. Several times I felt an impulse to drown myself, just to kill the monotony of paddling, but Eredani would encourage me and force me to swim on. We were attacked only twice, and we managed to fend the demons off. When I climbed out onto the shore, I collapsed exhausted to the ground.

"That's it, I'm done." It was hard to speak. "I came to Barliona to think with my brain, not swing my arms and legs around. I haven't lifted anything heavier than a tablet for years, and now it's constant physical exhaustion. I've lost nearly five kilograms. Another two days like this and I'll crash."

"You just need to take a rest. From work and from Barliona. Go somewhere with the family, it's the best kind of relaxation," said my partner, lying down next to me.

"I'm not married," I replied, thinking this was one fact of my private life I could reveal.

"Are your parents alive?" Eredani perked up. I nodded. "Are you on good terms with them?"

"Yes, but I don't see them often," I said, pillowing my head with my hand. "Although we speak virtually. We're in contact once a week."

"Once a week?" Eredani snorted, before either ordering or advising: "Go and see them. It'll take your mind off Barliona, and it'll be nice for them. Spending the weekend at home sleeping isn't relaxation. And your parents deserve some respect."

Eredani cleared his throat and was silent. I had no doubt he had a family and they meant a lot to him. He probably used to see them much more than I saw mine.

After tying my character to Eredani and asking him to carry me to the barrack, I exited the game. I found Matty in the kitchen, conjuring up a new culinary masterpiece. For some reason he'd become keen on cooking, and if to start with the results hadn't been great, his progress was more noticeable with each new dish. I began to wonder what course he was taking – technical maintenance or cookery?

"Hey, Bro!" He was pleased to see me. "Would you like some Italian meat balls in tomato sauce?"

"Sounds edible, but let me try it first. Matty, why are you bothering? The robocook works fine."

"Um, no reason. It relaxes me. Gives me something to do when I climb out of the pod. When I get the hang of it, I'll take the kids for a picnic. That'll be a big surprise."

"Fine. Knock yourself out. Are you going to see them this weekend?"

"No, they can't this weekend. Liz wrote that it's the end of the school year, exams and whatnot, not a good idea to distract them."

"Then I have an idea. Let's visit my parents. Together. I don't even remember the last time I saw them, what with one thing and another."

"You go. I'll stay home. I'll do some cleaning or something." Matty looked around in vain for something that needed tidying up. The management company's Imitators had the cleanliness of the sector-two house well under control.

"You'll get by, you fiend. Mom hasn't seen you in ten years. You can share the load of parental concern and care," I said, giving him a hug. He was all skin and bones under his T-shirt. "And it wouldn't hurt to feed you up."

"You could just say I need to do some eating for you," he laughed and went to pack his things.

Despite our longstanding friendship, our families had never met and were completely different. Matty's dad had drunk himself to death when we were still at school. Straight after we graduated his mom married again, moved to another city, and broke contact with Matty, figuring he was grown up, and she had a new life, a new family, new children. It must be said he'd never demanded her attention or help. Even before we finished school he'd spent a lot of time at our place. My mom loved him, fed him, and mothered him when the need arose. Then he went to college, started earning himself a crust, moved into a rented room, and met Liz.

My family was great all round. Dad was a government clerk, Mom kept house and looked after me and my sister. Dad's job didn't provide us with riches or flats, but he earned enough to give his children a good education. So, unlike Matty, I had a comfortable, mama's-boy childhood. So what? I was always proud mom loved me more than my sister, but I took it in my stride that Dad was more devoted to Emily. It happens in a lot of families. After Dad retired, we had enough for a nice house in the suburbs, and his pension allowed us to maintain the standard of living we were used to.

The further we got from town, the more markedly the view from the car window changed. The commuter belt, not to mention the countryside, was a sharp contrast to the large cities in terms of development and way of life. The Imitators hadn't reached that far. There was no social housing, and no plans to build it in the near future. But it had nothing to do with a shortage of cash, only the good judgment of the establishment. All they needed was to wait for the results of natural processes: the young and ambitious would move to the city in search of opportunity; if they could stand the pressure, society gained intelligent and flexible new citizens; if not, they supplemented the never-ending ranks of vagrants. Provincial degenerates were first ensconced in prison pods on the vaguest pretext, and later switched to special social contracts. The remainder of the population went about their business – the business they subsisted on from generation to generation: growing and selling seasonal fruit and vegetables, keeping small shops, providing services such as transporting goods or people, and so on. They lived in relative comfort, as long as there were people who needed to pay for products or services provided by the hands of a living being instead of an Imitator. It wouldn't be long before such people disappeared, taking with them most of the provincial entrepreneurs. Small islands of life would remain, necessary for the manufacture of premium-class products for rich and pretentious people.

The government understood this and was in no hurry to invest money in the suburbs or rural areas. For the time being, the Imitators reigned exclusively in the megalopolises, but Barliona already hung like an ominous shadow over the whole of the human world.

"Brody, my darling... Matty, it's great to have you here!" Mom couldn't rejoice enough at our unannounced arrival, by turns embracing us and scolding us that we hadn't called ahead. At first Matty was a bit flustered, but then he relaxed into her human contact and unassuming affection.

Even dad, usually so stoic, scuttled out and hugged us both hard. I'd never thought he was so concerned for me. You couldn't say we were close, but I'd always been able to count on his tacit support.

"Chaps! You deigned to show up after all! Mother, feed the men. Then we'll go fishing. They need to get away from work and the bustle of the city."

"Yes, yes," said mom, fussing, as I swallowed a lump in my throat. I loved them so much.

Two days flew by in a wink. We hung out at

the lake, wandered around the locality, chatted, and enjoyed a bit of home cooking. That's why I was so fat – Mom was fantastic in the kitchen. Sitting on the sofa by the fire, they asked me about my new job, and Matty about his life in general. He and I exchanged a quiet look and agreed not to go into too much detail. It was impossible to hide it from my father's attentive eyes, but he merely closed them approvingly. There was no reason to alarm mother.

On Sunday morning, after a hearty breakfast, we were already out of the door when Mom took my hand. Engrossed in conversation, Dad and Matty didn't notice and went outside.

"Brody, I heard Jackie died," she said.

"I can't say I'm heartbroken," I said, not sure what she was getting at. "But I won't speak ill of my ex-mother-in-law."

"Brody, don't make me ashamed of your upbringing!"

"Mom, don't make me lie. You know what we thought of each other."

"I'm not talking about that." She calmed down a bit. "You could at least call Andrea. You did live together for five years."

"Mom, why? To express my commiserations? There was enough hypocrisy in that relationship to last another two lifetimes. I'm sad my ex-wife has lost her mother, but I'm not sad Jackie's been driven out of this world to command devils in her own. Conversation closed."

"Catherine, are you harassing Brody again with your ideas about marriage?" Dad came back in time to save me.

"No, of course not. I was just asking him to call more often," protested my duplicitous mother. She knew how to plead for sympathy.

"He'll call when he has some free time." Dad embraced me and added, "Don't listen to your mother. She never washes twice in the same water. Bye!"

We pulled away, leaving them standing by the door in each other's arms, watching us go and gently ribbing each other.

"You're lucky."

"I know. It's a shame they're growing old."

"Why did your mom remember Andrea?"

"She wants grandchildren. When my brother-in-law whisked Emily off to another continent, Mom decided I needed to get married.

"What about you? Don't you want children?"

"Sure I do. But not yet."

Breakfast was taking its toll, and we shamelessly slept the whole journey back. We were awoken by the radio accidentally coming on.

"And now the sensation of the year, the Rock Messengers with their new hit, *Take Cover, it's a wipe!* We would like to remind fans the group will be playing in Anhurs next month, so hurry to see Lorelei the bard on Malabar's main stage."

Lively rock with pleasant female vocals blared from the speakers. The lyrics were crude, but with tangible social overtones – a jolly description of an unsuccessful raid which ended in a wipe and the dismissal of players considered useless. Just like real life. Lines such as, "A bad raid leader only has his raiders to blame," were not all that inoffensive.

"That's witty," laughed Matty, stretching. "Have you heard of them? Funny guys."

"No, but they sound okay. If they don't get banned."

"By the way, when can you give me those books back?" said Matty. "You said soon, but it's been two weeks. I haven't finished them."

"What the hell are you reading that garbage for?"

"Screw you, Brody! I read what I want. If you don't like it, give it back."

"We forgot about them. Otherwise we'd have given them back."

"Who is *we*?" He said, tensing up."

"Me and Eredani. Sorry, my head's a mess with all those dances. I borrowed them for him."

Matty had heard a lot about Eredani. Living under the same roof, I'd told him the details of our meeting and the agreement. He was concerned about my partner's character, but I didn't care, as long as he was being of use. Why get involved in others' misfortunes when you have more than enough of your own?

"S-o-o-o! Eredani isn't returning the books because he finds them useful."

"Matty, people like Eredani find only money useful, not books."

"Maybe you're right. Who is he anyway?"

"What does it matter? While he's working for us, he's useful to us. Thanks to him we've earned three hundred thousand toward establishing a clan."

Matty fell silent and turned to look out of the window. I thought he was upset about the books.

"Bro, that money, is it really for the clan?"

"Yes. We talked about this. We must establish a clan."

"Yeah, we talked. Can you buy me some demon ore? I need a hundred and twenty pieces."

"Why so much?" I asked, surprised.

"That task I told you about – there's a chain. To go on to the next level, you have to make fifty pins. I've done ten, but all my money went on them. Then I started studying and I don't have time now."

"A hundred and twenty pieces of demon ore is nearly six thousand gold," I calculated. "Are you sure you want to get involved with this right now?"

"Yes. No one has a task like this. No one is making these pins. While the opportunity's there, I have to try. I understand it's a lot of money, but if it's for the clan..."

"The clan doesn't exist yet," I reminded him.

"No, but it will, yeah?" Matty looked at me.

"It will," I said decisively, brushing away unnecessary thoughts. "Okay, let's say you make fifty pins. What next?"

"I don't know," he answered honestly. "It's the first step. Then there'll definitely be a second. The teacher said I'd have to go and see the engineers. I can tell it's something serious. It's a unique task."

"I need a description of your task, a description of how you received it, and what exactly the instructors told you. Can you do that? No offense, but I have to discuss this with Eredani."

"Yes... I... understand."

"I understa-a-and," I teased. "Firstly, we earned that money with his help. If I throw it around all on my own, the partnership might not work out, and we need him. He has more experience. And secondly, the opinion of an outside expert in the game won't hurt."

I convinced Matty, and when we got home he dove into his pod to send me a description of the task. I looked at the time – almost nine in the evening. Matty would do everything quickly, and we could sort out the business with the ore there and then.

Enter!

"Couldn't stay away, holiday-maker?" Eredani was lounging on his bed and leafing lazily through a book. As promised, I'd supplied him with enough reading matter for several months. "Has something happened? It's a bit late for training."

"Nothing's happened, but I am here on business. Remember I told you about Matthew and his task? We need some advice. It's a unique task, or to be more precise, a chain of tasks. Connected with Engineering and Smithcraft. Maybe something else. We need to buy a hundred and twenty pieces of demon ore now, and that's just the first step. What'll become of the enterprise later, God knows."

Eredani was interested, and he perked up and put his book aside. I gave him everything Matty had sent me, and he got stuck into studying it.

Book One: A Second Chance

Task: step one. Training

Description: *Unique. A chain of manufacturing tasks. In order to prove your worth as a master, you must first do some preparatory work. You must create fifty cylinders from demon steel. Diameter: 1 cm. length: 10 cm. There are no instructions; you must do it by yourself.*

Reward:

- *Experience: +5*
- *Reputation with all Malabar factions: +1*
- *Progress to next step*

"So... it's some component part." Eredani set to thinking. "First step – simple rivets."

"Where did you ever see rivets that thick amd long?"

"It's a standard beginning of a chain," he explained. "Half will be rejected by the master, another quarter will break. Matthew will cut the rest to the required length and use them. I want to ask your friend a couple of questions. Can you organize that?" I took out the communication amulet and buzzed Matty. He picked up immediately. "Matthew, greetings! My name is Eredani. Brody's told you about me. I have a quick question. What's your current Craft score?"

"Craft?" Matty was surprised. "They removed

it six months ago."

"Removed it?" Eredani's voice wavered from the unexpected news.

"Yes. Straight after the battle of the gods. They explained it had something to do with Carmadont. He thought up the characteristic, and took it with him when he died."

My partner's face grew long and froze; I knew a powerful thought process was in motion and didn't need disturbing.

"Did they replace it with anything?" I asked Matty.

"No, they paid out some cash and left the characteristic empty. I used the money to level Smithcraft and Engineering up to four hundred."

"Thank you, that's all." Eredani gesticulated for me to switch the device off. "Bad news," he said. I could tell he was still thinking over the problem. "I was pinning a lot of hope on craft."

"What do you want with it?"

"Not me, you. Luck, charisma, craft, and empathy – an ideal set of extras for the head of a clan."

"That hasn't made things clearer at all. Craft for me?"

"It was a cunning characteristic. It boosted everything its owner touched. I'm not just talking about manufacturing, but gangs of workers, mercenaries, the castle and its custodian, everything. Empathy helps you establish relations with locals. Manipulation is easier to gain, but it doesn't work with everyone. It's not worth meddling with anyone higher than Governor. Empathy doesn't have that restriction, it can even affect the Emperor. The main thing is to be in the right place with the right words. Apart from that, don't forget you're a tiefling. By default the locals will hate you as a half-demon. Empathy doesn't only allow you to establish contact via compassion, it also speeds up the growth of agreeability. Add in luck, charisma, and trade as a main profession, and you have a powerful mixture to barter with the locals for rare tasks and objects. Now there's no craft, we'll have to think what to replace it with."

"Interesting. In the beginning were the questions. Then Eredani came along and answered them – and then there were heaps more. Do you always work this way?"

"What are you talking about?"

"I came to you with a specific question: is it worth investing in Matthew's task or not? Now we're onto characteristics necessary to a clan chief. Let's decide questions in the order they arise."

"What is there to decide? Invest. Whatever it is, all expenses will be covered by selling the instructions or the end product to top players. Six thousand for one step is peanuts. The difficulties will come later, on step three or four. He'll have to go to a high-level dungeon to find some inconceivable part without which nothing will work. And then find something rare and unreal. It's a classic. And the six thousand you invest now in the first step will seem like peanuts compared to hiring a respectable posse in the dungeon. Is that clearer?"

"Much. How do you boost empathy?"

"Just like in reality. By showing compassion for somebody. Sincerely." Eredani saw my baleful look and added, "Meaning you yourself must believe in your compassion. I repeat, manipulation is N times easier to receive, but the result is N times worse. Is that a problem?"

"Yes, it's a problem."

People in the city had long since lived separate lives, preferring not to notice the ups and downs of others. At first it was called "respect for others' personal space," and later it was somehow reborn as indifference. The ability of contemporary people to be compassionate has been lost during the process of evolution.

"I know. I can share a personal experience with you. The game senses deception, so for some time you need to change. Not in Barliona, in reality. Take interest in the lives and business of others. Imagine yourself in their shoes, feel their emotions. Call someone who's not expecting it. Show some sympathy. Find out how they're doing, what's new. It won't immediately awaken empathy in you, but it'll lay the foundations. Read sentimental books. Foster a pet from the sanctuary—"

"I get the picture. Is that how you opened empathy?"

Eredani nodded, but once more warned it wasn't a quick process.

After saying goodnight, I logged out. Matty was waiting for me by the pod, looking ready to press the emergency exit button and drag me out if

I'd stayed in there another couple of minutes. I rummaged around in my PDA memory and found the number of an auction employee.

"Good evening. You have reached the Buy-Sell company. How may we be of assistance?" said a pleasant female Imitator voice.

"I need the services of an auctioneer." Responding to the machine's greeting would have been superfluous.

"Provide a description of the goods, the quantity, and the maximum cost for one unit."

"Demon ore, one hundred and twenty units, sixty gold."

"One moment. Please touch a finger to the scanner. Thank you, Brody West." The system had identified me. "Enter in the text box the name of a character to receive the goods."

I handed the PDA to Matty and he entered his username.

Your application has been accepted and placed in a queue for processing. May I help you with anything else?"

"Yes." Weighing up the pros and cons, I'd decided to risk it with Dheire's cookery. "Twenty pieces of meat from the depth rats of Anhurs. Maximum cost of one piece – twenty-two gold. That is all."

After entering my own name and confirming the order, I replaced the receiver, by which time Matty had already disappeared. On hearing he would soon have some ore, he'd shaken my hand and run to his pod, pulling his T-shirt off on the hoof. If only I had a fraction of his enthusiasm! Since Barliona had appeared in my life, the only thing which aroused me like that was sleep. On that pleasant note, I went to my bedroom and, without getting undressed, collapsed onto my bed.

Another week – another new group. Old questions, unconfident looks, and a keen interest in one question: will they be taken on or not? I decided to trust the teaching of the next group of candidates entirely to Helen, and to my surprise she managed well and I scarcely needed to intervene. Noticing proudly how quickly my students were developing, I relished the thought of an idle future where Helen worked for the two of us. The problem came from a completely unexpected direction. Due to the alignment of the stars, the little girl began to display a strange, even unhealthy interest in me. During recess she would bring me coffee and doughnuts, inquire about my wellbeing and weekends, smile for no reason, and violate my personal space. To begin with it seemed like nothing, but I sensed it getting worse. If at first I'd thought conversing with her would be excellent for developing my empathy, I now changed my mind, and scurried shamefully out of the hall before everyone else.

In Barliona, Eredani was already tired of training for the final obstacle, but I dug my heels in. The mere thought of dancing gave me the creeps.

"Look what I bought. Let's go and see Dheire first, then we can train." I opened my mailbox and showed him my purchase.

"You decided to go for it after all?" He was

pleased. "What made you change your mind?"

"Practicality and the simulator courses. Looking for demon-rat meat, frightening Dheire with it, and fighting for your preferences is a long and impractical process. The results of recent trades have shown that prices depend on the current relevance of the goods."

"Kvalen, it's nice to work with somebody driven by common sense." Eredani clapped me on the shoulder. "Let's go level up!"

The instructor met us with a dismal look, but I understood him. The NPC was just tucking into a delicious meal when we ambled into his box room. In order to defuse the potentially ugly situation and not lose agreeability, I hurriedly dumped the meat on the table.

"Here you are, master Dheire. The best in Barliona!"

"The best?" he asked suspiciously as he poked it with a fork. "You're lying, you goat-legged skunks. You think I don't know what meat is the best? You can't dec... O-o-o! This is Anhurs depth rat meat! Where did you get it?"

Rat Meat Supplier task completed
- *Experience: +43*
- *Reputation with Light of Barliona faction: +18*
- *Basic agreeability to Dheire increased to 40 points*

"This changes everything. Master Dheire will

now reveal to you the sacred meaning of cookery."

Reference information

Agreeability to NPC

A character parameter fluctuating from 0 to 100 is determined by the attitude of the NPC to the player. Unlike reputation, which applies to a whole faction, agreeability affects each NPC individually, including NPCs of factions with a negative reputation. You can see the current agreeability of your character to an NPC in the NPC's properties. The parameter can be altered by using temporary buffs, changing your clothes, interacting with the NPC, or doing something for the NPC.

Agreeability levels:

- **0-19: NPC does not converse with you or react when you speak. You do not exist for NPC.**
- **20-39: NPC converses with you, gives you tasks, tells you how to get to places. 20 is the basic agreeability value for all NPCs you encounter, friendly or hostile.**
- **40-59: NPC begins to trust you. You may receive a task to help NPC.**
- **60-79: NPC trusts you. You are permitted to enter NPC's**

> *house without their consent.*
> *• 80-99: NPC may suggest to player to visit a house of assignation. NPC may tell player some of their secrets.*
> *• 100: NPC is completely open with player, trusts them with all their secrets.*

"Rat meat is valued for its aroma," the master began, sniffing the meat with a blissful look on his face. It was definitely tainted. "The longer the rat lives in sewage water, the more aromatic the dish. Eredani, peel and chop an onion. I can't be doing that, can I? Kvalen, you do the ginger. You're going to help me."

"But we can't cook," I reminded him gently, but he waved me away.

"A minor problem."

New speciality available: cookery
Description: *A manufacturing speciality. You are becoming a true cookery master. From now on you are able to create dishes that restore health and activate certain buffs.*

"Do you have chef's kits?" Dheire asked and waited for our nodded replies, before continuing angrily, "So why aren't you getting busy? Meat doesn't just cook itself. Look lively! Chop-chop!"

Vasily Mahanenko. Invasion

Where was Matty when you needed him? He would have organized the potion brewing in a trice. Swearing, I chopped, more than cut, the brown root as best I could.

"Hey, are you a tiefling or a ram? Who's going to skin it for you, dipstick?" Dheire stamped his feet. I was afraid I'd spoil the whole show and agreeability would drop.

"Sorry, master. Thank you for the lesson. I'll skin it now." I bowed just in case.

Eredani wasn't having much luck either. The onion had activated a Maiden's Tears debuff, and he was smearing them all over his furious mug as he sliced it. Dheire clicked his tongue and shook his head as he silently watched the prisoner with one-hundred-percent sensations shower the unfortunate onion.

"Finished?"

"Yes," Eredani sighed.

"Well done! Now bin it. I have no use for your salty onion. You might as well have spat or blown your nose on it!" I clearly heard the scrape of Eredani's teeth, but he quietly threw the onion away and took another. The barrage, however, continued: "Hey, dipstick! Wet it with water! Do I have to teach you everything?" Eredani removed the debuff with water, and the self-satisfied master came to inspect my work.

"Now the most important thing – spices. Salt, pepper, and my secret ingredient – helirium pollen. Kvalen, you'll find everything on the second shelf, sugar too. Eredani, get soy sauce from the fridge.

Bring it all here and remember the proportions. I'm only going to show you this once."

Dheire mixed the onion, ginger, and spices, then added the meat to the resulting marinade, stirred it well, covered the container, and weighed the lid down. "Ideally, meat should be marinated for at least twelve hours, but I'm so hungry today ten minutes will be enough. Just enough to draw out the flavours of the rat meat and sewage. What are you doing just standing there? Light the fire and put the wok on it. You're dawdling like snails!"

He didn't let us rest for a minute. Even while the meat was frying in the strange pan, he found things for us to do. Standing in front of a huge mountain of dirty pots, I was irritated and grumpy. Why the hell did I have to clear away the leftovers after the whole training camp? I was about to refuse rudely, when Eredani shushed me.

Kvalen: *It's like he hasn't washed up for a month! Does his toilet need cleaning too?*

Eredani: *If it does, you clean it! Don't be stupid, Brody. There's not long to go, so don't ruin the whole game.*

Kvalen: *Thanks, adviser, but you're on your own this time.*

Eredani: *Whatever the clanless clan chief says.*

He sniggered and pointedly began washing the dishes, humming a song scandalously out of tune.

"Stop that! I'm helping already, so stop singing! I graduated from music school with distinction. I have perfect pitch."

"All the worse for you," he said, singing higher. "Wha-a-t is our life? But a ga-a-me!"

Eredani: *Sometimes it helps to get down off your high horse.*

Kvalen: *Uh-huh. I hope he's not going to make us eat this.*

Eredani: *Why? Are you a vegetarian?*

Kvalen: *No, but I have tried tofu and green eggs. Now I don't eat anything that stinks of hundred-year-old socks.*

"Hey, your hooves are on your feet, not your hands. Why are you taking so long?" Dheire complained after half an hour. The pile of dirty dishes had receded by just a half, on top of which we'd started with the cleaner items and left the pots and other heavy artillery for later. Plus it turned out we needn't have bothered anyway because, clicking his tongue, the master made a pass with his hand, and the door of a dishwashing machine opened to our right.

"Hey, dipsticks! Who washes the dishes by hand when there's a machine? You can tell you haven't eaten for a while. Your brains have shrunk."

Eredani: *Sly son of a bitch!*

Now both our teeth were scraping, and it didn't go unnoticed by the instructor. He giggled in delight at his excellent prank, and one minute later the sheen of the washed dishes made our blood boil.

"Hey. You'll never make true chefs. All you can do is waft your tails around and stamp your hooves. Get some forks, or are you going to eat with your horns?"

Grousing like an old man and shouting at us, the master opened the lid of the wok, and my belly produced a doleful rumble. The smell of freshly cooked rat was fantastic, just like that of any superbly prepared meat. Skewering a piece on a long fork, Dheire wafted the steam toward his nose with a hand and inhaled deeply, listening to his internal sensations.

"Yes! As I said, if you know how to cook it, rat meat is better than any delicacy. Attack!"

Boost received for 1 hour
- *+5 to Intellect*
- *+5 to Stamina*
- *+5 to Agility*
- *Speed of regeneration of Health increased by 30%*
- *Speed of regeneration of Energy increased by 30%*
- *Chance of Critical Strike increased by 10%*

You have learned a new cookery recipe: stewed marinated Anhurs depth rat
Description: *An epic recipe. <**description of preparation process**>. The player or NPC eating the dish receives a boost for 1 hour: <**description of boost**>. Preparation time: 10 minutes.*

Ingredients:

- *1 Anhurs depth rat meat*
- *2 pinches of helirium pollen for the marinade*

Restrictions: *The player must be at least level 200, or cook the dish themselves. You may create no more than 20 copies of the recipe. You may not create a copy from a copy of the recipe. You may not study the recipe independently.*

"Thank you for the lesson, master Dheire." Eredani bowed so low he almost butted the master with his horns. Our humiliation had been worth it for the result. "You are truly a great chef. Teaching us a recipe with three boosts is invaluable."

"Hey," Dheire said, waving away the compliment, but we could see it had fallen on fertile ground. "You did well too. You brought me the best meat, so I did my best. Now go, I like eating alone. Don't just stand there! Shoo, I said!" The change in mood was so sharp we shot out of the workshop like bullets.

"Epic strength!" Eredani said. "Three boosts! Brody, I have a task for you. Buy me some rat meat and pollen. We won't sell the recipe yet – prices for ingredients will go through the roof. I have nothing to do at night, so I'll learn some cookery. Ten percent crit via food is fantastic for raiders. Chop-chop, as Dheire said, meat doesn't just cook itself. Call the man!"

Book One: A Second Chance

"There's no man there, just an office full of Imitators," I muttered, pressing the Exit button. Eredani's enthusiasm was understandable – we might be looking at a stable, if insignificant income. First we'd flood the market with our meat, then start trading recipes. Before calling Buy-Sell, I looked at the online auction – you couldn't buy anything, but you could scope out prices and the availability of goods. There was a lot of depth rat meat, at twenty-two gold a piece. Not so much luck with seasoning – only just over two hundred helirium pollen, at forty-two gold per unit. Elementary mathematics calculated the prime cost of our meat at one hundred and six gold. Not bad. I had to search to find out where the pollen came from, and it wasn't good news. You couldn't buy it from NPCs; you had to collect it from bushes growing in level-two-hundred locations or higher. After giving a Buy-Sell employee a task to buy a hundred pollen and fifty meat, I returned to Eredani. He had all night ahead of him, so he could do some work.

Afterwards we started training. Eredani's expectations didn't bear out. He thought I would need four days, but in the end it took eight. It's not fun recognizing how wooden you are, but you can't fly in the face of facts – flexibility was simply not my strongest point. The players who'd paid us for passing had already long since completed the training camp and were now doing what Eredani did – training youngsters. The only positives from all this hassle were agility increasing by a point, and strength and stamina shooting up.

We also marked out a nice bonus from Eredani's culinary success. He stewed fifty pieces of meat, twenty of which we split evenly between ourselves, and thirty I sent to auction, where they sold like hotcakes for 420 gold per piece. The auctioneer took his ten percent, leaving me eleven thousand gold richer. We would have to set a task to buy up pollen as soon as it appeared at auction. No matter how much it cost, we would reclaim our outlay and make a profit on top.

At long last came the happy moment when Eredani announced, "You're ready. If not now, then never. It's pointless teaching you any further. Let's go."

Achievement received: unparalleled high level

Description: *You passed a minimum of twenty obstacles on the high-level course at the first attempt. Before leaving the training camp you will receive a High-Level Demon Hunter buff: a sixfold increase in experience, reputation, and characteristics growth rate.*

Bonuses:
- *+8 to all main characteristics for completing 20 obstacles in succession at the first attempt*

Step 4 task "High-Level Training" completed

Book One: A Second Chance

- *Experience: +43*
- *Reputation with Light of Barliona faction: +18*
- *You are permitted to leave the training camp*

I couldn't. I tackled twenty-one obstacles easily, but I couldn't go on. Lying on my back after crashing out of the course, I looked at the sky with one thought – I couldn't muster the strength to complete it to get the bonus. Not now, not ever. Fuck it all. I wasn't a dancer.

"Twenty-one out of twenty-five!" said Tarlin. The high-level course was supervised by the disfeatured instructor. "Waste of space! I always said a tiefling couldn't become a worthy demon hunter. You can leave the training camp. You're not going to learn anything else here. Next!"

He didn't mention Eredani, who had easily completed all twenty-five obstacles. My partner was waiting for me by the entrance to the course. He'd seen my inglorious attempt, but kept quiet about it, instead distracting me by pointing out a twinkling bulletin board. "We have tasks available. Shall we take a peek?"

There was a crowd around the board. While we were still listed as "minnows," the system painstakingly safeguarded us from unnecessary looks. Players leaving the training camp gates entered a new phase where they couldn't be seen, and now we'd reached that point ourselves, we in turn stopped being able to see the minnows. Only for the daily parade did the system consolidate all the spaces, showing there were more than enough players in the training camp.

The notice board was a new object for me; I'd never seen it before.

"Tieflings, come with us to farm demons!" As soon as we approached the throng, we were urged to join various groups.

"Don't listen to them!" another player shouted. "They're noobs. They want a mass free ride when there's no control at all. Join us. There are five of us. We'll make it ten and go hunt out N'Got. He resurrected yesterday. We'll level up to five and then go find L'Kri."

The phrase "We'll level up to five" made us look more seriously at the players. Most of those crowding round the board were level three. A few level two, but no one matching us. With level five we were welcome guests in any group.

"Let's go alone," said Eredani. "There's no point getting involved with minnows, we won't gain experience. It'll be easier to call Diabettis and hire him. Take the task to purge L'Kri's lands. It's on our way."

"Minnow yourself!" the players shouted resentfully, and one added with barefaced scorn, "Donators!"

Task received: purge the lands of L'Kri
Description: *A regular task. Destroy 20 demons in L'Kri's location.*
Reward:

- *Experience: +5*
- *Reputation with Light of Barliona faction: +1*

No bonuses, no restrictions. An ideal task for training-course graduates. L'Kri's demons were level four or five, so they should be no problem for us.

Half an hour's journey across red sands, and we were standing by a deep crater, like a mining quarry. A serpentine road led down its sides to a leaning tower at the very bottom. The place was a hive of activity – octopus-like demons were working the quarry, trying to dig out the tower, and some on the side cuts were obstructing the road with blocks. Not far from us a group of players was steadily butchering demons, and on the far side of the quarry a second group was doing the same. They worked in a coordinated fashion, assuming key positions, but not particularly advancing on the bottom of the crater. I picked out a demon roughly halfway up the quarry – level six – and everything fell into place: at the top were level four-five demons, a bit lower – level six, and at the very bottom – level seven-eight. There was nothing for level fours to do down there.

"Let's go to the Barrows first. Both the slopes are busy," I said.

"We can pick some herbs on the way," Eredani agreed, after checking with the map. Bear left and we can get some clover. It's this way."

We skirted round the L'Kri pit. There was a demon clover patch a hundred meters from the quarry, at the edge of a tapering gray wood. I had already bent down over it, when the system suddenly threw a fit.

Damage sustained

Health level decreased by 162: 162 (Bolt from the Abyss) - 0 (magic protection). Life remaining: 3,638 out of 3,800

Health level decreased by 162: 162 (Bolt from the Abyss) - 0 (magic protection). Life remaining: 3,476 out of 3,800

Two dark bolts of lightning impaled me and knocked me away from the flower, and Eredani began to wheeze alongside me – he'd been hit too. Jumping to my feet, I summoned Aniram and scanned around for our assailant. If some beastie thought it would be easy to deal with us, it was sadly misled.

Another two bolts in my direction. Taking them in the chest and being thrown aside again, I nonetheless saw where the fire was coming from – our adversary was hidden among the trees. Barely had I landed when I leaped up and charged toward the wood.

"Now we'll see who's going to get who!" came Braksed's voice. "Payback time is nigh!"

Debuff received

Deceleration: *Your speed is decreased by 50%. Duration: 30 seconds*

Book One: A Second Chance

On top of the deceleration, four more bolts pierced my body, leaving me just a third of Health. Those little bloodsuckers learned all too quickly, and this time they were well prepared.

Chapter 6

W E LAY FLAT on the ground and tried to blend in with the background. The system appreciated our effort and offered a Camouflage characteristic, but remembering Eredani's lecture yesterday about the harm of accidental characteristics, I had to decline. My partner, swearing quietly, rubbed his lightning wounds. It hadn't cost him much Health, but the strike was painful enough.

"Tieflings, where are you?" shouted Kurtune with familiar schadenfreude. "Coming, ready or not!"

Eredani gingerly raised his head and was immediately hurled a couple of meters away from me, four lightning bolts in his forehead. His HP almost halved, and he landed unconscious. I counted five seconds between the shots, which wasn't much, but it was breathing space. Raising my own head directly after the shots, I beheld the enemy – demons, Elder magi of R'tan, level nine. They were similar to N'got's snakelike cronies, but if the latter provoked laughter and the desire to coo over them, R'tan's magi were only terrifying. Brawny bodies supported by tails bound in brilliant scales towered high above the ground and threatened to flatten small beer like me. It was the first time I'd seen demons in armor, and I now understood where graduates got their bloody chestplates and shoulder protection from. Sixteen red eyes on four demons worked no less efficiently than laser sights, but worse was the dark energy simmering in their cupped clawed paws.

Hiding behind the magi's backs hovered the delighted Vartalinskys.

After five seconds, more dark lightning was dispatched in my direction. I hugged the ground and felt a light tingle a millimeter from where the missiles whizzed past. It was time to counterstrike. Aniram appeared instantly, compliant and ready to aggress, and, singling out the nearest beastie, I activated demon strike.

Damage inflicted

You have inflicted 162 damage: (212 magic attack) - 50 (protection from R'Tan's magi). Total Health remaining: 738 out of 900

Not enough against six.

"Hi, boys!" sang Aniram sweetly in the language of the demons, thrusting forth her virtues. In unison, the demons turned their heads in her direction and extinguished the fire in their hands. I had never seen such harmonious gallantry in my life. "So, R'Tan has also gained a foothold here?"

"Move aside, Elder." The demon closest to us spoke in a drawn-out hiss, rippling its muscles. Superb timing! Although on the other hand, for the sake of all the myrmidons of the Abyss, anything was preferable to more lightning. "We must kill your master."

"Have R'Tan's servants drawn up a contract with non-demons? It's unthinkable." Aniram voiced her conclusions and added schemingly, "Does your master know?"

"They offered suitable payment," replied the magus without going into specifics. "What do you choose, Elder?"

"Hey, what are you chatting about over there?" called Kurtune. "Attack the Tieflings!"

I made use of the hold-up to ask, "Aniram, can you devour them?"

The demoness uttered a sigh and scratched between her horns with her tail. "I cannot. They do not belong to you." There was chagrin in her voice. "I cannot devour anyone if they are bound by a contract. Defeat them or repurchase them, and I will gladly take them."

"Why are you so useless?" I asked.

"*I'm* useless?" she said indignantly.

I employed another demon strike and, seeing the same disappointing result of 162 damage points, looked at her pointedly. She huffed and retreated from the line of attack. Bitch! The next volley of lightning convinced me to take decisive action – run! The deceleration debuff was already deactivated, and to realize my superintelligent plan I simply had to distract the enemy and grab Eredani. My conscience wouldn't allow me to leave him to be torn to pieces by those misfits. Besides, I had big plans for him.

"Can you at least distract them?" I asked, crawling away toward my partner.

"Why of course," the Demoness said and unfastened the top clasp of her leather corset. A synchronous male exhalation resounded. Forcing myself not to be distracted, I reached Eredani, slung his lifeless body over my shoulder, and ran.

"Where are you off to?" The cries of the Vartalinskys mingled with the magi's shots. Eredani took three bolts, and I the fourth, but it merely spurred me to accelerate.

"After him!" yelled Braksed. "Don't just stand there, he's getting away!"

"Deceleration!" added Kurtune.

"It's still recovering. After him! He's getting away!"

"We don't run. We are only used for ambushes." The demon's voice was so loud I heard it clearly above the sound of my own ragged breathing. The demon magus could communicate passably in the common language of Barliona.

"Agreement!" said Braksed.

I dismissed the demoness and accelerated until my ears buzzed. The longer they argued, the greater my chances of escape.

"Bear right. The Barrows are over there." Eredani's voice came so unexpectedly I nearly stumbled.

"How are you?"

"Not good. They're running. Three hundred meters. Speed up."

"What about the demons?"

"And the demons."

I suppressed my desire to look back, and began to pick my route more carefully. There were too many rocks and sharp anti-cacti around. Eventually the Barrows loomed in the distance – three small mounds of red sand, nothing out of the ordinary. If you didn't know it was a hidden location, you could easily pass it by. I was sprinting, but Eredani kept prodding me, saying, "Two hundred metres. Crank it up. Right! Right!"

The dance training was paying off, and I dashed off to the right. I didn't know how rhythmical it looked, but I was happy with my speed and reactions. Lightning grazed some rocks away to the side. Only one thought pounded in my head: not far now. I ran and ran, almost on empty, driving myself to keep going, to fight to the last. This was more than just a silly game now. Then without warning I was gasping for breath, and my viewer was occluded by a system message. Bad timing!

"You're losing speed," Eredani wheezed. "They're gaining on us!"

I would gladly have swiped the warning to the side, but bitter experience told me to read it.

Warning

You have been running flat-out for 2 minutes 30 seconds. The safe time for flat-out running with Agility 40 and character level 5 is 4 Minutes 30 seconds. If you continue to move at the prescribed pace, your Health value will decrease by 5% every 10 seconds. Time until value reset: 30 minutes' rest.

"Can you run? I'm going to drop soon. Warning."

"I can't. Weakening. Left!" Another black cluster flew past. "They're splitting up. A hundred meters. Right!"

The third lightning strike was wide of the mark too.

"Summon the fish!" My breathing was very labored. "I have two minutes!"

"It's too far. A kilometer. Step on it!"

A kilometer in two minutes. Even my frugal knowledge of sporting records was enough to know that a time like that would challenge for an Olympic medal. They hadn't removed liveliness completely, they'd just hidden it, which was perfectly understandable – who would let players run about for free? Let them pay for transport or portals, but not just run. Within the confines of the world of Barliona it was bad for your health.

A minute later my breathlessness was joined by uncontrollable tears, and it was now harder to jump from side to side and keep track of rocks. Dodging lightning for the umpteenth time, I tripped over a stone and fell, scraping my face on the rough sand. Eredani flew arse over tit from my back and rolled away. I had no strength even to raise my head, but my partner grabbed me by the scruff of the neck and dragged me on, groaning. The barrows loomed close, but I didn't care anymore. The system had twice taken five percent, leaving my HP in the red zone. One hit from the demons and I would be sent to my first rebirth. I wondered if it would be painful.

Access to the Barrows of the Fallen confirmed

The guardian has confirmed your access to the Barrows of the Fallen. The entry point to the Barrows is marked on your map.

A golden veil along the entire border of the barrows separated us from our pursuers. Eredani turned me onto my back and helped me sit up. Breathless, we watched the magi approach, gliding smoothly over the sandy hillocks. With about ten meters to go, they abruptly stopped, as though they'd stumbled into a barrier, and shortly afterwards the Vartalinskys joined them.

"Why have you stopped? What the hell is this?" said Braksed, approaching the veil, kicking it angrily and howling. The guardian would not forgive such harsh treatment of his property.

"We can't get through. We're leaving," announced the demons.

"What do you mean *leaving*?" Kurtune was beside himself with rage. "We paid you, and you haven't fulfilled the contract."

"We are not omnipotent. We don't want to end up in the Abyss. We are cancelling the contract." The demon magi about-faced and zipped away.

Eredani: *Look at the properties of those thugs.*

The Vartalinskys' clothes had changed since we'd last met. They'd given themselves a none-too-shabby tweak, involving reinforcements, patches, knives twinkling as a green mist on their belts, flasks for restoring health and energy, and ninja stars. The outfits were now more suited to levelled-up raiders than nursery inhabitants. But the most interesting thing was in the pair's properties.

Player Kurtune Vartalinsky. Dark demon hunter. Level 11.

When did they manage to turn dark?

"Made it to safety, did you, you animals?" Kurtune asked us. Pissed yourselves in the fight?"

"Kurt, shut up." Braksed knocked him down a peg. "Return the ring, and we walk away."

"What, without any money?" His brother's offer came as a surprise to Kurtune.

Braksed spat on the ground and added, "A hundred thousand should do the trick. We'll consider it compensation for the emotional distress, and payment for rental of the object."

His manner was surprisingly laidback, which only served to irritate. "Are you sure that's enough? I asked, unable to resist. "If you need the ring, suggest a price."

"Just keep wisecracking, you goat-horned asshole!" Kurtune's control of his emotions was a weak spot. "The ring and a hundred thousand. Otherwise we bury you here. And you never leave the fucking camp. If you don't return the ring, we'll find you in the wide world."

Kvalen: *Hermit owes us an object. There was*

an ambush by the clover. Luckyrain must have told them about the herb.

Eredani: *Forget that. Those two changed their class and parleyed twice with demons. First the ambush, then the chase. There's just one thing I don't get – why are they so hung up on the ring?*

Kvalen: *I wondered that too. With their financial situation the ring shouldn't be such a big loss.*

Eredani: *Unless it has sentimental value to them.*

Kvalen: *Engagement? That would explain a lot.*

"What, are you deaf?" The Vartalinskys weren't best pleased with our silence. "Where's the ring?"

Eredani: *We've digressed. How did they change class and parley with the demons?*

Kvalen: *We have to try and milk them. I'll start, and you join in when you think it's right.*

Eredani: *I like the way you think! My school!*

Kvalen: *I'm self-taught.*

"The ring is ours," I said. I rose to my feet and approached the sparkling veil, stopping right by the Vartalinskys. You'd think they could reach out an arm and drag a cocksure tiefling off to the light of Eluna, but it wasn't that simple. "There's no need to try and scare us. You can see we're not faint of heart. Let's come to an arrangement. If we can agree on a price, you get your ring back."

"Have you gone freaking mad?!" Kurtune lost it and threw a punch at my chin. The result was superb – he recoiled, howling and shaking his fist in pain.

"I repeat. If you want the ring back, name a reasonable price. Or we'll name our own."

"We're gonna mess you up good, you fuckers! You're gonna eat dirt. You're gonna crawl to us on your knees with the ring between your teeth." Braksed didn't look like somebody willing to negotiate, and Eredani understood that too. We'd done the main thing: explained to the jerkoffs how to solve the problem. When they cooled down, they would realize it was the only way to get their ring back. There was no point wasting more time on them, so we headed to the Barrows.

"Stop, you cowards! You can't come out of there." Every decent word of Braksed's was set against a background of obscenities, which lent him a new whimsical shade. The player liked to cuss and did it well.

On the map, the reason for our foray lay somewhere up ahead, directly behind a large and very steep hill. If from a distance the hill could have been mistaken for a natural structure, from close up it was clearly handmade. It concealed another two just like it, and together they formed an equilateral triangle, with saddles where they joined, and the entrance to the barrows in the very centre. The closer we got, the more I grasped the structure's true dimensions – my house would have fitted inside ten times over, if not more.

After walking round the first hill, we began to scramble up toward the saddle, assisting each other. When we reached the highest part we looked around, and an unintentional exclamation of enchantment escaped from me. Not being spoiled in either reality or virtuality, I was easily impressed by picturesque panoramas.

On the inside, the peaks of the hills were cut away to form perfectly circular platforms, the larger part of which was occupied by monumental marble compositions. A bright sign with fiery flashes asserted that the event depicted was the "Battle of the Demons with the Forces of Light."

Three winged creatures of the Abyss were pitted against representatives of Barliona's light races, and judging by the sculpture, the outcome of the battle was predetermined. Their massive wings spread out above the light creatures, the nearly defeated demons were petrified in eternal agony. The centrepiece of the composition was an orc, who, with a demon in each hand and a third between its teeth, was fearlessly enduring the pain from the talons of the rampaging beasts.

A she-elf stood to the side. The priestess's hem blew up, revealing her stockings and coat, which were hung all over with flasks and magic objects. The sculptor had captured her in the process of weaving a spell to fend off accidental tail strikes. Her face was so concentrated I could only feel sorry for her – in that manifestation she would never finish weaving. Just as the human next to her would never bring down his hammer, which was cast high in the sky.

The scale and attention to detail were

impressive. You could easily make out the veins on the demon's wings, the bulging veins on the neck and arms of the orc, even the beads of sweat on the human's face.

The entrance to the main complex, which was underground, was at the feet of the orc.

"It's like they froze at the moment of battle," I said, breaking the ringing silence. "Do you know them?"

"No. I've never even heard of such a battle, but I do have a sneaking suspicion I've seen the paladin somewhere. I just don't remember where," said Eredani. Lost in thought, he approached the sculpture.

"That's normal at your age," I quipped. The composition was oppressive, and I wanted to lighten the mood. "It's called sclerosis. If you like I can bring you some crosswords tomorrow as a preventative measure."

"Kvalen," sighed Eredani. The last deer knows that if there are no names on a monument, there's a reason for it. It has nothing to do with sclerosis."

"But I'm not a deer, I'm a tiefling."

"You're a clown," he said good-naturedly and turned halfway to the monument.

"Where are you going?" There was nothing else around worthy of attention.

"You go on, I'll be there in a minute," he said, waving me away. I looked doubtfully at the entrance to the barrows and set off after him. His air of detachment was disquieting. His gaze fixed on a sheer wall, he began to mumble under his breath. I came closer and listened in.

"Well, well, well. What have we here?" He had his nose against the rock and began running a finger over the wall. On closer inspection it turned out that, red as it was, it was also covered in a dark-maroon pattern, which was scarcely distinguishable even close up. Personally I thought it was simple abstractions, but Eredani had other ideas. He walked along the wall, spellbound, gazing at the intertwined lines and geometric figures.

"Are you an art lover too?"

"Eh?" He was momentarily distracted and looked at me up vacantly. "Art? Yes, yes, I love it."

"Eredani, you're scaring me." I observed him closely. His behaviour was strange, like he wasn't all there, and I'd never seen him like that before. Hugging the wall and fingering it, he was talking to himself absently. "Victor! Snap out of it! Have you been given a task?"

"There is no task. It's a map," he whispered. "Part of a map."

However hard I tried to see something resembling a map or a diagram, nothing happened. It occurred to me that Victor had gone insane from constant immersion in Barliona, or was close to it. Or maybe it was the start of burning up? Both possibilities were cause for concern.

"What map? There's nothing here, just scribblings. Maybe someone immortalized the winner of a kids' drawing competition in Barliona, and you got hooked in," I said, seriously worried. He didn't respond. "Tiefling Eredani, first position! The advanced course will not wait!"

It didn't help. He continued to rave and run his hands deliriously over the wall. "It's a map. It's definitely a map. How can I tell? It's too bluffy... indecipherable... Who are they? How do I know? Where's the beginning? Maybe over there?" He shot off toward the next hill, where the same patterns were repeated. "A copy. It's just a copy. A bad one. Where's the map itself? How do I find out? That way!"

I supposed he would run to the third wall, but instead he turned toward the statues and disappeared into a passageway, where a metal mesh was immediately lowered behind him. I ran to catch him, but when I got there I saw only his shadow running down a spiral staircase. "Victor, wait!" I didn't hold my breath for an answer. "Damn you and your unhinged brain! I've gone and got involved with a simpleton!"

A brief inspection of the entrance produced no levers or buttons. In my anger I kicked the cage, but it didn't help. Wait! I had to try and knock it down with a demon strike.

"Holy Tiamat! It's..." whispered the newly rematerialized demoness.

I didn't manage to activate demon strike before Aniram froze, and the surprise reflected on her face had nothing to do with it. A quick glance at the report log informed me that a second before the debuff Aniram had begun to cast an essence-consumption spell, but the guardian of the barrows had stopped her.

"Aniram, I forbid you to consume any essences in the Barrows!" I said, and the debuff was deactivated. With a swish of her wings, the demoness flew up a meter and rained an incensed tirade down on me:

"Three highers! Three higher demons lie here! Allow me to consume them, and everything will change. Mostly for you. I will be obedient, just as you wish. I will take the place of Ireness, which is due to me."

Notification for player Kvalen

On consumption of the essence of any of the three higher demons, the archdemon Aniram will be destroyed, and you will have to dive into the Abyss for a new demon. We are obliged to inform you that your bonus for random generation has been used, and you will have access to a rank 1 demon.

As if Eredani wasn't enough, the developers and their tests were pissing me off so much it was beginning to irk. I should tell everyone where to get off, feed all three essences to Aniram, and take the higher demon as a pet. Naturally with the protection of a squadron of lawyers who would assert my client's rights in Barliona.

"You're in the barrows. Can we consider our agreement fulfilled?" I asked Aniram, knowing I had no choice as such. I didn't want to risk it and jump for a rank-one demon.

"Don't banish me! There are three highers here," she said, alarmed, but nevertheless added, "You have fulfilled your part of the agreement. But with my help you can become stronger."

In lieu of a reply I activated demon strike.

Warning

You have inflicted 0 damage. Magic attack is not applicable to objects in this location.

"Permit me to take just one!" Aniram continued to beseech me. "I will give you three months of peace and quiet."

"Aniram, you are not going to consume anyone in the barrows, period. You wanted to come here, and I brought you. There was no talk of anything more, so shut up! I have enough problems without you."

Demonstratively encasing herself in her wings, she went into a sulk and sat down on the orc's foot. She could not disobey a direct order from her master. Nobody could make me put up with her pouty expression, so I dismissed her. Like I needed a capricious madam for total game happiness!

Pick! I had a pick! Since magic attack was useless, maybe physical attack would work? Retrieving the weapon from my inventory, I took a swing at the mesh. The crossbar severed, and my mood improved. Five minutes later I'd managed to make a hole big enough to climb through.

The steep stairway led down to a very narrow corridor. So narrow that, far from being able to run,

I had difficulty moving sideways along it. I stood there hesitant. Enclosed spaces were my second greatest phobia, after heights. The grinding pressure of the walls unnerved me, and even my horns itched with reluctance to go on, but I couldn't leave my partner alone in that condition. If he didn't recover his senses in ten minutes, I would write to tech support. Although I had to find him first. I was terrified. If this continued, we would be recuperating our mental health together.

Duty won. Breathing deeply, I squeezed ahead, circles dancing in front of my eyes. The system had picked up on my fear and was visualizing it in this hilarious fashion. The corridor seemed to turn into a crypt, the walls formed from huge vertical tombstones. Time had nearly worn away their inscriptions, but from what remained it was surmisable that the Great Warriors of Barliona were buried there. Definitely. Capital letters.

A turn. A second. A third. The passage snaked, and the farther I went, the more unsure of my direction I became. Eventually I turned into a small room, where I nearly stepped on Eredani. He was crawling on his knees along the mosaic floor, most of which was damaged. But that didn't stop me making out the general picture – in the middle of a stormy sea lay an island, in the centre of which yawned a pit. The contents of the pit were a mystery, for that part of the picture was missing.

"A map. It's a map. The entrance must be here, I can feel it." Eredani's condition hadn't improved – he was still oblivious to his surroundings.

"Victor, snap out of it!" I hauled him up onto his feet, giving him a fierce shake as I did so.

"Don't! Touch! Me!" On top of his lapse of reason, he had also become aggressive. He pushed me so hard I flew against a wall and smacked my head. Even stranger was that I was now a prisoner. Something held me to the wall.

My partner returned to the mosaic as if nothing had happened.

"Three heroes. An island. Two islands. No. One is a copy. I know where the start is!"

He jumped to his feet, and was illuminated by a bright white light. I had to turn away and screw my eyes up so as not to be blinded. Until now, the process of him levelling up had been infinitely more subtle. With a dull groan, he fell to the floor and curled up in embryo pose. It wasn't enough for the system, and a second wave of light engulfed him, after which the field clamping me to the wall disappeared, the torches were extinguished, and we were in total darkness. I fell to the floor in shock, trying to make out anything in the darkness, and crawled in the direction of where Eredani should have been lying. My spatial awareness didn't fail me, and I soon felt his hand. "Victor?"

"Brody?" His voice was hoarse, but calmer.

"What happened?" I asked, throwing myself at him. My emotions were making themselves known.

"Where are we?"

"Don't say you don't remember anything." A shiver ran through my body. The darkness of the

Abyss hadn't aroused discomfort, but here underground, the enclosed space was unbearable. Only the game interface punctuating the impenetrable darkness helped me get a grip.

"What I remember has nothing to do with the dark," he replied and, judging by a shuffling sound, sat up. "Do you have a video?"

I made a video clip of the crazy chase and sent it to him. "So that's how it works," he said.

"Since everything's clear to you, can you explain it to me?"

"What don't you understand? I've just enacted a scene."

"I thought you'd gone mental, or started to burn up. What was the task? Was that seizure at the end from leveling up?"

"Not only that. I'm not a Barliona thrill seeker. It was the first time like that," he chuckled. "I don't know how to explain it clearly. I started boosting Cartographer and saw a map on the wall. Don't ask how I knew it was a map, but I just had to find the start, and looked for a symbol to find it. Everything else became unimportant. Signs on the walls led me to the mosaic. I deciphered it and whited out. There's no rational explanation and you can't control it with your mind."

"A unique task?"

"Yes. Multi-layered, like your Matthew's. And it requires good clan support."

"Sounds like a load of nonsense. How does it fit in with your conspiracy theory?"

"God knows. I'll insist to the commission it

was an accident."

"Maybe we could sell the scene?"

"You can't sell something like that," he said with a sigh. "Usually players with tasks like that are specifically sought out and offered membership of a clan. It's mutually profitable."

"Write to the developers," I said. "It's too dangerous—"

"Brody, I'm a prisoner on a special deal, not an idiot," he cut me off angrily. "I know better than you what threat such a task poses me. I've already written everything and refused. Let's get out of here."

"You cannot refuse," the darkness roared. I assumed it was a prompt response from tech support. "The path is difficult and challenging, but it is yours alone. Give peace to the stricken!"

"Me?" Eredani asked in disbelief. It seemed to me the whole scene had shell-shocked him. "What a twist!"

The torches were rekindled to show us the way out. Eredani stiffened, reading a message.

"Listen, I have a feeling all the most interesting stuff in this Barliona of yours happens to prisoners," I said and clapped my partner on the shoulder. He didn't respond. The torches flickered their displeasure; we took the hint and headed for the exit.

When we emerged under the glorious Barliona sky, I sighed hugely with relief. Eredani sat down in the shadow of the statue and motioned for me to join him. "Brody, we have to alter our plans slightly. Somewhere here on the island is a high mountain, and inside it is a deep lair. In that lair..."

"Is a crystal coffin?" We'd had to read Pushkin at school. "It's too early for you to be thinking about that, Victor."

"I'm not thinking about a coffin, Brody. All I can think about is Snow White," he sniggered, amused.

"This has shades of necrophilia."

"Almost. In that lair is an explanation of where to find information about these heroes." He nodded toward the monument. "They vanquished the great Evil and incarcerated it on the island. They didn't tell anyone exactly where, but they couldn't die without at least leaving a clue. So they created a map with the coordinates of the island, divided it into three parts, and each of the heroes took their third to the grave. The task is to find out who they are and where they're buried, find and assemble the whole map, and go to the island to cast Evil down into Chaos. The heroes made a mistake by not returning it there immediately. It's a long task, but doable."

"How did you manage to get mixed up in this?"

"Cartographer, damn it. Hermit said there were loads of barrows, even in the wide world. The player has to obtain access from the guardian and have Cartography as their main speciality. Arguably nothing unique. The developers didn't take into account that I might also fit the criteria. I just received official confirmation from tech support that nothing critical happened. They strongly recommend completing the scene. Everything's agreed with the commission."

"Congratulations," I said, hiding my sadness with difficulty. "So you have a straight path to the top clan. They can use your knowledge and abilities, and in turn help you find the map."

"Stow your congratulations," Eredani sighed. "That would be too easy. I have a restriction. Look."

Restriction: *Search possible only together with player Kvalen. Task may not be given to another player.*

"I didn't get a notification." I frowned.

"And you won't. You must go with me voluntarily. It's a requirement of my... curators."

"Aaah," I said, pleased. The cockles of my heart were immediately warmed, firstly because it's nice to be cajoled, secondly because I wasn't the only one with socialization problems, and thirdly because I had become accustomed to the walking Barliona encyclopedia. "Are you going to cajole me? And if so, how?"

"In the classical manner. I'll give you a bribe."

"Okay then."

"Here you are."

Task received: Evil doesn't sleep
Description: *A unique scene.*
<Complete description of legend>
Figure out who the three great

*heroes of the past were, find all
parts of the map, connect them,
find the secret Island of Keshin,
and cast Evil down into Chaos.*

Reward:

- *Experience: +5*
- *Reputation with Light of
Barliona faction: +1*
- *Access to Island of Keshin*

Restriction: *Search possible only together
with player Eredani. Task may not be
given to another player.*

"Wait, I don't get it, where's the bribe?"

"Are you blind or something? You should be
looking at it."

"In the terminology of the Vartalinsky
vampires, you've played me for a fool, yeah?"

"Yep." Eredani nodded, pleased with himself.

"You're not much of a bribe giver. That's a
'What the hell do I want with that?' kind of task," I
mumbled. "Fine, let's go see Argalot. He owes us."

You'd think it was easy – get your ass in gear
and run to Hermit. However, a surprise from reality
was waiting for us as we approached the saddle. The
perimeter of the barrows was cordoned by an army
of demon magi.

"That pair have really got me interested now,"
Eredani said. "How boldly they work with demons!
They're not demonologists. They're not Tieflings.

Bro, have a look out in reality and see who they are."

"You think they're not going to hide? I'll have a look, of course. But what for?"

"To learn their weak spots."

In my cluelessness I turned to my partner. The game was the game, and reality... Perhaps it was time to ask myself who Eredani was. I'd forgotten that the person next to me wasn't just my partner, but also a criminal.

"We won't get through here. Demons aren't players, they're not here to chill. I don't want to die. How are you for time?" Eredani was inadvertently waving his tail from side to side, but his eyes were scanning me.

"I've got a couple of hours. Any ideas?"

"One. Let's go, I have something to show you."

For some reason Eredani took me back underground. I followed him, nervously trying to brush aside suspicious thoughts and walls closing in. Back in the mosaic room he pointed to a narrow alcove.

"Climb in. Head first. Squash yourself in as far as you can go."

"I'll get stuck." Then it hit me: "I'll get stuck!"

"Two hours of doing nothing and you can press the Character Stuck button. That's yours, and this is mine. Let's crawl."

For the first few minutes I was rent with fear that I wouldn't be able to move. It was dark and tight like a coffin, with but the lightest relief in the form of multiplying multi-digit numbers and Eredani's salacious balads. When he tired of singing out of key, the tales began – far preferable to his singing, and the time flew by.

When the safety button appeared in settings, I pressed it with such mental force that, had it had been a physical object, I would have smashed it. A progress bar appeared, the stony space swam and transformed into the temple of our training camp, and the system transported us to the only point of rebirth on the island.

"At the double, march!" I commanded and trotted to the exit, Eredani right behind me.

After leaving the camp we made a detour, just in case, to confuse casual witnesses. We ran one and a half kilometers due west, made certain there was no one around, and headed due north. We soon found Hermit in his cave, asleep upside down like a bat. Opening one eye a crack, the demon grumbled:

"Oh, it's you, is it? What kept you?"

"We got ambushed. Demons were waiting for us by the clover. You owe us."

"That's impossible!" Argalot spread his wings and glided down.

I told him about coming across the demons, and he listened, not interrupting, save for the odd guttural interjection. Near the end of my tale he dove into the report log.

"The demons were expecting *you*, not just any Free demons." A hint at the injustice of our demands. "An ambush like that could be set up anywhere. The clover's irrelevant."

"But it was bang next to the clover!" I argued, switching into clever-dick mode. "And you said—"

"Don't split hairs! I know what I said." Argalot waved a hand, and Eredani and I found ourselves holding a massive red object each. They looked like cuirasses. Unfortunately a message prevented us from studying them in closer detail.

Search for Trouble task completed
- *Experience: +43*
- *Reputation with Light of Barliona faction: +18*
- *Epic object from Hermit's collection*

Breast plate from Unending Happiness set
Description: *An epic object. Part of a set (1 of 4). Material: thin leather.*
- *Protection from physical and magic attacks: 50*
- *Luck: +5*
- *Intellect: +5*
- *Damage sustained reduced by 10%*
- *Duration of debuffs reduced by 25%*
- *Probability of critical strike increased by 10%*

Bonus for full set: *None*

"I knew not to get involved with Free citizens," said Argalot, flying back up to his perch. "I'm not teaching you today. Come back tomorrow. Or in two weeks. Or not at all! They're going to blame me."

Eredani shouted after him, "Two Free demon hunters have gone dark. And they can parley with demons!" Argalot turned sharply in the air and glided back down to us, mild interest vaguely discernible on his face.

"Were their wrists bare?" he asked Eredani.

"That's the thing. They weren't manacled. The demons were helping freely."

"Strange indeed." Argalot frowned. "Where could Free beginners get such strength?"

Eredani and I exchanged disappointed glances. "We thought you'd know."

"I'm not omniscient." He sat down on a rock and was still, staring into space. A few minutes later he blindsided us with some news: "Uldaron doesn't get it either. They attacked the training camp."

"What? Who? When?" Eredani and I asked in chorus.

"Your friends, the dark demon hunters, rocked up with fifty level-nine elder R'Tan magi. Tarlin and Drumm beat off the attack, but Uldaron forbade them to leave the camp. The demons set up a blockade and are slaying everyone who dares show themselves. Not a good situation."

"How can we help?"

"You?" Hermit cast a look at us and waved a dismissive hand. "Level five, no weapons, no armor, no elixirs. Elder magi shoot from two hundred meters. You shoot from fifty. How can you help? This is not about harassing river demons."

"So teach us!" It seemed a suitable moment to

remember the purpose of our visit. "Give us the possibility to deal with demons."

"Well," Argalot thought. "Suppose I give you Aura of Despair, Retreat, and Wicked Strike. You're not ready for the rest. But against level-nine demons that's just barking, not biting." He thought a while longer. "To cut your teeth, you'll have to cope with your own demon essence. You must fully accept yourselves. Tieflings usually do that at level one hundred, when they get to rank one. But this is a special case. I don't remember demons ever blockading the camp and not letting anybody out. It's a disgrace. Are you going to risk your inner peace?"

"Hell yeah!" we replied in unison. A tad dramatic perhaps, and Argalot limited his reaction to a wry grin.

"Well, lads, what can I tell you?" He scratched his horns pensively. "The training camp was opened on this island for a good reason."

"Yes, we know." Eredani interrupted the archdemon, urging him on and trying to show off his own knowledge: "Your island, like many others, is a reproduction of Keshin, yes? Somewhere here is a cave where we can find a clue to those three heroes."

"Well I never! Good lad!" Argalot grinned. "That makes the job considerably easier. You need to go to that cave. If you're lucky, you'll take the essence, be promoted to the rank of demon hunter, and find a beacon with information about one of the heroes."

"And if we're not lucky?" I asked, latching

onto his subjunctive mood.

"Then the level-eleven demons together with all four archdemons will chase you out of the Cave of Knowledge and away to the Gray Lands."

"How can we make sure the archdemons don't find out anything about us?"

"You can't. That's why they're here." The chances of this escapade ending successfully had just slimmed drastically.

"Does anybody else live in the cave?" asked Eredani, as usual not letting even the most unobvious details slip away.

"No. Nobody alive. Only dead. Not ghosts, though." Argalot faltered, distracted.

"Is it another Barrows of the Fallen?" I asked, to which he shrugged his shoulders ambiguously. "Is there a guardian?" A shake of the head.

"Kvalen, what guardian has an army like that?" Eredani asked me, while trying to make a call. "Diabettis, greetings! Are you in the camp?"

"We've got an order for T'Mir. Get a move on," came the speakerphone response.

"The training camp is surrounded by demons. Fifty elder R'Tan magi." A heavy sigh from the amulet. Mobs were well known to Diabettis and his fighters. "You can't go back. We need covering fire for about eight hours. We need everyone there is, plus whoever you're boosting at the moment. We're going for R'Tan's lands."

"How are you going to get through Dorel's Frontier?" the player asked. We looked at Hermit – we'd never heard of it, but because the conversation was between players, we had to repeat the questions to Argalot:

"What is Dorel's Frontier, and how can you pass through it?"

"It's a wall dividing the island into two parts. It's protected by level-nine-ten demons. You can't just walk through it. The only way is underground."

"Did you hear that?"

"Uh-huh. Count us in! We haven't been beyond the frontier. Six hundred gold an hour, and we're all yours. I'll just ask the others." Nobody turned down free experience.

Eredani looked at the map, pinpointing the place, and said, "We meet at the westernmost point of the Lake of Tranquility in one hour." Diabettis confirmed and signed off.

"Brody, I know you have to work today, but right now we can't pass up this chance. With the Vartalinskys at the camp, we can get to the cave. By the system clock it's one o'clock in the morning. We meet at two, but we should be finished by six."

"I'm in." I nodded as casually as I could. I had always considered myself pragmatic, devoid of emotion. Every last action was measured, contemplated, recorded. But the thrill of the chase had gotten to me, and I was beginning to understand how people became hooked on Barliona – the yearning for new experience and sensation worked better than any marketing manager.

"You have to work out for yourselves what to do in the Cave of Knowledge." Hermit waited for the end of the conversation and started our lesson. "I'm only going to improve your chances."

Abilities received

Wicked strike: *You jump toward the enemy from a distance of no more than 10 meters and inflict damage to their feet, decelerating them for 6 seconds by 50% and inflicting 20% damage from your Attack parameter. Application time: 0 seconds. Recoil time: 30 seconds.*

Retreat: *You recoil 10 meters, invoking Demon Snares. All enemies entering snare coverage area (1 meter) decelerate for 6 seconds by 50%, and sustain 10% damage from your Attack parameter. Snare duration: 3 seconds. Application time: 0 seconds. Recoil time: 30 seconds.*

Aura of Despair: *Accuracy of enemy inside aura coverage area reduced by 10%. Coverage radius: 15 meters. Aura duration: 20 minutes. Application time: 0 seconds. Recoil time: 60 minutes.*

"There's no time to train you." In one fell sentence Argalot denied us free experience, without granting us the standard tasks. I placed two buttons on the quick access toolbar and checked they worked. There was nobody to test Wicked Strike on, but Retreat had interesting mechanics. After activation, my feet jumped by themselves into the depths of the cave, with no effort whatsoever on my part. After waiting for the recoil, I used it again, this time jerking backward with full force. The result was fantastic: I flew back much farther than ten meters – although the dimensions of the Hermit's dwelling didn't allow me to get a precise reading – until an unexpected wall got in the way of the experiment.

Eredani: *Finished prancing, goat-boy? Get a move on, we're out of time.*

Kvalen: *It needed testing. What do you think "understand essence" means?*

Eredani: *What do you mean what? We're tieflings. We've just fought demons and raked it in big time. That shouldn't happen. +50% to damage to demons and -50% damage from demons, that's what it was about. The specifics of our race haven't been activated yet.*

Kvalen: *Hmm... I hadn't thought of that.*

Eredani: *That's Barliona for you. You either jump, or you think. It's hard to combine the two."*

"The passage was dug a long time ago, when the frontier still belonged to us. Nobody knows who or what might have made it their home since then, but it's the only chance for a small group to pass through. The entrance is here."

Map updated
Description of changes: *Entrance point to underground tunnel under Dorel's Frontier.*

"Kind of pointless training, but it can't be helped," Argalot sighed. "You'll have to study the rest by yourselves in the wide world."

Continue Collaborative Tuition task completed

Reward:

- *Experience: +43*
- *Reputation with Light of Barliona faction: +18*
- *Agreeability to Hermit: +20*

"Dearest Argalot, I am banking on your wisdom and magnanimity. Permit an unworthy to ask a question," Eredani piped up, bowing. His tone was so out of character Hermit and I could only gawk at him. Satisfied he had the NPC's attention, he continued, "We are but dust beneath your feet, O Supreme One! Share with us your wisdom, O mightiest of demon hunters! Tell us how we may gain the remaining objects to complete the Unending Happiness set. Help us save Barliona!"

Argalot squared his shoulders, seduced by the player's crude flattery.

Kvalen: *Who's a clown now? Are you all like this here?*

Eredani: *The end justifies the means.*

Kvalen: *End? Flattering a digital code in order to receive another digital code is an "end" in your book?*

Eredani: *Brody, it's a game, a farce, a fairy tale. That's the whole point. Twist and turn to get a* result. *At the end of the day, I'm flattering, not ass-licking! Do you feel the difference?*

Kvalen: *I feel it, but I don't see it.*

Eredani: *Shut up!*

"The remaining objects are not so easy. You have to accomplish a great deed."

"We shall return Dorel's Frontier," Eredani suggested, thrusting out his chest. "We shall annihilate all the demons and raise the banner of the Light of Barliona. The passage will once more belong to Barliona."

I was never going to understand these people. What nonsense! I prayed for someone to kill me before my eardrums burst from the pathos.

"There are currently 222 level-nine demons at the frontier. If you can banish them to the Abyss and hold out until reinforcements arrive, another object will be yours," announced Argalot. The system reacted instantly.

Task received: Dorel's Frontier

Description: *A class-specific rare task. Destroy 222 demons at Dorel's Frontier and fend off attacks until supervisor Tarlin arrives.*

Reward:

- *Experience: +5*
- *Reputation with Light of Barliona faction: +1*
- *1 object from Unending Happiness set*

"There's no need to raise the banner. Go, tieflings, and may the Light be with you!"

Buff received
Argalot's blessing: *Your characteristics are increased by 50% for 1 hour.*

I couldn't help laughing, but a blessing is a blessing. At that moment Eredani and I were the terror of the local demons, but as soon as we arrived at the meeting point, the buff would be disabled. Argalot was the epitome of bureaucracy – useless rewards while-u-wait.

Diabettis and the Tishkin family had managed to level up to thirteen. Their previous hirers had boasted level seven. With our modest five we soon became lost in the crowd, but only until Diabettis's eagle eyes clocked Argalot's breastplate. From then on, the mercenary couldn't help giving it the occasional appreciative glance as he and the Tishkins whispered among themselves. In the end he succumbed: "Can you show me its properties?"

I was going to refuse, but to my surprise Eredani promptly sent him a description of the object. Diabettis, impressed, scratched his head and made another suggestion: "We boost you up for free, and you tell us where and how you came by this object. Deal?"

Poor Diabettis! I could only feel sorry for him when Eredani unleashed his profit-securing skills. The savvy tiefling demonstrated Argalot's task, which had no restrictions on being passed to other players, and the hired guns were ours, lock, stock, and barrel. The situation played out very amusingly – Diabettis was ready to pay us to participate in the task. Eredani, however, didn't get too brazen, deciding that the partnership was worth more than a couple of hundred gold. In the end we agreed they would help us for free, and we'd divvy the loot up fairly, the only restriction being that we would not become sidetracked – the sole purpose of the trip was to slaughter demons.

Four stray players also wanted the task, but Eredani wasn't down with it. Five thousand gold, or stand aside and don't attract unwanted attention. They had free experience and mob loot to spare.

Dispensing with the formalities, we jogged toward an accumulation of bald cactuses, christened the "Forest of Valor" on a whim of the developers. Yasya and Maestro went ahead as icebreakers and took the first mob strikes on themselves, but the plan soon went awry. Eredani and I were the juiciest morsels for the level-five beasties, and every last parasite considered it their duty to spit a web or something grosser at us, if not actually catch us and eat us alive. Three groups of ten demons held us up for ten minutes, although they did bring us our long-awaited level six. Shame there was no loot, only worthless garbage, unusable and unsalable. After boosting Luck and Trade, I pointed in the direction of a small clearing.

"The entrance is there."

"You got lucky, we've already cleared this wood." Diabettis stood with us and sent Yasya and

Maestro on a recce mission. "Every seventy-two hours, a particularly fat spider is reborn in this clearing, and you have to mess with it for a while, because it spits spiderwebs. It was whacked just yesterday. Have you all got Health elixirs?"

Everyone but myself and Eredani nodded.

"We'll settle up later." Diabettis gave us two flasks of a red liquid each. "It restores five thousand Health, and is only to be used for emergencies."

Eredani: *Now that's concern for the success of an enterprise. In terms you might understand, minimization of basic risk by drawing up a smart response strategy. Learn, student, learn!*

Kvalen: *I already get that you're a shitty adviser. Should I deduct your bonus or something as a precaution? Why didn't you say I'd have to buy it?"*

We were distracted from our potential shouting match by Maestro, who, leaning over the roots of a tree and raking twigs aside, shouted joyfully, "I've found it!"

In among the roots was a brown stone trapdoor, well hidden – if you weren't looking for it, practically invisible among the red sand and stones. Maestro and Yasya dragged it aside to reveal a dark narrow vertical shaft. And from deep under the ground came a bone-chilling groan. We all exchanged glances.

"First man go. Torch," commanded Diabettis, and Maestro didn't hesitate to dive into the hole. Commercial players were proving themselves more and more to be real pros, prepared for any hardship.

Maestro: *Clear! Come on down. It's a wide*

corridor.

The tunnel recalled a sewer shaft. Hewn from the rock, it had sturdy metal steps making the descent easy, and led down three meters to a wide and rather gloomy cave. The light from our one torch was not enough to chase the darkness completely away, but we could see hanging chains, spiderwebs, and tree roots breaking through the bedrock.

"I put the stone back. You never know." Diabettis came down last and produced a second torch. "Yasya, you take point. Maestro, you bring up the rear. Eredani and Kvalen go in the middle. It's that way."

"Light over here!" said one of the players, bending down to the floor. I craned my neck to look over their shoulders, and saw a decomposed human skeleton. The lightest brush and it would crumble to dust. The long groan repeated from down the corridor, and this time we could clearly make out the word "Alive." The players backed up, but not our hirelings. Yasya raised the torch above her head, trying to shed light as far as possible. Which wasn't far – three meters.

Diabettis said, "Maestro, go with Yasya. Take the torch. I'll go last. Move forward slowly."

"Let me out of here!" One of the players screamed hysterically and clung to the wall. "I'm not going any farther. Where's that damn ladder? Let me out!" Before we had time to react, he ran back into the darkness. A short cry, the sound of someone hitting the ground, and the player's frame went blank.

"A dumb way to die," Diabettis said matter-of-factly and looked at the other three. "Are we going to have problems with the rest of you?" Their simultaneously shaken heads were like something from a synchronized swimming program.

"Excellent. Yasya, move out."

"Careful with the walls." Eredani warned. "The ceiling didn't fall down accidentally. Find a clip from a second before the collapse."

Yet again my partner demonstrated the advantage of intellect over action, figuring out what had happened in a matter of seconds. I watched the video clip. The panicked player had run with his arms out wide, knocked something protruding from the wall, and triggered a rockslide. Maestro studied the wall and delivered a clear-cut verdict that it was the lever of some mechanism. We moved cautiously forward and found several more traps, some with triggers on the walls, some on the floor. You had to give the frightened player his due – he helped us avoid a bunch of problems.

Fifty meters on, we encountered a difficult situation.

"Which way do we go now?" Diabettis was standing at a T-junction. The passage split into two identical corridors, to the right and left, although according to the map we needed to go straight ahead. We hesitated, a brief examination of the corridors making nothing clearer. A decision needed to be taken, so I took the responsibility upon myself and said:

"We go right." All seven players stared at me

expecting me to justify my choice. "The right hand rule. The principle of getting through a labyrinth. When there's no other logical choice, that's the rule to go by."

While everyone was figuring out how to react, a strangled whisper emerged from the left-hand corridor: *Alive here! Quickly! Come to them! Alive!*

"Yasya, quick, but careful!" ordered Diabettis. "Maestro, rear guard."

The right-hand corridor weaved like a drunken hare. Tripwires, levers, and slabs to avoid stepping on – it was more like a treasure trail than a secret passage. Unfortunately, we lost another two players. Accident or simple lack of diligence, one slipped next to a pressure slab and sat down on it, triggering a huge spear to fly over his head. He got away with a slight scare, but the friends walking next to him were skewered, ready for spit-roasting. Their recently acquired level eight didn't help. Diabettis gave a heavy sigh. Three fighters down, and we hadn't yet reached Dorel's Frontier.

The evil whisper was a constant reminder to keep moving, and eventually we came out into a wide hall. Diabettis cross-checked with the map. "Dorel's Frontier is directly above us."

They are close! Quicker! They're alive! The whisper was very close now, coming, it seemed to me, from the entrance to the hall.

"The staircase!" shouted Diabettis. "Up! Maestro, stay here and cover us!" And so the sacrifice was determined. Yasya flew up the steps and busied herself with the upper hatch. Dull thuds and scattering dust indicated progress being made, but time was pressing.

"Let me have a go," suggested the last of the random players. "I can barely stand. I want to sleep."

We are here! Alive! There they are! Light streamed into the hall from the passage, radiating from the ghosts of humans, elves, orcs, and dwarves. Even in death the defenders of Barliona could not come to terms with defeat. They swept toward us in a great white tidal wave.

"Everyone up!" shouted Diabettis, before falling flat on his face and activating Retreat. The function worked superbly, throwing him high toward the ceiling and leaving snares where the player lay. An interesting use of the mechanics. Eredani and I looked at each other and did the same. Diabettis caught us in the air and dragged us into the passage, Maestro followed us, and Yasya quickly pulled the heavy stone back into place. The frame of the player left below went blank instantly; the ghosts were anything but well-meaning. A stupid death. Completely unnecessary.

"There's a spell on the rock. It's safe here," said Yasya, speaking for the first time since we'd met. Low, as though three-packs-a-day, her voice was better suited to a worldly-wise lady of fifty than a young girl.

"Location Dorel's Frontier." Diabettis looked at the properties on the map. "You guessed correctly with that right turn."

"I reckon the result would have been the same

if we'd gone left," I said. "The ghosts started whispering after we took the turn."

"A door." Diabettis again spoke brokenly, before lifting his torch and illuminating the space we found ourselves in. It was a stone oubliette, a few metres square. One door, one passage. Nothing else.

"I propose we continue tomorrow," Diabettis said after checking with the clock. "We need sleep. We've been working non-stop for nearly three days. Our reactions are slow."

"No complaints here," said Eredani. "Tomorrow after four. We need to chill too."

Diabettis left Eredani the torch and nodded to the Tishkins, who immediately melted away to reality.

"Can I ask a question?" I managed to say, before the hired killer followed his troops out. "Was it you who levelled up Braksed and Kurtune? What are they like?"

"Yes, twice. Thoroughly okay guys. They have their foibles, but who doesn't? Quiet, responsible. I had no problems with them. They paid and went on their way. Good clients. Sorry, I can't give you any more details, we have our principles."

"No worries," I replied, surprised. It was strange that our image of the Vartalinskys was so inconsistent with Diabettis's.

Eredani stayed to while away the night in solitude, and I stepped out of the pod, didn't undress, and fell onto my bed. My alarm clock went off three hours later, telling me to get up and off to work. My body protested, as did my eyes.

"Bro, are you going to work?" Matty's voice penetrated through the layers of sleep. "Hey, Mr. West!"

"Eh?" I sat up, abruptly awake. Alarm clock! My phone showed half an hour had passed. "I'm on it. Thanks for the call."

"No problem." Only now did I notice he was standing in the doorway, cleanly shaven and dressed to kill.

"Where are you off to?"

"I've got to pop out for a couple of hours. I'll tell you later." He took a swig of coffee, looked at the clock and, on the way out the door said, "Don't go back to sleep!"

Coffee and breakfast would have to wait until the office. I climbed into the car, pressed the Work button on the GPS, and fell asleep.

At work I was met with the unpleasant news that my group had been reshuffled, just the one problem child remaining from yesterday's newcomers. He didn't react to any attempt to establish contact, answering irrelevantly and withdrawing into himself. The new kids were a quiet lot too, as if they'd been selected for a failed facsimile of yesterday's group. I was forced to take the reins from the newly self-effacing Helen and manage the group myself. The lesson wasn't great and I let the students go early. When everyone had dispersed, Helen came to me.

"Brody, do you have any homework for me?"

"No. The next topic's easy. Go home and chill."

She sighed and stepped closer. "Brody... Bro, are you busy this evening?" Her full-on gaze made me feel uneasy.

"Very."

"What a pity," she sighed again. "You know, I've wanted to tell you for ages... you're so clever. It's so interesting to be with you. I'm so glad you came to our company and we're together now. I've never met a man like you before."

She extended a hand to my chest, and I took a couple of steps back. That was all I needed! The pause dragged – she drew her horns in but didn't retreat. Not good. I took her hand and led her to a huge mirror. "Helen, what do you see?" I asked in my office tone.

"We-e-ell, I see a respectable, interesting man and... a no less interesting girl," she said, batting heavily lined and shadowed eyes at me. She flirted so childishly I felt sorry for her.

"Someone has a problem with their perception of objective reality," I said harshly. "Personally, I see a mature old Winnie the Pooh and a little Piglet. The best I can offer is to buy you a big balloon. Would you like blue or green?"

Helen blushed and retracted her hand. "Pi... piglet yourself!" she threw back, turning and running out. The only thing I regretted was not having done it the day before. You had to nip these things in the bud, and without excess snivelling. I wasn't interested in children.

Maria came in. "Brody, it's good I found you alone."

"Maria," I interrupted. "There were no hints from my end."

"You mean Helen?" She adjusted her glasses quizzically and waved a hand. "I've just seen her in tears. Pay no heed. You're her third prince this month. It's an age thing."

"Yes?" I was surprised at her womanish levity. "Well, that's okay then. I really don't need that right now."

"God bless you. We have more important problems. A suicide case has made himself known."

"And what do we do?" I was shaken by the news. It's not that such events were rare for the times. On the contrary, statistics showed big mental health problems emerging in society. Usually sufferers were put in a pod for therapy under total control of special Imitators.

"You do nothing. I'm just letting you know so you can make allowances in your lessons. Psychologists are already working with him – in the guise of the fellow candidates you saw today. Don't hinder them, just present your material and forget about it. They know what they're doing. And don't let Helen into that group."

"I hear you loud and clear, Maria. I'll be discreet. Can I ask you something?"

"Why?" she guessed. "Because he's a genius, Brody. Such people need looking after. They're chosen by God, and we need them."

She made her exit and left me to my bewilderment. What other surprises could I expect from the company? I didn't want to think about it.

And I had no desire to keep coming to work. Perhaps I should become a Diabettis and live solely for pleasure?

Returning home, I opened the auction and flicked through beginner spell scrolls. Five players against 222 demons wasn't an easy ratio to reconcile oneself with. I chose the most indispensable one and called Buy-Sell. The time had come to splash a little cash.

Chapter 7

WHEN I ENTERED Barliona, Eredani was entertaining himself with his demon fish.

"Now round!" The beastie span on the spot.

"Good boy! Beg!" The handler teasingly lifted the tidbit higher.

"Fo-o-od!" the pet responded plaintively.

My partner expertly mimed a deep three right into its maw, which was followed by satisfied chomping and a yawn.

"And you had the nerve to complain about your demon," I sniggered. "You can chill in front of the fish tank, enjoy a water show, play basketball, all the while levelling up your marksmanship. Advantages all-round!"

"Carl, sleep!" he ordered, and deactivated the demon. "Kvalen, clever people are clever because they find the advantages in everything. Why are you so early?"

In lieu of an answer I opened my mailbox and pulled out a stack of spell scrolls. I hadn't taken many, because they were pricey, but even a dozen frost strikes, decelerations, and weakenings significantly increased our chances of crossing the frontier.

Eredani reacted coldly to my purchase,

merely nodding and taking his share. When I produced the remaining objects, however, he perked up. Not at the thirty health-restoring elixirs, but rather at the bags. A somewhat expensive luxury at fifteen hundred per item, but any self-respecting player was obliged to acquire decent storage space. You never knew when Barliona would present a gift.

"I figured you wouldn't buy clothes," he grumbled, attaching his five bags to his belt.

"If you're going to whine, I'll take them back," I warned him before reporting: "It looks like everyone's gone mental with kit. Any overlooked unusual object costs upward of three hundred gold, and no one gives a shit that it's beginner. Never mind rares. Do you know how much a replica of my pickaxe costs? Three thousand! Three fucking thousand gold! What for?"

"For the possibilities, Kvalen, for the possibilities," Eredani laughed. "There's not many can mine demon ore. I'm surprised it's so cheap."

"There's nothing surprising about it," said Diabettis out of nowhere. "When they introduced the new materials, almost every raid produced objects to mine them. And the lower the level, the more frequently. They stopped giving away freebies three months ago, but everyone who needed them got their objects. Guys, is it okay if we start a bit earlier?"

No objections. Within a minute Yasya was working her magic with the lock, cursing her hands colorfully. Lockpicks flared up and snapped one after another, and only at the thirtieth attempt was the girl illuminated in white, opening Burglar for herself.

The door flew open so quickly the hireling didn't have time to move, and it smacked her in the face. In the doorway stood a level-nine R'Tan guardian demon pointing a spear at us, and stuck out to the sides were the weapons of demons crowded behind him. Outwardly the mob was not so different from the magi I'd seen, except he had more armor. He was just the same immense four-eyed creep.

Without dramatic pause they attacked. A coordinated strike from seven lances pierced the protection of the nearby Maestro, and his HP went yellow. "Bastards! Bet, agro!" he shouted, jumping aside.

Diabettis dealt the demon a wicked strike, knocking him back a couple of steps, before jumping away so the enemy spears had only empty space to penetrate. Regaining her bearings, Yasya repeated her boss's actions and shoved the horned foe back further. A black flourish appeared by the mob. Eredani had summoned his pet to assist the hirelings.

Berating myself for my confusion, I tardily summoned Aniram and activated demon strike. Everything had to be done carefully, because in that tight space coordinated actions risked turning into pandemonium.

Damage inflicted
You have inflicted 211 damage: (291 magic

attack) - 80 (protection from R'Tan's guardians). Health remaining: 116 out of 900

This was followed by another strike from Eredani, which dispatched the first demon to the Abyss. The doorway was immediately occupied by a second, not allowing the hirelings room to maneuver, although having one spear less to deal with was a blessing. The demons defended themselves well, valiantly even, but only at close quarters. Two long-range weapons afforded them no chance. Diabettis and his guys jumped about like grasshoppers, eluding lances and allowing us to do our work. Three dark flourishes, and my Experience points crept up, easing me toward level seven. The last two demons were felled by the hirelings, the difference in level coming into play. Without the support of their brothers in arms, the beasties couldn't defend themselves properly, and the agile players were able to duck the spears and zero in on their torsos to finish them off. Even an inoffensive flick of the finger from a level-thirteen player would cause fatal cerebral concussion to a level-nine creature.

Dorel's Frontier task progress
You have destroyed 7 out of 222 demons.

"Level seven? That was quick." Maestro was surprised and looked me up and down, before asking, "Gems?"

"Maestro, keep your mind on the job."

Diabettis reined him in.

"Yes, yes, I get it." Maestro backed down and added flippantly, "Whatever. I don't care. What's the difference to me if we have donators with us or not." If this last remark was addressed to me, the hireling would be waiting a long time for an answer. I couldn't give a damn what he thought about me.

"Kit yourselves up. It's stupid going any further naked." Diabettis pointed at the bodies on the floor. Yasya had already examined the guardians, and returned her pithy verdict:

"Junk." She was right. Demon blood was completely useless. There was so much of it at auction that a set of ten measuring cylinders cost a gold.

Trophy clothing and weapons were packaged as universal blanks. A belt, for example, was called a "standard-quality belt suitable for your class." With plugs like that, a heavyweight could find plate armor, nimble and artful players – leather, and all the rest – cloth. You took the blank in your hands, pressed the Embody button, and it was transformed by the system into a common object.

"What level is your Luck?" asked Eredani.

"Twelve now."

"Open all blanks then. We'll see how much the system likes you."

"Why don't you do it yourself?"

"Resilience was more important for me. I'm dead meat without it. Open them."

There were only seven significant objects among the loot. I began to embody them, and the first results didn't inspire optimism.

Demon guardian pauldrons
Description: *A   common   object.*
Material: thin leather
- *Protection from physical attack: 10*

Objects made from cheap materials were useless, providing no real protection, esthetic value, or pleasure. If I was wearing so much as a single rag, I wouldn't look at that garbage. However, naked as I was, ten protection points was more than I had. A belt, a pauldron, and another belt. Common objects appeared one after another, which was utterly demoralizing, so when a bright sun materialized in my hands, I nearly cast it aside.

Demon-guardian gauntlets
Description: *An   unusual   object.*
Material: thin leather
- *Protection from physical attack: 15*
- *+1 agility*
- *-10% damage from demons*

My Luck shot up by six points. Diabettis was by my side in an instant with a questioning look. The properties of the object had been relayed to the group chat, and grabbed the interest of the hireling.

"Intellect is more important for me, agility second," I replied to the unspoken question. "Are they better than yours?"

Diabettis hesitated before sending me a description of his outfit. On his hands he wore a common object of thick leather with +20 to physical protection. No bonuses.

I looked back at the loot. Three hundred gold, and with that bonus it would be five. Something unpleasant was beginning to stir inside, reminding me of my own personal gain – I could collect scores of objects and furnish Matty with an extra five months of life in reality. Even if he didn't find work within six months. While the hirelings rejected the loot, logic dictated that the better equipped they were, the greater our chances of pulling off the mission. I gave the gauntlets to Diabettis. I had never been begrudging, but on occasion I could reasonably niggardly. There was no need for that now.

"Take them. Consider them our contribution to the common victory."

"Consider them considered." The hireling happily accepted them and swapped them for his own. My Charisma scale, which had idled the past two weeks, leaped into life. The same six points, but the ball was rolling, which got me thinking about levelling up. Magnanimity and absence of miserliness toward other players were unprofitable, but entirely instrumental.

Next was the turn of the common objects, which delighted me infinitely. Eredani explained that if you had luck, each standard embodiment increased your luck percentage in the future. Which is why I approached the last and seventh object with hope. A weapon.

Don't let me down, baby! I said to myself and pressed the button. A bright sun burned in my hands. Barliona had graciously answered my call.

Demon guardian glaive

Description: *An unusual object.*

Material: aspen

- *Damage: 50 (physical)*
- *+1 intellect*
- *+15% damage to demons*

"Mine!" I shouted after reading the description. Flailing the glaive about in the narrow corridors of the frontier was awkward, but it was the additional parameters of the weapon that were more important. The hirelings laid no claim to it, but Eredani sighed peevishly – it would have been handy for him too.

While I was inspecting the objects, Yasya examined the room. She looked in every drawer and every corner, knocked on the walls and inspected every cranny, and even shifted the table in the hope of finding a secret passage. Nothing. Her scrupulosity was winning me over rapidly.

When she opened the next door, she immediately sprang back, instructed by bitter experience. No strike followed, and she cautiously pulled the handle toward herself. "Corridor clear. Cover me." Assured there were no obstacles, we piled through. Prison cells lined both walls, looking like cattle pens with floor-to-ceiling steel bars providing a wonderful view of the phlegmatically chewing beastie inmates. At the will of the Creator, these fluffy yellow basketballs had three eyes and a long beak. Our presence did not affect their behaviour one iota and, eyeing us vacantly, they continued to annihilate the dry branches carpeting the floor.

"Prixis," Eredani whispered and stepped closer.

"Some kind of household pet?" I asked, brushing a cobweb from the bars to get a better view.

"Nah, vermin. Omnivorous beasts, a notorious plague – they eat everything in sight. I know a dozen locations in Malabar alone fighting a constant battle with these pests. They breed faster than rabbits and aren't picky. Leave one pair alone, and in a week there'll be a hundred. But what good are they to demons?"

"How clever and perceptive am I?" I snickered. "Remember when I was parleying with Aniram, she was surprised archdemons stay in Barliona and aren't exiled to the Abyss? Well, here's your answer. Bog-standard sacrifice on a mass scale. They steal their souls and feed their remains to lower demons or the prixis themselves."

"Possibly, possibly...," Eredani shrugged, not wanting to acknowledge this obvious fact.

"Thirty cells. All clear. No demons. No loot. Two doors." Yasya had managed to slip to the end of the corridor and back while we stared at the prixis.

Her manner of speech amused me. It was as though she'd just flown in from Lakoniki. Pragmatic and concise. I wondered if Maestro knew how lucky he was.

Both doors opened onto a spiral staircase running steeply upward. Choosing the right-hand one, we ascended two full turns and came up against a massive mesh gate. No levers, no locks. The landing was empty and the other end was blocked by an identical barrier.

"Maestro, lend me a hand." Diabettis and his partner leaned their shoulders against the thick wires and tried to raise the gate, but it was a non-starter – it didn't a budge a millimeter.

"Do my eyes deceived me, or is that a rope?" asked Maestro, peering into the darkness beyond the mesh. We all pressed our faces to the wires.

"Definitely. Look, it's a counterbalance," said Diabettis, pointing up to the ceiling at the hoist mechanism. The rope was tied to an extinguished torch and merged excellently with the wall.

"Is there anything to cut it with?" Eredani asked.

"You won't reach it with a spear. Maybe throw something... It's too thick. A knife won't cut it."

"How about like this?" My partner squeezed his hands between the wires and activated a frost strike. The torch and the wall became covered in hoarfrost; the spell had hit right at the base. Seeing no result, Eredani tsked and shook the grate.

"Fire would be a good thing at this point. Burn the freaking rope and be done with," I griped.

"We're missing something," said Diabettis, leaning his back against the gate. "They can't have designed the frontier so you can only cross it with a crossbow. Think, guys think. What did we see on the way here?"

A ruckus from below – the prixis had evidently polished off the twigs and begun gnawing the fat trunk of the tree. The sound triggered an associative chain reaction in my head. "We're missing the prixis! It's obvious! We let those rapacious beasts in here, and they'll eat the rope."

"Ridiculous. They can't fly, never mind climb the walls." Eredani waved away my suggestion, and the others were also sceptical.

"All that deep three practice wasn't a total waste of time then?" I was proud of my stroke of genius and wasn't about to back up. "Maestro, shall we go and fetch a couple of prixis?"

The hireling raised his eyebrows questioningly at Diabettis. The latter nodded, and the former followed me, bringing Yasya with him. Subordination was above all else with true hired guns.

"I think a couple should do, Maestro," I ordered, standing aside.

"Eh? Oh no, after you, messieur! We're here to help you, not to do the work for you," the hireling snorted and folded his arms.

His words had an element of truth. It was my idea, and I had to set an example. Drawing the bolt, I entered the first cell. The fluffballs began to growl their suspicion, then huddled together and froze.

"Quack-quack, peck-peck!" I slowly herded them into a corner, trying to recall how to address pet birds. "Come here, you yellow bitches! Maestro, don't just stand there. Do these beasts bite or anything?"

"Sharp as a razor, I see. Act first, ask questions later," the hireling guffawed. Don't fret. They can only peck you, but you can butt them with your horns. I'm off for a hunt in the next cell." Yasya went with her husband, while I readied myself for the final push. My tactic was: bide my time, then lightning quick grab a pair of prixis by the beak, effectively defending myself by doing so.

When a branch snapped loudly under my foot, the beasties warbled a warning, and it occurred to me that since they could make such short work of a tree, my legs would be a couple of bites' worth.

"You hairy bastards! What's with all the clacking?" Maestro's frustration could be heard through the wall.

"That's a system bonus for your eloquence," I shouted and launch myself at my prey. It all happened very quickly, and not very fortuitously. When I seized my preselected samples, the remainder of the flock kicked up a commotion and laid into to me, battering me with their beaks and feet. I strode to the exit, picking my knees up high like a heron, and burst from the cell with a victory holler.

"Aloha, dilettante!" My feeling of triumph was replaced with pique when I saw Yasya and Maestro waiting in the corridor, both with a brace of prixis in each hand.

We launched them by turns. The plan was to throw the prixis at the torch and convince them to chew through the rope. Never before had I experienced such sporting fever. Under my breath I swore my kinship to each prixi and asked it to die for us in the field.

Kvalen, Yasya, and Diabettis threw wide of the mark. The first hit was Eredani's, but his prixi only got a nibble of the torch before falling to the floor. Only Maestro's pet hit the target and clung there until its purpose was served. The gate lifted with a shrill rasp, and the yellow ball descended to its fellow tribesmen with the end of the rope still in its beak. Before moving on, we shooed all the beasties onto the staircase and kicked them back down so they wouldn't get under our feet.

"What's all this noise?" wondered a voice in the language of the demons, before the gate at the other end of the corridor swung open. I stepped back. In the doorway stood a two-meter demon, similar to Hermit, but for bigger muscles and no painful dark veins on its skin. Mighty, two-winged, with a thick tail and bloodshot eyes, it commanded trepidation, and the long flaming sword in its grip lit the room better than any lamp.

Groundskeeper of Dorel's Frontier. *Level: 9. Class: rare. Health: 9000.*
Abilities:
- *Fireball (recovery time 10 seconds)*

- *Dark entanglement (recovery time 30 seconds)*

Uh-huh. Groundskeeper indeed. *Somebody's either got an original sense of humor or a poor imagination,* I noted to myself. But why "groundskeeper," and not "frontier manager"?

The blazing strokes of the two-handed sword described a danger zone for players – a semicircle that almost reached the opposite wall. It stood to reason that level thirteen wouldn't save anybody from a direct strike, and it wasn't worth asking the hard-baked groundskeeper the way to his office.

Diabettis clutched his glaive so hard his knuckles cracked. A demon with nine thousand HP was not something to be trifled with. We were all going to feel the heat.

Maestro was the first to charge. Bending low, he avoided one swish of the sword before leaping high and striking the demon across the eyes. Or trying to. The groundskeeper wasn't so easy. As a consummate combat aurochs, it met the player with its horns and a stentorian snort, and with a shake of the head threw him against the wall with such force he couldn't get up. Seconds later a fiery sphere flew at the stunned player, giving him no time to duck or run. His body flashed like a sparkler, and a second debuff was added on top of the stun – Burn Up.

"I'll cover! Yasya, fix him!" shouted Diabettis, drawing the agro on himself. The girl tended to her husband, dousing the flames. After a second's confusion I hit the demon with a weakening spell. It bawled menacingly and once more sliced the air with its flaming weapon. Diabettis danced in front of it, dodging sure-footedly, not moving closer. Eredani joined the fray, alternating demon strikes with me.

Damage inflicted

You have inflicted 361 damage: (461 magic attack) - 100 (groundskeeper protection). Total Health remaining: 7,766 out of 9,000

"Woah!" Eredani croaked and looked in surprise at his demon fish. He had happened to deal the groundskeeper a critical strike, and himself become target number one on the agro list. The demon reeled and lowered its sword, allowing the hirelings to skip closer and strike a few times, before it shook itself out of its stupor and glared at Eredani. The tiefling stepped back and swallowed hard. "Quick, somebody take it!" he tried to shout, fear straining his voice as dark root-like sprouts emerged from the floor and enwreathed him up to his waist, bereaving him of the power of movement. He struggled, but became more entangled. Even Retreat didn't help – the bindings slackened but didn't break, and Eredani flew a meter and immediately sprang back. Diabettis distracted the beast with a yell, but it was too late. A deadly burning ball had already left the demon's hands in the direction of my partner.

As if in slow motion, I watched the Tiefling's

eyes widen in terror. He shrank away, throwing his hands up to protect his head, just as Yasya hurled herself at him, hoping to tear him free. She wanted to save her client from a direct plasma hit and rebirth, but she'd never make it in time.

And me? I saved a person from being burned alive, by stepping forward into the path of the fireball.

Damage sustained

Health level decreased by 1,750: 2,000 (fireball) - 250 (magic protection + damage reduction)
Remaining Health: 2,250 out of 4,000
Burn Up debuff received: you receive 200 fire-damage points once every 5 seconds for 1 minute.

It was hot. My ten percent pain threshold let me cope collectedly with the strike, but the ensuing steam-room sensation made me tense up. It was difficult to breathe, and I was forced into a long slow inhale-exhale routine. My eyes watered as if sand had been kicked in them, and my head buzzed. Yasya reacted instantly. Deserting the almost freed Eredani, she skipped over to me, forced my jaws apart, and poured two potions into my mouth: one to restore Health, the second to remove the debuff. Meanwhile Diabettis and Maestro continued their offensive on the demon. Although in truth, not to great effect.

"I'll wait down below," Eredani said out of the blue and disappeared down the stairs. He didn't want to put his health at greater risk, which was understandable.

The absence of one player drastically reduced the speed with which we could destroy the demon. After thirty seconds the groundskeeper began to hammer us for all it was worth, making us flit around it like moths. One careless move and its scorching wings would prevent us from ever completing the task.

However, I was a bee with a demon-strike multi-use stinger.

Damage inflicted

You have inflicted 822 damage: (922 magic attack, critical hit) - 100 (groundskeeper protection). Total Health remaining: 1,934 out of 9,000

"Take that, beastie! The desk jockey is on the warpath! Barliona will be ours!" I emboldened myself.

The critical hit had made me a priority target, and the groundskeeper raged, "Die, traitor!" before ensnaring me for ten seconds and launching a fireball. If the half-weakened strike knocked my Health down by two thousand, it was gruesome to imagine what a full-strength hit might have done. I lurched forward as far as I could and activated Retreat, flying a couple of meters into the air before crashing back down. My restraints didn't snap, but the required result was achieved: the fireball missed. When the dark shoots fell off, the demon hurled another one, which I easily evaded. The tactics for dealing with the boss now clear, I felt confident. A few minutes later I had my baptism of fire with a powerful mob. The beastie fell.

Reference information

Specifics of Barliona mobs

Common mob

- *Health: level * 100*
- *Number of abilities: 0*
- *Experience   coefficient received by player: 1*
- *Size of loot: 1*

Rare mob

- *Health: level * 100 * 5* (number of players / 5 + 1)*
- *Number of abilities: 2*
- *Experience   coefficient received by player: 5*
- *Size of loot: 2*

Raider mob

- *Health: level * 100 * 10* (number of players / 5 + 1)*
- *Number of abilities: 4*
- *Experience   coefficient received by player: 10*
- *Size of loot: 3*

Epic mob

- *Health: level * 100 * 20**

(number of players / 5 + 1)
- *Number of abilities: 6*
- *Experience   coefficient received by player: 20*
- *Size of loot: 4*

When the death toll of Dorel's Frontier demons reached eight, the first thing I did was remove the tally of sustained and inflicted damage from settings. System messages were very off-putting when they repeatedly obscured the viewer.

"Aha! Boots!" exclaimed Maestro hopefully, and an entry appeared in the group chat:

Player Maestro Tishkin discards 57

The hirelings' footwear was common, with no enhancements: minimum protection, maximum discomfort.

Player Kvalen discards 97

"They're collecting luck, while regular guys are running around barefoot," said Maestro in a fit of anger. His mood had plummeted.

"Nobody's stopping you boosting luck too." Eredani was back and on my side.

"Yeah, wicked. One's boosting luck, and the other – cowardice!" Maestro lost his rag and aped Eredani: " 'I'll wait down below!' Jesus!"

"Maestro!" The group leader tried to knock the

crabby hireling down a peg.

"Maestro what? We're all adults here. I don't have to censor myself." Self-restraint evidently ran in the female side of the Tishkin family. Maestro continued to bawl Eredani out: "Do you need it spelling out just what you are? He puts his ass on the line for you, and you do a runner!"

"Diabettis, chill your fighter out. The agreement explicitly defined your work, not our participation. Eredani hasn't violated anything." I understood it was no solution to the conflict, but I couldn't reveal the truth, because it wasn't my secret. Eredani was silent, not wishing to justify himself, which was his right. Curiously, it was Diabettis who came to the rescue.

"A hundred?" he asked Eredani, all attention on the tiefling. The latter's eyelids closed a fraction. "You have to warn us about things like that. We don't poke our noses into other people's business, but we have to consider them in our game plan."

Maestro waited in silence for a righteous decision.

"Yasya, Maestro, we rely only on Kvalen."

"What, that's it?" Maestro was restive. "Then we take all the loot as compensation. That's fair."

"No. We leave everything as agreed," retorted Diabettis.

Maestro didn't react, which spoke of Diabettis's cast-iron authority as leader. Respect! Yasya didn't give a hoot about the infighting. As a true hostess she was sifting methodically through the loot.

"Anything there, Yas?"

"A ring. Rare." She posted a description in the chat. Everybody cast their dice, and the object went to Eredani. The system was taking the piss. He clenched his fists in victory, transforming the blank ring into an object with +1 to Resilience and +10% to pain reduction. For him it was a gift from the gods.

My boots also turned out not half bad. Fashioned from thick leather, they added +6 to Stamina and Intellect, and an extra +5% to critical strike, and basically turned me into a killer. They fitted like a second skin; so comfortable and natural I didn't understand how I'd ever lived without them. Only my hooves remained naked.

"There's more." Yasya continued to gut the groundskeeper, and posted the next object in the chat.

Key. 1 of 4

Not a word more.

We exchanged quizzical looks. No one knew anything.

"There's a secret room somewhere at the Frontier?" Eredani ventured hesitantly, and put the key in his inventory. "What kind of groundskeeper doesn't have a key? We're losing time. Come on, move out!"

Our demon victim had a separate suite of rooms, strewn with all manner of junk. Wading through the mountains of furniture, appliances, and other clutter, we were able to identify the groundskeeper's workplace. Another touch of humor from the developers. For bad is the groundskeeper who considers himself not a general director! In the centre of the huge storeroom stood a no less huge... throne! Behind a desk. Funny.

Yasya set about emptying the drawers, tipping the contents on the floor, and the small objects turned to digital dust before they could reach the mosaics under our feet. Objects in the office were not meant for players.

While the hirelings and Eredani were combing the premises for anything saleable, I scrutinized the documents on the table. Floor plans, graphs of analytical data, descriptions of logistics flows. How I missed all that! Not long ago I'd been a normal person; now I was a fool with digital boots on my digital hooves.

Thumbing through the papers, I found three key points. The graphs were becoming more interesting. Ireness had granted us the ability to understand not only the speech, but also the script of the demons. The first graph showed the dynamics of prixi consumption by year. The second was a breeding plan to supply the frontier with the beasties. The third was a prediction of demon growth. And the fourth – their required feeding volumes.

"What are you doing?" Eredani stood next to me. "We have to go."

"Wait." I was totally engrossed in the papers. Ignoring him, I returned to the table and the floor plans. If this really was the frontier, we were standing at a concentration point of key lines. Which meant the last page was a plan of the floor we were on. A small, yet pivotal moment in understanding what was written. I looked back at the graphs. The dynamics of prixi consumption. Four spates clearly stood out on the overall graph, repeating every month. Four. But only three nodal points. What if the groundskeeper was one of the points? That meant there were rare mobs in possession of the remaining keys.

"We still have three to find," I concluded, proud of myself.

"You only just got that?" said Maestro. "If a key is the first of four, there are three left. True?"

"True, but I know where to look for them."

Everybody stopped. "Did you read that in those papers on the table?" Eredani asked. I nodded and showed him my discovery. My cartography skill did not allow me to visualize the map for the others, but he could do it.

"So what is it?" A 3D projection of the frontier lit up in front of us. The data was incomplete, and much of the space empty, but three red dots immediately arrested all eyes.

"In front of you is a layout of Dorel's Frontier, as the groundskeeper needed it. The dotted line is the way from the place of consumption, i.e. the prixis' enclosure, to the three rare mobs."

"Yasya, not too hastily, but open the door. It's some kind of hall, judging by the size." Diabettis instantly found an application for the map. The girl nodded and set to tinkering with the locks. A quiet click, and through the narrow gap we saw a training room. Just like all creatures in Barliona, demons also needed to hone their skills. The presence of such a hall next to the prixi stables was thoroughly logical. Tired hungry demons had to fortify themselves without having to go too far.

A good few demons were training. We couldn't count them all, but there were definitely several dozen regular warriors.

"Maestro, you take the right flank. Yasya, left. I'll take the middle. Go!"

At last I saw with my own eyes the advantage of our class. Demon hunters specialized in skirmishes in open spaces, where there was room to maneuver, accelerate, and retreat, rather than skewering their chests on lances in a tight corridor. Three lightning flashes danced around the hall, leaving nothing but bodies and loot in their wake. The difference between thirteen and lowly level nine was catastrophic for the latter. Eredani and I could do nothing other than enjoy the process of levelling up. Sixteen demons got me to level eight; nineteen – to level nine. We ran out of opponents before making it to level ten. I couldn't imagine how I was going to live after the nursery without a sixfold increase in Experience.

Dorel's Frontier task progress
You have destroyed 53 out of 222 demons.

"Embody," said Yasya, sending me an

exchange and showering me with blanks. Chestplates, shoulder protectors, belts, gauntlets, weapons. Forty-five objects, all for me, and absolutely gratis. The only downer was the lack of pants and footwear. Eredani continued strutting around the parquet with bare hooves, clip-clopping like a horse.

You could say I'd done my best. As soon as a fantastic common object appeared, the players drew lots and the system automatically took the embodied object from me. Seven out of forty-five – such was the result of my embodiment. I drew myself a pair of gauntlets. Only +1 to Intellect and +15 to protection from physical attack, but thanks all the same.

"Diabettis!" shouted Eredani from somewhere to the right. "Come here!" The whole group responded to the call. He pointed at a door and said, "That entrance was definitely not on the map." Indeed, according to the blueprint there should only have been two exit points from the hall, leading to our key points. The unmarked third door was intriguing.

"This oversight needs correcting," said Diabettis. "Yasya?" She had boosted her burglary skills so much that locks seemed to pick themselves as she drew near. Behind the door was a staircase leading down, and a breeze of cold and nastiness wafted up from wherever it led.

"But we're on the ground floor," exclaimed Maestro in surprise. "Where does it lead? Back to the prixis?"

"Or to the ghosts in the underground passage," Eredani offered. He took out the map of the frontier and added the new route. "Not happening. It's too far."

Yasya leaned over the first step and studied it closely. "It's a trap," was the authoritative verdict. Gesturing us all to move aside, she placed a foot on the first step and activated Retreat. The ceiling caved in, and from among the rumble of crashing stone we heard the clicks of booby traps discharging. When caustic smoke began to belch from the rubble, we hastily retired.

When all was calm and the smoke had dispersed, we approached. The stairway was gone, as was the entranceway.

"At least we don't have to worry about what was down there," noted Maestro joyfully. Eredani didn't share his delight.

"Kvalen, get your pick out."

"What freaking pick?" the feisty player jumped in. "We agreed to cross and clear the frontier, yes? So what's the deal?"

Frankly, the hireling had begun to bore. And although I had no desire to smash rocks, I also couldn't publicly take his side. "Maestro, I've had enough of your shit. Were you hired to clear the frontier or not? So get clearing, and do it quietly. We'll do it like this: when you realize it's no good without me, holler. Meantime, I'll be twirling my pick." I showily produced my tool and hefted it around in my hands.

Maestro gritted his teeth when he heard the

hint at his ineptitude. Diabettis shrugged and said, "We'll cope by ourselves. But this was a bad idea. Do you think the door's just after the first flight?"

"Why not?" Eredani asked. "We're in the nursery. This doorway should be a decoy. To show there's something down there and it's valuable. The traps are evidence of that. I don't doubt there's another entrance which doesn't require digging, but it'll be better protected. We'll stay here."

"Suit yourself. If you get bored, come and join us," said the chief hireling before commanding, "Guys, the right-hand door. Move out."

Before they were out of sight I made the first strike. It was sonorous and accompanied by a shower of sparks, and the pick flew off to the side. This was no demon ore – it needed striking accurately, but straight away I saw the results of my actions: a durability bar appeared by the stone.

Boulder. Durability: 948 out of 1,000

I waited until the hirelings had disappeared from view, before rounding on my partner. "Why the hell am I waving a pick around instead of fighting? You're no warrior, but what does this have to do with me?"

"Brody, chill out. If you want to vent spleen, there's your rock. It'll even do us some good," he replied. "Don't be too hasty in your conclusions. We'll gain experience anyway while the hirelings are keeping their side of the bargain. You're not that much use to them, never mind me. They're just like you and I, earning with their brains. Remember that. You're a future clan chief, not a warrior."

"Is that why I'm swinging my axe now and realizing my own uniqueness?" I nodded at the stone. "Where's the logic in that, Victor?"

"The logic is that while the hirelings are boosting our experience, we're also boosting Strength, Stamina, and Mining. And we'll probably get an extra task too," he said, taking the pick. "Out of the way, grunt! Let the old guard show you how it's done!"

I accepted the partial truth of his order, laughed, and made way for the experienced showoff. We'd see how right he was. I already understood he wasn't your average raider.

We swapped over every three rocks. Not so much because of fatigue, as the monotony. Information concerning acquired experience and the progress of the task continually flashed up before my eyes. The hirelings worked efficiently as a team, and in thirty minutes halved the demon personnel of Dorel's Frontier, gifting myself and Eredani level twelve. I continued to hack away, while keeping yearningly abreast of their achievements.

Dorel's Frontier task progress
You have destroyed 128 out of 222 demons.

"Here was a booby trap with arrows." Another rock glimmered and evaporated, letting us down a step. Fragments of crossbow bolts protruded from the wall. Lots of stones were piled in the doorway, blocking up every hole and unable to fall away.

"Acid over there," I said, pointing out a corroded step.

"And fire there. Look how cunningly the demons hid the flame thrower." A thick layer of soot on the wall confirmed the observation, and a buckled muzzle in the ceiling was still emitting smoke. "Curiouser and curiouser."

"Why demons? What if it was the former proprietors of the frontier?"

"Because the work is crude, as if it was built by migrant workers."

Another rock faded away, and a pile of stones now robbed of support cascaded forward, accompanied by more clicks. A concern suddenly crossed my mind. "Don't you think maybe not all the traps disappeared in the rockfall?"

"No," Eredani barked, smiting the final stone. "No time to think. Only dig."

"Then this is just the right time," I muttered, trying to make out anything at all beyond the dark turn of the stairway. Pressing on without thoroughly checking would be extremely stupid.

We reached the second flight quicker by rolling the stones ahead of us instead of smashing them. The stairway turned again, revealing that our goal lay deeper than the underground passage. At the bottom of the last flight was a door. A perfectly normal door, wooden, with steel rivets and no frills, not even a visible lock. Just grip the round handle and open. Having first, of course, descended forty death-laden steps without a single stone – by this time they were all gone. I estimated we'd dug deep enough and the door should be on the same level as the prixis.

Diabettis: *Kvalen, Eredani, what have you got?*

Eredani: *Nothing yet. Still digging. What about you?*

I sniggered. Goddamn conspirator.

Diabettis: *We're past the first mini-boss. A rare ring. Roll the dice.*

While we were digging, I was interested to observe the traffic lights of the hirelings' frames. From green, denoting relative safety, they fell to yellow or even red, only to return immediately to green. They dropped to red only after the battle with the mini-boss, which spoke of its strength.

The ring went to Yasya, and I would have given my right arm to be next to her just then to see her reaction. I wondered if she accepted the loot with her inherent aloofness, or jumped for joy like a normal woman. Did she take joy in rings at all? Eredani was absolutely delighted with his.

Diabettis: *A rare belt. Roll the dice.*

This time Eredani got lucky, but as soon as he received his loot, he gave it to me. "Take it, it's only fair." I didn't know if it was gratitude for my fireball, but it was silly to refuse. I activated the button, and the sun shone in my hands.

Maestro: *Jeez! Have you dug up someone you can sell your souls to for a wad of cash?*

The hireling's stupefaction was understandable – an epic object was beginning to fade in my hands. Although what was the big deal? I'd seen such things before. Way more important were the properties.

Trainer's belt

Description: *An epic object. Material: thick leather*

- *Protection from physical and magic attack: 40*
- *+8 stamina*
- *+8 intellect*
- *Growth rate of all characteristics increased by 10%*
- *Value of all characteristics scales decreased by 10%*
- *Experience increased by 5%*

Diabettis: *We've got the second key. You can have it later.*

Eredani: *Okay.*

"You know, I'm beginning to think game intellect somehow tells on a player after all. Only plus eight, but I've found an alternative to rocks," I laughed, having thought of a way to deactivate all the booby traps. "The prixis."

"In for a penny, in for a pound," Eredani sniggered. "You're right. Let's go hunting."

He turned out to be a better hunter than me. After quickly catching eight creatures, he offloaded half on me, and we returned to the stairs. The prixis died like heroes, but moved toward the sacred door with the zeal of donkeys. The tree was more appetizing to them than a Big Mac and supersized Coke. The first eight went very quickly, and we had to go back for another eight. Four times. Somewhere in the middle of the process the system peeped that level thirty had been attained, but we weren't to be distracted. The goal was in our sights.

"Ready?" Eredani lifted the handle with his trophy spear. No lightning, no fire, no rockfalls. I nodded. Aniram appeared alongside, and I was ready for the apocalypse.

"Open!" He stepped away from the door, letting me go ahead. Unhurriedly, I pulled the door open. A cold draft; the torches on the walls flickered. The darkness beyond was impenetrable; Eredani passed me one of the torches. The breeze settled, allowing me to squeeze into the doorway and have a nose around.

"Fuck!" I stepped back. It was a crypt. An abundance of decomposed corpses crudely piled into two eternally long mounds disappeared into the black.

Alive! Come quickly! The gruesome moan beckoned. Away in the distance it grew lighter, as an army of undead souls streamed toward us.

"Brody, let's get out of here!" Eredani about-faced and darted back up the stairs without looking round. But I didn't flinch, for I understood that ghosts moved quicker than tieflings. They'd catch us on the second flight. I needed to delay them somehow.

Is it DC day or something? Full-on heroism in underwear, I thought. The torch flame twitched again, and a tiny spark flew into the air and immediately died. With the thought that I had nothing to lose, I lobbed the torch into the middle of the left-hand mound. My chances of being right were one in a million, but today was a day for split-second decisions to produce the right results. The mound burst into flame, and the fire reached the ceiling with such noise and thrust that I stepped back and covered my face from the searing heat.

The ghosts stopped and looked spellbound at the incarnate segment of hell. The fire spread quickly, taking a few seconds to reach the souls, pass them by, and surge on to the end of the crypt. The room was incredibly long, like an aircraft hangar. Surprisingly the second mound didn't catch from the raging armageddon next to it. The aisle down the middle provided complete protection and did not allow the other bodies to ignite.

My hopes were not destined to be realized. The ghosts marched freely through the fire with no consequence whatsoever. It began to die down, and the incorporeal beings remembered their calling – to kill. I turned on my heel, reprimanding myself for not doing so directly I'd thrown the torch, and stopped rooted to the spot, as a transparent, though utterly palpable lance dug into my chest. While I'd been admiring the flames' hypnotic gallopings, a squadron of otherworldly warriors had crept up behind me. The poke intensified, making me shuffle backward.

Alive, a rustling voice called right by my ear, and I span around to see a delegation of three souls standing in front of me. Time and altered state had not withered their charisma. The pellucid beings oozed strength and overwhelming might.

The middle one slowly unsheathed its sword and raised it. I held my breath. My first rebirth would be exotic. Not by the hands of the Vartalinsky thugs, nor by the paws of demons, which would be natural. No, I would have my first rebirth at the hands of those who should not even exist in the nursery. It was kind of absurd. I hadn't crossed the frontier, or entered the cave. I awaited the strike with a deep sense of vexation.

It didn't come. Instead, the ghost saluted me, raised his sword to the ceiling, and vaporized. A sigh of relief echoed around the hangar, and the light dimmed a fraction as half the ghosts vanished in their commander's wake.

Alive! Release us! whispered the remaining beings. An image from a classic film seen long ago swam up in my head – a fighter gains an army of just such ghosts and in doing so decides the outcome of a global battle.

Since I'd been lucky so far that day, I had to try that possibility too. "Help me clear the frontier of demons, and I'll free you. Have your revenge on those who brought this curse upon you."

We can't leave. Seal. Release us.

I could only sigh wailfully and think what else to ask.

Eredani: *What's taking so long?*

Kvalen: *Take a torch and come here. Preferably as quickly as you left.*

"Have you decided to become Aragorn?" Eredani understood the situation instantly.

"My desire alone is not enough," I said and explained how I'd established contact with the ghosts. "They can't leave the dungeon. Display your mastery of negotiation with NPCs. Prove your kung fu is more hardboiled than mine."

"Observe." He took a swing and heaved the torch to the top of the right-hand mound. Flames once more licked high to the ceiling, calling forth a many-voiced gasp of relief, and another marshal of the spectral warrior host took his soldiers off to find their peace.

"I don't get it. What about treasure, secrets, chests, knowledge?" I was dumbstruck.

"Some things, Kvalen, need doing immediately and permanently. I have bitter experience of dealings with ghosts. Two locations completely deserted for a month. My advice to you is, if you see a ghost, dispatch him to the Gray Lands at the first opportunity. No agreements."

The hangar was in near total darkness, the dim light that there was provided by the dozen remaining immaterial beings. *Release us too!* They whispered. I looked around in puzzlement and kicked one of the mounds of ash. There was nothing left to burn. I ran to fetch another torch and walked around the crypt. No niches, no passages. Where were the last of the bodies?

"Do you think running around will make corpses stand up and move?" Eredani laughed.

"So we have to comb the frontier for them?"

Book One: A Second Chance

He nodded and looked at the rest of the castaways. "We'll help you. We'll search for your bodies just as soon as we finish off the demons."

Too long. Release us now!

"You've waited centuries. One more hour won't hurt."

We are drained. Help us!

"Demons first!"

No!!! You help us now, or you'll never help anyone! The ghosts encircled us.

"That's what I was talking about," said Eredani. "Deals with ghosts always come back to haunt you. Okay, okay, we're looking already." This last phrase was meant for the ghosts, who ransacked the dungeon but found no way out. Fortunately the souls themselves wanted to join in the search.

Over here! the ringleader whispered and swam off to the far end of the crypt. Hovering by a wall, it pointed unequivocally to massive rock. With great effort Eredani and I shifted it aside to find another secret passageway or vault. It was dark, so I threw in the torch to give us something to see by, and it landed right in the centre of a "Leap of Faith" installation. Hundreds of tall spikes grew out of the floor and were hung with petrified skeletons. Fire erupted from the hole and scorched my face, making me stagger back and cover it with my hands. It was a good job we didn't have to crawl anywhere. As long as all the corpses were there.

The ghost that led us there whispered, *Tha-a-nk you! The alive helped us. The alive must know.*

Three-two-five-twenty. Search here! Then it saluted and vaporized, departing for its long-overdue rest. The Gray Lands accepted all the defenders, and our maps began to flash furiously, informing us of updates.

Dorel's Frontier task progress

You have completed an additional task, allowing the souls of fallen warriors to find peace.

A hidden bonus for task completion has been activated:

- *+1 object to the Unending Happiness set*

Maestro: *That was just now?*

"An object lesson in the advantage of 'man the thinker' over 'man the raider'," my partner muttered, though he wrote something else in the chat.

Eredani: *Clearing the frontier. What's happening with you?*

Diabettis: *The third boss fell. Arm shields and a belt. Cast the dice.*

Both objects went to the hirelings, which grated somewhat.

The point which now appeared on the map was situated in the lair of the fourth rare demon, so we caught up to the hirelings. They were squatting down by the entrance to the next room and heatedly discussing tactics. Which was odd – level-fourteen players were deciding how to kill the remaining sixteen mobs at the frontier.

"Problems?" I asked, coming closer and peering into the room. Assessing the disposition, I was slightly stunned. The fourth rare mob was a demoness! Which wouldn't have been a big deal, were it not for a number of peculiarities.

> *Groundskeeper's elder wife. Level: 9. Class: rare. Health points: 9,000.*
> *Abilities:*
> - *We gotta talk (recovery time 15 seconds).*
> - *Kiss of jealousy (recovery time 30 seconds, less than 70% of boss's Health required).*
> - *I want one (recovery time 60 seconds, less than 50% of boss's Health required)*
> - *Ballbuster (recovery time 60 seconds, less than 30% of boss's Health required)*
> - *Summon mother-in-law (recovery time 90 seconds, less than 10% of boss's Health required)*

The demoness was standing in front of a mirror and trying to don armor that was obviously too small. Working herself into a frenzy, she pulled so hard the armor burst, enraging her still more. At this point the heinous woman gave the nearest R'Tan magus a weighty clip round the ear, slamming him into a wall, and demanded new apparel. If the magi were not sufficiently compliant, the swish and snap of her whip would be heard. The rare mob had a formidable weapon and used it with filigree precision. The demons did not die, but received lacerations which prompted them to start running quicker around the room.

"Why does she have so many abilities?" I was surprised. "Rare mobs only have two."

"We were surprised as well at first. Presumably a specific of the frontier. Each successive rare mob has one more ability than the previous one. She's the last."

"So what are you sitting here for?"

"The magi. We've got to get them out of the way before we deal with the boss. We're deciding how to do that. It's a small room. Touch one and the rest will get involved," explained Diabettis patiently.

"Have you tried this?" Eredani pulled a prixi out of his inventory. The yellow ball was unconscious, a player's inventory not being the healthiest of places for an NPC. When I looked at him in surprise, I was met with a provocative grin. Like hell there was only one prixi in there! What a diversionist. He'd collected a boatload of the yellow plague so that if necessary he could release them somewhere and initiate a series of elimination tasks.

He flicked the prixi awake, and it immediately began to clack its beak indignantly and try to bite him. The demon closest to the entrance stopped and listened to the strange sounds. Eredani pinched the prixi, making it chatter all the louder, and the magus crept toward the bait. Eredani touched the prixi again, but the demon activated dark lightning in preparation for an attack.

"Fuck!" Eredani swore and shook his hand. The prixi twisted and turned, and bit his finger.

"Have you been collecting loot?" I asked Yasya in a whisper. "Give me a weapon blank." She didn't argue, and I prayed for Barliona to gift me a common object. The system was taken aback at such a strange request, but responded without query. No bright suns or titanic flashes. Everything standard and casual.

"Gnaw on that," I said, putting the glaive on the floor and making it accessible for interaction. Eredani understood me and held the fluffy ball to the shaft, and the corridor filled with the loud crunching of wood. The prixi's beak worked more efficiently than a pulverizing machine.

The demon's four eyes widened in surprise, and it rushed the pest. Although... that's a lie. The demon's eyes widened decidedly more when it was struck simultaneously by three level-fourteen players. It didn't have time to squeak before being dispatched to the Abyss to rail against us indiscriminately.

"Give!" With effort I managed to tear the piece of wood from the prixi's jaws. It squealed angrily, which attracted the attention of the next demon. The situation repeated itself down to the last detail, except that there was nothing left to snatch away from the prixi. The beastie had gobbled the handle of the glaive whole, and the blade vaporized as a now unnecessary element.

"You've got to take it quicker or you won't save up enough loot," said Eredani amiably, watching out for the next magus. The clearing tactic was working.

"Where are my servants?!" screamed the demoness, and the last magus left alive got bustling, upending tables in the process. The waiting phase came to an end, and we proceeded to the active phase. I took aim at the creeping low-life and whacked it with a demon strike, sending it scuttling off to the Abyss. It didn't have a hope against my level thirteen.

"What the hell is going on today?" the demoness said in a huff, before defining her personal space with a crack of her whip. Closer than three meters was dangerous. The hirelings entered the room one by one, pressed up against the wall. The demoness watched them, but didn't react.

"We're staying put." "I'm not going in there." Eredani and I spoke together. The demoness's passive behavior was vexing. And not only for us. Diabettis was turning his head, assessing the situation in the room, and pointing to ledges which could be jumped onto in order to avoid the whip.

"Darling, we gotta talk." The demoness waited a while longer and switched on her first ability. I was drawn into the room against my will. Clutching at the stone projections, I tried not to move, but my legs opposed me, wanting to deliver me to the fair lady. Seizing hold of the doorframe, I also managed to grab Eredani. He was delirious and also gravitating toward her for a serious chat. The We

Gotta Talk debuff was active for just three seconds, but it was plenty for all her enemies to come within striking distance. A swish of the whip, and for the first time I could remember, Diabettis's composure betrayed him.

"Bitch! Attack! Destroy the beast!" The boss's strike was dreadful. All three hirelings lost the power of sight for ten seconds. The whip slashed across their eyes, invoking Blindness, and I squirmed to imagine what they were feeling. Approaching the demoness was not a good idea.

"Tail! Bind!" I shouted. My partner reacted quickly, winding his tail around mine. Aniram and the fish appeared at the same time, and we went to hirelings' much needed assistance. The demoness handled with consummate skill not only the whip, but also her body. The hirelings had only been able to touch her using wicked strike, which they directed at her legs and either sprang immediately back, or felt the sting of her whip. Diabettis waited before nipping at her from close range, but she easily jumped aside and again called her ruthless weapon into action.

A double demon strike made the elder wife totter. Rubbing her breast and pursing her lips, she hissed, "You hurt me, and I trusted you. We gotta talk. Come! I have a kiss for you."

I clung to the door, and my tail immediately tensed. Eredani was still trying to communicate with the demoness. While dragging him back, I noticed she had her sights on Yasya. We Gotta Talk acted on her too. She'd got too close and was now being strangled in the demoness's embrace. She tried to wriggle, but couldn't break loose from the boss's iron grip, and the kiss was reducing her HP. The demoness was drinking the player, like liquid from a vessel.

"I'll kill you, beast! Leave her alone!" Maestro roared. He slipped under the mob's arm and flung a spear at her head. It was a spectacular crit: the elder wife began to rock and released her victim. Nevertheless, she somehow reacted to Maestro's second shot, batting him to the far side of the room with a swing of her arm. Diabettis pulled the dazed Yasya to the wall and ran at the boss to distract her. The Tishkins were temporarily out of action.

The second of the boss's abilities didn't impress me. At all. So little, in fact, that I cussed immodestly, imbuing my words with maximum vulgarity. For the demoness, cracking her whip for the nth time, began enthusiastically to clap her hands: "Oh, how charming! I want one! Darling, we gotta talk urgently."

The epic breastplate – my pride and joy – flickered and disappeared as though it had never existed. The exclamations, "Hey!", "What the hell?!", and "Where...?" indicated that each of the players had lost something valuable. So valuable that their ability to challenge was powerless in the face of their wrath.

Damage dropped substantially. The countdown timer started, and we had fifty-five seconds before the next I Want One.

"Everyone back!" Diabettis's cry heralded a

new Kiss of Jealousy, coupled with a challenge. Ostensibly the players had learnt to avoid these abilities, but each time the demoness reached out to one of them with a kiss, Yasya noticeably quaked.

The minute flew by so quickly I had no time to gather my wits. The next time I struck the demoness, I stared incredulous at the timers. All three of her abilities had recovered, but she was in no hurry to employ them. The reason for this became clear a few seconds later – her HP was down to thirty percent. At a rate of knots she dashed to Maestro and hung over him, staring into his eyes. He could neither avert his gaze, nor jump away.

"You don't love me! At all. You don't buy me anything, or give me presents. My sister's husband takes her to the lava crater, showers her with gifts. I want one! You're cheating on me. We gotta talk urgently. Come, I have a kiss for you!"

The combo of four abilities plus Ballbuster was brutal. Maestro didn't stand a chance, his body melting from the kiss. Yasya attacked next and, despite Diabettis, Eredani, and I covering her, she got a good thrashing.

The second I Want One relieved me of the glaive, which reduced damage even more. Were it not for the difference in level, the demoness might already have been celebrating victory. But there were four of us, all level thirteen-fourteen, and we were pissed off. Almightily so.

"Mama-a-a!" the beast wailed a summons, and there was another being in the room. An exact copy of the elder wife, the only difference being that its HP was full.

"My girl! Where is this wastrel? Who have you wasted your best years on? He's not worthy of you. I warned you."

A superb new character! If I'd had the time, I would have stopped to applaud. The replica was, of course, a tad beaten up, but perfectly recognizable, and enough to distract the players for split second. I hesitated, not knowing who to shoot at, and that was a critical mistake. The elder wife's abilities were restored, and she was back with Yasya. "You don't love me..."

"You don't love her..." the mother-in-law chimed in, pouncing on Diabettis.

A Weakening scroll appeared in my hands when the shimmering Yasya was already melting away in the boss's arms. Diabettis survived by activating Retreat right as the mother-in-law was kissing him, but it wasn't easy: he slammed into the wall, slid to the floor, and froze. The list of debuffs was so long that if he didn't urgently neck a potion, he would definitely be joining his gang. Minus the belt and gauntlets, but that only served to put me on my mettle. Making one last appeal to Aniram, I administered a devastating strike. Crit!

Dorel's Frontier task progress

You have destroyed 222 out of 222 demons.

Phase 1 completed.

Commander Uldaron has been informed of your success. Supervisor Tarlin has been dispatched to you with reinforcements. Arrival time: 2 hours.

Book One: A Second Chance

Phase 2: Fend off 3 waves of demons before supervisor Tarlin arrives. The first wave will arrive in 20 minutes.

Potion in hand, I moved toward the hireling, but Eredani intercepted me. Skewing his eyes to the side, he shook his head and raised his eyebrows in question.

"Think of yourself and the future of the clan," he whispered. "They've fulfilled their part of the bargain. We're on our own now. Nothing will go to waste." He pointed to a pile of objects that had appeared, among which I recognized my red chestplate and all the other items which had been taken. "Don't worry about the hirelings. They'll be fine. They have their own clan." The tiefling continued to work me. "We'll soon be leaving the nursery, and the bonuses won't hurt. Two epics. You've dismissed people from projects because you didn't need them, yeah?"

"Yes, I have," I confirmed, staring hard at the loot. I made my decision on the spot and was in absolutely sure of it. My rational mind agreed that my partner's suggestion was right and beneficial to the general cause. However, aside from the benefits, other factors also affected the decision, and they could also sway me. "You're right, Eredani. But it's one thing to dismiss employees for incompetence, so as not to harm the project; it's quite another to leave people unpaid for their good work. That's something I've never done." I freed my hand and went over to Diabettis.

"That's why you were dismissed yourself," he called after me in irritation. "There's no place for the righteous in business."

He was mistaken. It wasn't so much moral principle, as a desire to set a few things straight in our relations. At that moment I was ready to make a small sacrifice, and I didn't think the hirelings had anything valuable anyway. But Eredani would understand I wasn't going to follow his orders blindly.

Leaning over Diabettis, I forced his mouth open and poured in a restorative potion. I had nothing for removing the debuffs, and had to wait a minute for them to remove themselves. The hireling came round and jumped to his feet. His look, at first lost, soon became comprehending and, seeing the pile of objects and identifying his own things, he looked questioningly at me. I nodded, acknowledging his right to take what was his.

"Two rings." Diabettis gutted the demoness. "And a key. Yasya had the others, so..."

"There they are." Eredani pointed to where the girl had died. Two keys twinkled on the floor. I picked them up and extended a demanding hand to my partner for the first. Eredani slapped the key into my palm, Diabettis handed over the fourth, I put them together, and...

And nothing. No flash, no system notification, no reward. Just four cold heavy metal objects, lying silently on my palm.

Player Diabettis discards 34

Book One: A Second Chance

Player Diabettis discards 71
Player Diabettis discards 63

"For me, Yasya, and Maestro." The hireling explained his actions. "Let's roll dice for the rings."

"They're dead and can't be involved in the carve-up," I said. Standing off to the side, Eredani sniggered and took my response as an attempt at rehabilitation. I told him mentally where to get off. He could think what he liked.

Both rings went to Eredani. I looked at the timer: there were just over ten minutes until the demon attack. We had to have time to sort out the ghosts' reward. I approached the wall. The map reiterated emphatically that there ought to have been a doorway in front of us, but the wall was as plain as could be. A standard, run-of-the-mill wall, just like all the frontier's other walls.

I took out my pick and, imagining what the door looked like, picked a spot and struck it. Not hard, but enough to produce a sheaf of sparks. Previously there hadn't been such a bright lightshow. I looked thoughtfully at the tool – it was in good order. I struck again, this time without swinging back, and created no fewer sparks. When I merely scraped it along the wall, the effect was identical.

"Move aside," Eredani ordered, producing a Frost Strike scroll. I scarcely had time to run before an icicle hit the wall. "Now strike!" The pick sank halfway into the wall. I pulled it back, knocking out the nearest brick. The wall soon rid itself of the hoarfrost by turning the spark-sprinkler back on. Thrusting the pick into the hole, I pushed, and picked out another brick. To paraphrase Archimedes: "Give me a place to stand, and I'll knock down any wall." Swing by swing I widened the entranceway, uncovering a heavy metal-plated door. It wasn't locked, and it led into a miniscule room, or rather a niche, where on a stone plinth stood a trunk. As we approached, the lid flipped open, presenting us three neat, named sacks. The loot turned out to be pukka gold.

"Kvalen, I give you full access to my share," said Eredani. He didn't want to take the gold himself. Each sack contained five thousand gold coins. Not a bad haul for newbies!

I stepped out of the niche and regarded the pick. How many more secret rooms were there at the frontier? The guardian, the ghosts... Who said we'd fulfilled all the bonus tasks? What if a legendary card was hidden somewhere? Just reach out a hand, and it was yours. What I really needed to do was trace the entire perimeter of the frontier, scraping the pick along the wall in search of sparks. But that would take forever, and there were no guarantees. Still, you could sell the idea!

An unsettling droning sound reverberated around the frontier. The first wave of demons had arrived.

Notification for players at the Demon-Hunter Training Camp location
A local event, the Cleansing of

Book One: A Second Chance

Dorel's Frontier, has been successfully completed. From now on players have access to tasks concerning the protection of the Frontier from hordes of demons. See supervisors for more detailed instructions.

Be prepared! Demons will attack in 48 hours! Are you ready to face the beasts of the Abyss?

The message indicated that supervisor Tarlin had arrived at the frontier. I sat down on a wall and sighed with relief. Three waves of demons had utterly drained me. They weren't strong and they weren't powerful; they were just too many. But the main problem was that demon hunters didn't have a single mass-damage spell, so we had to beat the beasties individually, chasing them all over the frontier. They didn't give experience either, because they were only level seven. Kids' stuff, but you had to catch them first. Which we did.

"Well, well." Tarlin found us at the wall and looked disparaging. "Two Tieflings decided to become heroes, hey? Did you think folks would treat you better if you took back Dorel's Frontier?"

"We didn't think anything," I said wearily. "We were just doing our job."

"We did it well too," said Eredani. "We freed the restless souls of former defenders."

Tarlin screwed up his disfigured face. It was hard for him to admit we were right. He turned to Diabettis: "I'd like a word with you. I have a task."

Dorel's Frontier task completed

Reward:

- *Experience: +45, until next level: 92*
- *Reputation with Light of Barliona faction: +18*
- *Reward: Pants from the Unending Happiness set*
- *Bonus reward: Helmet from the Unending Happiness set*

"Hey, you! There are pens full of prixis down there. Destroy them all! Don't let that plague spread!" Demon hunters and priestesses began to run all over the frontier, fulfilling Tarlin's orders. I didn't want to know where they'd all come from. There were definitely not that many NPCs in the camp.

"Diabettis, can I have a word?" I put my hand on the hireling's shoulder, stopping him from leaving. "Tarlin gave you a shoulder protector from the set. I want to buy it. Ten thousand."

"Are you kidding? I could sell it for two or three times that at auction."

"No, I'm absolutely serious. Ten thousand gold, and not a single coin more."

His eyes bored into me long and hard. "I accept your unprofitable offer, but only because I heard you," he said to my surprise. "I appreciate that. It's nice to work with people like you. But... ten thousand – and the question of the keys we decide

427

together. Deal?" I nodded my agreement, and the system winked to signal the transfer of ten thousand to the hireling and the receipt of the new object.

I asked my partner to get out the map of the frontier. I had an idea of what to do with the keys, and had to convince myself I was right. The three key points glowed red. "Add the groundskeeper." A fourth sign appeared on the map. "Now connect the points to make a cross." Two dotted lines stretched between the bosses, intersecting in a corridor. We hot-tailed it there to find the wall already firing sparks, an indication it was concealing something. Frost Strike hit, I pulled out a few bricks, and we were presented with another niche. Instead of a chest, the plinth bore three scrolls, one for each of us. Eredani took his first and burst out laughing. The reward was a full map of the location.

Map updated
Description of changes: *You have received a full map of the Demon-Hunter Training Camp.*
Familiarization with current location: *100%.*

The system showed entrances to a dungeon, a strange prixi settlement, the Cave of Knowledge, and all the demon ore, clover, and pine patches. It was ideal, and for that very reason, almost useless. For both my own and Eredani's location familiarization readings were close to seventy. The remaining thirty could be made up by ourselves in just a couple of days, by boosting Cartographer concurrently.

Two things remained to do – exhale heavily, and enjoy the updates.

Shoulder protectors from the Unending Happiness set

Description: *An epic object. Part of a set (4 out of 4). Material: thin leather.*

- *Protection from physical and magic attack: 40*
- *Luck: +5*
- *Intellect: +5*
- *Damage sustained reduced by 10%*
- *Chance of avoidance increased by 10%*
- *Probability of critical strike increased by 5%*

Bonus for set:

- *2 out of 4: Experience increased by 10%*
- *2 out of 4: Luck +10*
- *4 out of 4: Chance of embodiment of a +1 object increased by 15%*
- *4 out of 4: Luck +20*

After short deliberation we decided we needed a break. I would relax a little in reality, and Eredani would explore the frontier fully. Then we would set out for the Cave of Knowledge. After all, I had to find out sometime what was so unique about tieflings. So far the advantages of the race were not obvious to me. Although the tail... Yes, the tail ruled!

Chapter 8

MATTY'S IRONED shirt and shaved face annoyed me with their perfection. He was going somewhere again that morning, but didn't deem it necessary to share his plans with me. I don't know what upset me more: his secrecy or the fact that I hadn't slept, but the morning was definitely lacking in festive colors.

"Bro, has something happened?" I just barely raised my head, not concealing my displeasure. I wondered if he was playing dumb or really didn't get it. "I'm not great," said the new-sprung fashionista, staring at his plate.

"What's not great? Problems with studying?" I tensed up, and my cup didn't even make it to my mouth.

Since the very start of the venture, I had suspected the learning process would be hard for him, but I'd forbidden myself to think about it. Matty's lack of confidence could scotch more than one Napoleonic plan. I hastened to comfort him. "You can always retake the exam. Nobody's demanding top marks."

"Huh?" Matty ceased his long contemplation of his breakfast. "No, you've got it all wrong. Everything's fine there. I reckon I'll pass everything.

It's something else."

"The kids? Liz?"

"No. I've got a problem with the task. I made some rods and took them to a master, and he turned his nose up at them. He said they needed tempering, and not just anywhere, but in the bowels of Mount Shatri. The dungeon there is level two hundred, and first I have to deal with the boss."

Now I knew the gist of the problem, I could relax. Eredani was right: the further along the chain the task, the greater its demands on resources.

"What about your buddies? The ones you used to hang out with. Surely there must be someone?"

"They've all disappeared for two months, so I'm a bit stuck. I tried getting some dodgy guys together, but the only ones who'll do anything for free are either small fry, or cowards. Or cowardly small fry. I've been there five times, but haven't got further than the first boss. Last time I went with a bunch of serious headcases."

"That's it!" I blurted out, fully awake now. Matty blinked a couple of times in his confusion.

"What's *it*?"

"Headcases! We need to find out about the Vartalinskys." I remembered Eredani's request and made a note in my phone.

"What do 'Vartalinskys' have to do with anything?" he asked, offended. "I was talking about my task."

"Yes, I get it already. You need steamrolling through Shatri, right?"

"Right." He nodded dolently. "But I can wait

until you leave the nursery."

I promised I'd think about how to help him, and hurried to work. Solving Matty's problem was a priority. Unfortunately, that depended on two variables: the situation at work, and the unforgivingness of a certain fickle character.

"Good morning, Helen." I greeted my subordinate with overt politeness. She was preparing the hall for our lesson. "I shall be giving the lesson myself today." She stiffened, a chair in her hands, and didn't hurry to return my salutation. After a second's confusion, she carefully put the chair in its place and came toward me with a very resolute air.

"Good morning, Mr. West." The tone was cold and composed, although her hair, ever the bird's nest, ruined the whole image. Definitely a Gorgon as a child. "Is that because of what I said?"

"No, why?" I hurried to mollify her, thinking up an excuse on the spot. "Nathan wants to see how I'm getting on."

"Fine." Helen nodded, still scowling, and continued, "About yesterday. Let's put this to bed now. You were right."

"Yes?" I was surprised but, being a man of experience, wanted to confirm: "About what?"

"You are old." The little monster put the record straight.

Her conclusion was so unexpected I perched myself on the edge of a table. "Ri-i-ght!"

She was rattled now and added, "No, I don't mean you're really old and I'm just not old. Um, I wanted to say..."

Book One: A Second Chance

"I understand already," I said, cutting short her torment. "Let's pretend I didn't hear anything yesterday, okay? I'm old and hard of hearing."

"Okay." She agreed quickly. We both felt a little uneasy, and it was just the time to close the subject and take advantage of the situation.

"Great." I gave her a friendly smile and rubbed my hands. "Helen, I seem to remember you offering your help with Barliona. Is that offer still open?"

"Of course!" Helen gladly agreed to assist Matty, without me having to talk her round. After all, a paladin is not just a character in a game; it's also an internal philosophy. At least it was with this little brat.

Throughout the whole lesson I couldn't stop myself contemplating the problem genius. A lanky lad with a far-off look. His kind were either self-reliant, or eternally misunderstood, both of which made them awkward to their nearest and dearest, and avoidably weird to strangers. You had to at least try to understand them, and I never wanted to.

Looking at the busy circle of psychologists, I thought they definitely did not have a problem with empathy. It was impossible to work effectively in that sphere if you couldn't understand what another person was feeling. It was difficult for me to even breathe the same air as, much less interact with, the genius, so, understanding my effectiveness working with such a contingent, I transferred management of the process to the team of shrinks, and settled down to observe. I really wanted to open Empathy in Barliona.

Vasily Mahanenko. Invasion

By the end of the lesson, I'd realized the key thing was the desire to share another's feelings and strive to show compassion. I gave myself such a tongue-lashing that I felt for the unfortunate boy in every way until he left.

I was itching to take pity on somebody else, but there were no ideal candidates in the office. By way of a chain of association, I did arrive at one possibility. No big deal, of course, but I considered that yesterday's boss in Barliona was a sign from on high.

"Hello!" A familiar voice came from the speakers. Andrea hadn't changed her phone number, and I hadn't deleted it, but it had long since migrated from "favorites" to the general mass of several hundred contacts, and got lost there.

"Hi! It's Brody."

"Hi... Has something happened?"

"Ummm, no," I muttered, becoming aware of the idiocy of what I was doing, but it was too late to back down. "Mom told me a few days ago about Jackie. I was just calling to express my condolences."

"Oh, thank you..." Andrea was shocked. "It's just a little strange you're calling now. Mom died two years ago."

"Oh, Really?" *Great, thanks mom!* "I didn't know. My commiserations anyway." I wasn't lying. At that moment I really was hurting. From realizing my own stupidity.

"Come on, Bro," she chuckled, not buying my sincerity. "You couldn't stand her."

"It was mutual."

"I'd have to agree with you," she laughed softly, no anger or offense in her voice. "But she never said a single bad word about you. She respected my choice."

"Yeah? Strange. When we were alone together she never held back."

"I can imagine. A practicing psychologist has to be able to do that expertly."

"Well, it's water under the bridge now. How are you?"

"I'm good. Married, happy. Before you ask, Mom managed to approve the candidate. What about you?"

"I'm happy for you. Me too. I mean I'm a bachelor and no less happy."

"Still quite the joker, I see. You're married to your job and you won't betray it. I remember."

"Something like that." I had nothing else to say, and there was an uncomfortable pause. Evidently that particular means of opening Empathy wasn't happening. I wasn't experiencing compassion, or any other emotion for that matter. Which I was glad about. "Well, Andrea, I've said what I called to say. I should be getting off. Thanks for hearing me out."

"Thanks for calling. It was nice to hear from you."

"You too. Bye."

The beeps left me alone... with Victoria, who was looking disapprovingly askew at me. The secretary had for some reason entered the hall and become witness to my conversation. "Hello, Brody.

How's your socialization coming along?"

"Hello, Victoria. Just fine, thanks."

"Am I to understand you're trying to rekindle relations with your ex-wife? Bad idea."

"Are you going to condemn all my intentions? What's with all this poking your nose into other people's affairs? And anyway it's rude to eavesdrop."

"Brody, it's a bad idea not because I don't like it, but because your ex-wife is expecting a baby soon."

"Yes? What's that got to do with me? It's not mine."

"I did warn you. Attempting socialization by means of your ex-wife will not be perceived in your favor."

"Victoria, I called my ex-wife to express my condolences on the death of her mother. What's wrong with that? And how the hell do you know what's going on in Andrea's life?"

Amazingly I managed to embarrass the impenetrable secretary. "I beg your pardon," she said, pursing her lips in embarrassment. "The Security Service wanted to speak with her, but didn't want to disturb her again. I thought—"

"I get it," I cut her off. What the woman thought was of no interest to me. "If it's all right with you, I'll be off home. I have unfinished business in Barliona." I left the hall, escorted by Victoria's silent gaze. What, I wondered, had she come in for in the first place?

At home I was greeted by a beaming Matty. "Brody, I passed the mid-course exam! Ninety–two out of a hundred. I never got results like that in school."

"Congratulations!" I didn't have time to cringe away before my friend had me in a bear hug, and there was nothing for it but to hug him back. I was truly thrilled with his success."

"Thank you!" Matty relinquished his hold on me and grumbled, "It was nicer hugging you before. Have you noticed how much you've sagged in a month?"

I squinted at the mirror. He wasn't joking. Four weeks of intensive dancing in Barliona had shown themselves. My spare tire hadn't gone anywhere, of course, but it was noticeably deflated. And my belly had stopped greedily sucking my belt buckle into my belly button. Soon I would be able to see all of me without the aid of a mirror.

"I'll never catch you though!" I couldn't resist a sarcastic retort. "You beauty, running every morning. Where do you go?"

"I thought you'd never ask." He paused, feeling my support, and admitted: "I've been going to see a psychiatrist."

"What for?"

"I'm learning to look at the world again. Prophylactic measures against burning up and stuff like that."

"No, I get that bit. But why in reality?"

"Because I don't want to do it in a pod. I was given a choice and I chose reality. I don't go into town very often. I see the kids out of town. It's an excuse to wander round the streets. Brody, shit, I had no idea how much everything's changed. Three years, and it's like landing on a different planet."

"Probably. When you see it every day, it seems natural. Why do you go to the psychologist in a shirt and shaven?"

"I'm working on myself," he said enigmatically, scratching his poor chin. I decided to leave it at that. It was no time to try and solve both our problems at once; it wouldn't work.

"I found you some raiders. Here's the number. Her name's Helen. She promised to speak with her guys, and they'll help you get through the dungeon." The jubilation on Matty's face was so genuine that this time I didn't hold back and hugged him myself. Man, it felt good! I hadn't really done anything to speak of, but he was happy as a pig in shit. I needed to learn to get sincerely excited about nothing too.

Matty and I discussed our current business in the game and reality, while I searched for information about the Vartalinskys. Only a month of our allotted time had passed, yet we had already attained certain intermediate results. Granted, the work was preparatory in nature, but it was impossible to achieve our stated goals without it.

After making sure Matty called Helen and arranged to meet, I finished gathering my mini-dossier on the Vartalinskys. Eredani displayed his visionary skills there too. Finding Braksed wasn't particularly difficult, all the less so because that representative of the small town's golden youth had not deleted all traces of himself: the character's contact details were on his social network pages.

A couple of search engine clicks, and I had a

bunch of photographs of a twenty-year-old Alpha-male in his daddy's cool wheels. A couple of links, and I had an entire atlas of this loud and primitive being's weak spots. It was time to hit Barliona.

"What are you lounging around for, not working?" I found my partner snoozing on the groundskeeper's throne, feet up on the table.

"Do you have an appointment?" He opened his eyes. "I can only see you if you have an appointment. What can I do for you?" The tiefling was in a playful mood I'd never seen before. A brisk analysis of potential reasons led me to the only real possible conclusion: he had found something.

"Reveal all." I kicked a nightstand toward the table and sat down.

"Did the ghosts not strike you as a mite unusual?" Eredani began from a distance.

"What struck me as unusual was their presence in the nursery."

"No, not that. Two mounds of corpses, three commanders. Let's suppose one was in charge of scouts and went with them to the mountains. Then the other two each had their own battalion or company. Make sense?" I nodded. "But why were the remains divided up so exactly? Why not heaped all together, which would be natural if they'd been slaughtered?"

I recalled the episode with the ghosts. Directly after the ascension of the first leader, he was followed by everyone on the left. As though they were trying to be as close as possible to their bodies. Or not get mixed up with those on the right.

"Maybe that's just how they die?" I scratched my ear pensively.

"Piled into two neat equal ranks?" Eredani was amused. "By who? Demons? Those beasties that devour everything indiscriminately and aren't even averse to prixis? Don't forget we have two commanders."

"And the stairway with the booby traps, the first of which blocks the entrance." I added my two cents' worth. "Or the last, if you count backwards."

"Plus ten to Attentiveness," Eredani said praisingly. "So, what are the options?"

"There aren't any," I sighed.

"Then let's watch a film!" My partner rubbed his hands in glee and took from his inventory a glaive emanating a noxious green mist.

The Cursed Glaive of Seth

Description: *A legendary object. Seth, the ancient god of war and death, has desired since time immemorial to capture Barliona. His servants were not able to break through the defense of the Creator, so Seth created the Cursed Glaive. Whosoever possessed it would acquire incredible strength, but would be Seth's slave for all eternity. Material: Almaryl.*

- *Intellect +40*
- *Stamina +40*
- *Strength +40*

- *Agility +40*
- *Luck +40*
- *Damage inflicted increased by 40%*
- *Probability of critical strike increased by 40%*
- *Attack speed increased by 40%*
- *All basic characteristics increased by 40%*
- *The race of the owner of the object changes to Cursed Werewolf, and the owner himself becomes an acolyte of the god Seth and founder of the cult of the dark god in Barliona.*

I had scarcely touched the object, when Barliona disappeared. For the first time in my short virtual life I'd found my way into an explanatory video. I felt a little lost. I was thrown right into the thick of things, yet at the same time my character did not exist for those around. A strange feeling.

At first I was running among warriors, chasing a higher demon. We caught up to it easily in the Cave of Knowledge, cornered it, and finished it off. How we rejoiced in the victory! How we crowed over the loot we found in the trunks! How we ran riot, showering our friends with the gold received! It was a celebration. A celebration of the Light of Barliona warriors.

Nobody remembered who found that damned glaive, or where, but it was forwarded to the Frontier together with its loot. Only a week had passed since the victory, but trouble was brewing in the ranks of the defenders. Half of them had fallen under the influence of the weapon and begun to prepare for the coming of the dark god, while the other half tried to hamper them, by killing their friends of the day before. Ten people survived the confrontation. They hid the glaive, dragged everybody down to the dungeon, and set booby traps. Against themselves. The survivors understood that reason could not oppose the subjugating power of the weapon for long, and they would soon be disciples of Seth. In order to save the world, they killed themselves by falling onto stakes. However, they didn't account for Seth not setting them free even in death, the poor wretches. So they'd been castaways. Until we showed up.

The surrounding space winked, and I returned to Eredani. My hands threw the glaive away by themselves.

"Now that's something I understand – visualization," I said, still mesmerized. "How did you find it? Just by scraping the pick along the wall?"

"Exhaustive search is not my method. Three-two-five-twenty. The ghost's words wouldn't give me any peace. He quoted a combination, but it wasn't used anywhere. That doesn't happen. What he showed us on the map was a decoy. The real loot was somewhere else. Third floor, second corridor, fifth room, twentieth niche! Simple as that."

"And what do I do with this godsend now?" I looked at the glaive. I absolutely did not want to become a cursed werewolf.

"Now that's a good question," said Eredani disappointedly. "It would be stupid to give such a powerful weapon to anybody. You won't be able to sell it for a fair price, and in keeping it we'd risk going mental. That thing is only of value if we destroy it and gain a big plus to reputation with the gods. It's not the most cutting-edge thing in Barliona."

"So much hassle for so little result, "I said, understanding Victor's disappointment. "Feed it to Aniram?"

"That's the most logical suggestion," he agreed. "Trade it for a couple of months' peace and quiet. No less. That thing is extremely energy intensive."

The demoness needed one glimpse of the glaive to make her cower in the farthest corner. When she began to hiss violently, we realized our plan had developed a flaw. Flattened against the ceiling, she trembled wildly, and her eyes and nostrils were wide with terror. Her long claws scratched at the stone walls, leaving deep marks. She looked dismal, so I deactivated her to keep her free from danger. The last thing I needed was to give her the kiss of death.

"Hmm... An interesting reaction," said Eredani, looking perplexed. "We must tweak our primary intention. I'll put the glaive away in the inventory, and you summon Aniram again. We're going to torture."

Aniram activated, immediately ready to clear out as far as possible, but glancing around hauntedly and not seeing the weapon, gasped with relief. "Don't do that again!" She spoke to me for the first time since our visit to the barrows.

"What exactly? I just wanted to give you a present. You were offended because of the guardian, and I wanted to placate you with the glaive." I played dumb.

"No!" Aniram jumped away again, thinking she would see the weapon. "Don't you dare!"

"I won't, if you tell me the reason for your reaction. And please, make your answer comprehensive." I had to scare her so she wouldn't think of holding back information. She nodded obediently.

"The demons are avoiding the dark god Seth."

"Avoiding or afraid of?" Eredani asked, but in reply received only a viperous cackle. I pointedly cleared my throat, and Aniram hurried to continue.

"His world is the only one where the Abyss has no dominion. They exiled the demons from there and set a disgraceful tithe until the dark of night has the same rights as the light of day. Anything to do with Seth is taboo. Forbidden! No! Over! Choose the word you like best. If you wish to continue having anything to do with me, never mention Seth and never use his objects. Now let me go. The proximity of his power weighs heavy on me. I must resolve my consciousness."

I deactivated my pet and considered the new information. A timer appeared, indicating I couldn't use Aniram's abilities for the next twelve hours. I shared this news with my partner and suggested postponing the jaunt until the next day, but the tiefling rejected the idea. "No, we go now. The cave contains level-eleven demons. I'll cope even without you. I only have a couple until fourteen. But first we must decide what to do with that thing."

"Leave it here?" I shrugged.

"It'll be found by locals or players. Not good either way. We can't destroy it. Or throw it back into the niche – I destroyed it when I was hammering the wall."

"The abyss?"

"I thought about that, but it has people diving into it all the time. What if somebody pulls it out?"

"Then it won't be our problem anymore... Wait! There's a much simpler option – we take it to the Barrows and hand it over to the guardian. It can stay there."

"Good idea!" Eredani nodded thankfully and hid the glaive. "That's what we'll do. Let's go. It's time to become full-fledged tieflings."

We were lowered down from Dorel's Frontier by rope. I reckoned Tarlin was relieved to see the back of us. Checking with the map all the way, we jogged to the closest mountain. The entrance to the cave we needed was right on its peak, way above the clouds. My partner kept turning round, on the lookout for demons, but we didn't come across a single antagonist, even the most mediocre.

Dorel's Frontier divided the location into two large parts. On one side was a wide lake, prides of four archdemons, Hermit, and the training camp; on the other side a high mountain range covered the entire territory from north to south.

"We go that way," said Eredani, checking with the map and pointing somewhere upward. We stood at the foot off the cliffs and, throwing our heads back, endeavoured in vain to see the top. Everything was obscured by mist.

"Are we going to look for a path or head straight up?" I assessed the cliff, which rose at a very steep angle, promising a long and arduous ascent.

"We'll lose time, and we can't be sure a path exists. We climb," Eredani replied and, for some reason spitting on his palms, rushed to storm the forbidding crag. His zip and enthusiasm lasted for precisely five meters, at which point his bare hooves proved themselves inappropriate for conquering mountainous heights, slipping on the rock and whisking the hapless climber back down. Were it reality, he would have smashed himself up good and proper. As it was, he shook himself down, swore, and set off upwards again.

"How persevering you are," I noted after his third fall. It was quite dramatic: flat on his face from ten meters up, and a rock landing on him to add to the spectacle. He was saved by his level thirteen, but his HP dropped into the red zone. "Maybe we should look for a path after all?"

"Fine," he growled, shaking himself down and drinking a potion. "Right? Left?"

"According to the map it's straight up. Let's go right."

We spent a good hour walking in circles in search of a gentler slope, but all we saw were overhanging scars, so we went back. "Shall we try locking tails like we did at the frontier?" I suggested, and he nodded his agreement. We interlaced our tails, turning them into safety ropes, so that if one of us fell, he'd take the other down with him and it wouldn't be so galling.

Eredani soon noted it was much easier climbing together, because if a rock slipped from under the hoof of one, the other could help by dragging him back. Mainly I was the unlucky one, but I did have to assist him on a few occasions, saving him from pain or rebirth. The problems started when we reached the snowline. I had to give him my boots, for his feet were mercilessly frozen. Scrambling up snow was harder than up stones, and we fought doggedly for each centimeter.

How long were we climbing? An hour? Two? A day? Working on full autopilot, I lost track of time. When my hand reached out and didn't meet with rock, I collapsed forward and thought that was it – falling and rebirth. But an unpleasant sensation in my coccyx made me look up, and I saw my partner pulling me away from the cliff edge. We had actually made it to where we needed to be.

"D-d-demons," Eredani stammered with the cold. It was a way to the top, and it was still concealed in an impenetrable whiteout, but the goal of our venture was elsewhere. We found ourselves on a small flat space which led into an ice cave, the entrance to which was guarded on either side by demons. Or rather what was left of them. Unable to desert their posts, the beasties had frozen to death.

"Quick." My partner pulled me inside the cave. The penetrating wind and cold, blowing sharp ice particles instead of soft snow, had caused him no little discomfort, and he was desperate to escape the elements.

"Just a second," I yelled over the noise of the wind, and activated Aniram. The demoness quivered and looked questioningly at me through unfocused eyes. Such snowy heights were not her favourite places.

"Is there any call for warriors like that in your army?" I motioned toward the icy sculptures. She looked at the demons, extended a hand, and two semi-transparent threads drew themselves into it. The petrified idols crumbled to snowy ashes.

"Thirty minutes for each," she said and sheltered herself behind her wings. The timer twitched, dropping at once by an hour, and I dismissed her.

As soon as we stepped inside the cave, a system window popped up.

Notification for players entering the Cave of Knowledge

Be ready, traveler, for battle draws near! You have entered the Cave of Knowledge, and the archdemons will spare no effort to kill you. They have already gathered their multitudinous forces and will soon be here.

"We still have to survive until the archdemons," Eredani noted philosophically, in confirmation of which a spear flashed out from the depths of the cave. We dropped to the floor as one and rolled away to opposite sides of the entrance. Following the spear came a crowd of level-eleven demon guardians dressed in prixi hides.

"Charge!" I cried, bracing myself and drawing the glaive. My other hand reached into the inventory for a Frost Strike scroll. Unfortunately, I couldn't activate it, since the system was categorically against it.

Magic is inaccessible in the Cave of Knowledge.

Eredani's swearing, which sounded in unison with the piteous "Eat!", was the last thing I remembered before the start of the death dance. I can't argue that in terms of physical attack I was one hell of a fighter, but the camp had given me one or two close-combat skills too. Employing all the dance moves I'd learned, I skipped nimbly away from the enemy's direct strikes and managed to do some attacking myself. We would have spent four strikes on in each demon instead of one, if I'd had Aniram's abilities. By the end of the fight I'd lost a third of my HP, but I could be proud of myself: I had ten dead demons to my name, precisely half the attacking squadron.

The snow-white light of level fourteen overcame me and Eredani simultaneously. After rejoicing in my new level for a moment or two, I rushed to disembowel the demon's remains, having learned from Yasya's infectious experience. Oddly, there were no blanks. Only coats and gauntlets of thin prixi leather to prevent frostbite. I was sceptical about the gear, but Eredani perked up and immediately tried on the new acquisitions.

"We take everything. We can sell it later," he said, his teeth chattering. Evidently the cold had had a negative effect on his brain power. What player in their right mind would buy such crap? No armor, just ten percent protection from the cold. I didn't manage to open my mouth to make the frostbitten fool see sense, before another system notification popped up.

Notification for players at the Demon-Hunter Training Camp location

Call to arms! Demons have attacked Dorel's Frontier! There is a direct teleport link with the training camp; see instructors for tasks and additional instructions.

A reward to everyone who answers the call: a rare object, consistent with your level and specialization.

Eredani was surprised they'd reached the frontier so soon.

"It's probably the first wave. R'Tan's forces," I suggested, recalling the map. "They're not far from the frontier anyway. I think we should take this staircase."

Eredani picked up the glaive and trotted after me. The descent was quite steep, and we had to hug the wall. What we took at first for a stairway was actually just a small serpentine stone ledge. The lower we got, the warmer it got, and soon it was so hot Eredani risked removing his coat and gauntlets, nearly falling in the process.

Taking small unhurried steps, we arrived at the next guardians' position. Peering out from behind a rock, I saw ten demons sitting by a fire, and a strange creature hanging in a cage above it. The poor thing opened its mouth, but no sound came out.

Kvalen: *What's this mummery? We can see the unfortunate devil screaming, so why can't we hear anything?*

Eredani: *We can't hear because its howl together with its feelings of pain and fear are being absorbed by the demons. They're feeding.*

Cursing Barliona's scriptwriters, I spotted another cage in the far corner, and emitting from it was the already familiar crunch of wood being worked over. The prixis were awaiting their moment of glory on the fire, though they didn't appear too worried about it. With Eredani gripping the glaive more comfortably, we attacked swiftly. The demons had no chance.

"It's empty," I said, examining the loot disappointedly. "What's up with that poor soul?"

"Nothing good, I suspect. It's some kind of dwarf." Eredani kicked the cage from the fire and examined the screeching creature. The fire had burned all its hair, which made the fat little fellow look nothing like the average representative of the piedmont people. It groaned at every touch, and there was no evidence of intelligence in its eyes. Its properties introduced it as an "Anonymous Dwarf."

"Help me." Eredani pulled out the pickaxe and

struck the lock. The cage flew to the edge of the chasm, and I barely caught it to stop it falling. We were on an intermediate level, but the main a goal of our trek remained somewhere below.

Two strikes, and the lock clicked, allowing the door to be opened and the obstinate Dwarf to be removed. Ignoring the protests and bleating, Eredani forced open the martyr's mouth and poured in a restorative potion. To our chagrin, nothing changed – it didn't come to its senses.

"What now? Leave it here?" I asked.

"It'll get eaten. In theory we should take it with us."

The dwarf slipped from his hands and went to find a dark corner among the rocks to hide in. Which, honestly, it did well. Were it not for its shiny bald spot, its body would have been impossible to spot against the background of the cliffs.

"Then we need to get it to the camp somehow. Uldaron will know what to do with it."

"Uldaron," the dwarf piped up suddenly and was quiet again. Shit! Now we couldn't toss the mental case until the head of the camp had seen it, even if we wanted to.

Notification for players at the Demon-Hunter Training Camp location

Call to arms! Demons have attacked Dorel's Frontier! Say: "I want to defend Dorel's Frontier," and the power of Barliona will transport you to the wall.

A reward to everyone who

answers the call: a rare object, consistent with your level and specialization, +10 to reputation with the Light of Barliona faction.

"It's hotting up there," I noted, before saying to my partner, "I'm going down, you follow with the dwarf."

The target seemed to take forever to reach. I reckoned I should have been able to descend to the foot of the mountain in that time, if not burrow deep into the earth. Eredani and the dwarf were already several tiers behind. Occasionally I heard their squabbling, and the odd rock flew past me into the chasm. Rounding the last of many hairpin bends, I eventually saw it: the red eye looking up from the bottom of the shaft; the end point of our journey. The light down there did not flicker like a torch, but was still, white hot, and absolutely captivating. After scrambling down the last ten meters, I stood transfixed. In front of me opened an enormous lake of bubbling red-hot lava, in the middle of which was an island. Ironic though it was, there was a coffin. In the very centre of the rocky isle stood tall columns, suspended from which, by chains, was a swinging three-meter sarcophagus hewed from a single piece of rock. There was no evidence of demons or guardians in the vicinity.

Looking at the rock, I was seized by a feeling of unity with my birth element. This was it – my vine and fig tree. Here we were glad, here we were expected and loved. My knees buckled, and I was unwittingly plunged into a state close to meditation.

The approaching footsteps of Eredani and the dwarf jerked me from my reverie. The dwarf began to moo, and wrestled its way out of Eredani's arms. Attempting to protect itself from the heat with its hands, it hastened to take refuge deep in the rocks, but not before its skin managed to redden and blister. My partner and I did not suffer from our proximity to the molten lava.

I approached the very edge of the lake, which grew more tantalizing with every second. It struck me as the only place where I could discover peace and contentment. Helpless to restrain myself, I hunkered down and scooped up a handful of lava. The guardian gauntlets dissolved momentarily, unable to withstand the high temperature, and my bare hand bathed in the comfortably warm, incredibly soft, and somewhat viscous liquid. The pleasant sensations enthralled me totally, and I continued to pass my hand aimlessly over the surface, playing with the lava as I had with water in childhood.

**Race-specific chain of tasks received:
Fireborn
Fireborn: Step 1. Merge with your birth
element and undergo a test.**

"What have you got there?" Eredani approached cautiously, ready to spring back to safety at any moment.

"I lost my gauntlets," I sighed, and in a single stroke threw all the objects I was wearing into the inventory, keeping only the pristine white drawers. My partner giggled, but was in no hurry to join me in stripping. He preferred to wait and see what would happen.

I knew studying the guides was pointless – they had nothing to say about tieflings – and consulting with Eredani was just as pointless. He hadn't been in this situation, even in his previous life. Added to which, I needed to sort myself out by myself. With these thoughts, I leaped up and tucked my legs in. My partner didn't have time to react before I cannonballed into the lava, spraying him from head to toe.

I was a tiefling, born in half-blood lava, taking up arms against demons at the will of NPCs. My element was fire. My mother was the higher demoness Ireness, my father – an anonymous paladin. That's why I could survive in Barliona and the Abyss. I was a child of both worlds, and only I was fated to decide who I would become in that game. Not Uldaron, not Abigail, not Ireness. Only I. For I was my own master!

Notification for player
You have begun the Fireborn:
Step 1 task.

Kvalen! At last I can speak with you! Welcome home, Grandson! I am Baal.

My body shuddered in involuntary ecstasy. I had been honored by the attentions of a higher demon, one of three leaders meddling in Barliona.

One who had power. And one I had to bow to, in obeyance of demon law.

I was betrayed by my body, but not my mind. As in previous times, it refused to follow primitive instincts. First and foremost I was Brody West; only then was I a tiefling, a player, and whatever else.

"Greetings, Grandfather." I saluted the demon and said nothing more. Let him take the initiative, and I would see which way the wind blew. Baal was silent for a long time, apparently expecting more homage from me.

I have kept track of you. I watched you grow, take your first steps. And now I am sure you will achieve great things.

"I am flattered, overjoyed, and startled, Grandfather. Flattered by your attention, overjoyed at the potential prospects from our acquaintance, and startled that you kept tabs on me like a madman. What do you want from me?"

From you? Nothing. Quite the opposite. You get everything.

"Allow me to clarify. Everything means absolutely everything, or are there restrictions?"

You shall stand at the head of a new empire!

"What empire? Will I be absolute monarch, or will the system of government be close to parliamentary?"

We can discuss that later. I am presenting you with a mighty army for your future conquests.

"One more question: will the army answer exclusively to me, or to anyone else also?"

You disappoint me, Grandson. I am offering you

my support and might.

"Listen, I'll stop interrupting you, and you tell me everything you want to offer me, only without the dramatic pauses. I ask just one thing: I need details, not ardent battle cries. Tell me exactly what you are proposing. Objectively."

You are insolent!

"I'm pragmatic! If I am being offered something, I want to know exactly what. Let's agree that all offers must be numerated and with absolute ownership rights. Deal?"

Do you doubt my word?!

"Who would I be if I did not doubt the word of a higher demon?"

You will receive gold; hundreds of millions in gold pieces.

"Will I be able to transfer it to my game account?"

This gold is needed for the fulfilment of a great purpose! The conquest of pathetic creatures!

"I'll take that as a no. What else?"

I will give you an army of hundreds of thousands of warriors. You will vanquish all of Barliona!

"Will I be able to manage them at my own discretion?"

They will serve only the great purpose!

"Another no then."

The best demons will work for you and create inconceivable objects!

"Will I be able to trade these objects with other empires? If not, I'm not interested. What's the point if I can't increase my own prosperity? Grandfather, are you listening to what you're saying? You promise me mountains of gold, but as such you're not offering me anything personally. How were you thinking of buying me?"

What do you want? There was a note of displeasure in a Baal's voice.

"Now that's a different matter altogether. I want twenty percent of all the loot I receive as head of the empire. I want to transfer that loot to my game account and do with it as I please. I need open trade with those we are planning to invade. They can spend their money on us, rather than on war with us. I need the coordinates of twenty as-yet-unpassed dungeons and, please, a full set of celestial-level attire for the new class. Do you see how I'm listing things that can be counted and evaluated no matter whether the result is achieved or not. No attractive pledges or taglines. Distinct and concise.

Your demands are unfeasible!

"I'm open to conversation!" I snapped. "If twenty percent is too much, I can come down to fifteen. But no lower than thirteen, even out of respect for our kinship."

Silence.

Congratulations! You were able to resist the temptation of a higher demon.

Fireborn: Step 1 task update. Task completed.

Player race update: tiefling updated to fire tiefling – you have opened all your race abilities.

Player class update: demon hunter updated to demon destroyer.

Fireborn: Step 2 task will be accessible to you at level 100 or during particular class-specific scenes.

I emerged from the lava with a deep sense of frustration. Was that it? Would I have to go through fire and water too? Empty conversations like that always maddened me. Baal was no salesperson.

Eredani was nowhere to be seen. Figuring he would appear on the surface any minute, I swam to the island. But I didn't hurry to climb out – approaching the sarcophagus without cover would be the height of stupidity.

Victor surfaced right by me and, paying me no attention whatever, climbed quietly from the lake and began rushing around the island like a recently caged animal. I took a peek at his properties, and saw no obvious reason for such behaviour: he had also become a destroyer and a fire tiefling. Evidently he hadn't been able to parley with Baal either. His condition concerned me. He kept smoothing his hair down and lashing his legs with his tail. His movements were fidgety, his whole being seemed disturbed, if not angry, and he wasn't aware of his surroundings. He wasn't interested in the sarcophagus, next to which he was describing his manic circles.

"How did you find the test?" I asked, but he either didn't hear or was ignoring me. He was away with the fairies. "I didn't think much of it personally.

Offering world domination and piles of gold, but actually selling air? What a crock of shit." He continued to hold his tongue, so I tried a different tack. "Victor! Stop crying! Pull yourself together!" He twitched. "Go on, you have a good cry. Everything's shit, nobody loves you, you had to choose between your family and your personal safety."

"What would you know, milksop?" he said, trotting down to the edge of the lake and standing before me in a threatening pose. I swam a couple of meters out; after all, I didn't know what he was in prison for. If he went nuts, he'd run out of steam chasing me and come to his senses.

"Spare me the scenes of self-castigation. Positive emotions are for chicklit. I need a level-headed adviser for the clan. Get your act together!" The look he gave me was full of meaning. Even Aniram couldn't do that. "Excellent. Now sit down and pull yourself together. We need to figure out who's hiding beneath the paladin's mask." With apparent calm he folded his arms across his chest and nodded. He wasn't remotely interested in the sarcophagus; indeed he seemed not to give a damn about anything. I didn't want to leave the warmth of the lava, but I had to risk it and join him.

"What was that all about?" he asked in an entirely normal voice.

"I thought you needed some support." I shrugged.

"You call that support?" he said, surprise in his eyes.

"I helped the way I knew how." I frowned. "You

clammed up and turned nasty. You needed pulling out of your state. Which I did. How is my method worse than a dumb pat on the shoulder and a no less dumb 'What happened? Wanna talk about it?' ?"

Eredani chortled. And again. He began guffawing loudly, which echoed like thunder around the cave. Problem solved. The stress he experienced from the lava was gone.

"Yes, empathy's not going to be easy for you if that's what you call support," he chuckled. "Let's go, supporter, it's high time we found our paladin."

"That's gratitude for you." I knitted my brow at the mention of that mysterious ability. I was more and more convinced that empathy was a genetics thing.

The stone sarcophagus, wrapped in black chains, hung at the level of our heads. Demonic writings covered the sides and told of the deeds of the higher demon that lay at rest within. Only victories and accomplishments, only feats and glorification. All in the best traditions of any "never speak ill of the dead" burial: imbibed the souls of hundreds of thousands, enslaved and raped many more...

"And where's the clue in all this demonic eulogy?" I said, after reading the glowing heresy carefully to the end. In all that was written, there was nothing that could be perceived as a reference to a specific figure or occurrence.

"We're missing something." Eredani didn't get it either. "We can't shift the lid, it's too big." It occurred to me we ought not to move anything anyway, so as to avoid unpleasantness at the hands of the higher demon.

Notification for players at the Demon-Hunter Training Camp

Dorel's Frontier has fallen! Supervisor Tarlin has taken the defenders back to the training camp. All participants in the event are awarded an unusual object consistent with their level and specialization. All tasks connected with the Frontier are canceled.

Eredani and I looked at each other. If the demons continued to move with such determination, they would be at the summit in half an hour. We physically wouldn't be able to escape.

"We need help." I summoned Aniram and immediately forbade her to consume anyone. She ignored me, dropping her jaw and staring exuberantly at the coffin. Her lips stirred in a rambling whisper:

"O, Abyss! It is he... His spirit is here... I want... Oh how I want..."

"We're looking for a reference to a paladin." I interrupted her panegyric, but she had already regained control of herself. She fell to her knees before me and clasped her hands in prayer.

"Allow me to consume him, master! I beseech you! Then I shall become mighty! The strength you gain through me will increase from three to five. You will become an invincible destroyer! Do not refuse me this time!"

She was evidently talking about the coefficient in the formula of magic damage.

"Let's do this in the right order. First me, then you. First we look for the paladin." I spoke slowly, emphasizing each word.

"There was never a paladin here," said Aniram, shaking her head. "There was an object belonging to a light warrior. But it is not here now. Permit me to consume the demon, and I will tell you where to find the object. It is here, on the island. Ma-a-ster!"

"First tell me where," I persisted. My intuition screamed there was a hitch somewhere.

"I swear with all my soul," Aniram snarled hotly, bowing her head low and scorching me with her look. "If you do not let me consume the higher, I shall tell you nothing. Ever. I swear I will do everything to escape, and annihilate you. I'm going to smash the lid, and you will know the might of his wrath!"

How quickly she changed her tune when she didn't get her way. She'd even started threatening.

"It's a set-up," Eredani concluded. "I don't like her ultimatum. Don't accept."

"Do I have a choice? The clock is ticking. Now she's going to set the hellish chimera free, and in half an hour the entire jet set of relatives will be here with four archdemons at their head. Then we definitely won't learn anything. We'll be reborn and have to leave the nursery."

My partner thought. "Well... yes, you're right. You decide. The responsibilty's all yours."

The demoness understood I was wavering, and

once more began with her whiny supplications.

"Aniram, I want to be sure you aren't bluffing, and that we'll definitely find out the new location of the object."

"I swear on the Abyss, I know where it is." The Demoness was covered by a dark cloud. The drawling call of a horn sounded from somewhere far away: the demons' advance guard had reached the mountain.

"Consume!" I said, and two black lightning bolts struck Aniram. She bent over, eyes rolled back in ecstasy, raised her head, and cried. But instead of a shriek, dark light burst from her mouth. I had always considered darkness to be the absence of light, but Barliona convinced me otherwise when I saw dark energy with my own eyes.

The sarcophagus shattered and disintegrated into sand. The loosened chains clanked loudly against the columns before crashing to the ground. Aniram collapsed too. I ran to my pet, and her hands clutched me. "Ma-a-ster!" she said listlessly. Her eyes were red, and a smile meandered over her face, portending nothing good for me. It wasn't the rapacious scowl I was so used to, but the giddy amusement of a woman so drunk she's convinced the sea is knee-deep.

"Master, you are so handsome! Come to me! Have a kiss from a real archdemoness. I've never had a tiefling." Her hands reached for my tail and pulled it down toward her.

"Aniram, where's the object?" Trying for an affectionate tone, I carefully extricated my appendage from her grasp.

Book One: A Second Chance

"Which object? Ah, the object... A kiss, and I will tell." The drunk released my tail and slapped me painfully on the buttock. "Come here!"

"How about you kiss me later?" I snarled, hearing the horn again.

"I want to now!" In a heartbeat she rose up and locked herself onto my lips. It took no small effort to release myself. "Do you refuse me?" Tears welled in her eyes.

"Where's the object?!" Eredani and I shouted in one voice.

"Wasteling!" The affronted demoness pushed me away so hard I nearly flew to the other side of the island. It was a good thing one of the columns got in the way. "You will rue your rejection of me! What a... You don't deserve me! I'm leaving!"

"Aniram, you can't leave. I haven't dismissed you. Where's the object? You swore on the Abyss," I answered severely.

"Ha!" In a wink she was by my side, tottering, the tip of her tail describing pirouettes, like that of a rabid cat. "You have made a mistake, ex-master! Now nobody can forbid me anything! I am strong enough to destroy Ireness and take her place, you traitor! I remember my word, wasteling! Do you see that sign?" She pointed to an arrow-like symbol carved into one of the columns. "That is the sign of G'Rot. He was here and he took the object. Back to his lair. If you need it, follow the arrows. They will lead you to him. I have honored my oath and said what was demanded of me. Nothing can stop me now. Farewell, ex-master! When I become a higher, I shall return to suck out your soul, and you will be my slave!"

The beastie flapped her wings and disappeared with a deafening clap.

Notification for player Kvalen

The archdemoness Aniram has consumed the essence of a higher demon and ruptured the bonds between you. In order to use demonic abilities, you must dive into the Abyss again for a new demon. Your bonus for random generation has been used, and you have access to a rank-1 demon.

"Oh, Brody, Brody. Who wines and dines a girl without planning to sixty-nine her?" Eredani said, at which I couldn't contain myself and burst out laughing.

"Do you need support?" He continued to scoff. "Or can you cope alone?"

"Alone," I confirmed, struggling to suppress my mirth. I had no desire to argue with the system. They took her, and that was fine. I'd find myself a demon hamster or toad and be thankful for small mercies.

"If you say so. Let's go. It'll be better to greet the demons where we found the dwarf. We can take them one at a time."

It was a fair point. We swam quickly to the shore, dressed, and only then noticed something was amiss. "Where's the dwarf?" The piedmont personage was nowhere to be seen. We peaked down into the shaft – everything was clear until level two. The demons hadn't reached and the cave yet.

"Tracks!" My eagle-eyed partner saw footprints disappearing into the shadows. Curiosity got the better of us, and we followed them. Behind a rock we found a small cave, and we crawled after the dwarf, flat on our stomachs. The narrow passage wound, and overhanging rocks threatened to fall and crush us, but when the black hole ended, we came out onto a flat area under the sky. The dwarf lay with its face to the dull sun, and hadn't noticed the long caravan of demons scrambling up the mountain behind its three archdemon leaders a stone's throw from us. By the looks of it, the fourth hadn't survived the standoff at the frontier, but it was cold comfort to us.

Beasties fell and stones slid, causing rockfalls, but the demons clambered tenaciously upward. Split into groups of ten or fifteen, half the troops had passed the first milestone and almost reached the snowline. Hidden conveniently behind some large boulders, Eredani and I lay on our stomachs and observed the beasts of the abyss. I wasn't convinced the training camp would hold out if it was attacked by that army.

"Wow! *They*'re here too?!" Eredani whispered and elbowed me. At the very end of the cohort, riding atop strange creatures, was a pair of painfully familiar level-fifteen players.

"They're not just here, they're in command," I said, noticing the Vartalinskys' instructive gestures to the archdemons. "Oh yeah, I completely forgot. Meet Arthur Vartalinsky, twenty years of age, single, dumb, has a relatively rich daddy. The youngest and least prosperous son of a second-rate small-town businessman. He really does have an elder brother, but it's not Kurtune, who I don't think is actually any relation to the Vartalinskys. The devil knows what was on their minds when they were choosing a name. Anyway, the eldest son is the pride and hope of the family and daddy's business. He's with daddy: his right-hand man in the business, and in the clan, which was established several years ago and is successfully run by his esteemed father, Andrew. In a nutshell, that's it."

"That's pretty much what I thought," said my partner. "Sonny boy swipes daddy's ring from the safe. Daddy gets wind of it and gets mad... That's all very well, but as yet useless. If they come after us when we're done with the nursery, we'll think about it. Should anything happen, we can use jealousy and envy toward the elder brother. Arthur will do anything to show his father he's worth something."

"Who are you?" The deep voice from behind us came so unexpectedly we nearly jumped. The dwarf had recovered consciousness and was looking distrustfully at us two tieflings. Experience had taught it that horned and tailed beasties didn't bring happiness or good luck, but our behavior did not measure up to its expectations – we ourselves were hiding from demons.

"Be quiet!" hissed Eredani. "We're not your enemies."

"But you're not friends either." It demonstrated incredible shrewdness for a witless dwarf.

"We're demon destroyers," I explained. "We

just don't look like it."

"You're pretty cruddy destroyers. The demons are over there, and you're over here," it said, casting a sidelong glance at the climbing beasties.

"Y'know, Kvalen, maybe we should return the honorable gentleman to the cage we so pained ourselves to free him from?" The dwarf started and took a step back. The stones beneath its feet crackled treacherously, and I hurried to calm the NPC.

"He's just joking. Nobody's going to send you anywhere. But be quiet! Don't disturb our recce mission."

"So you're spies?" It was overjoyed. "I'm... I'm... My name's..." The dwarf blushed and choked up, digging around in its memory. It remembered how to speak, but not its name. All in a day's work for an amnesiac.

"Kvalen, a sign." Eredani was pointing at the overhanging wall of the peak closest to us. There, standing out vividly, bang in the centre and pointing south, was the symbol of G'Rot.

"Aniram wasn't lying. The object really is in the dungeon."

A prolonged howl came from the passage we'd recently crawled through.

"The first wave of demons has reached the lake. How long will it take them to find the tunnel?"

"Give me a hand." The dwarf rushed to the entrance and pointed at a small rock, saying, "Strike here!" Hoping the child of the hills knew what it was doing, I gave the stone a hoof. A rumbling came from the depths of the mountain, and the dwarf covered the entranceway with its body and said, "Pile on me!" Eredani and I flattened it against the rockface. There wasn't enough of it to seal the opening, so we were bombarded from all around by gravel and dust. Its HP dropped. When the dust had settled, we dragged the martyr out of the hole. Its back was covered in welts and scratches from the sharp stones. I carefully cleaned it up and fed it a restorative potion. We couldn't lose such a useful NPC at the very start of the journey. "They won't find it now," it smiled sluggishly and switched off.

"Bad timing," whispered Eredani. We left our savior to regain its consciousness and went to evaluate the situation again. The Vartalinskys continued their ascent, following the archdemons. Their transport creatures took on the crags no worse than mountain goats, bringing trouble nearer. A guard of five dozen magi tailed the players relentlessly as their personal bodyguards. The archdemons waited for the Vartalinskys to reach the first milestone, before heaving their wings and flying to the cave entrance.

"The frontier's occupied, we can't leave the dwarf there." I looked at its lifeless body. "Can we put it in the inventory?"

"It'll perish. The higher their intelligence, the less time mobs can spend in there. We'll carry it in turns. You first, I'll repel."

"Okay. Did you see the sloping path? Do we take that or go straight up?"

"All the demons are on the mountain, so we'll risk the path. Let's go."

Book One: A Second Chance

I hoisted the dwarf onto my shoulders, and we slid down the scree slope. Stones skidded down to the foot of the mountain, making a fearful racket.

"Run!" Eredani shouted, setting off southward at full steam. The horn blared again, and I had a gut feeling of someone's hostile glare boring into my back.

"Three kilometers! We have to hold out for three kilometers!" my partner shouted, just before we heard a blood-curdling howl. He turned around and bared his teeth: "Dogs! A pack of lower demons, fifty of them. They'll be on us in five minutes. Get moving!"

For the second time in as many weeks I ran like a bat out of hell. Against my better judgement, fear simmered inside me. Not because I might be reborn, but because of bad luck. We had been given too much to deal with in the dungeon, and to lose it all because of an NPC would hurt. The howling was gaining quickly on us, and we could distinctly make out the snapping of jaws and the scraping off claws on stone. One level-seven demon dog would do us no serious damage, but a pack of fifty, when one bite would remove one HP, could easily hamper our plans by simply delaying us. Plus we couldn't forget about the Vartalinskys, who were also no doubt hot on our tails. That was a force against which we had no cogent argument. Apart, that is, from the Glaive of Seth, but I didn't want to lose the character, because I already had too many bonuses. It would be a shame and not very practical.

"Run, I'll hold them up!" Eredani came to a screeching halt and summoned his fish. The howl of the dogs changed key. At first joyful (the prey entering their chops by itself), then surprised (it beginning to bite back), and towards the end – frightened and charged with pain. Each demon strike removed one beastie, but it wasn't enough for my partner. Swiping the glaive from side to side, he hurtled through the pack like a hurricane, scattering demons asunder.

"I said run!" he shouted, noticing I had slowed down to watch the fight. A deceleration scroll appeared in his hands, and the dogs turned into crawling tortoises. He hoofed the nearest one away, jumped aside, and activated Retreat. Now I knew for sure those two actions worked together. In that free space, the tiefling flew thirty meters and almost caught up to me. The horn blast repeated, and the main cavalcade of demons appeared from behind some trees. Up ahead, traitors that they were, galloped the Vartalinskys.

"Mire! Run!" Eredani all but kicked me to spur me on. In front of us was a vast, even plain, bordered on all sides by mountains. The standard landscape of the location, in shades of blood. The rocks, the sand, the mountains – everything was red. With the exception of the plain, which was an intense black, making it similar to the River of Darkness. The map gave it a simple and unpretentious name: Mire, and our path led directly into it. It was time to choose between the lesser of two deaths: suffocation by oxygen deficiency, or dismemberment alive by cankered beasties. Help came from where it was least expected – my shoulder. The dwarf had had the grace to wake from its blackout, and it now whispered:

"It's safe on the bubbles. Walk over the bubbles."

Hoping that, despite forgetting its name, the mountain child might still be an orienteering star, we pelted across the swamp, leaping from bubble to bubble. The debuff on the dogs ended, and they resumed their pursuit. Only they couldn't follow our tracks anymore, because there weren't any in the mire. They charged straight ahead and didn't get ten yards before sinking beneath the dark surface with a dull "glug".

"Two hundred meters!" I reminded Eredani of the magi's shooting distance, while seeking out my next bubble. The mire was loath to let go of our hooves, the marshy ground being viscid and syrupy. We had to fight for every step, but we had done enough. The mire swallowed the next wave of pursuers, making the demons tarry. The system interpreted the effort we'd expended as a maximum-level battle, and flashed a warning. Planting the dwarf down on a neighboring patch of bubbles, I sat down in the sludge. I urgently needed rest. Thirty minutes.

The Vartalinskys dispatched the next cohort after our heads, but the unwitting demons merely upped the mire's victory count. It was happy to accept any and all. The cumbersome archdemons rose into the air and tried to fly at us, but Eredani's frost strike relieved them of that particular desire. The spell struck the nearest boss from fifty meters. It nosedived into the mire like a plane shot down, and the remaining two suddenly had a much bigger problem than us. They dived to fish out their partner, while their compadres kept their distance from us.

"Tieflings, we must talk!" shouted Braksed. "Return the ring!"

"Perhaps it's not the Mahan's after all, but the Absolute's?" I muttered. "We should have tested it in the lava."

"One ring to rule them all," said Eredani. "Dreams, dreams, dreams. It's a pity the Mahan hasn't read *The Lord of the Rings*."

"Dismiss your demons!" I shouted. "We'll talk."

The Vartalinskys really could command the beasts of the Abyss. The latter stepped unquestioningly back from the edge of the mire, leaving us alone with the assholes. I approached to fifty meters from the shore and stopped. Any further and I might have been within range of their scrolls, which I certainly didn't need. Eredani remained standing where he was.

"Return the ring!" repeated Braksed.

"What do we get in return?"

"Are you taking the piss? We're gonna get you and..." Kurtune was fuming, but Braksed assuaged him:

"Shut up! Ten thousand! Here and now."

"Are you having a laugh? You've been chasing us around for three weeks for ten thousand?"

"Twenty! That's twice the value of the ring. We get the ring, you keep moving."

"I seem to remember you asking a hundred thousand for it," I said.

"That was my mistake, it can happen to anyone." Even from fifty meters we could hear the player gnashing his teeth in ire. Nevertheless, he was exercising self-restraint.

"I'm not really interested in money." I read aloud Eredani's message. "I need information."

"What information? Just say the word and you will receive it." The real Vartalinsky agreed like a shot and stretched his mug out into a smile.

Eredani: *We're leaving. It's a trap!*

Kvalen: *Why? I can't see anything amiss.*

Eredani: *The kid screwed up. He's making concessions too quickly. Let's get out of here.*

"Where are you going?! Stop, motherfuckers!" Braksed yelled, losing all sense of aplomb in a split second. Which gingered me up. Seizing the dwarf, I hightailed it toward the mountains, whereupon the mire bristled.

"Get down!" Eredani shouted, throwing himself face down in the muck. I followed his example, allowing a wave of fire to pass above my head. Acrid steam rose. The dwarf considered delirium the best cure for surprise, and promptly nodded off. I would now have to keep pouring restorative potions into it, as the volatile mire had inflicted considerable damage. A tailed figure flickered in the green haze, and I was a hair's breadth from blasting it with my glaive, when I recognized Eredani's crooked right horn.

"What was that?!" I threw the dwarf to him. "How did they do that?"

"Run! They're draining the swamp. Let's

move!" He took off along the bubbles with the frolic of a kid goat. I followed close behind, but choosing my own route – after being used once, the bubbles burst, and you had to find new ones.

"We'll get you anyway!" Braksed's threatful cry carried through the mist. "It's not going to be easy!"

"You asked what they hit us with? I tell you I have no idea. Some local version of a meteorite shower. It wasn't a scroll. The Vartalinskys sacrificed their entire guard by sending them up against that strike. I'm a little concerned by their abilities. It looks very like they've found some version of the Glaive of Seth."

"I thought about that too. But they didn't find it, they bought it. Or took it from their father. Damned donators!" I pronounced this last word aping Maestro's accent. He had literally spat it out, expressing his disdain for misfits pouring their own money into the game.

The mire wasn't big, approximately five kilometers in length, but we were forced to waste several hours on it. There were no opponents, other than the tacky gloop. We even took rests, when the system began chewing away at five percent of our HP. The distant specs of the Vartalinskys and the demons embarked upon a circumvention of the mountains. You couldn't get through from the side of the Abyss, because the mire bordered too close on it.

"The saddle!" Eredani pointed ahead and threw me back the dwarf. The mire came to an end, taking the most important thing from me – the will to win. Right then I wanted to press the Exit button, collapse onto the sofa, and stare at the ceiling for a few hours. However, I had yet to work myself literally to death. Even in reality I could feel a real body resisting that particular excess. That night I would again leak out of the pod like a puddle.

"Come on. Let's go!" Eredani shouted. "The Vartalinskys'll be here in half an hour!" The determined players had already covered the greater part of their journey. The array of dark spots was gaining on us, threatening to bury us in an avalanche. Exhaling heavily, I slung the dwarf onto my shoulders and shuffled off after my partner. The saddle was within spitting distance, along with the dungeon. But we were catastrophically short of time. Realizing we wouldn't make our goal on time, we left the road and hid behind some rocks. Up ahead bristled a cactus patch, but we couldn't poke our noses in there – it was the first place they would look.

"Quiet!" whispered Eredani. The dwarf placed his hands on our chests, activating some magic known only to him, and we blended into the rocks. A couple of adroit demons flew low over our heads without noticing us. There were no more dogs – they had petered out back at the mire – so the beasties couldn't follow our scent. The Vartalinskys positioned themselves in the center of the army, ceaselessly throwing out commands left and right with wild gesticulations. All the players' attention was focused on the forest. They knew full well we wouldn't get far, because we had to hide somewhere. However, it didn't even enter the whippersnappers' heads that our strength would run low much sooner, and they'd begun their search too late. Never mind, experience comes with time. The main thing was to learn by your mistakes and, as far as we were concerned, allow those mistakes to repeat themselves.

"The dungeon's here. A kilometer and a half." Eredani unrolled the map. The dwarf whistled as he appraised the scale of our preparations. The entrance to G'Rot's lair was situated to the side of a large track, and it was logical to suppose that initially the Vartalinskys would charge straight on, and only later begin to spread out their forces.

Hopes and dreams... No sooner had we crept out from behind the rocks to follow the army, than demons appeared in front. We just managed to dive back in, trying to merge with the wall, but the beasts of the Abyss paid us no attention. They were bolting from the valley, driven by fright, eyes bulging, and trampling one another underfoot in their haste to get to the saddle quicker. Several octopuses ran right over us, taking a shortcut through the boulders. A stroke of the glaive put one of them out of its misery, but its mates paid no heed to our aggression. Far from it, they were well pleased with the freed-up space.

"Kvalen, let's get out of here!" Eredani succumbed to the general panic, hauntedly surveying the forest. The far trees began swaying and cracking, as if a gigantic creature was marching through them. The kind that frightened even demons. The archdemons appeared from around the bend and, flapping their wings heavily, the lumbering fat-asses flew away, ignoring us again. It was more than their hides were worth. The next giant trunk crashed to the ground, and before us stood the initiator of the army's stampede. A colossal demon, five or six meters tall, very similar to the groundskeeper of Dorel's Frontier. The heavy swished its fiery sword from side to side, mowing down those beasties that didn't duck in time. The trees were no hindrance to that fearful weapon, snapping like reeds and bursting into flame at the very touch of it.

"This is my domain!" the monster bellowed in the wake of the fleeing archdemons. "Out!" Its next strike took down another dozen less vigilant runts, after which the satisfied giant heaved its flaming weapon onto its shoulder and trudged off on its way.

"For some reason I'm having doubts about the success of this venture." I watched the fifth archdemon of the island go, and didn't understand which side to approach it from in order to beat it. G'Rot was terrible, strong, and mighty. Level fifteen, a raider. Its HP was through the roof, but largely because it had just slain swarms of demons. In passing, the monster stuck out a hand to grab a fat magus from the crowd and bite its body in half. It was hungry, and its food was running around beneath its feet.

"That's not the boss itself. It's an avatar," said Eredani comfortingly. "The real thing is more terrifying. Let's go, we mustn't waste time. I can't see the Vartalinskys anywhere."

"Maybe they're resting?"

"It's not worth underestimating an enemy. Especially a well equipped one."

Exercising extreme caution, we followed the monster. It didn't turn around, but every so often it would select one of the fatter demons scurrying around and devour it, replenishing its spent energy. In sending the archdemons packing, G'Rot had confirmed his right to the valley. None of the smaller demons dared contest it, so nobody paid us any attention. All the beasties' desires boiled down to one thing – avoid the boss and scuttle off home, where it was warm and there was a constant supply of prixis.

The dungeon was exactly where we expected to see it. G'Rot's avatar walked up to a glimmering shroud and disintegrated into miniscule stars. The archdemon had dismissed its embodiment. We had one final sprint to go before the entrance, but Eredani laid a hand on my shoulder and said, "The Vartalinskys."

Braksed and Kurtune had survived the encounter with the monster and, having forfeited their guard, were now standing in front of the entrance to the dungeon and making a call using the amulet. We couldn't hear whoever they were talking to, because they were too far away, but Braksed's visible outrage was telling.

"Yes, a glimmering shroud. Shit, I'm not stupid, I can read! That's what's written here: 'Path to Enlightenment Dungeon'! No, I don't have the ring yet. Yes, I know. No, you don't need to do anything, I can manage by myself. I said, I'll manage! Yes, I'm with Kurtune. Send the scrolls. No, the sphere has no effect on him. Shit, brother, this is the final boss! I'm waiting!"

Braksed rang off and kicked a stone, which flew off to the side. Kurtune came closer, and they sat down together right by the entrance.

"Can we follow them?" I asked my walking encyclopedia. "I mean enter the same copy of the dungeon with them?"

"Why?"

"Now they're going to collect ridiculous amounts of various things, and clear the path to G'Rot for us. We can't beat these goons directly. I'm not willing to pour so much money into a local conflict. But... what if we wait until the boss starts fighting them, wait for just the right moment, and... Get the idea?"

"And he looks such a decent human being." Eredani was ostentatiously surprised, smiled and said, "Yes, we can get into their copy of the dungeon. Because the leading clans always put a guard at the entrance, so nobody can frustrate their plans. There is a minus – the Vartalinskys will know we've entered. We can't hide that."

"Let them know." I shrugged. "It's their problem. The main thing is to give them time to get tangled up in a fight with the boss. Then knowledge of our presence won't help them."

"Yes, that might work." Eredani perked up. He was also looking for a way to wangle a First Kill, and my idea fell on fertile ground. "Only we shall do things a wee bit differently. Look..."

The letter to Braksed arrived half an hour

later, which allowed me to relax properly at last. The Vartalinskys exchanged scrolls, elixirs, and objects, then dove into the shimmering veil. The clock counted down ten minutes, and Eredani galloped off after the youths like a high-spirited goat. The dwarf did not lag behind. It had decided that things would be easier hanging around us. We didn't complain – we had no plans for the anonymous thing, so it was free to choose its own place of death.

Notification for player

A new territory is open: the Path to Enlightenment dungeon. The probability of finding valuable objects is increased by 49.999%; experience gained is increased by 20%. You have joined a group to pass the dungeon under the leadership of Braksed Vartalinsky. Number of bosses killed: 0 out of 1.

The Path to Enlightenment was indeed a path. Hundreds of walkways twinkled above a green lake which effused unpleasant vapors. They interconnected with each other on columns or massive rocks, then scattered in all directions. I counted four levels, forming a humongous 3D network. You could move between them via the columns, which is what the Vartalinskys were doing – shinnying up to the very top level.

"We go that way." The experienced Eredani motioned toward the far wall, where, adjoining the third level, yawned a dark cave. I glanced down – a long way. My chest itched, and the unpleasant sensation was gradually making its way lower. I hated fairground rides.

"I'll wait for you here!" The dwarf appreciated the epochal nature of the structure before stepping toward the entrance, where he found a boulder to hide behind, away from prying eyes.

We were spotted immediately. Kurtune drew his thumb across his throat in demonstration of his plans for our afterlife. The Vartalinskys clambered up, ran between the columns and began to look over their shoulders distractedly. Not all the columns had a way down, and not all the stairways led in the right direction. There came a soft whispering, and to the clarion cussing of the Vartalinskys, the stairways began to rotate, changing their points of contact with the columns. The stones anchored themselves in their new places with a dull thud. The structure of the connecting stairways was fixed for the next five minutes. We stepped up to the start of the stone labyrinth.

"Now, Kvalen my friend, a small lesson," snickered Eredani. "There are two ways to pass through labyrinths like this. One – act like our young foe, leaping hither and thither in the hope of getting lucky. Two – wait for your moment."

"What's with the edifying tone all of a sudden?"

"You have to pass your knowledge on some time. Surely that's precisely why you took me on?"

"What chance are you talking about?" I decided to put aside Eredani's true desire to turn on Teacher. Let him do what it wanted. The main thing was that it was of some benefit.

"We have to get in there, right?" Eredani indicated toward the dark passage and waited patiently for me to confirm. I was forced to nod, and only after that did my partner continue, "The stairways reconfigure themselves every five minutes. All we have to do is wait for a direct route to form."

"What, for two weeks?" I was pretty good with graphs, and estimated when the system would align itself in the right order.

"Half an hour, maximum fifty minutes." Eredani threw me a curveball. "The standard cycle of rotation is one hour. We've already seen two variations of the path, and there are ten left. So I'll repeat the question, what are we going to do? Gambol about or wait patiently?"

"You've already made your choice, yeah?"

"I'm too old for all this." He stretched his back theatrically. "Agility's not what it was."

"Well, let's enjoy the Vartalinskys' acrobatic études. By the way, what's that green gunk?"

"It smells like acid. I wouldn't want to fall in there. At all."

We had to wait seven reconfigurations before Eredani ordered, "Let's go!" and shot off. His decision was counterintuitive to me, but I didn't bother contesting it. If an expert says it's time, you either have to trust him, or come up with arguments of your own. I didn't have any.

"Up!" Eredani quickly climbed up to level four, where he saluted the Vartalinskys, who fired a Weakening at us. Then he about-turned and sprang chicly back, after activating Retreat. He performed a graceful airborne U-turn, before landing on a level-three stairway about twenty yards from me. He was one flight away from the entrance.

"Don't just stand there! Jump!" he commanded.

The tightening and coldness were there in my chest again. Jumping over an abyss... That was... pretty shitty. And terrifying. There must be a direct route. I looked at the Vartalinskys. Those two were definitely not going to jump. They would jump between the levels and search for the correct route. Damn it! How long was I going to hide my cowardice behind attempts at logical explanation? Hang it all! "Retreat!"

"And who's going to turn in the air?" My partner caught me by the tail and tugged me sharply to my feet. Stars danced before my eyes, and I collapsed, clinging to him like a lover. That I should ever again jump like that of my own volition! Never!

"Had a little lie down? Now onward and upward! Realignment minus one minute!"

Eredani was unpitying. Without releasing my tail, he hauled me toward the passageway. The noise of the shifting rocks was drowned out by the Vartalinskys' swearing. The boys had found a way to get to the entrance, but the scheming labyrinth scuppered all their plans. The area we were standing on broke out in hoarfrost – one of them had lost control and flashed a frost strike at the rocks.

The long journey down led us to a wide platform, the central part of which was approximately twenty metres, smooth, and even. Further on was a forest of fat cone-shaped stalagmites, deformed by time and the owner of the cave. A green fluorescence to the side of the platform suggested we were floating on a lake of acid. G'Rot was not as enormous as its avatar. It was a typical two-meter-tall demon, and it sat in state upon its throne, snoozing, eyes closed, flaming sword across its knees.

"*That* is the groundskeeper's elder brother?!" I was surprised. The throne, the blazing sword, the external appearance – all signs indicated that the boss was a more progressive copy of the demon we had killed.

"I don't think so." Somebody's been cutting corners and used two identical models in the nursery.

Archdemon G'Rot. *Level: 15. Class: raider. Health points: 28,500.*

Abilities:

- *Acid spit (recovery time 10 seconds).*
- *Target selection (recovery time 30 seconds, less than 70% of boss's health required).*
- *Death dance (recovery time 30 seconds, less than 40% of boss's health required).*
- *Armageddon (recovery time 20 seconds, less than 10% of boss's health required)*

Book One: A Second Chance

Quick steps behind us – the Vartalinskys were able to bust through the labyrinth after all. "Hide." Eredani pointed at the stalagmites. We'd scarcely taken cover, when the hoodlums appeared.

"Where are they?" Kurtune held a scroll. He clearly wanted us out of the way there and then.

"Fuck 'em! Brother said fuck everything and just take down the boss. Woah! Why's it so fat?"

"So we let the tieflings go just like that?" Kurtune wasn't going to be pacified.

"Shut up and do what's required of you!" Braksed reacted harshly.

Even in my amateurishness I was able to appreciate the Vartalinskys' know-how. They were surprisingly savvy and worked well together. They separated and got out their scrolls, before Kurtune slowly approached the boss to measure its agro-radius. Ten meters. The monster opened its eyes and looked in bafflement at the player creeping toward it. When the latter was within arm's reach of the throne, the sword came into play – the boss slashed it snappily at his head. But he was already gone – the Vartalinskys' Retreat worked just the same as that of any other demon hunter, common or dark. The blade plunged deep into the rock, but G'Rot drew it out with ease and strode to the centre of the platform.

The first battle phase had begun.

"That's exactly why I'm going to stay out of the way," Eredani said quietly, before swearing floridly. The boss was unpredictably swift for its size. An instant, and it stood with Kurtune. The Retreat was for recovery, so the player could not avoid the first acid spit and the monster spewed green goo on him. Kurtune was enveloped in a cloud of fumes and began to scream atrociously – his face was being eaten away by the acid. A brisk roll to the side and some recovery potion spared him dreadful wounds, but they couldn't do the same for his equipage. His chest was decorated with a huge bald patch, after the acid had dissolved the armor. It wasn't utterly destroyed, but doubtless all its characteristics were tellingly dented. Braksed kept his eyes peeled. While the boss was busy with his partner, he flashed it scroll after scroll. Frost strike, electric strike, block of ice, rock fall – the thoroughness of his preparation for battle commanded respect. The boss skipped over to Braksed to repeat his acid spit, but he was no longer there. He'd activated Retreat – and the boss's ability went way wide of the mark.

Whirling its sword, G'Rot rushed to finish off the speedy player, which was precisely what the Vartalinskys were expecting. Braksed hared around the platform, not even attempting to attack, while Kurtune got busy with the scrolls. Then a switch, and now Kurtune ran and Braksed attacked. A well worked tactic against an NPC. It wouldn't work with players.

"I'm going to do justice on you!" the demon yelled and abruptly grew to one and a half times its size. It cast a green glow, its eyes streamed fire, and its appearance became downright abominable. It was Kurtune's turn to run, which meant he would also get Target Selection. The boss was next to him in a flash, teleport-like, and swung with his sword. The attack was so blistering the player had no chance. He was struck right in the chest and launched in the direction of the stalagmites, smashing them all to smithereens. He didn't quite make it to the edge of the platform, although his HP was down to a hundred units. The boss shook himself down and, turning its attentions back to Braksed, made him run around the platform some more.

"Not now, we need him alive." To be on the safe side, Eredani warned me against doing anything rash like liquidating Kurtune. He lay not far from us, and one strike would have been sufficient to give Braksed some privacy. Eventually Kurtune came round, revitalized his Health, and rushed to assist his partner.

"Are we just going to sit here twiddling our thumbs?" I asked. Kurtune was sent flying another five times, doing significant damage to the stony forest, but the brothers still managed to reduce the boss to nearly forty percent. The waiting game was beginning to bore me. The youngsters tried and fought hard, but the boss, who was rated at four players, wasn't going to give up that easily. Despite the fact that its HP was dropping, it was doing so slowly and unsurely, like a girl on a first date.

"Patience, my friend, is the cornerstone of any success. When the time comes, we... Shit!" Eredani shrieked wildly and sprang away from me. The third phase of the battle had come into effect.

The boss had stopped chasing the players. Standing in the centre of the platform, it raised its paws to the ceiling, muttered something, stamped its foot, then lowered its paws sharply. The sword rent the air with a whistle, and we all felt the force. Next to each player G'Rot created a small copy of its own weapon, which rotated maniacally in the manner of a circular saw, grimly chopping down our HP. Stone chips from the shattered stalagmites enhanced inflicted damage in the form of shrapnel. Even a leap to the side did not guarantee safety, for following the target was a fiery shrapnel vortex. The ability lasted for a mere ten seconds, but it was enough to halve what was left of the protrusions. The boss immediately ran to catch Braksed and douse him in acid. The demon never forgot his duties for as much as a second.

"It's time!" Eredani commanded, summoning his fish. The Vartalinskys gave us a nasty look, but didn't refuse our help. It was all quite lively: Eredani worked not only for the two of us, but also for the Vartalinskys. Despite the brothers' good kit, damage to a higher-level player was considerably greater. And that would be his undoing.

However hard I tried, I could not attract the demon's attention. Without demon abilities I was a hopeless fighter. Unleashing yet another death dance, G'Rot caught sight of Eredani fleeing the swords and was beside him in a twinkling. Retreat saved him from acid spit, but he had nothing to counter Target Selection. The stunning strike of the sword threw him to the side, but there were no stalagmites left there, and he flew toward the edge of the platform.

He didn't panic. A wicked strike returned him

to the demon, although it brought no dividends to speak of. Another swing of the sword, and the abilityless tiefling flew into the air. There was no point pretending – the end of the beginning would be acid and all that went with it. A tornado of thoughts instantaneously formed itself into what seemed to me one logical and sound idea. I took a run-up and thrust the glaive into the edge of the platform. Physics did not fail me – the weapon entered the rock and stuck fast. In truth, I did not actually see this, for I immediately took a mighty leap after Eredani and managed to catch hold of him by a horn. My tail, wound around the glaive, threatened to snap, but I did not let go of my partner. He ceased twitching, and the only evidence of sentience was his wide open eyes and irregular breathing.

"Let me go, and finish off the boss!" came an unexpected order.

"I can't. I don't have any abilities!" The glaive was tilting treacherously, and my tail slipped to the end of the shaft, where I hung on for grim death.

"They're not going to hide. Whatever you do. That's First Kill." Eredani squirmed, trying to free himself. He even used his hands.

"Stop it!" I shouted. "What freaking first kill? Get back up here!"

"Kvalen!" He lowered his voice threateningly, as if he wasn't hanging over a lake of acid. "Killing the boss is the most important thing! It's a game! I'll lose consciousness from the pain in five seconds. Put your brain in gear!"

Vasily Mahanenko. Invasion

Danger!

"Twenty seconds! You idiot, you're going to screw everything up!" Eredani completely flew off the handle. "Kill the boss! Do it!"

I was hanging on by the skin of my teeth. My tail was seconds from slipping off, and Eredani was struggling berserkly, wanting to fall, but I wasn't having it. My entire being insisted that ultimately I was surrounded by a game, and the feelings of any human in it were worth more than a tick in a box in a data table. My partner did not understand that. We were too different.

"It's stupid, Kvalen. It worked out too stupid," sighed the tiefling as he stopped trying to break loose. We had both seen the Vartalinskys catastrophically not manage to destroy the boss in the time allotted.

"Do you trust me?" I asked him.

"No!" he snapped.

"Excellent. Drink some elixir!"

I blissfully relaxed my overworked tail, and we dropped into the acid. An explosion. My back burned seriously. Rubble rained down. Something crashed somewhere, but it didn't concern me overly, because I had other plans. Hitching Eredani to me, I activated Retreat literally a few meters above the acid, by drinking the elixir. Diabettis had taught me, and the ability did not let us down – we were flung back, almost out to the very edge of the boss's platform. Emphasis on the "almost". We didn't even make it as far as the protruding glaive.

At the apex of our flight's parabola, before we

began to fall, I flipped over and turned Eredani so his back was toward pit of hell. "Retreat!" I yelled. "Activate it! Drink!"

How pleasant it was to play with someone who could stifle his emotions. No matter what Eredani had said to me before, no matter how he'd begged me to ditch him, no matter how he suffered from the fire scorching his back, nothing could affect his ability to react to the situation. The next ability threw us another ten meters, and we were almost on the ceiling. Luckily, the fire had already moved on from there.

The boss had survived. Staggering and leaning on its sword, it was holding up a pile of rocks that had fallen from the ceiling. Remarkable. We flew down. A fall from ten meters would guarantee us the unforgettable experience of our first rebirth, were it not for one "but": I still had a wicked strike. My heart was in my mouth when I activated it, and the abrupt change of direction opened a fair array of debuffs and caused a nagging pain in my groin. Nonetheless, the main deed was done: we were next to the boss.

"Die already!" I growled, and dug my horns right into its face.

I had neither the energy nor the ability to do anything else. An elementary physical attack would inflict minimal damage, pointless in normal confrontations, but it was big enough for G'Rot. Stones crashed to the floor, entombing the vanquished boss.

Achievements received
Better than us only...

1 rank: *You have destroyed your first Barliona boss. Your ability to find a way out of difficult situations is impressive. Damage to all bosses is increased by 1%. To gain the next rank you must destroy 5 bosses (progress: 1 out of 5)*

First kill of the archdemon G'Rot of the Path to Enlightenment dungeon

Reward for achievement: *During embodiment, probability of receiving improved-quality objects is increased by 10%.*

Information for player: *In five months you will be teleported to the Emperor's reception of the joint forces of the continent of Stivala. You can take with you two escorts, and you must give them an invitation within five months. Tickets are available at any branch of the Bank of Barliona.*

The number 1 appeared alongside Eredani's name, inside a gold star. My partner restored his HP and looked about. The Vartalinskys were nowhere. Surviving in the center of Armageddon was unrealistic.

"Minus fifty percent from fire damage..." said my partner thoughtfully, turning me to face him. The debuffs had turned my body into a feeble-minded doll, so for a whole minute Eredani could do whatever he liked. For example, ask: "Do you understand the risk you took? Do you understand you nearly blew everything? Why did you jump?"

"Because I decide what I do and when. I felt sorry for you." The words didn't come out easily. I was having to fight myself, but my actions required explanation. Eredani made a face, wanting to say something, but he waved a hand and turned away.

New characteristic available: Empathy
Description: *You are a sensitive person. Your ability to sense the pain of others and show them support is impressive. Every characteristics point increases your original Agreeability to NPCs from 0.1% right up to 50%.*

The window popping up was such a shock I burst out laughing. "And you said empathy would be difficult for me to open." I explained my reaction, and Eredani shook his head incredulously.

We sat a while longer, looking at the archdemon's rocky burial mound, but in order to receive the loot due, we had to clear away the rubble.

"I remember!" exclaimed a happy voice. We'd completely forgotten about the third member of our expedition. The dwarf was jumping nimbly among the stones, trying to get to the burning throne. In there, among the rocks and firebrands, an object shone. The dwarf got to it, snatched it up, and held it in the air with two hands. "I have remembered my name! I am master Bartulun, apprentice of master Borh Goldenhand! And this is my work! I remember! Ha-ha-ha!"

A shield twinkled in the dwarf's hands. Time had not been lenient to it: whatever it was created from many centuries ago, now it was just stone. Of the onetime great shield remained only the name: "Shield of Tamerlane; used only by paladins." Seated next to me, Eredani swore.

"Kvalen, we have problems. Tamerlane the Great is a mentor of the Luciferous, the founder of the paladin class, and nobody in all of Barliona knows where his tomb is. And that's a fact. It's a rotten business."

"Or a new scene has just started," I said.

Eventually the debuffs fell away, allowing me to move normally around the platform. First off, I went over to dig up G'Rot. I needed just a small patch of skin in order to take the loot. I had to use the pickaxe and absolutely decimate the rocks, but it was worth it. Just as from a raiding boss, three epic blanks fell out of the archdemon: two rings and a pair of gauntlets. After muttering that he had more than enough rings anyway and the gauntlets would suit him just fine, Eredani withdrew to allow me to receive all the objects. Before carrying out the embodiment, I went to retrieve the glaive, but either the fire had destroyed it, or the explosion had sent it into the acid. I was weaponless.

The blanks were made of a beginner material, so I wasn't expecting anything unique. Even the extra twenty percent to improvement did not help create anything better than epic.

Two identical rings, reducing damage sustained by five percent and increasing fire resistance. Instead of +5 to intellect, this time I got +5 to agility, which significantly decreased the rings' value to me. It was the same story with the gauntlets: the bonuses were the same, except there was more magic protection. Thirty, as opposed to the rings' ten.

"So all that fuss was about that number?" I pointed at the star by my name.

"That star turns us specifically into wealthy people," Eredani explained. "At the beginner levels our bonus is useless. Garbage no matter what. But starting from three hundred you can't imagine what objects there are. Having an extra ten percent probability of turning an epic into a legendary... The clans will do anything to get hold of us. They'll put us on a salary, and not let us out of the castles so the competition won't happen across us.

"Do I detect a note of enthusiasm in your voice?"

"Why would there be? We are now a priority target for any clan. They're going to be looking for us. No way are we going to find the island. Tamerlane... Where are we going to look for him?"

The dwarf said it could make it to the camp by itself, so we decided not to worry about it. Finding a suitable niche, Eredani and I used a tried and tested means of return – by getting stuck.

At the temple we were expected. Tarlin stood a couple of meters away, arms folded across his chest. Without a word he walked toward the camp. Clearly we were meant to follow him. When we approached, a gong sounded, and an announcement echoed around the camp.

General muster! Two minutes to general muster! Everybody stop training and go to the square!

The light column designating our place was in among the graduates. There were now substantially more demon hunters. Approximately a hundred newbies, twice as many training at various levels, and only five graduates. Standing alongside us were Diabettis and his gang.

"Brothers! Today we present the world with five demon hunters!" Uldaron began his speech triumphantly. "Just the five, but these heroes deserve the highest praise. They were able to take back Dorel's Frontier, albeit for a short time. This gives us the chance to hope that their followers will be able to repeat the deed. The frontier will be ours! But that is not all. Two of these heroes were able to find the fifth archdemon on our island and..."

And what? remained a mystery. For at that very moment right in the centre of the square opened a portal, and out of it, sprawling on the ground, tumbled Aniram. Beaten up, wings covered in scorched featherless patches, one horn broken, eyes swollen and bruised, the demoness was a picture of colour.

"Master! I beseech you, take me back!" she implored, and made a dash for me, but it was not to be, because another demon followed her out of the portal and trod on her tail.

Notification for player

You have the opportunity to get Aniram back in return for the Cursed Glaive of Seth that you found. The rank of your fosterling will not be lowered; the amount of strength necessary for discarding shackles will be reset to zero. Decide wisely.

"Uldaron, what a delightful surprise!" said Mother sweetly. The higher demoness Ireness was honoring the demon-hunter training camp with her presence, not remotely concerned for her fate. Here, away from key developments, nobody stood a chance against her. A fact which was confirmed by what happened next.

"There is no place for you here, beast!" Tarlin reacted first, but was cast aside by a nonchalant flick of the demoness's wrist. I was far less concerned with the appearance of Ireness – Barliona was full of surprises – than the presence of the Discard Shackles ability, about which there had been no information. Aniram would need shaking down to get it out of her.

"I don't remember inviting you to my island!" the voice of Argalot resounded. Hermit had returned to the camp to defend his territory.

"I didn't come here to fight, Traitor." Ireness was geniality itself. "I care not for your petty intrigues. I came for my new bondmaid. This numbskull found a vanquished higher somewhere, got high on a surplus of energy, and decided to dethrone me. The stupidest suicide I've ever heard of. She deserves a separate punishment."

"Master!" Tears ran down Aniram's face. "I implore you! Take me back!"

"No, sweetie pie," laughed Ireness sanguinously. "Nobody's going to take you back. You're going to experience the full beauty of my vengeance at first hand!" Ireness almost shouted these last words, and the surrounding space darkened. The demoness's fury could blot out the sun.

"Master!" Aniram's voice had weakened, but she fought on. "I can be of use. I know where a paladin is buried." With that, her strength failed her, and she became a spineless doll. The battle with the higher was lost.

"Don't stress it, Traitor, I'm leaving." Ireness hauled the body of the archdemoness onto her shoulder and turned toward the portal. "Teach them well. I shall enjoy turning all demon hunters into my children. Farewell!"

"Stop, mother!" I shouted. "Our deal!"

"Deal?" she said and turned back. "What are you talking about, misguided child? Do you want to return to me?"

"I want to take my slave from you," I said, pointing at Aniram. "She belongs to me."

"Is that so?" Ireness raised her eyebrows ostentatiously. "You allowed her to get drunk on borrowed energy, and she terminated the contract. That alone warrants disembodiment."

"I can offer you something in return. Something that will make you stronger."

"You?" she laughed. "What can you do, pipsqueak? You live only because I am interested to see when you will turn tail on this world and return to the demons. You cannot fight your nature for ever. He couldn't," she said, pointing at Eredani.

Kvalen: *Give me the Glaive of Seth.*

Eredani: *I should probably have told you about my test earlier...*

Kvalen: *Later. The glaive!*

"I can do lots!" I raised the glaive above my head, eliciting a gasp of amazement from the NPC. Unlike players, NPCs could see the properties of the object. Of course it came out somewhat melodramatically, but that was just fine. "I propose a swap. Aniram in exchange for the glaive."

"Oh really?" Ireness twitched, but didn't recoil as my demoness had. Throwing Aniram's body to the ground, the higher came closer to me. "Where did you get that?" she asked keenly.

"Where I got it... it is the only one. Shall we swap?" I replied simply.

"An exchange, my son! I will gladly see your bondmaid back with me when she becomes supersaturated with energy. Feed her more often."

The glaive melted away in my hands, and a system notification immediately informed me of the return of my demonic abilities. Aniram was unconscious, so I deactivated her just in case.

"Farewell, traitor!" Ireness smiled at the darkling Hermit, while demonstratively ignoring everybody else. "Make more warriors! My army needs fighters! As for you, children of mine" – her gaze rested on me and Eredani – "we shall meet soon. Barliona will know the wrath of Seth!" With a dull clap the demoness disappeared.

Argalot plonked himself down wearily on the rocks and looked at us reproachfully. "You've made a big mistake. And the whole world will have to put it right."

"The Glaive of Seth," Uldaron chimed in. "I considered it a myth. A children's spooky story. You have brought pain and suffering upon Barliona. You placed the personal higher than the whole world. You are not worthy of the honorary ribbon of a graduate. I do not want to see you in my camp anymore. Get out of here! Abigail was mistaken – a tiefling will always remain a demon, no matter how much you purify him."

The mass of demon hunters ran to form a living tunnel to the portal. Eredani chuckled and shuffled off after them.

Evidently our adventure in the nursery was at an end. It was a shame we didn't manage to get a handle on the dwarf; after all, a student of the incomprehensible Borh is an interesting story. An NPC prodded me, wanting to rid the camp of our presence. I sighed, and dived into the portal. It was time to end the farce.

Information for player

You have left the nursery and been

transferred to the town of Lok'dar, continent of Stivala. We wish you a pleasant game!

"Let's go!" Eredani was already waiting for me. Lok'dar was a huge city decked out in medieval style. Taverns, bakeries, workshops, babble, din, and hubbub were integral features of its streets. And our appearance did not go unnoticed. A detachment of guardians stood nearby, their eagle eyes fixed on us.

Eredani headed straight for the commander. A couple of phrases, and the general tension eased – it was negligible, but our reputation with the Light of Barliona faction had done its thing. Having got our bearings, Eredani guided me through the windy streets of the city as surely as if it were his home town, and few minutes later we stood at the entrance to the registrar's chamber.

"Make a clan. We must show we have serious intentions," he said, pushing me inside. "Don't forget to put ten thousand into the account. When we buy a castle, we'll choose its location."

The registrar, an elderly and portly human with fabulous whiskers and a no less fabulous belly, was standing by a board and unhurriedly writing something on it. Registering a clan was absurdly simple: pay five thousand gold and choose from a list of available names. Job done. The system automatically generated patches, which you could edit if you could be bothered, and inserted the clan logo into the names of the players. Strictly speaking that was all.

After paying the required tax, I opened the list. The name of the clan, just as the names of players, were theoretically unique within one continent. And with very few clans on Stivala, the list contained more than ten thousand possibilities. I had long had a name in mind and, to my delight, it was free:

The Pareto clan has been created. Clan leader: Kvalen.

And that was that. The registrar gave me a piece of paper confirming my right to ownership of the clan and the possibility to choose a location for the castle. I opened my properties to admire my successes. Not bad for the nursery, not bad at all.

Characteristics window for player Kvalen							
Main parameters					**Additional parameters**		
Experience		912	of	1,000	Item	Unit	Quantity
Player level		14			Account balance	gold	187,409
Race		Fire tiefling			Physical attack	units	245
Class		Demon destroyer			Magic attack	units	823
Main speciality		Trade			Protection from physical attack	units	305
Learning speed		0			Protection from magic attack	units	260
Health		7,300			Chance of critical blow	%	51%
Energy		7,550			Chance of avoidance	%	14%
Main characteristics					Fire resistance	%	65%
Characteristic	Scale		Limit	Base	Total	Rank of subjugated demon	rank	4
Stamina	1,187	of	2,400	11	73	Reduction in damage sustained	%	45%
Strength	1,466	of	1,600	11	44	Reduction in debuff time	%	45%
Intellect	2,990	of	3,200	17	84	Reduction in scale value	%	20%
Agility	1,668	of	2,400	19	67	Bonus to experience gained	%	15%
Additional characteristics								
Characteristic	Scale		Limit	Base	Total			
Luck	887	of	2,400	14	64			
Charisma	546	of	800	2	2			
Empathy	1	of	800	1	1			
Not specified								
Specialities					**Specialization**		
Speciality	Scale		Limit	Base	Total	Specialization	Unit	Quantity
Trade	4	of	800	14	14			
Cartographer	566	of	800	2	2			
Herbalist	22	of	800	1	1			
Fishing	20	of	800	1	1			
Mining	16	of	800	1	1			
Cookery	6	of	800	1	1			

I didn't overlook my criteria either. Somehow or other, fulfilling them ought to guarantee me a job.

	Criteria	Numerical value	Fulfillment status
1	Reach level 50	50	14
2	Become a full clan member		1
3	Pass 20 dungeons of any level. Group must not be	20	1

	organized by you		
4	Receive Friend status from 5 players	5	3
5	Fulfil 50 socially important tasks	50	0
6	Help players fulfil tasks 20 times. One player must have no rights	20	5
7	Fulfil 10 requests from other players	10	1
8	Extended communication with another player. No fewer than 2,400 minutes in 6 months	2,400	2,400
9	Participate actively in 2 festivals in Barliona	2	0
10	Receive 80 Agreeability points from two Barliona NPCs	2	0

"An eloquent name." Eredani accepted the invitation to join the clan, and by his name appeared a pictogram: 80/20.

Wilfried Pareto, after whom I named the clan, formulated a well-known rule of thumb: twenty percent of the effort yields eighty percent of the result. Which means superfluous stress should be avoided. An ideal law for making a profit.

We approached a wall on which three ratings were displayed: the game's best clans, continents, and locations. We were last – 250th place. A clan of two players.

"First we rise to here." My partner and now official adviser pointed to the line under number 1 of the local rating. "Then further."

"Do you have a plan?"

"I have more than a plan. I have experience, desire, and an understanding of what must be done. How are you with stepping on people's toes?"

"You know I'm all for it."

"In which case, operation "Rip 'Em to Shreds" begins! The province of Lok'dar will be ours!"

End of Book One

Want to be the first to know about our latest LitRPG, sci fi and fantasy titles from your favorite authors?

Subscribe to our **New Releases** newsletter:
http://eepurl.com/b7niIL

Thank you for reading *A Second Chance!*
If you like what you've read, check out other sci-fi, fantasy and
LitRPG novels published by Magic Dome Books:

Reality Benders LitRPG series by Michael Atamanov:
Countdown
External Threat
Game Changer
Web of Worlds
A Jump into the Unknown
Aces High

The Dark Herbalist LitRPG series
by Michael Atamanov:
Video Game Plotline Tester
Stay on the Wing
A Trap for the Potentate
Finding a Body

Perimeter Defense LitRPG series by Michael Atamanov:
Sector Eight
Beyond Death
New Contract
A Game with No Rules

League of Losers LitRPG Series
by Michael Atamanov:
A Cat and his Human

The Way of the Shaman LitRPG series
by Vasily Mahanenko:
Survival Quest
The Kartoss Gambit
The Secret of the Dark Forest
The Phantom Castle
The Karmadont Chess Set
The Hour of Pain (a bonus short story)
Shaman's Revenge
Clans War

The Alchemist LiTRPG series by Vasily Mahanenko:
City of the Dead
Forest of Desire
Tears of Alron

Interworld Network LitRPG Series by Dmitry Bilik:
The Time Master
Avatar of Light
The Dark Champion

Rogue Merchant LitRPG Series by Roman Prokofiev:
The Starlight Sword
The Gene of the Ancients

Project Stellar LitRPG Series by Roman Prokofiev:
The Incarnator
The Enchanter
The Tribute

Clan Dominance LitRPG Series by Dem Mikhailov:
The Sleepless Ones Book One
The Sleepless Ones Book Two
The Sleepless Ones Book Three

The Neuro LitRPG series by Andrei Livadny:
The Crystal Sphere
The Curse of Rion Castle
The Reapers

Phantom Server LitRPG series by Andrei Livadny:
Edge of Reality
The Outlaw
Black Sun

Respawn Trials LitRPG Series by Andrei Livadny:
Edge of the Abyss

**The Expansion (The History of the Galaxy) series
by A. Livadny:**
Blind Punch
The Shadow of Earth
Servobattalion

Point Apocalypse *(a near-future action thriller)*
by Alex Bobl

Moskau by G. Zotov
(a dystopian thriller)

El Diablo by G.Zotov
(a supernatural thriller)

Mirror World LitRPG series by Alexey Osadchuk:
Project Daily Grind
The Citadel
The Way of the Outcast
The Twilight Obelisk

Underdog LitRPG series by Alexey Osadchuk:
Dungeons of the Crooked Mountains
The Wastes
The Dark Continent
The Otherworld

An NPC's Path LitRPG series by Pavel Kornev:
The Dead Rogue
Kingdom of the Dead
Deadman's Retinue

The Sublime Electricity series by Pavel Kornev:
The Illustrious
The Heartless
The Fallen
The Dormant

Citadel World series by Kir Lukovkin:
The URANUS Code
The Secret of Atlantis

You're in Game!
(LitRPG Stories from Bestselling Authors)

You're in Game-2!
(More LitRPG stories set in your favorite worlds)

The Fairy Code by Kaitlyn Weiss:
Captive of the Shadows
Chosen of the Shadows

More books and series are coming out soon!

In order to have new books of the series translated faster, we need your help and support! Please consider leaving a review or spread the word by recommending *A Second Chance* to your friends and posting the link on social media. The more people buy the book, the sooner we'll be able to make new translations available.

Thank you!

Till next time!